Praise for *Zoey Punches t*

"[*Zoey Punches the Future*] is at its bes
ture of wealth and power. In the ch.
against the fairy-tale cliché where the downtrodden (through super-
natural means or otherwise) are rewarded a life of carefree prosperity."
—*Locus*

"The future is simultaneously familiar and utterly ridiculous in *Zoey
Punches the Future in the Dick,* the second Zoey Ashe thriller from [Jason
Pargin] . . . a fun house mirror of modern society viewed through a
superhero comic or a James Bond movie. . . . Rich with commentary
on celebrity culture, social media, and toxic masculinity, readers will
be laughing too hard for it to ever feel preachy."
—*Shelf Awareness* (starred review)

"[Pargin] once again achieves the perfect balance between sardonic
humor and satirical digs at the digital age."
—*Library Journal* (starred review)

"[Pargin] sneaks a nuanced examination of the surrealist nature of the
digital age into the nonstop action, whipping technological, philosophi-
cal, and ethical questions into a wild romp that satirizes everything from
the men's rights movement to gaming culture to the cult of celebrity.
This is a brilliant modern parable disguised as pop fiction."
—*Publishers Weekly*

"[Pargin's] trademark imagination and humor remain, but it's his ground-
ed sense of humanity that elevates this work." —*Booklist*

Praise for *Futuristic Violence and Fancy Suits*

"With verve and velocity, the story moves . . . one cinematic set piece after another, strung together with twisty fun and wit."
—*The New York Times Book Review*

"Like Jonathan Swift for the internet age, [Pargin's] novel offers an engrossing journey and razor-sharp wit inside of an uncanny prediction of an American future. His newest is only more proof that he will be remembered as one of today's great satirists."
—Nerdist

"All right, grab some popcorn and strap in. We're in for another profane and funny roller-coaster ride from [Pargin]."
—*Kirkus Reviews*

"[Pargin] unabashedly trolls everyone and lampoons everything in this beautifully outrageous science fiction adventure. . . . Biting humor and blatant digs at modern society overlay a subtly brilliant and thoughtful plot focused on one young woman's growth and survival against all odds."
—*Publishers Weekly* (starred review)

"A sofa-clutching read from beginning to end and a great look at the constantly growing world of social networking."
—*Starburst* (9 out of 10 stars)

ALSO BY JASON PARGIN

John Dies at the End

This Book Is Full of Spiders: Seriously, Dude, Don't Touch It

What the Hell Did I Just Read

Futuristic Violence and Fancy Suits

ZOEY
PUNCHES
THE FUTURE
IN THE DICK

JASON PARGIN

ST. MARTIN'S GRIFFIN
NEW YORK

Published in the United States by St. Martin's Griffin, an imprint of
St. Martin's Publishing Group

ZOEY PUNCHES THE FUTURE IN THE DICK. Copyright © 2020 by Jason Pargin. All rights reserved. Printed in the United States of America. For information, address St. Martin's Publishing Group, 120 Broadway, New York, NY 10271.

www.stmartins.com

Designed by Steven Seighman

Library of Congress Cataloging-in-Publication Data

Names: Pargin, Jason, 1975– author.
Title: Zoey punches the future in the dick / Jason Pargin.
Description: First St. Martin's Griffin edition. | New York :
    St. Martin's Griffin, 2021.
Identifiers: LCCN 2021028409 | ISBN 9781250833488 (trade paperback) |
    ISBN 9781250195814 (ebook)
Subjects: LCGFT: Science fiction.
Classification: LCC PS3623.O5975 Z44 2021 | DDC 813/.6—dc23
LC record available at https://lccn.loc.gov/2021028409

ISBN 978-1-250-19579-1 (hardcover)

Our books may be purchased in bulk for promotional, educational, or business use. Please contact your local bookseller or the Macmillan Corporate and Premium Sales Department at 1-800-221-7945, extension 5442, or by email at MacmillanSpecialMarkets@macmillan.com.

First St. Martin's Griffin Edition: 2021

10 9 8 7 6 5 4

IN A FUTURE IN WHICH EVERYTHING IS POSSIBLE,
IN A CITY IN WHICH ANYTHING GOES...

1

Zoey Ashe surveyed the carnage and said, "Sorry we're late, it was my cat's birthday."

The man who greeted her on the sidewalk was named Hank Kowalski. He was bald and had the eyes of a man whose favorite joke is just a shrieking child falling down a flight of stairs. He wore a jacket with a flashing logo that said ASHE SECURITY—WILL USE DEADLY FORCE.

Looking a little too amused for the occasion, Kowalski said, "So, the good news is, the hostage taker knew to ask for you by name."

"Why is that good news?"

"If it's somebody you know, that raises the chance this ends in disaster and creates a cool scene for when they eventually make a movie about my life. Maybe the guy's an old boyfriend? You like psychopaths, right?" He stuck a finger into the air. "He's up there."

Zoey looked up and then down, then up again, trying to make sense of what she was seeing. All of the buildings downtown were skinned with display panels and synced so that a giant, obnoxious ad could scroll down the whole block. For example, right now an animated banner was hopping from building to building promoting the beginning of Halloween Month in Tabula Ra\$a, warning/promising that the city would not be enforcing public nudity laws for the duration of October. But the panel on the building in front of her was dead, leaving a dim gap in the display. That was presumably because of the ragged hole in the glass a few floors up, like a Godzilla had stooped down and taken a bite.

Directly below the hole at ground level, the main entrance was blocked by an overturned food truck. Zoey was familiar with the truck, just by its shape. It sold lightly charred strips of Korean barbecue on little sizzling, self-heating metal plates with a side compartment of melted cheese for dipping. It was one of the five best food trucks in the city, so this incident had already taken a terrible toll.

"Did . . . the food truck *fly into the building*?"

"Don't be ridiculous," Kowalski replied. "A guy knocked over the truck with his bare hands, then shoved it across the door there, to barricade it. Then he ripped a parking meter out of the ground, jumped straight up, and, while dangling from a ledge with one hand, smashed out the glass on the fourth floor, using the parking meter like a club. Then he entered the building and declared that everyone inside was his hostage."

Then, Zoey thought, he'd demanded to speak to her. This time last year, she'd have been restocking the muffin case at the coffee shop where she'd worked for minimum wage plus tips.

"Oh. Well, that's, uh, *pthththhbb*," said Zoey, fear causing her mouth to just give up halfway through.

"I agree," said Kowalski. "I'm thinking either he's gotten some implants to make him stronger or else he's *really* pissed off."

"Not an old boyfriend, then. I don't think I could make somebody *that* mad."

"Maybe you gave him a disease."

Kowalski took a bite of a hot dog. There was a nearby vendor who was doing brisk business with the crowd of gawkers who'd shown up to watch the hostage situation unfold. The hot dog guy, who'd apparently acted quickly to seize the Korean BBQ truck's territory, had a grilling apparatus strapped to his torso, complete with a rack of condiments. He wore a beat-up metal exoskeleton to help him carry it all and Zoey thought he looked like an old-timey one-man band. On the side of his grill was a looping animated logo of a smiling, sentient hot dog happily taking a bite out of a smaller, regular hot dog. Zoey tried to puzzle out the grossly unfair rules of the society depicted in the hot dog logo, then realized she was still a little bit high.

In words filtered through chewed hot dog, Kowalski said, "Nice outfit."

He didn't mean it. She was still wearing her party clothes, a black pleated skirt that an asshole at the party said made her look like a table lamp (he was right) and a black T-shirt bearing a symbol of a Jolly Roger, only the skull was replaced with a cat's face, and the two crossed bones were a pair of fish skeletons. Her black hair was in pigtails because she had thought it was funny earlier, but it now seemed inappropriate for the situation. She had arrived in a leopard-print BMW convertible, though she could never put the top down as it made her huge, fat head a target for snipers, according to Will Blackwater and her other advisors, who did nothing but sit around imagining worst-case scenarios all day. The car could be any color she wanted (she'd sprung for the programmable skin) but she'd left it leopard print for the last month only because it seemed to annoy Will, who at the moment was emerging from the driver's side. Will was an unreasonably white man in his late thirties wearing a suit the color of a wet sidewalk and the expression of a man who's just realized the wetness is piss.

Will "suspiciously fake-sounding menacing surname" Blackwater shot an annoyed look at the crowd of gawkers behind him, each one representing a potential complication, and asked, "How many hostages?"

"Sixty-eight employees," said Kowalski, "and fifty-two sad-sack customers."

Those numbers punched Zoey in the gut. It would not be good if she got sick here in front of the onlookers and their many cameras. Not good at all. It should be noted here that no one involved in this conversation was a police officer and none were coming. In Tabula Ra$a, you got the policing you paid for. And sometimes not even that.

The building the pissed-off guy with superhuman strength had smashed his way into was the Night Inn Cuddle Theater. For $250, an attractive member of your preferred gender would curl up with you in pajamas and watch a movie in a small private room with a wet bar, snacks, and a fireplace. There was no sex. That theater was down the block and they actually charged a lot less.

Kowalski took another bite before speaking, as if he preferred to talk while he chewed. "Entrance from the parking garage is blocked, too, from the inside. We can unblock it, but the guy says he's got a sonic device that will scramble the brains of everybody in the building if we try."

Zoey, utterly failing to sound unsettled by this, asked, *"Is that a thing?"*

"Who can say? They're inventing new things all the time. I even remember an era when a guy couldn't jump thirty feet in the air carrying a parking meter he'd plucked from the concrete like a dandelion. Are we waiting for the rest of your people to get here?"

Will said, "They're getting into position."

They were all in the process of executing a plan that had been hastily thrown together after they'd gotten word that the hostage taker would talk only to Zoey. Will had advised against her coming to the scene at all and the sensible part of Zoey's brain enthusiastically agreed. But then a key piece of information had been relayed to her: much to her surprise, she apparently owned the Night Inn Cuddle Theater. Thanks to a large inheritance, Zoey owned a lot of things she still wasn't aware of, some of which were just *incredibly* illegal. So this was in fact her problem and there was just no getting around it. Still, they intended to stretch the guy's "Only talk to Zoey" rule as far as possible. Will said hostage situations were like bad marriages, one party trying to subtly force the other to surrender, inches at a time.

Kowalski said, "I'm gonna finish my hot dog and then go supervise crowd control, unless you want me to climb up and shoot this guy real quick."

Will and Zoey both glanced back at the gawkers. The crowd was being kept in check by large men in suits with black pants and bright yellow jackets. They weren't Zoey's people, they were from a popular security service called the Vanguard of Peace, its logo a glorious sunrise over the silhouette of a waving child. They'd been called in to help control the crowd and billed by the hour. They also were quick to get brutal with anything they arbitrarily deemed to be a "riot" (those yellow coats really showed the blood). The prospect of this turning into a night of car-flipping chaos was part of what was turning Zoey's insides to jelly.

Will said, "Yeah, control the crowd. And the VOP." Will noticed something over Zoey's shoulder and said, "He's here."

A second vehicle pulled up, a panel truck with an animated ASHE DEVELOPMENT logo on the side, cartoon workers assembling the letters out of girders. The truck parked and the rear door lowered like a drawbridge, revealing its cargo to be a gleaming black metal object roughly the size and shape of a crouching rhinoceros. A butterfly-sized drone buzzed in front of Zoey's face, bearing a tiny camera that was probably one of five hundred tiny cameras watching her at the moment. If you enjoyed livestreamed human tragedy, Tabula Ra$a was an all-you-can-eat buffet.

Zoey smacked the drone aside with her hand and said, "Can everybody hear me? Are you all in your spots?"

From a nearly invisible earpiece in her right ear, four voices spoke at once, rendering all of them an indecipherable jumble until one person finished their sentence with "hot link."

Zoey said, "Let's try that again, one at a time. Budd?"

A man with a Texas drawl said, "The hostage taker's name is Dexter Tilley. Twenty years old. Frequent customer of the Night Inn. You've never met him. Inherited a house from his gramma, sold it a week ago, and used the cash on bootleg skeletal and musculature Raiden implants. Can't find anybody who'll admit selling him a brain zappin' contraption but they do exist."

Will said, "We're obviously going to assume he has it."

Budd said, "Echo's with me."

The voice of Michelle "Echo" Ling chimed in. "Every time Tilley came here, he requested the same girl, a nineteen-year-old named Shae LaVergne. She is currently in the room with him. So you've got over one hundred hostages but it's looking like this is about her."

Oh, god, Zoey thought. The guy fell in love with one of the professionals. She now feared the sheer awkwardness of this encounter more than death.

"Well, that all sounds terrible," said Zoey. "Where are you now?"

"Budd and I are both inside. Trying to keep the inn's staff calm."

"You are? How did you get in?"

Zoey had been told they were waiting at the scene, but didn't know they were, like, *in* the scene.

Budd said, "We were here before Tilley. Been tailing him all day."

"You were tailing him, but arrived before he did?"

"You do your homework," Budd said, "and you can tail from in front."

"All right, way to earn your paycheck. Wu, you in position?"

Wu was Zoey's personal bodyguard, who the hostage taker had specifically demanded not accompany Zoey to the meet. Again, they intended to push the envelope as far as possible on that demand.

A hushed voice in her ear said, "I am."

"Where?"

"The fourth floor of the Hyatt, across the street."

Zoey turned and looked behind her, the front of the hotel flashing an animation of a waterfall cascading and breaking over the main entrance. There was a world-class seafood joint on the top floor and there were animated fish swimming around up there. Occasionally one would go leaping out of the "water" and a shimmering silver tuna would break the boundary of the roof and soar into the actual night sky, a projected hologram picking up the animation as one smooth motion. The tourists loved stuff like that.

Wu said, "When you turn to look at me, anyone watching will immediately know why, that you are looking to your sniper."

"Oh. Right. Andre?"

From her other ear, she heard, "I'm right next to you, getting a hot link."

She turned and there he stood, a large black man with a shiny bald head, squirting mustard onto a sausage he'd just bought from the one-man band.

He said, "See, now you're giving away *my* position. Already this thing is a train wreck. And did you see that Halloween Month ad that ran up there? Since when has this city had public nudity laws?"

Andre actually was in position. His job was to remotely pilot the shiny black thing in the back of the panel truck.

Zoey looked it over. "I thought you were supposed to get the scariest drone you could find? This just looks . . . *fancy*. It's piano black. It looks like a sculpture some old rich guy would have in his parlor."

"It's scarier in motion. SWAT teams in Israel use 'em for hostage negotiation all the time. Well, they don't really do all that much *negotiating . . .*"

"So the hostage taker can talk to this thing and I can talk back through it?"

Will said, "Even better, it'll display a live hologram of your face to the front end there, that way he gets facial expressions, too. That's important for building rapport. When I talk, it'll switch to mine."

It sounded like Will had used one of these before. Zoey would have to remind Will to never tell her that story.

There was a scuffle in the crowd behind them, some of the spectators getting roughly shoved back by the yellow jackets. The agitators were mostly guys in their twenties, and they were mooing at Zoey, like cows. Zoey was well known in the city, but not necessarily well liked, and at some point her detractors had decided she was a cow. They sold T-shirts and everything, depicting her head on a cow's body, only drawn to mimic Zoey's in cartoonish yet hurtfully accurate ways (they even included her missing tooth). The first time she'd seen one of the shirts, she'd been eating at a cafe with her mother and bodyguard.

She had rolled her eyes and snickered and actually made it all the way back to the car before she burst into tears.

Zoey said, "Can we push those people farther away or something? And by 'something' I mean have Kowalski shoot them? In the crotch?"

Will looked surprised. "I'd bring them closer if I could. If the guy is near that opening, I want him to hear the chants."

She thought about asking why, but ultimately decided against it. Will liked to hear himself explaining things a little too much, so she tried to ration it out.

From her earpiece, Budd said, "Get to a screen, looks like the hostage taker is about to make a statement."

As Will went for his phone, Wu spoke from Zoey's earpiece. "He has reentered the room. He has the girl with him. He just moved behind the window frame, trying to stay out of view."

Will brought up Blink, a searchable network of just about every running wireless camera on Earth. The top trending stream was titled "Night Inn Hostage Crisis, BIG Death Toll Assured—ALERT: POSSIBLE COW SLAUGHTER!"

Dexter Tilley appeared on-screen. Well, sort of. He was using a digital "mask" to cover his face on the feed and it replaced his head with a fairly realistic animated skull. Unless the guy actually was a talking skeleton, which if so, Zoey thought it was weird that Budd and Echo left that out of their summary. When Tilley spoke, his voice had been filtered, too. It was a high-pitched, taunting tone, about what you'd expect from a skeleton possessed by some kind of evil spirit.

"I see you down there, bitch! No negotiation, no tricks. You hear me? I'm ready to die, I'm ready to take everybody with me. Are you?"

Reading the concern on Zoey's face, Andre said, "I think they all say that."

Will said to her, "I'm in contact with a rapid entry team, they're ninety percent sure they can take him out before he triggers whatever device he's got, if he even has one at all. They don't even want to get paid, they'll do it for the exposure. Last chance."

"Ninety percent? Would you board a plane that had a ten percent chance of crashing?"

"I once boarded a plane that barely had a ten percent chance of *not* crashing because, like now, my other options were worse."

"And what are the odds the hostage makes it out of a raid intact?" Shae. That was her name. "I've seen what those ribbon guns do. No, this requires finesse. Andre, send in the giant robot monster."

Andre tapped some icons on his phone and the shiny black thing in the truck blinked to life. It whirred and beeped and birthed itself from the cargo hold on unseen wheels. Once free, eight mechanical legs sprang from the sides, lifting its body six feet off the ground. Every inch was covered in that reflective black shielding, like it had been sculpted out of a moonless night. It was the most terrifying thing Zoey had ever seen.

Andre said, "It's patched into your phone. It's calling you now."

Zoey dug out her phone, then physically recoiled when a full-color hologram of her face appeared where the spider's head would be.

"Holy god."

Andre said, "Whoa, that's actually even creepier than I intended."

"Private military groups also use these things to take out tanks," said Will. "The two front legs have plasma cutters that will slice through two inches of armor. It can take a direct hit from a railgun. Skin will heal itself from damage, you could riddle it with fifty-caliber fire and watch the holes disappear in ten seconds."

Zoey stared at the thing, transfixed. "Wait, where did you get this thing, again?"

Andre said, "Rented it from a friend. Though you wouldn't know he was a friend based on the deposit he demanded."

"Do I want to know how much?"

"Can you really put a price on something like this?"

"Oh god. All right. Let's do it."

2

The piano-black Zoey-ghost-face spider-drone monster clicked along the pavement to *oohs* and *aahs* from the crowd. It hopped onto the overturned food truck and then, without hesitation, skittered right up the building's darkened facade, toward the ragged opening in the fourth floor. It pulled itself into the room with a quick, jerky movement that was much more arachnid than robot.

Zoey held her breath.

Even from street level, they could hear the terrified shriek of a young girl from inside. *Well,* Zoey thought, *we've already traumatized the hostage.*

She watched the machine's camera feed from her phone, and saw a brief, blurry glimpse of a young woman before a figure stepped into view and the screen went dark.

"What happened?"

Andre said, "He covered the drone's camera. Threw a blanket over it or somethin'."

"Can we uncover it?" If not, Zoey thought that seemed like an inexcusable design flaw.

Will said, "We can, but won't. We don't need to see him, not yet. As long as he can hear us, go ahead and let him think he accomplished something. Open the line. I'll do the talking."

Zoey found a "Speak" icon and pointed the phone toward Will's face. Drones swarmed around them and just about every bystander had a Blink camera pinned to their clothing. Everything they said was being streamed to an audience of maybe millions, from dozens of angles, everyone watching their follower counts tick upward. Zoey saw several people in the audience with Gadflies, the little drones everyone had been buying this year that hovered around their shoulders, livestreaming their lives in a way that could also get their face in the shot.

Will asked, "Can you hear me?"

From the phone, a normal human voice—the dumb skeleton filter only worked on Tilley's own camera—said, "Who's this? Put the cow on."

"My name is Will Blackwater. I work for Zoey Ashe, solving the problems that aren't worth her time. Listen closely, because I'm not going to repeat myself. Each breath you draw from this moment forward is a precious gift granted to you by Ms. Ashe. After each said breath, I want you to silently thank her and appreciate the grace she has bestowed upon you. Her patience, however, is not boundless. I am not here to listen to your demands. I already know your demands, your *true* demands, even if you do not. You demand to remain alive and to be forgiven for your trespasses.

"If you leave immediately, we will all return to our respective homes and I will plead to Zoey on your behalf for a reasonable punishment. I cannot offer any guarantees as to what her response will be. If you do not leave immediately, however, the machine before you will cut off your head and rip those implants off your bones. It will do it so quickly that you won't even register the movement—the speed of its limbs is restricted only by air resistance. This is an A-8 Disruptor, made in Germany. It took exactly three of them to disable an entire division of Iranian tanks during the Blue Sky Raids. So let me be absolutely clear. You can still win here. But only if you define victory as leaving that building with your body intact."

Will stopped talking and muted their end. No response. Zoey

wondered if his attempt to paint her as a cruel, omnipotent overlord was undermined by her outfit. She had wanted to change clothes, but Will had advised against it for reasons that he hadn't had time to explain. She needed to remind herself not to accidentally press the spot on the seam of her T-shirt that would make the cat start singing a sea shanty consisting entirely of meows.

Zoey said, "If he tries to detonate the sonic gadget, or do something else stupid, how are we going to fight back if we can't see him?"

Andre said, "The Disruptor's own AI will take over and kick his ass. A human operator would just slow it down anyway."

In Zoey's ear, Wu said, "I do not have a clear shot, the A-8 is between me and the target. I can just make out movement beyond the—whoa! I, uh, think the negotiation phase has ended."

There were crashes from inside the building. The crowd gasped. Some people even backed away, realizing that there was, in fact, no reason this conflict couldn't spill out of the building and wipe out a dozen of the gawkers before they even had time to crap their pants. Zoey, realizing she'd made their same mistake, took a step back from the noise.

"Uh, just to be clear, the brain-melting device he said he had, it can't penetrate the walls of that building, can it? We'd be safe out here?"

Will looked surprised. "Who ever said that?"

From inside the building came a noise like a car being stomped down a manhole by an angry giant. The battered carcass of the 8-8 Disintegrator or whatever Will had called it came flying out of the hole in the wall. The crowd below screamed and scattered. Zoey ducked. The mangled black monstrosity crashed onto the sidewalk and rolled into the middle of the street. A self-driving bus detected the obstacle and braked in time, then a cherry-red human-driven convertible on monster truck tires rear-ended the bus.

A boo went up from the crowd and there was a brief euphoric

moment when Zoey thought they were booing Tilley, having come around to her side. Then she figured out that they were mooing. Will stood up and straightened his suit, standing in the spot where he'd quickly placed himself in between Zoey and the wreckage. Zoey took a long breath to steady herself and pushed her bangs out of her eyes.

To Andre, she said, "So, do we just lose the deposit, or do we now have to pay for the whole thing?"

"I think it's important to remain calm in these situations, so I won't go into detail about the exact financial toll of tonight's operation until it's all said and done."

Tilley's animated skull appeared on the Blink feed again and in the silly skeleton voice said, "My patience is done! I want the cow. Not her lawyer, not her bodyguard, not her pathetic toys."

Will shot a quick, almost imperceptible glance at a nearby drone before saying, "Wu, do you have the shot, or is he back behind the window frame?"

"He is behind the frame and also I have the shot. These rounds can penetrate the steel beam and then detonate in a spot of our choosing, perhaps inside one of Tilley's eye sockets. The problem is the female hostage is sitting right next to him."

Zoey said, "Plus if you miss, or just hurt him, he's going to activate his brain gadget for sure. You'd be giving him no choice."

"If he has it," muttered Will, casting an annoyed glare at the building.

Zoey followed his gaze and said, "Look, I know how you say you hate unknown variables more than Abe Lincoln hated ceiling fans—"

"I'm sure I've never phrased it like—"

"But I'm obviously going in there. Everybody wants something; we'll make him an offer. It's by far our best chance of this not ending in utter disaster."

There was nothing in the world Zoey wanted to do less than she wanted to do this. At this point in the night she was supposed to be extremely drunk and full of sushi, sloppily hitting on some high-society kid who was looking to do something his parents wouldn't approve of.

"Zoey, if you give in to this guy, next week you'll have another one just like him holding up another of your joints making bigger demands. You'd be laying out the welcome mat."

"Well, tonight I'm worried about tonight. Now how do I get in there?"

"I'm going with you," said Will, never taking his eyes off that ragged hole in the building. "He has to know that only I can make the kind of decisions he wants made."

This wasn't true, but Zoey knew why Will had said it. If Dexter Tilley was watching literally any feed about his own hostage situation, he also was listening to everything they said right now, including the exchange with Wu moments ago. Being on camera every moment you were outside your home meant every conversation, facial expression, and mannerism was a performance. It was an adjustment that Zoey found difficult, because only a psychopath would find it easy. Of course, Tilley himself had to know that Will knew Tilley was listening in, and would thus deduce that this could be a performance on Will's part. But he also knew that Will knew that he knew, so maybe Will's performance was intentionally inauthentic, so that Tilley would think Will was lying, when in reality, he was telling the truth. Zoey was starting to get a headache.

Will looked her in the eye, getting serious now. "You know what to do?"

"I've been in a hostage negotiation before, Will. Multiple times."

"As a hostage, yes. This end is more complicated."

"Sure. So, again I ask, how in the hell do we get in?"

It turned out their method for reaching the busted-out hole in the side of the building was, in fact, just a big-ass ladder. The fire department was on hand (they always came when called but would send a bill later) and they had one that could extend from the top of the overturned food truck up to the opening. Unfortunately, nobody had a second, smaller ladder to get them from the ground to the top of the truck, so Andre rolled over a trash can they could use as a step stool. Zoey stumbled six or seven times on the way up, even with Will awkwardly trying to help her. It was almost like Andre had picked the single clumsiest option possible. The crowd loved it.

Will then led the way up the ladder, disappearing into the spot where most of the floor-to-ceiling window had been bashed away. Zoey followed, the rickety ladder shaking with every step. She was coated in cold terror-sweat before she was even halfway up. There were drones swarming below her and they probably had a great view of her black-with-white-polka-dot underwear (the pervs who zoomed in would find the white dots were tiny skulls). Live female wardrobe malfunction. Blink also never lacked for content or audience.

Finally, she climbed through the opening into the room, tumbled across an end table, and thumped to the floor. She stood, brushed broken glass off herself, and smoothed down her skirt. She accidentally brushed the wrong spot and the cat on her shirt started meowing to the tune of "Blow the Man Down" ("meow-MEOW meow-meow-meow . . .") until Zoey found the off switch in the seam about two full minutes later. When she finally looked up, there were three sets of eyes staring back at her.

Zoey said, "Uh, hi."

Huddled in the corner was a weeping woman Zoey assumed was Shae LaVergne. Thin, pale skin, huge brown eyes, auburn hair cropped into a pixie cut that swooped down across her forehead. She had ears that stuck out a little, giving her an elven look. Silk pajamas with little cartoon bunnies. Zoey suspected the Night Inn Cuddle Theater kept Shae very, very busy.

Sitting on the ornate bed was a chubby guy who didn't actually look twenty years old, which was the age Budd had given her for Dexter Tilley—she'd have guessed an awkward fifteen or sixteen. Slumped shoulders, acne, hair he'd buzzed off, presumably after realizing he couldn't do anything trendy with it. He had a wispy failed mustache. On his hands were black armored gloves, designed to let an overpowered person punch through metal without pulping their fists.

Along his shoulders and elbows were ugly, inflamed surgery scars. The aftermath of an in-and-out back-alley procedure with no post-op care. Zoey had seen body scans and, in one case, the actual skeleton of a guy who'd gotten the implants. It was a super-strong black mesh woven through bone and tendon, like their innards were wearing sexy fishnets. Somewhere in there was also a little thumb-sized device driving it all, the tech that made the whole thing possible, called Raiden. It could generate enough power to bring down a building. She'd seen it.

Will, softening his tone so radically that it physically startled Zoey, said, "You're Dexter, right? How are you doing?"

"Not good."

She had seen Will do this before, adopting a manner that implied he'd entirely forgotten a vicious conflict that had occurred just minutes earlier. Someone told her the technique was called "gaslighting." Zoey assumed they called it that because it really confuses people, just like if you stopped in the middle of a conversation to suddenly light a fart.

Will nodded. "Let's see what we can do about that." He turned to the girl. "And you're Shae? How are you holding up?"

In a tragically hopeful voice, the girl said, "You're with the police?"

Zoey said, "No, I actually own this business, much to my surprise. I'm Zoey, this is Will. He works for me."

"*What?* Where are the police?"

Zoey said, "Ah. You're new in town, aren't you?"

Dexter answered for her. "Shae moved here in the spring." He turned to Shae and said, "Ain't no laws in Tabula Rasa."

Zoey said, "I'm new myself, I got here less than a year ago. This actually isn't even technically a city. And the laws do exist, whatever is illegal in the United States or the state of Utah is also illegal where we're standing. But it turns out laws only mean something if there are flesh-and-blood people around to punish the bad guys. Most of the police here stopped showing up to work a long time ago, so security pretty much falls to whoever owns the property and, like I said, I'm told I own this place. Mr. Tilley here apparently knew that, so, here we are."

Will went to the wet bar and poured himself a scotch.

Without looking up from his glass, he said to Tilley, "You seem to know who Zoey is; do you know who I am?"

"I know enough. You're one of her people."

"One of *her* people? Open your eyes. Zoey is twenty-three and is wearing a cat shirt and a necklace with a pendant that says MY EYES ARE UP THERE. You don't wonder how she ended up in charge of an organization that owns buildings like this and has 'people' like me?"

"I don't think I give a shit."

"You should," said Will, in his eerily friendly voice. "You see, before Zoey came along, this, and many other establishments, were owned by a man named Arthur Livingston. He helped build this city. This was all a bunch of dusty construction sites just twenty years ago. A whole lot of people tried very hard to stop him at every step of the way. None succeeded. Arthur passed away last year, unfortunately, leaving his fortune and businesses to his daughter, Zoey, who prior to that had been living in a trailer park in Colorado and working as a barista. Some parties who had previously known better than to cross Arthur wrongly decided that his passing was the time to strike. They have since found out otherwise. Do you understand?"

"You people say 'business,' when you mean organized crime."

Zoey said, "It honestly isn't that organized."

A swarm of camera drones buzzed outside the hole in the glass behind them. Surely tens of millions were watching by now, waiting to see if this situation would explode. Hoping it would.

Will sipped his drink and seemed unimpressed. Zoey didn't know if he was annoyed that the bottles were too watered down, or that they weren't watered down enough.

"Do you mind if we sit?"

Dexter shot a glance outside. "We're not staying here."

"We're not?"

"You think I'm an idiot? My general intelligence is in the ninety-eighth percentile. Look it up. You have a sniper on the fourth floor across the street, behind the fish. Room 412. Chinese-looking dude. Do you not see my people out there, on the street? Do you not hear them? They tracked him all the way up to his perch, reported back to me every step, listening to every word he whispered in your ear. So we're moving to another room, away from that opening, away from your sniper, away from those cameras."

Tilley picked up a backpack that looked like it'd never seen a day in the wilderness. If his lethal brain scrambler existed, it was presumably in there, though it looked to Zoey like it was bulging at the seams with clothes, like the kid had packed everything he owned.

"You're coming with me," he said to Zoey. To Will, "You're going to turn your ass around and take the long, sad climb down that ladder. This is between me and her."

Will said, "You don't want that. You're not negotiating with her, you're negotiating with me. She doesn't even know what she has to negotiate with."

"Stop with all that. I know all about this bit, the negotiation, you saying you're going to do all the talking. I've seen the streams, I know what you're trying to do. And if you say one more word in that direction *I will punch your balls into space*."

Will stared down Tilley and in a horribly casual voice asked, "Wu? You have the shot?"

Dexter's eyes went wide. He snatched Zoey by her shirt and yanked her over to him, his arm around her neck, using her as a human shield. Shae screamed. Zoey didn't, but did think she was going to piss herself.

Will, calm as wind chimes, said, "Wu, if you hit Zoey two inches below her rib cage and one inch to the right of her spinal column, you'll punch a hole through her abdomen that she'll likely survive. Set the round to detonate about six inches later, inside Mr. Tilley's torso. It will blow him in half, implants or not."

Zoey said, "We're not doing that! Wu, do not shoot through me! Don't shoot at all! I'll go with him. Will, stay here, that's an order."

Dexter Tilley apparently didn't have too much faith in Zoey's unquestioned authority over her organization, as he kept her in the human shield position and quickly dragged her backward toward the door leading out of the room. He picked up the backpack and called for Shae to follow.

Zoey thought this would have been a perfect time for the hostage to hurl herself out of the window, jump down to the food truck, and sprint off into the crowd, leaving the problem to Zoey. Instead, Shae climbed to her feet and voluntarily followed them into the hall. Zoey couldn't blame her. When push comes to shove, almost everyone complies.

3

Tilley slammed the door behind Shae. Will did not follow them through. Zoey knew he wouldn't.

Tilley asked Shae, "Where are the showers?"

"W-what?"

"The employee showers. In the lounge, you mentioned it before."

"Th-thirteenth floor. It doesn't show on the elevator but I can make it stop there with an eye scan."

"Let's go."

Zoey spent the elevator ride up filling her mind with wild guesses about what this guy wanted to do in a group shower setting. She nervously fidgeted with her necklace. They arrived to find the employee lounge was locked behind a sturdy door that wouldn't even open for Shae—probably some automated lockdown system—but Dexter calmly tore the door off its hinges and tossed it aside. Inside was a break room with a few sofas and vending machines and a huge framed list of staff reminders on one wall. ("If a hand goes under your clothing, GENTLY resist and remind the guest of Rule #4. BE NICE.")

A couple who appeared to have been hiding out in the room recoiled at the sight of them. The guy was in a white suit with a white cowboy hat perched above unkempt eyebrows, the girl was a stunning Filipino woman half his age.

The woman, whom Tilley apparently did not recognize as Zoey's associate Echo Ling, screamed, "Oh, my god, don't kill us!"

Zoey thought it was . . . fairly convincing. The guy in the hat, Budd Billingsley, acted like a man who was frantically trying to size up the situation while remaining cool, which probably wasn't a performance.

Dexter nodded toward the door and said, "Out."

Zoey was hoping he'd demand they stay, as Budd and Echo both had way more experience with this kind of thing than she did. Apparently Tilley thought that'd be too many hostages to control. The couple hurried out of the room and Echo, in her "panic," left her purse behind. That purse, Zoey was sure, contained some kind of weapon or gadget she could use to disable Dexter in an emergency. Right as they reached the door, Dexter said, "Hey, you forgot your purse."

Nice guy.

Echo hesitated, but went back and picked it up. Her eyes met Zoey's, just for a second. Echo's look seemed to ask if Zoey was okay, if things were under control. Zoey tried to project confidence, but guessed that her own expression only communicated that she'd made a horrible, horrible mistake. Both of them left and Dexter led Zoey and Shae into a connected tiled room with a half dozen private shower stalls.

Tilley drilled his gaze into Shae and said, "You told me they have showers. I never asked you why. I want you to tell me."

"Tell you . . . what?"

"Why do you have showers?"

Zoey didn't understand the question and it was obvious that Shae didn't, either. The other thing Zoey didn't know at the moment was if Tilley was livestreaming this encounter himself. The cameras could be as tiny as you wanted—he could have one embedded in his belt buckle, or anywhere. It would help to know if she was still performing for an audience.

Zoey said, "Let's not get sidetracked. The clock is ticking before somebody on the outside, either my people or some other group looking to make a name for themselves, tries to storm this place. Let's work out a deal and then I can go back home. I think my party guests have left but there should still be food."

"Answer my question."

Shae looked pleadingly back and forth from Dexter to Zoey. "I don't . . . I don't understand. The showers are for the staff."

"You work up a sweat doing this? Lying there, watching movies?"

"Not always, but—"

"But sometimes you want to shower after doing it. After having to lay there with some damp fatass for two hours. Got his BO all over you. Right?"

Shae didn't answer.

Dexter said, "Or maybe you just need a shower anyway. Because you just feel gross inside, having some ugly guy rubbing up against you, his bad breath in your face. A shower, to try to put it out of your mind."

"No, it's not like that."

Still locking eyes with her, he asked, "Did you ever shower after our appointments?"

"No. No."

Zoey didn't know if Tilley could spot the lie in Shae's eyes, but Zoey could.

Without a word, he went to one stall after another, turning on the water. While he was distracted, Zoey surreptitiously pulled out her phone and typed in a search:

HOSTAGE NEGOTIATION STRATEGIES

In the thirty seconds she had to browse the list before Tilley returned, she saw something about reassuring the guy that any previous actions were easily revocable and making a big show of listening to demands. Then there was something about extracting concessions in exchange for meeting lesser demands, like food deliveries, finally just delaying until the bad guy got tired and gave up. God, she was going to be here all night. She heard his shoes coming her way and quickly put the phone away.

"There's recording gear that can penetrate walls," he said, "but it shouldn't work this far in and it can't handle that background noise. That means it's just us."

Dexter put his arm around Shae and pulled her close. She tried to suppress her tears, but failed. He said "Shh" and kissed the top of her head.

Zoey said, "First of all, the fact that this city is a lawless clown orgy works to our advantage here. Nothing has happened so far that can't be easily fixed. Nobody's been hurt or killed, and insurance will patch up the window. That's the big thing we all need to keep in mind. If we want, we can all go back to normal."

Dexter held up a hand to stop her. "See, here's the problem with that. Your 'normal' *is my Hell*."

"Okay. So, tell me what you want."

This stopped Dexter. It was like he actually hadn't been expecting this question. He suddenly seemed nervous, like he'd been put on the spot. Zoey thought that where most guys had at least a little confidence, this one only had a dark cellar where he stored his shame.

"So, every weekend I'm here. With Shae. I buy back-to-back sessions when I can. We talk, we hold each other, I pour out my heart to her. We cry. The first time in my life I've had this. I'm not ashamed to admit it. I've been invisible my whole life, until now. I feel her pressed up against me and I become real, for the first time. So two weeks ago all I did—*all* I did—was ask if I could see her outside of the sessions. If we could go have coffee. She says no, and that's fine, no big deal. Next time I come, they tell me I have to go with a different girl. Shae has blocked me."

Zoey knew without having to consult the hostage negotiation guide that this was not the time to tell a crazy man he's being crazy. Women get their faces smashed in doing that. Anything she said that challenged him, or made him feel small, would just be seen as an attack. So what in the hell *do* you say?

Zoey said, "That must have been hard." There, that should do it. "But you know that's not the fault of any of the hundred other people in the building, so how about you let us move the snack truck that's blocking the front door and start getting those people out of here. You don't want to hurt them."

"And what do I get in exchange for doing that?"

"What do you want?"

"I want Shae."

"You want them to let you make appointments with her again?"

"No. I *want Shae*. My only possible life is with her. If I can't be with her, I have no life, and I'm taking as many people with me as I can."

Zoey started to tell him that perhaps the terrified girl standing next to him should have some say in how she spends the rest of her life, then stopped herself. Zoey didn't have much of a filter but sometimes it did kick in during emergencies.

She thought for a moment. "Wait, if that's all you want, why did you ask for me? Why didn't you just grab her and go?"

"You have to let her out of her contract. The slave deal you made her sign."

"I'm sorry, the what?"

"You made her and all of the other hosts sign a deal that they have to work out their yearlong contract, or else your people track them down. She can't go with me unless you release her from it. We want that, plus some money. Enough to get away. Ten million."

The contract thing didn't sound right to Zoey. It's entirely possible some of her businesses had been run that way at one time, but that was the kind of thing she'd put a stop to. Then her eyes met Shae's and the obvious truth hit her: that had been Shae's lie to stall Tilley. She hadn't been expecting him to actually call the owner to get it voided.

"Ah. Right. But if you didn't find that out until you got here, it means you didn't come here planning to stage a hostage crisis. So what's really in your backpack there? Your lunch?"

That, it turned out, had been the wrong thing to say. Dexter pushed Shae aside and *flew* across the gap between him and Zoey. His fingers, coated in segmented metal, were instantly around her throat. He pushed her back against the cold tiles. He then swung his other fist and it exploded into the wall next to Zoey's head, leaving a hole the width of a bowling ball and sending ceramic shards spraying across the room.

Zoey's ears rang from the impact. Shae screamed.

"You know what these implants can do," hissed Tilley. "I can smash your skull against this wall, like cracking an egg. You know that, right?"

Zoey clawed uselessly around her neck. Then she reached down frantically with her left hand, digging into her pocket.

He said, "So it doesn't matter whether or not I have the device, not to you. Because you know I can smear these tiles with your brains without breaking a sweat. Right?"

Shae begged him to stop, told him she didn't want this, any of it.

Zoey's lungs burned, trying to pull in breath through her compressed windpipe. Her hand found her phone. She brought it up with her right hand, holding it so the screen was visible over Dexter's left shoulder. With a shaking thumb, she tapped the browser and brought up the list of hostage negotiation tips again. She found what she thought was the relevant sentence.

She croaked, "I . . . can take that request to my people. But . . . it will take some time . . ."

Dexter squinted in confusion, glanced back at the phone, then let her go. Zoey collapsed to the floor.

He said, "You're dumber than they told me you were. I know you own this place, I know you've got the money. Whatever I want done, you can do it with a word."

Zoey struggled to catch her breath. Her throat was throbbing. "I'm sorry . . . I'm used to being on Shae's end."

Shae said, "Can we please talk to that other guy instead?"

"I want half of the ten million in dollars," said Tilley, "and half in Spoils, transferred to my Hub account."

Still sitting on the tile floor, Zoey folded her legs under her and let out a sigh. Her neck was burning and she was starting to feel clammy all over from the shower steam. She pushed her hair out of her face.

"You know I can't let you take her."

"You can't stop us."

"'Us?' You're acting like you're running off together. You think she wants this? Look at her!"

"So what. For almost all of human history, this right here is how it was done. You wanted a woman, you acquired her, no different from livestock. I understand why, now. Women don't know what they want. *I can make Shae happy.* She doesn't know it now, because society has told her it's shameful to be with a guy like me. All we have to do is push through that. In time, she'll see."

Zoey found herself wishing someone had in fact activated a device to melt her brain.

"I, uh, understand where you're coming from, Dexter. And it's good that you're . . . honest about your desires—"

"No. You don't even live in the same universe as I do. You notice ninety percent of the customers here are male? All of us, starving for this."

"Yeah and ninety percent of the employees are girls, same as the sex workers in any of the thousand brothels in this city. You think they wouldn't prefer to be doing something else? Meanwhile, I have to do boring meetings with rich CEOs every week and guess what—*they're* mostly guys. That's the world."

Zoey had several vices in her life, perhaps none more dangerous than her addiction to pointless arguments.

"No," said Tilley, trembling with the anticipation of finally putting all of this into words. "Look at you. You're as fat as me and your face is nothing special, but even if you lost every penny you could always find a guy to take care of you. Men have wanted what you have since before you even knew what it was, begged you for it, done you favors. Meanwhile, I was treated like a slug on a sidewalk, told every day that no one wants me. You'll *never* know what that's like. So no, you won't talk me out of this. We're not even speaking the same language."

"I just came from a party, a bunch of people there I barely know. This gross old rich guy was hitting on me the whole time. Do you know what he liked about me?"

"Your tits? That you look like you have no respect for yourself and will do anything in bed?"

"He liked that I'm twenty-three. How many years can pass before that window closes? All that humiliation you went through in school, all those cheerleaders getting treated like goddesses, I get it, I was there, too. But each and every one of those girls is praying they can get their lives to a solid place before society declares them invisible. Meanwhile, a guy can get old and ugly and still pick up prom queens as long as he's got his life together. That can be you! Let Shae go, maybe we can work something out. Turn your whole situation around."

Dexter reached over and grabbed Shae, roughly this time. He pulled her in front of him. An arm around her neck, a gloved finger stroking her collarbone.

"I'm not giving her up to some fraternity douchebag. You have five seconds to tear up her contract, or I'll crush her windpipe."

Zoey's hand instinctively shot up to her own neck.

"There is no contract. She just made that up, to stall."

Tilley scoffed and shook his head, as if he was annoyed with himself for falling for it. "So we don't need you at all."

"Well, you do *now*. There's almost certainly a trigger-happy army waiting for you out there and your implants don't make you explosion-proof."

"Then they'll take out Shae, too. We'll die together. If that's how it's destined to happen, so be it. I still want the cash. We're done talking."

He raised his hand, putting his fingers around Shae's throat. Zoey reached up, touching the MY EYES ARE UP THERE pendant, rubbing it between two fingers.

Zoey said, "Stop."

"I said WE ARE DONE TALKING!" The shouts ricocheted around the tiles.

"I agree. Let go."

Tilley loosened his grip.

His eyes went wide. Confusion. Doubt.

Zoey said, "Take your hand away from Shae's throat. Drop it by your side."

He did just that, his eyes following his hand as it dropped.

Terrified.

His hand was acting on its own.

Zoey said, "I forgot to mention before now, but my company developed those implants. Well, one of my companies. One product we never sold publicly was the remote override. I've got one embedded in my necklace here. It's voice operated. Have a seat, on the floor. Let's talk."

Dexter Tilley did not move. He was trying to lunge at Zoey, she could see him flexing, trying to make his body obey. His face was turning red with the effort. For the first time in his life, his arms and legs were not his own. People have nightmares where this happens, right?

She touched the pendant and said, "Sit on the floor."

His body did as it was told.

"Thank you. Shae, if you want to slap him or kick him, now is your chance."

Shae had backed away, trembling. "I don't understand what— I just want to go. Can I go?"

"I don't want some private security dope out there to gun you down in the confusion. Give me a minute and we'll all leave together. Now, we have several options for what we can do with Mr. Tilley here. And

I'm leaving it up to you. If you want me to make him tear his own throat out, that's what we'll do."

"I don't want that."

"What do you want?"

"I just want him to stay away."

"And you don't want an army of angry trolls coming after you later. You heard the chanting out there, right?" It was clear from her expression that Shae hadn't considered that as a possibility. "Do you like living here? In the city, I mean."

"Not particularly."

"We'll set you up with something. Wherever you want." To Tilley, Zoey said, "You, on the other hand, deserve nothing. And right now, my associate, Will Blackwater, is telling the news cameras that we do not negotiate with terrorists, that I'm going to offer you the same less-than-nothing he offered, that your options are to give up or die. I know this, because we planned it in advance. Just as we planned to give you that cool-looking drone to smash in front of everybody, to show off how big and strong you are. But then you're going to walk out that front door and announce that *you're* getting everything you wanted. You're going to say that you demanded we give you a job. Fortunately, I have an associate named Rico Hierra, he owns a very successful materials recovery company, they go into buildings that need to come down and rip out all of the valuable stuff."

"You're . . . offering me a construction job? I don't—"

"Not construction. *Deconstruction.* You'll be smashing bricks, breaking glass, knocking down walls and listening to the wonderful sound they make when they fall. It's hard work, but the good kind. Rico is big on second chances, hires a lot of ex-cons and other shady types, and the job pays accordingly. But get on Rico's good side and you'll have your pick of jobs; his name means a lot around here. You can get your own place, have a reason to get up every morning. A new start. And you'll be surprised how fast you put on muscle doing it."

Zoey paused to give him a moment to take it in, to visualize it. Then,

"But Shae won't be there. That's not an option. We find you any-where nearby, if you show up in the same *city* as her, you'll die and I'll feel nothing. All I have to do is push a button and overload your implants, turn you into a pile of charcoal on the floor. If I ever hear you've pulled anything like this with anyone else, you die. If you tell anyone we have control over the implants, you die. That's information we're keeping under our hats, for now. Instead, you will say to the crowd that this was all your idea, that you've decided you want to work on yourself first, that women are all ungrateful harpies anyway. It'll be super convincing."

"Why? I mean, why offer me any of this?"

"Because I believe that giving people second chances pays off in the long run, regardless of whether or not they deserve them."

"Bullshit. There's something else here. You fear me. You fear my people. Otherwise you wouldn't be giving in."

"I can command your right hand to rip out your tongue and flap it against your scrotum for the rest of the week. Within fifteen minutes I could have your mother, brother, and nephews killed in their homes and I would not be inconvenienced by so much as a visit from the po-lice. I am giving you a chance, and it tastes like poison in my mouth to be giving you anything. But the private prisons in this city will just spit you out as twice the monster you are now, so there's this big, gross gap between what you deserve and what would actually make the world better. And even then, I'm giving Shae the right to take back this offer if at any moment she decides she's not cool with you going unpunished."

Dexter stared daggers into Zoey. Then he worked his jaw, and sud-denly burst into tears.

Zoey sat quietly as he did so. Her face was stone.

After a while, she said, "A year ago, I was living with my mom. We had nothing, because she had hitched her wagon to a rich psychopath who bailed before I was born, and I had hitched mine to a high achiever who eventually decided high achievers can't be seen in vacation photos with girls whose thighs look like this. My entire idea of the future was blown to pieces in a single late-night conversation conducted on my mom's back porch in a pair of lawn chairs. I didn't leave the trailer for three weeks. Caleb, his new girl, and all of our old friends all went on vacation in Cuba, streamed the whole thing on Blink, these quarterbacks of life and their giggling trophies. I sat there in my room and watched it all, every minute. I watched them *sleep*. I was too sick to eat but still somehow gained six pounds."

She shrugged.

"Skip forward a bit, and here I am. This life, Dexter, it crashes in on you. You get your heart broken and you get humiliated but the sun rises the next day. The difference is I never tried to hurt any of them, never tried to take what they have. You won't ever do anything like that again. You're free to move your limbs now."

Tilley tested his right arm. He wiped his eyes.

"Oh," she said, "also, don't activate your implants. Not even to knock over walls for Rico. None of the devices you can buy on the black market are safe, they either overload and explode, or else they're calibrated wrong and you'll accidentally twist your own ligaments off."

Tilley clearly wasn't listening. "What if Shae changes her mind? What if she wants to see me?"

"You'll never see her or speak to her again."

Zoey stood, her legs feeling unsteady beneath her. She was relieved, but only because she was, of course, unable to see the future, to know exactly what chain of events she'd just set in motion. She had no idea, for instance, that at least one person in that room wasn't going to live to see Halloween.

"Let's go," she said, "I have to get back home, my cat is going to be furious."

4

Zoey made it back to the gigantic ballroom of the enormous mansion she'd inherited from her ginormously corrupt father, only to find it empty of party guests. She heard a faint ripping sound and found her cat, named Stench Machine, under one of the circular white tables. He was casually shredding a cat-sized paper party hat with his claws. She reached down to stroke him and he allowed it.

In the center of the room was a giant cake shaped vaguely like him: a grumpy white cat with a dark splotch like a coffee stain on his face and chest and a studded collar around its neck. Only a few tiny pieces had been taken. Nobody eats at parties in Tabula Ra$a, they just drink and nibble and then talk about how full they are. Even so, Zoey had hired a master sushi chef who'd rolled in with a whole setup that had to be unloaded from a truck, including cartons of fresh mackerel on ice. All of that was now gone, too. At one end of the room was a pink, ten-foot-tall octopus wearing sunglasses, frozen in place behind a turntable setup—the animatronic DJ they'd rented that someone had mercifully turned off before Zoey arrived. Champagne flutes sat abandoned on tables, some with delicate lipstick kisses on the rim. Nearby was a pair of ruby-red high heels someone had left behind. These people just go places and forget their shoes?

Zoey sighed.

She hadn't actually known any of those people, she'd turned her cat's birthday party into a fundraiser for an extremely important cause that Zoey couldn't remember at the moment. The ballroom had filled with rich locals wearing practiced smiles and elaborate wigs who either wanted on her good side or who just liked to be seen at these things—there was a reason Zoey had downed a fairly large antianxiety cookie before anyone had arrived. A monitor on the wall was still showing a Blink feed of the hostage crisis aftermath. Zoey imagined her guests huddled around it, watching to see if Zoey would get killed so they'd have an excuse to leave early. Then they'd left early anyway. Eh, she'd have done the same.

Near the opposite wall was a green tarp covering a lump the size of a school bus. The hidden object was humming ominously, Zoey could feel it through the floor. To keep people from messing with it, a WET PAINT sign had been taped to the tarp. She wondered if anyone at the party had gotten curious and taken a peek.

Zoey pulled out her phone and tried to call her mom to let her know she was okay, but got no answer. That was hardly unusual, her mother had a hard rule about not breaking up in-person conversations for phone calls.

Carlton, the butler who Zoey estimated was probably older than America, entered and said, "Good to see you back in one piece, Ms. Ashe. I of course was unable to view the standoff itself but I did get to see some harrowing moments on the TV there. That was a very tall ladder."

"Where did everybody go?"

"Your mother and her friends left to go find a bar—I believe one of them is going through a difficult divorce and she felt she needed support. The sushi chef feared that if he stayed, you would not approve the overtime, despite my reassurances to the contrary. I had him save you a plate, though he was not happy about that, either—he asserted that even minutes-old leftovers do not represent the true quality of his work. Many of the remaining guests left as they assumed you would not be in the mood to deal with company after your ordeal. Others had already departed after realizing that they were not, as they had mistakenly believed, at a party hosted by world-famous blues singer Zoe Ashley."

Zoey picked up Stench Machine and squeezed him. "Crowds aren't his favorite thing anyway."

Will entered next—Zoey had told everyone to meet up back at the ballroom—and seemed relieved that the party had dispersed. He glanced at the frozen robot octopus, rolled his eyes, then made a beeline for the open bar to pour himself a glass of scotch. Next came Wu, dressed in clingy black with harnesses and carrying a rifle case, like an exotic assassin in an action movie. He was immediately identifiable as a sniper, which would have been a terrible choice for a mission in a public location unless his goal was specifically to get caught, which it had been.

Zoey said, "Could you have shot through me if you'd had to?"

"There were not actually any cartridges in the rifle. Even if there had been, I would have no idea how to program the proximity detonation triggers. I'm not trained in that type of weapon; a bodyguard who hides and shoots from fifty yards away is probably being a bit *too* proactive in his duties."

"No, I mean would you have been able to make yourself do it, if you had to?"

"Not shooting at the client is actually one of the very first lessons they teach you in bodyguard school."

Zoey heard Echo Ling's heels clicking into the room. She wore a jade sweater over leather pants that covered a physique that had apparently been designed in a lab specifically to make Zoey feel bad about her own. She'd recently added some gentle curls to her neck-length black hair as an additional insult.

Echo said, "That was crazy. Were you scared?"

"A little bit. What was in your purse you tried to leave behind? A stun gun or something?"

"A second override for the implants. It was on my key chain, we were worried you may have lost yours during one of the several times you fell down on the way in."

"Wait, how did you know he'd head for the employee lounge?"

Budd Billingsley was right behind Echo, and answered for her. "Tilley was takin' suggestions from his 'fans' on Blink chat. So we got on there and fed 'em the idea anonymously, told him it was a way to thwart long-range microphones. We had an entry team hacking the elevator to get back up there when you came out. Wouldn't have worked if we'd lost track of where you were in the building."

"Yeah, it's really sinking in now how much worse that could have gone. Could everyone see up my skirt as I was climbing up?"

Echo said, "Well, uh, the bad news is that, yes, a clip from the ladder situation went viral immediately. The good news is those skull-dot panties sold out nationwide within twenty minutes. There was an article about it. Probably an endorsement deal in it for you, if you want."

"And . . . yes, I want to die."

Andre Knox was the last to arrive, saying, "Thought you were gonna fall off that ladder." He glanced at a nearby table. "Anybody want some cocaine? Somebody left quite a bit behind. Aww, who turned off DJ Rocktopus?"

Zoey said, "All right, everybody gather around. I'm giving Wu an eight for his performance tonight."

Wu looked confused. "That's an eight out of . . . ?"

"Ten. You played a convincing sniper and also said you wouldn't shoot through me. Wu, you are allowed a piece of the cat cake."

Andre said, "Wait, is this something we're doing now? When did this start?"

"Yes, we're doing performance review scores. Budd and Echo, you both get a nine. You guys were so on top of this guy that you were at the scene of the hostage crisis before it was even a crisis. Incredible work, to the point that it's a little creepy. Actually Echo loses a point for telling me about the underwear thing, which I now can't stop thinking about. Echo, you should have lied. Make a note going forward. Still, you both get two pieces of the cat cake."

Echo gave the cake a slightly alarmed look. Zoey had never seen her eat anything but leaves, lab-grown seafood-style "meat," and endless varieties of protein shakes. She probably hadn't allowed herself to have cake since her ninth birthday party.

Budd said, "That probably isn't as impressive as it looked. Only two places in the city you can get the implants done and I've got somebody inside both, leaking to me whenever a patient shows up. Then Echo noted that our Mr. Tilley sent up every shade of red flag one can imagine."

"That's actually super impressive, guys. Andre . . . let's see. You get a seven."

"Oof. That's harsh, Zoey."

"On one hand, the spider tank thing was incredibly scary, on the other, I am getting the sense that you overspent on it. And also it got bashed into junk."

"That was the plan! As for the cost, there's two things to consider there. One, you always get shafted as a last-minute shopper, and two, do you *want* to live in a world in which any group of lowlifes can raise the cash to get somethin' like that? And really, it only added up to about two months' profit from one of the casinos."

Will choked on his scotch.

Zoey said, "Normally a seven would not qualify for cat cake, but Echo may let you have her pieces. Will, you get a four."

Andre said, "Damn, Will, you're dragging this whole organization down. Be honest with me, are you drinking again?"

Zoey said, "On one hand, this entire thing was Will's plan and it worked out exactly the way he said it would. On the other hand, Will's first plan, which was to splatter the hostage taker with a squad of guys with exotic weapons, was just shameful."

"I *still* think we should do it. Track him, take him out. The moment he leaks the fact that we can override the implants, somebody will come up with a workaround to counter it. We can make it seem like an accident, if that makes you feel better."

"Why would *that* make me feel better? It's a million times better to get a bad guy to turn his life around than to get exploded by a railgun or whatever you had in mind. And what about Shae?"

"What about all of the future Shaes? Our only alternative was to let the guy walk out with enough gain to save face. That creates incentive for others to do what he just did. The predators in this world can sense that weakness from across an ocean."

"So you don't negotiate, and then the guy triggers his bomb before you can kill him and a couple hundred people die? That's what we want?"

"*Yes*, because it saves lives in the long run. From that point on, everybody knows not to take hostages, because we've sent the message loud and clear that hostages are not valuable to us. If you care about the lives of innocent people, *really* care, you take away the financial incentive to hurt them. Otherwise you're just creating a bill that somebody else will have to pay."

"Enough with that, you're upsetting Stench Machine. As punishment for that dismal performance, you must eat the entire rest of the cat cake, all at once, with your hands tied behind your back. The entire time, the rest of the team will take turns explaining in detail at least one thing they don't like about you. If you try to refuse, Wu will be allowed to chop off one limb of his choosing."

Will finished his drink and set the empty glass on a nearby table. "I'm going home. I'll talk to the manager of the Night Inn in the morning, see what it'll take for the staff to come back to work. I'm guessing it won't be cheap."

"Ugh. *Fine.*"

He turned to go.

Zoey said, "Hey."

Will stopped and turned.

"How did I do? Tonight, I mean?"

"We're all still here, aren't we?"

That was all she would get from him.

As he left, Zoey let out a long sigh that devolved into a raspberry. "Well, I'm going to go soak in my bathtub until I fall apart like a corned beef."

"There is one last thing," said Budd, "unless you don't want to deal with one last thing in which case I can take care of it, but Shae is in the foyer. She wanted to have a word with you."

"Shae?"

Andre said, "You know, the hostage? From the hostage situation? That happened an hour ago?"

"Why does she want to talk to me?"

"Didn't feel right to interrogate her on the subject," said Budd. "Want me to send her away?"

"No, it's fine." It actually wasn't fine, Zoey wasn't in the mood to have this woman tearfully thank her and call her a hero, she'd find that just as draining as the standoff. Still, if Zoey could be said to have a job at all, this was it.

Zoey found Shae standing just inside the huge etched bronze doors of the main entrance, bundled in a long jacket that was too warm for the weather and definitely too warm for the foyer. Her arms were folded like she was hugging herself and her posture suggested that she thought the marble tiles around her were trapdoors. She clearly wasn't used to being in places like this and seemed afraid that one wrong move would result in getting mauled by guard dogs. Zoey remembered the feeling.

"Hey," said Zoey as she descended the stairs. "You holding up okay?"

"Yeah, I think so."

"You wanted to talk to me?"

"I'm really sorry. I just mentioned it offhand and your guy told me to wait here, it's fine if you don't have time, I didn't mean it like—"

"Oh, no, it's fine. I'm in for the night."

"It's just . . . your people are offering me all sorts of money and stuff and I don't want it. That's all. I don't want to go back to the inn but I'll find a different job. It's okay. I'm okay."

"Hey, I get it," said Zoey as she stepped off the bottom stair. "I don't like accepting help from people, either. But one thing I've learned is that sometimes the best thing you can do is say yes and then try to make the most of it. In terms of cost, don't worry about it. It's nothing compared to some of the other stupid junk we spend money on."

"It's not that. I don't . . . please don't take this the wrong way, but I don't want to be a part of this." She waved her hand around the room. "This . . . thing, what you guys do. I can't get wrapped up in anything like this. If I'd known you guys owned that place, I wouldn't have taken the job. And please, please don't get mad at me for saying that, I don't have any problem with you, I really don't, but I can't get pulled into . . . I just . . ."

Shae was near tears.

"Oh," said Zoey, letting out a nervous chuckle that was completely inappropriate in the moment. "You're talking about all the crime. You think if you take the money then you're on our payroll and somebody is going to show up at your house a month from now and say, 'Hey, we paid you, now you gotta pay us back by whacking this union organizer we got beef with.'"

Shae did not crack even the hint of a smile. *"I just want to go home."*

"Shae, you've got us all wrong. Or, well, you've got *me* all wrong. Can I tell you the story? It'll take like thirty seconds."

Shae didn't answer but made a face like she was bracing herself to listen to a sales pitch while simultaneously rehearsing how to say no to it.

"I want you to imagine," said Zoey, "that I gave you a piece of paper signing over everything I own—this huge mansion, all the businesses, everything—to you, right now. That's exactly what happened to me a little over a year ago. I'm not a crime person at all. I was a regular girl, just like you. So, what happened was a famous crime boss got a random stripper pregnant and never gave her the time of day after that. Twenty-two years later, he dies and leaves everything he owned to the stripper's baby that he had no relationship with whatsoever. That's me, I'm the stripper baby! And when I say everything, I mean everything. Hotels, casinos, apartment buildings, sex workers. That scary guy I showed up with? Will? He was my father's right-hand man. Same with the guy who brought you over here, his name is Budd. This is a team my father put together years and years ago, I inherited them along with all the rest. But I didn't know about any of this until last Christmas."

"I'm sorry that happened to you. And I get that you can't get out, but I can't get sucked into all of this. I can't wind up like you."

"What? No. I can get out. We could leave together, right now. Those people all work for me, they all have to do what I say. It's fine! It's all fine."

Shae was truly thrown for a loop by this.

"They're not . . . making you do it?"

"Ah, well, yeah, I see why you're asking that. Not to get into my whole sad history or anything, but if you could see what I had waiting for me back home you'd understand. We had nothing, I lived in a trailer and it had an ant problem so every once in a while you'd go to pour a bowl of cereal and you'd put the milk in and look down at your spoon and see a dozen ants floating in it. So I didn't have much of a life to go back to, is what I'm trying to say."

"Yeah, but . . . you couldn't just take the money and leave? You just, took over the Mob instead?"

Zoey crossed her arms. She suddenly felt like she was on trial. "We really have gotten rid of the bad stuff, I mean, a lot of it is still prostitution and gambling, but it's not the kind of thing where we're ambushing people in an alley and stealing their jewels. I wouldn't stand for that. Hell, that's why I stayed, to try to clean up the operation. They were doing some pretty terrible stuff before. And my father, he was a monster. *His* father was even worse, or that's what I hear anyway."

"But you kept all of those same people around? The ones who did all of the bad stuff?"

"They were the only ones who knew how to run everything! And trust me, they all know the rules, they step out of line and they're gone. I mean, I really am doing my best here. It's not easy."

It was clear Shae sensed she'd stepped over a line. It was also clear that Shae fully believed Zoey would have her killed and dumped into the river if she persisted. In the course of the conversation, Shae had edged back toward the doors by a couple of steps.

"Okay, okay," said Shae. "I believe you. Still, I don't want your money. I don't want it to turn into a thing at tax time, or if I could get in trouble for accepting illegal income . . ."

"First, it's not illegal. These are legitimate businesses with thousands and thousands of people on the payroll all around the world, it's all getting filed with the IRS, it's all aboveboard. Second, and this is the important part, we're not doing this as charity. If you stay in the city, you're going to bump into that guy, Tilley, at some point and who knows what he's going to do. Plus all the weirdos who were cheering him on out there, maybe they wouldn't do anything and maybe they would, but, you know, why tempt fate? We can even provide security staff, just for peace of mind. And these doubts you're having, they're the same ones I felt last year! But in the end, hey, the money is going to go to somebody, so why not you?"

"If I take it, can you promise that I'll never see any of you again? That scary guy isn't going to show up at my door?"

"You mean Will? Ha, yeah, I'll make sure you never have to see him. And he's not that scary once you get to know him."

"He's terrifying. And if you don't see that . . ." Shae abandoned the sentence, apparently sensing that it was heading toward dangerous territory. "Anyway, can I go? Please?"

"Of course, you're not a prisoner. Door's unlocked. One of my people will drive you—"

"No, I've called for a ride already. Thank you."

"Are you sure? We can—"

Shae was already pulling the door open. She slipped through and Zoey heard brisk, nervous footsteps fade into the night.

5

Zoey was still agitated from her conversation with Shae when she crawled into bed a few hours later. As she tossed and turned, she thought about a sign on the wall of her old workplace, posted back by the coats and Department of Labor notices. It was a supposedly motivational quote that said:

> [A] flaw in the human character is that everybody wants
> to build and nobody wants to do maintenance.
> KURT VONNEGUT

The manager had hung it there because she was always complaining about the staff not cleaning the espresso machines properly and it was probably the only "inspirational" poster she could find that seemed to be scolding people for not taking care of equipment. But Zoey thought about that quote constantly, especially in light of the turn her life had taken in the last couple of years. When you get sick of what's in front of you, yeah, fixing it is never as appealing as just walking away and starting fresh. It's the reason the landfills are choked with stuff that could easily be repaired and it's the reason action movies are always about killing psychopaths instead of helping them get better mental health meds. It's the reason Zoey's supposed soulmate, Caleb, had decided to just go find a girl with better genes and it's the reason, according to Will, that the city of Tabula Ra$a exists.

Mankind, he had told her, had spent much of the twentieth century dreaming of colonizing the stars (why fix civilization when you can just run away and build a brand-new one?), but by the 1980s or so everyone had soured on the idea. Colonizing Mars, everyone eventually realized, would be unbelievably difficult and the only reward for interplanetary trailblazers would be that they'd have to live on goddamned Mars. By the early 2020s, a new and better idea started to take hold among the ultra-wealthy and powerful: just recolonize the earth instead. Go find some sparsely populated area with a weak or disinterested government and just start building a brand-new city that would function under its own rules. Everything could be fresh, new, and efficient, free of the baggage and stagnation that was weighing down the rest of the modern world. And really, what's the worst that could happen, other than the new city descending into a dystopian hell of poverty, terror, and bloodshed?

These ludicrously expensive social experiments were often called "charter cities" and soon, every obscenely wealthy and/or powerful clique wanted one to call their own. Scientologists started one in Taiwan, some famous Communists did the same in Northern California, and a bunch of Libertarian tech billionaires were, at the moment, building a floating island nation off the coast of French Polynesia. Tabula Ra$a, by far the most successful and well known of the bunch, had been planted in southwestern Utah by a cabal of flamboyant criminals, apparently over a petty grudge.

Spearheading the project had been Arthur Livingston, Zoey's biological father, a self-made crime kingpin. And here, "self-made" means he gave himself a fake, WASP-sounding name to conceal his connections to his own wealthy Armenian gangster father. Arthur's group had been run out of Las Vegas and, mostly out of spite, planted their flag in a spot positioned to siphon away Sin City's most profitable tourists and whales. The founders played up the new city's lawlessness,

Arthur doing media appearances telling potential residents and developers alike to stay away if they couldn't handle it. "Tabula Rasa," he'd say while grinning and stabbing a finger at the camera, "is not for pussies. If you're not man enough, well, there's a loser's train to Vegas that leaves every hour." People couldn't move there fast enough.

Zoey stared at the ceiling. She really wanted to roll over, but Stench Machine was sleeping in the hammock formed by the blanket between her legs and disturbing him was, of course, unthinkable.

She didn't ask Will much about Arthur's early years; when she did what she got back were anecdotes that everyone at the table thought were hilarious but that Zoey found sickening. She knew that several years after Arthur got Zoey's mother pregnant, North Korea fell into civil war (the two events are thought to be unrelated). Arthur then used the war as cover for a human trafficking scheme that blatantly violated the laws of the DPRK, the United States, and common human decency. In the process, he encountered Will Blackwater, Budd Billingsley, and Andre Knox, who were doing equally illegal off-the-books PSYOPS work on behalf of the US government. Once back in the States, Arthur recruited all three to ill-defined roles in his organization that would take advantage of their unique training. Arthur had apparently once confided to Will that if one possessed the skill to craft sufficiently elaborate and convincing lies, then no other skills were really necessary.

Yet, over the next fifteen years, Arthur apparently began to have some minor regrets about the fact that his business practices had caused untold human suffering across several continents. He joined a church, started charities that actually gave money away instead of just laundering it, and grew an elaborate mustache (that last one may seem unrelated, but he saw it as a crucial part of his personal rebranding). This attempt to go legit, unfortunately, steered Arthur into unfamiliar waters he was ill-equipped to navigate. His enemies closed in, now possessing the power to make bricks shatter like glass and steel melt like wax. Thus, the man whose high school class would have voted him Most

Likely to Leave a Giant Smoking Crater When He Dies had such an award or his high school actually existed, did exactly that.

It was only after his murder that it was discovered he had left his entire empire to a daughter he'd only spoken to once in his entire life. Arthur had not discussed this decision with anyone and, predictably, chaos ensued. On several occasions Zoey nearly joined Arthur in that part of the afterlife reserved for people who die particularly weird and gruesome deaths. But she made it through, much to everyone's surprise, and that's how in the autumn of the following year Zoey wound up standing in her foyer trying desperately to explain herself to Shae LaVergne and probably doing a terrible job of it. Why *had* she stayed there, sleeping in the same home as her infamous father and doing a job with duties so alarmingly vague and varied that the news usually just referred to her as an "heiress"?

The real reason was one that she rarely articulated even to herself, because it was probably the same reason Arthur had left the business to her in the first place: sometimes, the story of your life gets so jumbled and messy that you just want to erase it completely. Like some kind of a, you know, clean slate.

Stench Machine found a better spot at the corner of the bed and Zoey rolled over, finally feeling herself drifting off. She thought that she'd dream of superpowered nerds smashing into her room and twisting her head off. Instead, she plunged immediately into the nightmare she'd had a hundred times since moving to the city. She was back in Fort Drayton, Colorado, late for her shift at Java Lodge. She was trying to start her old car and it was giving her that Battery Discharge error and she'd already been told if she was late one more time that she'd be fired and Cassie was managing and Zoey knew she wouldn't cover for her and she kept hitting the start button over and over and she was crying as she watched the time tick down on the dashboard clock and—

Zoey jolted herself awake. She rolled over and the last thought she had before drifting off again was that she'd rather die than go back there, to that place she was in her life less than one year ago.

Literally, rather die.

THIRTY

DAYS

LATER

6

Less than a year after promising to do only good with the fortune she'd inherited, Zoey Ashe had spent $4,500 on a Halloween tree for the foyer of her embarrassingly large mansion. In her defense, she thought she had actually done quite a bit of good with the money in the last ten months or so, and the tree provided easily $10,000 worth of holiday spirit. So if anything, she had saved $5,500. It looked like a fir tree that had gotten charred in a forest fire and was covered in little mechanical skeletons that climbed around the branches. Holographic ghosts swirled and moaned all around it, programmed to occasionally shriek and lash out with ghostly hands when sensors detected someone walking too close. The kids would love it at the Halloween party. Yeah, that's who it was for. The kids.

Zoey was in a business-y gray skirt and blazer, having just returned from a brutal day of meetings with people asking her for money or permission to do things she didn't fully understand, trying to appear attentive while her shoes were slowly grinding her toe bones to powder. She wanted out of these clothes before her soul asphyxiated.

She encountered Carlton, the ancient butler, at the foot of the twin staircase in the foyer and said, "I wish this house had a machine that would make my bra go flying off the moment I walked in the door."

"If such a device existed, Ms. Ashe, I'm certain your father would have had one installed long before you moved in. A package arrived at the gates this afternoon. It is marked for your urgent attention. It is currently at the guardhouse."

"Well, I think I'm out of attention for today."

"Understood, but I must make it clear that it is rather large, the size of a steamer trunk. It also appears to be armored and, in place of recipient information on the invoice, there is only a bloody handprint."

Zoey was not as alarmed by this as you'd assume.

"Thank you, Carlton. Considering there's a ninety-nine percent chance it's a box of cow turds or something from my 'fans,' I'm thinking Wu can open it tomorrow. Or, you know, never."

Zoey's hate mail was both plentiful and elaborate. The latest thing was to rig packages with cameras to try to stream her shocked/dismayed expression when she opened them, as if she was dumb enough to even open anonymous mail. The only reason Wu examined such parcels at all was to decide if they represented a genuine threat. If someone tried to mail a bomb, that package needed to be traced and the sender paid a visit. But otherwise, Zoey knew the harassers' game—guys like that weren't exactly an exotic species. She knew that her attention was their prize, that the idea was to occupy her mind, rob her of peace, to tie her in knots so that she couldn't live her life. Granted, it had taken a nervous breakdown and two weeks in a very fancy mental health facility over the summer for her to learn that lesson.

The trolls couldn't be ignored, her therapist had said, but they could be contained in her mind, locked in a little room until she chose to address them. For example: this scary package, which was undoubtedly from some bored sadists who'd adopted her torment as their hobby, was intended to ruin her Friday night and hopefully her whole Halloween weekend.

Carlton said, "I would suggest Wu give it a look sooner rather than later, the scan at the gate revealed no presence of known explosives, toxins, or remote detonation mechanisms. But this being Tabula Rasa, I believe the key word there is 'known.'"

"Sure, when he gets back from parking the car let him know to do that and to dispose of whatever's in there and never speak of it."

Zoey laboriously made her way up the stairs. She was going to submerge herself in her brand-new bathtub, one designed with an amazing set of incredibly precise pulsing jets. Her fling with that tub had actually been one of the most satisfying intimate relationships of her adult life. Zoey told the bath to start while she was still walking down the hall and left a trail of clothing outside her bedroom.

She was still soaking a half hour later, promising herself she wouldn't watch any street streams tonight. Tabula Ra$a was a hotbed for that genre, commentators narrating live Blink feeds of gunfights and Mob hits, riffing on the action and keeping score of which side held which territory. The feeds had first taken off in cities like Juarez, Jakarta, and Miami, but none of those cities had deviants who could pick up a car and chuck it into an oncoming train. If you liked watching real-time chaos, there really was no competition. It was an odd thing to take pride in, but the locals definitely did.

Zoey's phone chimed and a holographic text message hovered above it, Wu telling her he'd scanned the box and that it was important, to get back to him right away. Stench Machine, who was terrified of holograms, jumped up onto the toilet and hissed.

Zoey ignored the message.

She instead turned her attention to the monitor above the tub, which was still paused on the video she'd been watching (a haughty heiress in a marble mansion and her filthy, wiry, olive-skinned gardener) and brought up a street stream called Blastphalt, hosted by a quick-talking guy named Charlie Chopra. He was bald, with a two-foot-long beard twisted into elaborate braids. He was walking the streets, talking into his Gadfly, the little bobbing drone recording his face.

"So I know what you're asking, you're asking, 'Charlie Chopra, you golden beacon to mankind, why does a routine stickup make this week's Worst Ten List? Did you actually have less than ten crimes this week, and try to fudge some boring ones in?' Oh ye of little faith, grant me your attention for just one minute more and ye shall be rewarded. So this one occurred Monday night. Our degenerate approaches the old dude running the Human Bodega—you've seen him walking the sidewalks downtown, got the power assist rig with the display box strapped to the back, full of sodas and churros and, oh yeah, plenty of narcotics. And the degenerate's got some kinda plasma pulse zapper implanted in his palm and intends to burn Bodega's old-ass face off and then cut his way into the case. And we all know he's not there for the sodas.

"So the degenerate goes to fire his zapper and, as so often happens with those implants, it overloads, vaporizing his hand and most of his forearm in a flash, as if the Goddess of Justice herself had summoned a bolt of lightning and declared, 'Enough! This limb shall sin no more!' Then the little battery pack implanted next to the guy's degenerate spine catches fire and those tiny capacitors have got so much juice that once they start burning, they can't be stopped. My friends, that man's torso is *still* burning, five days later. They've got him in a special ward at the hospital and if you listen close, you can still hear his screams carried by the night wind. Though I'm sure that through it all, he is still beaming with pride that he has made number two on our Worst Ten List, certain that a mention by the great Charlie Chopra made it all worth it."

Zoey grabbed a cube of cheese off the tray mounted to the edge of the tub. She accidentally knocked a couple of olives into the water, where they vanished under the suds.

The phone chimed again. Another text message from Wu, about the box. Asking if she'd gotten the first message, then asking if she was still in the tub. Zoey lifted her feet out of the water and studied the black polish on her toes.

"So we've made it almost all the way through the list," said Chopra, "and no mention of the Suits. Will that end our streak? Have things honestly gone quiet on that front for a whole entire week? Not at all, my beautiful, yet hopelessly impatient disciples."

Ah, there it was, Zoey thought. All of the streamers were obsessed with Zoey's people, who everyone just called the "Suits," always sniffing around for any hint of palace intrigue. When she'd been hospitalized due to her breakdown a few months ago, guys like Chopra went wild with the idea that it was some sort of coup, a Will Blackwater PSYOPS operation that would let him seize power once Zoey was found mentally incompetent. Word had leaked somehow that he was the one who'd discovered her unconscious in her bedroom, Zoey having mixed the wrong alcohol with the wrong pills. The rumor mill immediately mutated this into Will having drugged her. Crazy, the things people make up.

Chopra stopped walking in front of a glowing construction site. His gadfly got a low angle, showing off the looming skeleton of a seventy-story skyscraper enshrouded by an enormous hologram. This would eventually be the new headquarters for Zoey's company. She was supposed to come up with a name for the tower, but she'd been stalling, since sticking her own dumb name on there just seemed weird (the whole idea of having her own building seemed weird, if she was being honest). They had decided it would be cool that if during the months-long construction process, they installed a bunch of hologram projectors that would show off the building as it would look once finished. As for the design, they had held a contest for people to submit their own and Zoey had ignored the professional renderings in favor of one sent in by a six-year-old girl. She demanded the finished building be built *exactly* like the winner's wobbly crayon scribble, complete with colors spilling outside the lines and giant squiggly windows seemingly placed at random. The press seemed to think the cartoonish hologram was just a joke and that the final building would be something more professional. Boy, would they be surprised.

Chopra said, "Get a look up behind me, Cammy."

His camera drone tilted its view upward to reveal that some clever jerk had gotten in and reprogrammed a few of the projectors so that what scrawled across the middle of the building in glowing red was a fairly sloppy Cow Zoey drawing. Under it were the words,

WAIT, THAT'S NOT MILK!

. . . which Zoey assumed was a reference so many memes deep that it'd take a half hour for someone to explain it to her.

"You talk to any old-timer in this city," said Chopra, "they'll tell you, if you opposed Arthur Livingston, if you had an expression on your face that implied you were even idly musing about it, bystanders would get quiet and slowly back away, as if waiting for a giant fist to crash down from the heavens and smite you. And you know what? The streets were peaceful back then. That first decade, the blank slate years, you didn't dare rob a Livingston business, you didn't dare intimidate his potential customers. You didn't hurt his escorts, you didn't *tag his walls*. And he owned everything. That, my children, is what kept the peace. Now, with all of the advisors in charge and his daughter, who I'm going to be frank, when they were handing out brains in Heaven she accidentally got back into the tit line, the inmates are running the asylum. It's the scariest thing in nature, my friends—a power vacuum. What do you get then? Anarchy. Or worse, *government*."

Chopra gestured to the glowing graffiti. "That's why this simple act of holographic vandalism takes the number one spot this month. It's an act that would have been totally unthinkable a year ago. Those of you who've been in town from the start, who saw this place grow up around a single casino in the middle of nowhere, could you imagine somebody striding onto a Livingston property and doing this, ever, in your wildest dreams? No, you could not. Or maybe you could. Okay, I admit I only had nine good ones this month."

Zoey turned it off.

Here's what really drove her crazy: if her on-site security had shot that vandal, it would have gotten ten thousand times more coverage than, say, the sliding scale housing project she'd spent months getting built outside the city. Nobody cared about that, or the endless meetings spent fighting with the bus companies to get them to set up routes out there, finally paying through the nose for additional security to calm drivers who were nervous about doing stops in the projects. That housing meant thousands of homeless and semi-homeless people were saved from the incredibly dangerous structures they had been squatting in. It meant heat in the winter, locks on their doors, and working plumbing. But it wasn't exciting, so nobody cared. People don't want solutions. They want novelty.

Her phone rang, from where it was perched on the lip of the tub. Wu's translucent head hovered over the phone and this time, she answered.

She said, "I'm here."

"Did you get my messages? I completed the scan of the package. It took forever, it was specifically shielded to block scans. Someone paid a fortune for that box. I actually had to drill a hole in it so I could run a probe through. I think you need to come see it."

"Is it a bomb?"

"No. It's a corpse."

7

Zoey stood in her pajamas and huge furry slippers, waiting in the foyer just inside the giant doors that probably both cost and weighed more than her old trailer in Colorado. The haunted Halloween tree moaned behind her, the little robotic plastic skeletons clicking around the branches. Zoey's eyes wandered toward a bowl of candy near those enormous doors and she had to force herself to look away. It was full of these golf ball–sized brownie things with an ice cream core. They sat at room temperature but opening the wrapper triggered some chemical magic that froze the ice cream inside in about ten seconds, while somehow warming the brownie exterior, creating a light crust. She'd had four of them today.

Wu pushed his way through one of the giant doors and she said, "Hey, I need you to protect me from those ice cream brownie balls. If I start to take one, chop my hand off."

"Wouldn't it make more sense to just throw them out?"

"Don't you dare."

"Carlton is bringing up the box from the gate."

The two of them stepped out into the chilly night to see Carlton rolling up the winding driveway in one of the electric carts the grounds crew used. He rounded an enormous jack-o'-lantern the size of a small house, the fiery interior casting an orange glow around the landscaping. Zoey hadn't bought that one, it was already in the storage building with the other seasonal decorations, including the dozens of bat-shaped drones with glowing red eyes that were currently flapping around overhead. She unwrapped a brownie ball and waited for it to cook/freeze in her hand. She had no memory of picking it up.

Carlton's cart skidded to a stop in front of them and from behind the wheel he asked, "Did you have a specific location in mind for the corpse?"

"I guess just plop it down right here. I definitely don't want it in the house. Should we wait for Will to get here?"

She'd texted him, knowing he'd be annoyed if they waited until morning to tell him that they'd been mailed a dead body.

"That is up to your judgment," said Wu. "The box contains no explosives, poisons, biotoxins, or booby traps that I can detect. Just the body. But those are all of the details I have, the best scan I could get just looks like a very blurry X-ray. It is clearly a person, though, and they are very clearly deceased."

"So no idea who sent it?"

"The return address is fake, it's the address of the construction site of your new office tower—a lot of the hate mail uses it. But right now, I am less concerned about the box's sender than I am its inhabitant."

"Well they're dead, so I think they're beyond earthly concerns."

"So . . . everyone is accounted for, then?"

Zoey didn't quite understand the question, then she went cold.

Somehow, the novelty of receiving a corpse delivery had completely obscured the possibility that this box may contain someone she actually knew, or loved. Zoey reached for her phone, found she didn't have it, then sprinted back inside the foyer.

Carlton had said the box arrived in the afternoon.

She hadn't seen her mother since yesterday.

Zoey found her purse where she'd left it at the bottom of the stairs, dug out her phone, then almost dropped it with shaking fingers.

She couldn't breathe.

She dialed her mother.

There was no answer.

That, again, was not strange. Friday night, her mother was certainly at some party, or at a bar, or passed out in some gross guy's bed. She tried again, no answer. Of course, she could just go out there, see who was in the box, see who her enemies had managed to snatch up and mutilate to death. But in that moment Zoey was seized by a superstition that what was in the box didn't become real until she set eyes on it, that if she could reach her mother, it would somehow make it so that it wasn't her in the box, that there was still a chance because the death wouldn't become final until it was observed. It was stupid, she knew. She wasn't thinking. Zoey put her hand on her forehead and tried to force herself to think, to be rational, to be like Will. She failed.

She didn't have any of her mother's friends' contacts in her phone, and in fact didn't know their names. She could try to find her on Blink, if she was in range of a live camera . . .

Zoey sensed Wu standing behind her.

He said, "Do you want me to open it for you? If it is your—if it is someone you know . . ."

"Yes. Please."

He went outside and, after several seconds, Zoey followed. She found Wu already at the box, working a latch. He glanced back at her.

"I changed my mind. I want to see. I want to see what they did to her. If it *is* her . . ."

Zoey hadn't had time to take inventory of who all it *couldn't* be. Will had been at the meetings with her all day, but not the rest of the crew. It could also be Echo in there. Or Budd. The box looked too small for Andre.

"Are you certain?"

She wasn't, but for some reason she felt like it was something she needed to do. If they'd rigged a camera in the box hoping to catch the moment of despair, she'd use it to talk to them, to tell them that she'd find them all and pound them into marmalade.

Wu opened one of the two overly complicated latches, then the other. Zoey's cat had wandered up from the lawn. They tried to keep him restricted to the enclosed courtyard out back but he always found a way out when he felt like it.

Wu lifted the lid. Zoey steeled herself.

The stench hit her first, a hot wave of it. She tried not to gag and made herself step forward, to examine the contents. It was a man, naked, compressed into the box in the fetal position. White guy, looked fairly young. Definitely dead and not recently, either. Maggots pooled in the bottom of the box. The last thing Zoey noticed before she turned her back to it was that his eyelids had been sewn shut.

Zoey put her hands on her knees and tried to catch her breath. It wasn't any of her people. Good. Then she felt a pang of guilt because of course this was still someone else's father, son, brother, friend, whatever. Had they killed a guy just for a dumb prank? Or maybe stolen a body from a morgue, or funeral home? Maybe that was it.

Wu was still standing over the open box, leaning into it, scrutinizing the contents for clues with a small flashlight and taking photos with his phone. Which, of course, is what she should have been doing, trying to gather information. Zoey had nothing to fear from what was in the box other than a very bad smell. And, if her enemies had killed this man in her name, this was now her responsibility, like it or not.

Zoey covered her mouth and nose with her shirt and joined Wu.

"Do you see anyth—"

The corpse reached up and punched her in the face.

Zoey tumbled back onto the cobblestones. Her eyes watered. She tasted blood.

Wu stood there stunned for the moment, unsure of what had just happened, looking back and forth from her to the fist that was still standing erect from the box. The naked corpse then raised itself up slowly from the steamer trunk. It moved unnaturally, not using its hands at all to climb to its feet. It just unfolded itself, like a machine. Dark fluids oozed from various holes, maggots dripped off of it in squirming clumps.

The corpse took a step out of the box. Wu sprang into action.

He pointed his closed fist at the figure and with a sharp mechanical *snap,* an unseen object launched from his wrist and whizzed through the night, punching the corpse in the chest. Blue arcs of electricity flickered and popped off the embedded projectile, the smell of cooked flesh filled the air.

The corpse was not bothered. It stepped out of the box and lumbered toward Zoey. Its face was slack, the head lolling around without purpose, the mouth drooping open stupidly. The sewn-shut eyelids were sunken, as if there were no eyeballs behind them. A viscous stream of dumpster water ran freely from its lips.

Wu ran in Zoey's direction, pulled her to her feet, and urged her through the doors, back into the foyer. She and Wu tumbled through and spun to close the door on the approaching corpse—

Zoey said, "Wait!"

Stench Machine the Cat was still out there, heading toward the door but not really showing the urgency Zoey would have preferred.

"GET IN HERE!"

Stench Machine, still traveling according to his own itinerary and no one else's, trotted through the doorway. The corpse stepped purposefully toward the door, just two strides behind him. Zoey and Wu shoved at the door—

Too late. The corpse effortlessly flung the doors open. Zoey and Wu staggered backward. The corpse stepped forward, then its left hand pistoned out and slammed Wu in the chest so hard that he fell and then slid backward on the marble tiles for several feet.

The corpse, Zoey saw, was wearing a glowing apparatus around its neck. It blinked and got brighter, then a hologram flashed to life, an image projected over the corpse's dead, slack face. It was another face, a translucent mask of light. It had chiseled features and a pompadour of sculpted, unmoving black hair. A cartoon face, not a real one.

The face smiled and in a modulated voice said, "Didn't think you'd see him again, did you? Everything comes back around, my dear. WE are RISING."

Zoey tried to process what it had just said. Then she noticed the sloppy surgery scars on the corpse's shoulders. It appeared that sparing Dexter Tilley had only bought another four weeks or so of life and Zoey was going to go out on a limb and say that he had not made the most of it.

Then Zoey realized that someone was remotely driving the dead body's implants and that, oh yeah, *it meant this corpse was strong enough to tear her in half.*

Wu jumped to his feet, making the simple movement look acrobatic. He waved at her and said, "GO!"

The problem was that the place Zoey needed to go—her bedroom, where she had both a panic room and a necklace that could shut down the corpse's mechanism—was upstairs. Tilley's resurrected robot corpse stood right between the two staircases, meaning he'd be able to easily snatch her before she hit the first step on either.

Wu knew her dilemma and urged her to just go, in any direction, to just get distance.

Zoey snatched up her cat and ran out of the foyer, toward the nearest hallway, which led to the west wing of the mansion. Behind her came rapid footsteps, each one beginning with a faint electrical whine and ending with a slap of rotten meat, the machinery inside doing its work. Wu was shouting instructions that she could not hear over the sound of her own frantic breaths and hammering heart. She put a hand on her neck, hoping her override necklace would have magically appeared there despite the fact that she'd taken it off an hour ago, before her bath. No such luck.

Zoey ducked into the first room she came to, a space walled with glass cases that had been Arthur Livingston's cigar humidor. The floor was now mostly occupied by a life-sized animatronic moose Zoey had accidentally won in an online auction while drunk and then quickly broken while attempting to ride it. Before she could turn and force the door closed, a hand grabbed a fistful of her hair and yanked her backward.

Stench Machine thrashed free, as usual deciding that he'd have a better shot on his own. Zoey tried to remember Wu's self-defense training. Don't pull away, turn and face the attacker, get your balance, strike back, go for the eyes. She twisted herself around, feeling hair getting ripped from her scalp, in time to see that the holographic face was grinning at her, the slack visage of the corpse lolling behind it. Well, clearly clawing at its sewn-up eyes wasn't going to accomplish a lot.

Wu burst into the room and pulled out a jagged, black knife. He plunged it into the corpse's shoulder and punched a button with his thumb. There was a flash from the blade and a meaty ripping noise. The corpse's shoulder exploded, sending bits of putrid meat flying. The arm went limp and Zoey twisted out of its grip, then stumbled and fell to the floor.

Wu reared back with his explode-knife again and tried to stab the ghoul in the lower back, as if hoping to sever its spine and paralyze it. Instead, the one-armed corpse spun on him, reaching out with its remaining arm and snatching his knife hand by the wrist. Wu tried to pull himself away, causing the pair of them to crash into a glass case, sending shards and cigars flying. They then toppled to the floor, the corpse on top.

The corpse's hand was still around Wu's wrist.

It squeezed.

There was a sound like a bag of peanuts getting crushed under a boot. Wu tried to suppress his scream, then failed. The noise he made terrified Zoey. The knife fell to the floor and his hand flopped over, now barely connected to his arm.

Zoey had to get that necklace.

She yelled, "I'll be back!"

Over Wu's protests, she ran and leaped over the two of them, stumbling into the hall and sprinting toward the stairs. She went up, nearly bowling over Carlton on the way. She made it to her bedroom, then pushed through into the bathroom. She always left the necklace next to the sink . . .

It wasn't there.

She looked around, knocking aside face creams and toothpaste. She faintly heard another howl from Wu, the noise rolling through the halls below her. The Tilley zombie could crush his skull any time it chose to.

She looked around the tub. Nothing. She stumbled back out into the bedroom. No necklace on the nightstand. Not on her dresser. Not on top of her mini-fridge, or Stench Machine's mini-fridge. Had it fallen under the bed? She dropped to the floor, looked.

There was a crash and tinkle of glass breaking from downstairs. But no more screams . . .

She went back into the bathroom. Had she checked by the sink? She checked again. Had she really checked the lip of the tub carefully? Maybe it fell onto the floor and got kicked under the bath mat. She looked. She was covered in sweat.

It wasn't here.

Okay. Okay. Plan B.

She needed a weapon. There was a cheese knife on the tray . . . no, it was flimsy.

She paused to listen.

From below, only silence.

Damn it. So stupid. Wasting time.

She grabbed one of the empty beer bottles from the floor. Through the bedroom, down the hall, down the stairs. Her heart drumming. She braced herself for what she would see when she arrived back in the moose humidor. For what she would do after she saw it.

She slowed as she got closer to the doorway. Creeping down the hall, she stopped about ten feet away and slammed the beer bottle against the wall, to turn it into a jagged weapon.

It didn't break.

She tried it again. It just bounced.

What the—?

She smacked the bottle against the wall again, and again. It just kind of made a hollow bonking sound. What the hell do they make these bottles out of?

"What are you doing?"

A confused Wu was standing outside the door to the humidor, clutching his left arm, the hand dangling at a gut-churning angle. Carlton stepped out of the room behind him, holding Zoey's necklace. She stopped bonking the beer bottle.

"I was looking for that!"

Wu silenced her with a head shake, then nodded toward the room behind him. She moved to where she could see inside, noting on the way that Wu now had a reddish-brown stain of corpse ooze on his shirt and neck, and a few wriggling maggots strewn across his chest. The corpse was flat on its back, the holographic face showing some confusion as it found the mechanism suddenly unresponsive. Stench Machine was sniffing the corpse and Zoey leaned in and picked him up before he could start eating it.

Zoey knew why Wu had silenced her. Whoever was operating Tilley was about to figure out that the implants had been remotely disabled—the big tactical secret Will had continually lectured them about keeping.

Zoey looked around and quickly said, "He, uh, stopped moving. I think it's . . . cats. The technology doesn't work near cats."

Wu said, "I managed to dislodge the Raiden capacitor with my blade, before we went down. We were fortunate."

"Right, right," she murmured, going along with this much better lie. "The power source is usually located in the, uh . . . butt . . . area."

The holographic face said, "There you are, cow."

"I have to admit," replied Zoey, "if this was all a prank, you absolutely win Halloween."

Will Blackwater walked up behind them, looking extremely

confused. Zoey watched him scan the room and it was kind of alarming how quickly the confusion dissipated.

"Someone operated the corpse remotely," he said. He looked the holographic face in the eye. "Who are you?"

"I am The Blowback."

Zoey said, "Great, do you have a name?"

"First name 'The,' last name 'Blowback.'"

"Oh. Of course. And your gimmick is you murder people and turn them into puppets? Is that just for your own amusement or do you have some other goal in mind?"

"Your feigned ignorance does not impress me."

"We know this is that Tilley kid. Did you kill him?"

"Dexter Tilley's murdered corpse was found Tuesday morning missing its eyes, stomach, heart, lungs, liver, kidneys, and testicles. Among other parts. He was found in the parking garage of Fort Fortuna."

That was a hotel and casino Zoey owned. The largest one, in fact. It was shaped like a sprawling medieval castle and its dining area featured entire animals being roasted over open flame, served by scantily clad wenches. Otherwise the only way it was period-accurate was that a lot of men probably contracted flesh-rotting diseases there.

Zoey said, "So you killed him to, what, send a message to me?"

The holographic face said, "Spare me. We know who you are. All of you."

"Wait, are you saying we killed him? Did you not watch us go out of our way to *not do that* like a month ago? Even though he totally deserved it? You, meanwhile, have just shown yourself to at the very least be capable of nonconsensual corpse puppetry."

"The very next night after Dexter Tilley was found missing his organs, your estate hosted a dinner party."

"Uh . . . probably? My life is a never-ending stream of banquets and functions with people I'm told are important. It's the main reason I secretly suspect that I died a year ago and am actually in Hell."

"I am sure you ate well that night."

"Is that a fat joke? You're losing me."

"It is very interesting," said the holographic face, "how every time you and your people plan a feast, another corpse is discovered missing key pieces. Which of you ate his liver? Or do you share it? I hear it's the best part."

"Oh, I get it. You're crazy."

Will said, "Just turn it off."

To the corpse, Zoey said, "Not that you're going to listen to anything I say, but while my deceased father was undoubtedly a pile of hot garbage shaped like a person, he wasn't *that* kind of garbage, and neither are we. Nobody is eating people over here. Especially not this kid. You think we gave him a good construction job just to make him taste better? The added muscle would just make him stringy."

"Like the rest of your team, you are a skilled liar."

"I'm really not."

"Tilley was one of us."

Will said, "One of what?"

"The Blowback. We know you killed this man and partook of his flesh in order to send a message, to try to quell the uprising. It has only birthed in us a new resolve."

Zoey said, "Wait, is your 'uprising' just all of those twenty-year-old dudes who keep mooing at me at public appearances? You think we cannibalized somebody in response to that? To the mooing?"

"You deny now, because you are afraid. You will soon have greater reason to be. The bounty went up on the Skin Wall one minute ago. One million dollars for evidence of your complicity in Tilley's murder. Sleep well."

The hologram disappeared, leaving only the slack, gray face behind. Even now, Zoey barely recognized the man.

Wu went to Zoey. "Are you all right?"

"Your hand is barely attached. Go tell the sedan to drive you to the hospital." To Will, she said, "We need to do something with that body. Does the city still do that?"

The machinery of justice existed in Tabula Ra$a, but was about 10 percent of what was needed. There was a coroner's office that tried to process the obvious murders but it usually took a bribe to get your case to the front of the line.

Wu, who had made no move to leave for the hospital, said, "They claimed he was their friend, but were willing to defile his body like this? I don't understand these people."

Zoey said, "Actually, if I get taken out one of these days, I want you to do exactly this with my body. Rig me up and unleash me on my enemies. Stick a flamethrower inside so I breathe fire. We need to notify his family, so they can arrange a funeral. And to let them know that we're going to find who killed him."

Will said, "We are?"

Zoey said, "It's the right thing to do. Also, it kind of sounds like we have to. Wu, if you don't go to the hospital right now, I'm breaking your other arm."

Wu reluctantly left and Carlton went to go get a mop. Will made like he was going to call someone about the body, but Zoey put her hand over his phone.

He met her eyes. "What?"

"Did you do this?"

"Did I do what?"

"Did you decide to finish the job on Tilley? Like you said you wanted?"

"And steal his organs? No."

She studied his face. "If you did it, because you thought it was safer, or whatever, just tell me. I won't be happy, but it's better than us running around in circles trying to answer a question you already know the answer to."

"You told me not to do it, so I didn't. I shouldn't have to keep saying it."

"But you wish you had done it."

"We wouldn't be in this situation if I had."

8

The next day was Saturday, October 29. Like most profitable holidays, over time Halloween had expanded to swallow up more and more of the calendar. The actual Halloween celebration had, as such, spread to two separate days and nights. October 30 the night before, was now Devil's Night. It was the naughtier of the two, the night for wild parties, drugs if you were into that kind of thing, vandalism, pranks, and a costume that was either incredibly inappropriate, gross, slutty, or all three. At midnight in Tabula Ra$a was the annual Black Parade, which Zoey was told was legendary, though she was dubious because parades by their very nature were sad and stupid.

The next morning, October 31, marked the beginning of the family-friendly part of the holiday. That's when the mischievous gifts from under the Halloween Tree were handed out by hungover adults. The rule was that if your gift was actually thoughtful or useful to the recipient, you had failed—these gifts were to be tasteless and worse than useless. They were also extremely difficult to shop for, you had to know a person pretty well to know exactly what they hated. For the kids, there were baskets of booby-trapped treats (say, a batch of six caramel apples, only one was secretly an onion). Everyone either had a separate costume for that day, or a tasteful modification to their Devil's Night outfit for the traditional haunted houses and trick-or-treating. At Zoey's estate, they were hosting a "haunted" maze in the courtyard for hundreds of mostly poor kids from the city. The point is, this had been cued up to be a hectic, stressful weekend even before somebody mailed Zoey a dead body.

She was still in her pajamas when she dragged herself toward the conference room at the obscene hour of seven forty-five A.M. These were different pajamas; she'd spent forty minutes in a hot shower scrubbing the corpse juice off herself before bed. She was carrying a mug of steaming Da Hong Pao tea.

She glanced back at Wu—his left arm now in a plastic cast that could also dose the area with pain medication—and said, "Can you smell me? I feel like I smell bad again. I think I was sweating all night."

"I would say you are within range of how you normally smell."

"That is an amazing answer."

They headed down a hall to a sturdy door labeled STAFF FARTING ROOM—DO NOT TURN OFF VENTILATION FAN.

The door automatically unlocked itself for Zoey, revealing the Suits' conference room. Echo was already inside, sitting at the long table, drinking some kind of morning post-workout shake probably made with oats and algae protein or something. There was an understanding that the estate was Zoey's home but also the Suits' workplace, so they had access but with a rule that she always be told whenever they were coming so she could put on some pants.

Zoey said, "You look awful. Do you have some sort of disease?"

She said some variation of this every time she saw Echo, who'd done something different with her hair, pulling the curls to one side so it formed a mop that cascaded down the right side of her face. It was adorable in a way that could almost be considered an act of violence.

"I actually am a mess this morning. Couldn't sleep last night, for some reason. Put on my gym clothes at three and just went to work on the heavy bag, to burn off the energy."

"Whose face do you imagine on there when you're hitting it?"

"Yours, of course. I've stuck a little wig on top."

When Zoey had first moved in, the conference room had been a dour space dominated by a beaten-up table and battered leather chairs, the room stinking of old tobacco and coffee, like they were all sitting inside a giant cop's mouth. The table had since been replaced with a new one with a built-in display along with new chairs that had on-the-fly body temperature adjustment to keep your back from getting sweaty. Along the wall to the right, opposite the main monitor, was a row of plants under grow lights, to freshen up the air. It was a whole different vibe. Will hated it.

Zoey set the mug of tea in front of an empty seat, then went and sat in another spot. Will was next through the door, in a suit the color of a ripe cherry that had been spray-painted flat black. He was carrying a fedora and went to set it down at his customary spot, when he found a mug of tea in its way.

"Is someone sitting here?"

"That's yours. It's that tea you like."

Will stood frozen for a moment. He did not like it when people gave things to him unexpectedly, because he hated being put in the position of having to choose between saying "thank you" for something he didn't ask for, or refusing an act of kindness and looking like a jerk. Will knew that Zoey knew he hated this, because he had told her as much.

He muttered, "Thank you. Where's Budd and Andre?"

It was still seven minutes until meeting time, so neither of them were late, but in Will's mind the meeting started whenever he happened to get there. He'd ask after whoever wasn't in the room when he arrived as if they were missing, no matter how much time was left until the actual appointment. Andre showed up a minute later, in a pinstripe suit with a tie woven with some kind of reflective red that appeared to undulate as he moved, subtle changes in light making it appear the colors were rippling across the fabric. He was carrying a huge pink donut box, bless him.

Andre glanced around the room, looked at his watch, and said, "Where in the hell is Budd? Must have overslept. Probably hungover."

Budd appeared five seconds later, clearly having been right behind Andre in the hall. They'd probably ridden together.

After everyone was seated, Echo said, "First order of business, we should talk about the sale of the Moutainview lot, they finally got financing squared away. I've got documents. Just need signatures."

Zoey said, "Wait, are you serious? I think me getting attacked by a mechanized corpse last night is probably the first order of business."

Will said, "Actually, we've been going back and forth with Ali-COM on this sale for months, we definitely don't want to give them time to change their minds."

Zoey said, "Sure, sure. Whatever it is, I'm confident you're on top of it."

"You have to give final approval and signature, Zoey. That's your land. You said you wanted to be involved in the business, this is the business."

"Then in my role of Queen of Business, I declare that we talk about the mechanized attack corpse and the organization who sent it to try to kill me because they think I ate the guts of their friend, who happened to be the very corpse they sent."

"The corpse wasn't trying to kill you," said Will, in an infuriatingly dismissive tone. "I'm estimating that the implants were operating at about one percent power. They just wanted to make you run around in a panic and get it on camera. That was the whole point. They don't want you dead, because then the show's over. You don't kill the cow as long as it's giving milk."

"Either way," replied Zoey, "the murder of Dexter Tilley is officially our problem. Now, with the combined brains of everybody here, I think we should be able to knock this out over the weekend. If we're lucky, maybe somebody caught his murder on cam—"

"They didn't," said Echo. "I checked. You had to know it wouldn't be that easy."

"He was found at a casino but nobody got it on camera? Aren't there cameras all over, to keep people from cheating and all that?"

"Your casinos are proudly camera-free zones," noted Budd, "and feature prominent signage guaranteeing it. No closed-circuit, no Blink, no nothin'. Your high-rollers who enjoy the company of mistresses and escorts appreciate the discretion, you understand. Cheating—casino cheating, not marital cheating—is monitored with sensors and algorithms that detect patterns they reckon are a bit too lucky."

"So if people win, we kick them out. Remind me that we need to get rid of the casinos next."

"In other words," continued Budd, "we don't even know that he actually passed at Fortuna, or that he was even found there. They could be makin' that up, to put his death at your feet. Coroner had no record of him."

Andre made himself a cup of coffee from the machine in the back of the room. He returned to his seat and opened the big pink donut box to reveal that it contained exactly one donut. He picked it up and took a bite.

Zoey said, "And I suppose his death isn't going to turn out to be something straightforward, like a jealous lover? The guy had issues with women."

"Someone who ate his guts afterward?" said Andre. "I don't think I've ever been that jealous before."

"I have," said Zoey. "Could it be organ thieves? Aren't there stories of people waking up in a bathtub full of ice, missing a kidney?"

Will shook his head. "Urban legend. There's no record of that ever happening for real, anywhere in America."

Budd said, "Just no market for it. As you can imagine, petty criminals are actually not the best at performing invasive surgery and dying patients aren't big on getting mysterious, possibly infected black-market organs screwed into their bodies. There are better ways to get them."

Will said, "And to that end, we talked to the organ dealers in the city. Nobody showed up with a garbage bag full of Tilley's guts looking to make a sale."

Zoey said, "Okay, then what's he been up to the last four weeks that would lead to this ending? We were keeping tabs on him, right?"

"Well," said Budd, shifting in his seat, "Rico had instructions to tell us if he didn't show up on the job site, or otherwise acted squirrelly. Said he showed up every day, seemed to like knockin' holes in walls well enough. There was one night where he showed up drunk at Shae LaVergne's momma's apartment, but was turned away without incident."

"What? He did?"

"Shae was in no danger, she wasn't there at the time; she was on a camping and hiking vacation in Moab. Otherwise, if Tilley made new enemies or got into mischief, there's no record of it."

Echo thought for a moment. "But if we're going with the revenge angle here, don't you start with Shae?"

Zoey said, "It's hard for me to imagine this dainty elven pixie girl hacking the guts out of a man."

Andre said, "Actually, I've dated some—"

"Stop," said Zoey, "we've already made that joke too many times."

"For all we know," said Will, "her dad is a psychopath. Or she's got a brother who's a two-hundred-and-fifty-pound ex-Navy SEAL . . ."

"She doesn't," said Budd. "But that don't mean she couldn't have hired it out. Maybe her vacation wasn't as relaxing as she'd hoped. Maybe a few weeks of PTSD and nightmares convinced her she wasn't okay with the creep getting a new life out of the deal. Maybe she was making a point, with what was done to the corpse. Saying he's gutless? Somethin' like that?"

Will nodded, just a bit. "That's the least crazy, as our current theories go. Who do we know who'd take a job like that, including being willing to go the extra mile with the organs?"

Budd said, "Ripper Genero, Stevey Bunson, Hack Pederson, Mike Cordry, Andy Smith, Donny Smith, Butch McCall, Holly Hollister,

Doc Menace, The Red Nightfall . . ." Budd continued saying names
for two minutes, then finished with, "plus a veritable stampede of
cash-hungry newcomers."

Zoey said, "I think I see why the cops all quit."

Will started to say something, then got an incoming message alert
on his phone.

He studied it, then said, "Well, Megaboss Alonzo's gang just put
up a video in which they chopped up and ate a human heart."

Zoey said, "Wait, did you say—"

"Yes, they ate a heart. On camera. Just now. Said it was Tilley's."

Zoey threw up her hands.

"Well, great. Go have them arrested, or whatever. Hot damn, we
got this done in less time than it takes to make toast. I'm going back
to bed."

Will said, "There are several problems with that, the main one being that eating a human heart is not a crime."

"It's not?"

Budd said, "No federal law against it, only state that outlaws it is
Idaho."

"Why do you know that? Actually, don't tell me. So, fine, call up the
crazy people who put up the bounty and tell them."

"Tell them what?" asked Will. "For all we know, Alonzo's people
bought the heart from the killer. Or it's somebody else's. We need to
go talk to him."

"Sure, let me know what he says."

Budd spoke up. "Actually"—he glanced quickly at Will—"you'll
get better information if Zoey tags along."

Zoey didn't like his expression. "Why?"

Will, clearly covering some kind of lie, said, "You're the queen, like
you said. Alonzo may feel insulted if you don't come yourself."

Andre asked, "You want me there?"

Will waved him away. "No, he'd see through that."

Zoey felt like she was clearly missing a bunch of context.

"Alonzo has sex workers," said Will, "maybe Tilley got weird with one of them, maybe even killed one of them."

Zoey went cold. The implication there was clear: if that was true, that woman's death was on her for letting Tilley go free.

"Or," said Andre, "he bumped into Alonzo on the sidewalk and scuffed his shoe. If so, he won't be shy about saying it."

Zoey said, "All right. Let's go talk to the flesh-eaters. Do we need to make an appointment?"

Budd stood. "I'll see to it."

"Anything else? I have to go figure out what to wear to a cannibal meet."

Will studied her for a moment with an expression she liked even less than Budd's look earlier. "You remember when they made you leave the refugee benefit banquet, because they said your dress was inappropriate?"

"Do I remember the most embarrassing thing that's ever happened to me? Yes."

"Do you still have that dress?"

"*What?* Why? I don't know."

From his spot by the door, Wu said, "The larger issue is making it to the meeting at all. We do have a bounty out there."

The million dollars had been offered on the "Skin Wall," a public board on which such contracts could be posted for any suitably awful person to claim.

"The bounty isn't for my death, it's for evidence of my guilt. Wait, it just occurred to me that this bounty is actually less than the last time somebody put a bounty on me. How am I going backward here?"

"And what do you think will be the easiest way for them to obtain said evidence of your guilt?" asked Wu.

"Oh. To grab me and beat a confession out of me."

About four different people in the room simultaneously said, "It's what I would do."

9

Zoey had decided that if/when the peasants finally rose up to over-throw the rich, she'd just put on some of her old clothes and quietly go join them. It'd only taken a few months of extreme wealth to real-ize that if everyone back home actually knew how these people lived, they'd have burned the system down long ago. First, there's the fact that at this level, debt is usually a good thing—it makes you richer. Zoey was getting loans on hilariously friendly terms and was pretty sure that if she failed to pay, the *bank* would apologize. She could borrow at a low rate, invest that same money in something with a much higher return, then just pay off the loan and keep the difference. If the investment fell through, it wasn't Zoey who would take the hit—Will said it was always done through an "LLC," an organization created out of thin air purely to absorb all the risk, kind of a financial bodyguard. Zoey had said it sounded like a free money hack in a video game, though Will insisted it wasn't that simple.

Then there's the fact that when you're rich, people just give you things. When Zoey was spotted at a concert drinking a bottle of some Ukrainian beer that a dude had just handed to her, the manufacturer sent her ten cases of it. She got gift baskets of makeup, phones, shoes, and bras that somehow fit perfectly (that last one kind of made her skin crawl when she stopped to think about it). Restaurants comped meals, she got offered free tickets to events. When she'd mentioned hiring a personal trainer, all of them offered to do it for nothing in exchange for weekly Blink updates from her saying what great results she was getting (she refused; she didn't need the whole world to know that she was always lucky to make it to the third session). She had a walk-in closet in one of the spare bedrooms that was literally nothing but band T-shirts. She had jewelry that looked so expensive that she was afraid to even touch it, let alone wear it out of the house. She had outfits for ritzy clubs and red carpets and other situations she intended to spend the rest of her life avoiding. She had two hundred pairs of skull-themed underwear in an unopened box somewhere.

She was not, however, going to dress to make this man-eating crime lord swoon. He wasn't getting the red dress that she'd decided to wear to that benefit banquet while in a particular mood. He was getting jeans and an ordinary black button-up shirt that could be worn with or without another top to make the cleavage more dignified, and today she was covering up to the collarbone. She would wear sneakers, shoes she could run away in. Not cute shoes. Action shoes.

Zoey passed Will on the way downstairs and he looked mildly disappointed but knew not to say anything. Zoey was pleased that he knew.

"Your mother's here."

"Oh, good."

"But we do need to go, soon."

"Yep, don't want to keep a psychopath waiting. Makes a bad impression."

Zoey had summoned her mother after the morning's meeting, as it occurred to her that she, too, was a potential target with this bounty out there, since they could easily snatch Zoey's mother in exchange for a confession. It's understandable if at this point one got the impression that about once a day Zoey flew into a panic believing that her mother was in some kind of mortal jeopardy. In reality it was only slightly less frequent than that.

Melinda Ashe was thirty-nine years old and would probably claim to be thirty-nine for several more years. She believed in the goodness of men, had arranged her life so that she'd had one male or another taking care of her since puberty. She'd been through three marriages that ended horribly but would never say a bad word about an ex. Zoey watched her mother excuse away bruises and black eyes, saw her lie to the cops about pulled knives and threats. When Melinda looked at these tattooed, sweaty men, she saw only the scared little boys inside.

It was last December when Zoey's mother had in fact walked into an abduction situation, shortly after Zoey came into her money. After having nightmares about her mother in a shallow grave every single night for weeks, Zoey had moved her to Tabula Ra$a, thinking that having her nearby would put Zoey at ease. That, Zoey now knew, had been stupid. What was she imagining, her mother living at the estate under the watchful eye of armed guards twenty-four hours a day? That she would sleep alone? That she would, in other words, live Zoey's lifestyle? No, Melinda Ashe would shrivel up and blow away without a flock of giggling friends to breathe life into her. And so she had insisted on her own apartment, on getting her own job (as a sex therapist—she could charge five times what she did in Colorado), and within a month, had made more close friends than Zoey had made in her entire life. Her mother seemed to know the names of all of the bartenders at every drinking establishment in the city. She'd had her first shady boyfriend before she'd even finished unpacking. This was how it would always be, Zoey knew: if someone ever wanted to get to Zoey, her mother would be there for the taking.

She made it downstairs and heard her mother's laughter from down the hall. Zoey turned to her right and followed the sound through the dining room and into the vast kitchen. Sitting at the bar was a woman who could pass for Zoey's sister if she didn't seem too pretty to be from the same bloodline, next to a weirdly tan middle-aged guy with neat white hair. Zoey had never seen this guy before. If he was a boyfriend, at any moment she would get the "I have a great investment idea!" conversation. So far, Zoey had paid for a food truck, a tattoo shop, and a rap video.

"Heeeey, Z!" said her mother. "Carlton made us brunch, though we told him not to bother."

They were picking at a tray of halloumi fries, sticks of hard cheese that were deep-fried, then served under ropes of white yogurt sauce and sprinkled with bright red pomegranate seeds. Carlton's cooking skills had been developed under Arthur, who'd required him to cook a cuisine Zoey thought of as "upscale county fair."

Before Zoey could speak, her mother said, "Your lashes look amazing today. God, you are just so beautiful. I wish I had your curves. I want you to meet Clarity."

Zoey decided right then that she was making a resolution: if somebody gave her a one-word name, or a name that was clearly a phrase or a slogan, she was not going to ask them to elaborate. That was, after all, what they wanted.

"Good to meet you, Clarity."

Clarity looked like he might possibly be nuts, but he didn't look like a scumbag or ex-con. Of course, you couldn't always tell an abuser from a glance. But here was the thing: in many cases, you totally could.

"You have a lovely home," he offered through a blinding white grin.

"Thank you. It was built with crime money." To her mother, Zoey said, "Don't freak out, but something happened last night."

"Oh, my god. What?"

"Somebody tried to . . ." She tried to think of a word for what had occurred. ". . . mail something to me. But we're okay."

"Oh, honey. Did you call the police?"

"Sure. It's, uh, all taken care of. But there might be more of them. Bad guys, I mean."

"Ugh, Z, this city, I tell you. Did you hear what happened last night at Zero Hour? Me and Maddie were at the bar, just minding our own business, and this guy just slams into me. They were fighting, the bar jammed me in the ribs. I have this huge bruise. Look—"

"Mom, I want you to stay here, for a bit. At the house. And to not go out without security. Just for a while."

"Well, if they come with me to class, they have to stay outside. I can't have scary guys looming over the—"

"You may have to skip the classes."

"I can't, I'm teaching."

"If they fire you, we will buy the clinic and put you in charge of the whole thing. A whole chain."

"Here, have some cheese, I'm full."

"No, thank you—"

"Drink? Coffee? Anything? I never get to do anything for you!"

"No, I just need to not be nervous, I've got a big meeting this morning with . . . I'm not sure what he is."

"Oh! I've got something for that, too. This is perfect. Clarity and I are selling these mood-enhancing skin creams, it's an amazing program and the product, oh my god. Here . . ."

Ah, there it was. Her mother pulled out a white tube the size of a fat cigar, animated flowers dancing on the label. She pulled off a cap and there was a spiral pattern of tiny slits in the end. When she twisted it, the cream squirted out of those slits in thin white layers, then a dotted yellow ball emerged, forming a perfect miniature daisy made of skin cream. Her mother swiped it off with her fingers and spread it between her palms.

"Give me your hands."

Zoey would have worried about applying a mood-enhancing anything to any part of her body if she for one second thought the stuff actually worked. She let her mother spread it on her palm and fingers. She felt a mild tingle, something they'd added to enhance the placebo effect.

"Great, right?"

"Yeah. So, I've got to run—"

"All we need you to do, if you can, is just use this on camera at some point. And say the name of the cream. The brand is Mood Food, there are twelve moods, this one is Amazey Daisy. It builds confidence!"

"Do I . . . have to say the whole thing?"

"No! You don't have to do it at all. But if you can that would be huge, I get a free set and fifty credits for a mention. And if you can say the whole thing, yeah, that'd be amazing."

Clarity said, "Also if you mention the effects, you need to point out that the health benefits haven't been verified by the FDA."

Zoey looked over the tube. "I'm almost afraid to ask, but how many tubes of this did they make you buy, as your starter stock?"

Her mother said, "Five hundred."

Clarity sensed the conversation was taking a wrong turn. "That's at only half of the sell price! Just moving this initial stock and she can clear twenty thousand dollars, easily. And for every sales associate she recruits—"

Echo walked into the kitchen and Zoey said, "Oh, thank god."

Zoey's mother took one look at Echo, then her eyes went wide and she said, "Oh my god, you look a-*may*-zeen! Look at your hair!"

"Will says it's time to go."

Zoey's mother sighed. "It always is."

Zoey took the chance to escape and as they entered the hall, Echo said, "Ha, I told him you wouldn't wear the dress."

10

It was decided that the envoy to meet Megaboss Alonzo and his gang of murderous cannibals was to consist of Will, Zoey, and Wu. Budd was going to go to Fort Fortuna to talk to the staff there, and Echo and Andre were going to try to track down any friends or family of Dexter Tilley, to try and figure out how he'd wound up losing both his life and all of his most important organs while he was supposed to be learning how to recover copper plumbing from defunct buildings. They were covering all of the bases in case the Alonzo thing was a dead end, since most things in life are.

Zoey owned multiple vehicles with various arrays of countermeasures (the leopard-print convertible, for instance, could launch a drone from its trunk that could do serious damage to up to a dozen bad guys), but obviously the first choice was to avoid detection/confrontation altogether. In a city with more cameras than people, this was not easy. In fact, Wu said that there were four drones with eyes on their driveway, either owned by bounty hunters or street streamers hoping to catch the ambush by said bounty hunters.

The three of them left the house in the convertible (by far the most recognizable of her vehicles) and pulled into a car wash that Zoey frequently used and also owned, one built with a Roman bathhouse theme in which scantily-clad animatronic slave girls would come out and scrub down your vehicle. A nondescript van had entered said car wash one minute ahead of them, and while both vehicles were progressing through the wash, the water and scrubbing girls abruptly stopped and allowed the three of them to exit the convertible and enter the van in front. They would continue on their way in the van and the convertible would then lead the spy drones through a series of leisurely stops around the city, the tinted windows hiding the fact that there was no one inside.

The nondescript van bore the faded logo of a ride-and-breakfast commute service, boasting it would serve pancakes and eggs while the vehicle waded through morning traffic. The entire exterior of the vehicle was in fact just a series of bolted-on panels that could totally alter its make and model, one of nine outfits they could swap out. The interior was that of a state-of-the-art transport designed to move high-value targets through war zones. Wu was behind the wheel (if someone had to take over the autopilot in an emergency, he was the one trained in evasive driving), Will in the passenger seat, Zoey in the back. She was seated in front of monitors that could display a list of potential threats, right down to any unusually aggressive facial expressions on passing motorists. She glanced at them and then started playing a game on her phone.

Zoey asked where Megaboss Alonzo's headquarters was and Will said, "The Styx."

"Like, outside town?"

"No, S-T-Y-X. Guess you've never been. There's a tunnel system under the city and Alonzo has laid claim to most of it. His rationale is that property deeds don't extend that far under the surface and also that no one can physically stop him from claiming it. He's right about the second part, which is all that matters."

"Underground? How do we get there?"

"There's an entrance in West Turner."

Zoey was from a small town of fewer than ten thousand people and the most confusing thing about moving to the city was how big of a deal people make about which neighborhood they're in. Back home there had just been the trailer parks (her domain), the one rich neighborhood around a lake, and then everybody else. Here, people identified their neighborhood as their location, rather than the city ("That's how we do it in Beaver Heights!") but the borders weren't official and bitter disputes broke out over whether a new housing development was in West Turner or the adjacent West Arlington (there was no East Turner). These disputes were particularly nasty when one of those was well established in the public mind as the "bad" neighborhood, as was the case with West Turner. Zoey, however, was not at all nervous about taking a trip there and quietly congratulated herself for not being nervous.

That didn't last. The moment they emerged from the fancy suburb and hit the city, Zoey thought she could sense a crackle of tension in the air, a sour mood. It had to be her imagination (the supposedly world-class sensors in the back of the van didn't note any direct threats) but she felt it in her gut. Hunched shoulders on the sidewalks, people staring at their shoes as they walked, the wound-up angst of a mutual, unresolved grievance. Even if her instincts were right, there was no reason to believe it had anything to do with her. These people led their own lives. Maybe it was the stress of Halloween shopping.

Still, she felt trapped in the armored vehicle, like there wasn't enough air. When they stopped at an intersection, she concentrated on the light, willing it to change, holding her breath. At one point a passerby stared a little too long and she wondered if they'd made the vehicle . . . but then they just kept walking. That was the thing—the moment a single person saw through the subterfuge, anyone and everyone who had bad intentions could know inside of a minute. That was the terrible magic of the Blink network.

Still, they crept along with the rest of the traffic and passed unmolested into West Turner, a place in which not a single door didn't have an armed guard and the doors they guarded wore metal bars. Zoey made a mental note of the plentiful neon and the cool clubs and restaurants and tried to shout down the small-town part of her brain that was treating this like a safari. Hell, it's not like any of these people were the angry nerds who'd put the bounty out on her. This was fine. Everything was fine. Look, there's a brick BBQ joint with a giant golden pig on the roof with smoke pouring out of its butt! That's pretty cool.

Will, who had an eerie and annoying ability to read Zoey's moods, said, "If Alonzo starts getting political, just move on to the next subject. Don't agree or disagree, just say that's not what we're here to talk about."

"Political?"

"If he starts talking about economic justice, racism, any of that. Alonzo is an activist, at least in his own mind, and your father had a . . . complicated relationship with the community. He'll try to go to work on you."

"Wait, the heart-eating guy we're going to meet was an enemy of my father? You're just now mentioning that?"

"'Enemy' is a strong word."

"And he had 'problems' with 'the community'?" She made air quotes with her fingers. "Is that your way of saying my father was a racist? On top of everything else?"

"No. Not in his opinion. Get ready, we're here."

For some reason, when it was said earlier that Alonzo ruled a system of tunnels under the city, Zoey was picturing stone walls lit by torches. Instead, they pulled up to a covered stairwell ensconced between two buildings that led down to a bustling, well-lit thoroughfare two stories high, with storefronts and food carts and people zipping around on electric scooters.

"Is there a whole other city down here that nobody ever told me about?"

"No," said Will, "only about eight blocks of it. This was supposed to be the start of a subway system way back at the founding, but Arthur was never big on public transportation, so it just sat dormant until Alonzo's crew came down and built it out. Five of the city's ten best restaurants are down here, so there's that."

There were sideways glances at the Suits and their bodyguard (who was in a black tunic with a katana on his back, Wu's Stay Away outfit) and for a good reason: their presence down here could not mean anything good. They soon arrived at a men's clothing store called Threads of Power, a gleaming storefront with gold trim and, in the display windows, six naked mannequins. When Zoey got within about ten feet of the entrance, the mannequin nearest to her blinked to life, the skin replaced by a hologram of Zoey herself, now wearing a striking crimson skirt-and-jacket combination. A floating price tag hovered over every item and she noted that the system's algorithm had, like every stylist she had worked with, determined she should be showing more chest.

Jazz music wafted from the store as they passed through. Zoey assumed that at some point they'd be ushered through some kind of armored door and wind up in a back room full of scowling henchmen smoking cigarettes and polishing bullets or whatever people like that do in between crimes. Everybody in the city did their dirty work behind some kind of legit storefront, even if the city's law enforcement situation barely made it necessary. Zoey thought it was partially a status thing for these guys, having the cool restaurant or whatever to slap their name onto. Either way, Zoey found her eyes darting around the racks of suits and dresses, studying the mannequins and nattily dressed salespeople for clues, trying to find the cracks in the facade. Unless this wasn't Alonzo's place and Will had just stopped to ask directions.

Will approached a counter helmed by a wiry young black woman with a shaved head and, before he could speak, she said, "You just won me a thousand dollars."

"How's that?"

"I bet Alonzo that you would bring her and her bodyguard both; Alonzo said you'd come alone. We made a bet, I won."

"Is he here?"

"Oh, he's here," said the woman. "He's been waiting all morning. Cleared his calendar, just for you."

She was at least four inches taller than Zoey, though from behind the counter it was impossible to know if she wasn't in heels or something. She wore a dress that was made of a delicate silver material that almost seemed like chain mail, draped over broad shoulders and bare arms. No polish or art on her fingernails. She had a tattoo over her left breast of some kind of falcon, like something you'd see in Egypt, and Zoey thought she could detect where it had been applied to cover a circular scar. The shape of an old bullet wound.

Will glanced up toward the ceiling and said, "Well, that was considerate of him."

"Yeah, he must really want to see you people. Or, he knows the winter lines are coming in today and that every inch of these shelves have to be swapped out and four girls called in sick, and that if he pokes his head out of his office I'm putting his ass to work. I'll bet you the thousand dollars I just won that when you go up there, he'll pretend to be on the phone. Here . . ."

She hit a switch under the counter. Behind her, a pair of mannequins slid aside, opening a hidden door and revealing a narrow staircase going up.

They circled around behind the counter, which immediately felt to Zoey like a dangerous trespass, then up one floor to find an enormous office that somehow felt bigger than the entire store below it. There was a black marble desk in front of a sound system that occupied the whole of the rear wall. A muscular man sat shirtless behind the desk, a thick beard jutting from his face, a tattoo of a teardrop under one eye. Zoey wondered if he was wearing pants. This, presumably, was Megaboss Alonzo.

Alonzo put down the phone he'd been pretending to listen to without even feigning a good-bye. "Welcome!" He looked at Zoey. "You're looking well."

Zoey was sure she'd never spoken to him before, but said, "Thanks."

"You're not letting the trolls get to you, right? I know you had some hard times over the summer."

"I try."

"Stay strong." To Will he said, "Do a magic trick for us! Break the ice."

Will had a reputation for being able to do magic but Zoey had only ever seen him do one coin trick. It wasn't something you asked him about.

Without breaking stride, Will said, "Look for your wallet. You'll find it's not in your pocket."

Alonzo's face froze. He reached for his back pocket.

"It's right here."

"But just for a moment, you had doubts. *That* is the trick."

"Touché! Have a seat."

There were three chairs, but Wu remained standing behind them. Behind Wu were two of Alonzo's bodyguards, each of them much larger than Wu, who also only had one unbroken arm. They stood so that they were blocking the door and Zoey thought this was all fine, just fine.

"So," said Alonzo, "why has the Lord brought us together on this beautiful day? Is this about that unfortunate virgin who held up your pajama theater a month ago?"

Will, already sounding impatient, said, "Yes, the one whose heart you say you ate for breakfast this morning."

Alonzo stared at him for a solid three seconds, as if trying to hold an expression. Then his eyes lit up and he threw his head back, laughing with his whole body. The sound filled the room. Will sat, stone-faced. From behind them, Alonzo's bodyguards joined in the laughter. Zoey felt Wu place a hand on the back of her chair.

After he caught his breath, Alonzo said, "Sorry, I couldn't hold it any longer. You think I eat human flesh, Willy? It was a pig's heart.

Just a little bit of theater. Saw the story on the news and thought we'd have some fun. It's almost Devil's Night!"

Will said, "So you don't know anything about Tilley? We'll let you get back to your business, then." He made like he was about to stand, but clearly had no real intention to.

"I didn't say I didn't know anything. I just said that wasn't his heart."

"Great. Did you kill him?"

"No sir."

"Do you know who did?"

"Before I answer, I want to ask you something." He looked at Zoey. "Why did you believe me and my boys would eat a man's heart?"

Zoey hesitated. "Because . . . you explicitly said so on camera? Several times?"

"I say the fact that you thought it was real says more about you than it does me."

"I don't know what you want from me, here." She glanced at Will, looking for a rescue.

In a friendly tone, Alonzo asked, "You know why I own a clothing store?"

"Uh, I'd say because you need a legit business to launder money."

"Aside from that. I sell the suits at cost, because they're needed for job interviews. I even rent out suits by the hour, for that purpose. Tell them they can pay when they get the job. Or not."

"So you're not a bad guy, you just pretend to be one for your videos?"

"Zoey," interjected Will, "you could fill an Olympic pool with the blood this man has spilled."

"Is that true?" asked Alonzo. "Or have I just made you think it is?" He turned his attention back to Zoey. "See, you can't get a job without a nice suit. You know why that is? It's because a job interview isn't really to see if you can do the job. It's to see if you can properly assume the role of a member of a higher class. And guess who gets to decide what *that* looks like."

Will said, "We're getting off the point here . . ."

"Are we?" Alonzo stayed fixed on Zoey. "See, that's *your* people's power. You've got all of the finest things locked away, accessed by a secret handshake that only certain kids learn growing up. The rest of us get left out in the cold, where asking the wrong person the time of day gets you shot. Not by a police officer, not in this city, but by a low-rent merc who answers to no one but some coldhearted millionaire looking down from way up high. Well, when all other kinds of power are denied to you, the power of fear is all you've got left."

"And so your only choice is to say you eat human hearts. Sure. So why are you mad at me for believing it?"

"Who's mad? I'm sitting here calm. I'm not raising my voice. Once again, you assume savagery. You brought that attitude in the door with you. As usual."

Zoey was sweating.

Will, on the other hand, sounded merely bored. "Look, if you don't actually know anything about Tilley, we need to go chase down other leads."

Still keeping his eyes on Zoey, Alonzo said, "You know three young men were shot outside the Kennelworth apartments last week? Private security did it, said they were trying to break in. They were visiting their grandma."

Zoey had not heard this, but Will jumped in. "Zoey doesn't own Kennelworth and those weren't our people. Those were VOP."

Zoey said, "And as for your job interviews and secret handshakes, a couple of years ago I heard a group of managers burst out laughing after I left an interview, then they posted my application on a 'Job Interview Fails' website. It was a job cleaning toilets."

Alonzo smiled.

Will stood and buttoned his suit jacket. "Let's go. He doesn't know anything."

"I know who you should talk to. How about that?"

"Who?"

To Zoey, Alonzo said, "Ah, your little heart is racing. Now look at your partner here, he's not scared. You know he's not even carrying a gun? See, he's got that confidence that comes with knowing that if somebody wrongs him, a whole lot of other people with guns will come along and exact unthinkable vengeance. What do you like to do for fun?"

The question caught Zoey so off guard that she wasn't even sure she'd heard it.

"What do I like to do for fun? Uh, these days I mostly get high and watch street streams. Or those Blink feeds where they've got the cameras tied to animals."

"Oof. That sounds depressing."

"Have you ever followed a squirrel's life over the course of a day? It's hilarious."

"See, I've already diagnosed your problem right there. You're carrying all of the stress and troubles of wealth, but *you're not having any of the fun.* You have Halloween plans? Why don't you come to the Lincoln Showroom? Doing a costume party. It's a jazz club, a little upscale, shouldn't be too scary for somebody like you, especially not if you're there as my guest."

"I can't tell if you're making fun of me or what you're doing here."

"No mockery at all, you can even bring your bodyguard. My parties are very subdued, all about fine music and soft conversation."

"My Halloween costume wouldn't fit in the door."

"Can't say I've ever heard that one before."

"I'll think about it."

Alonzo rolled his eyes. "Ugh. I know what *that* means."

Will said, "You've had your fun, give me your lead and let us get on with our lives."

"You ever wonder how your personal fan club put together a million dollars for the bounty?"

Will said, "Assumed they crowdsourced it. Zoey has thousands of people who hate her, I assume *some* of them have jobs."

"No, they do not. The money came in all at once. Single donor."

Will nodded, suddenly looking past Alonzo. Thinking. "Somebody's got money."

"The kind of money that they can throw out a million just to mess with you. Not that many of those people in the city. Find one who benefits from the chaos. Somebody who, I don't know, has a business interest in security."

"How do you know this?"

Sounding insulted, Alonzo said, "*Because I knew you were coming and didn't want you to leave empty-handed.* Made some calls."

Will nodded. He'd gotten what he'd come for.

Zoey said to Will, "Wait, if we just get Alonzo to confess, does that mean we win the reward money?"

Alonzo said, "Oh, no, the reward is specifically for anyone who can prove *you* did it. Doesn't pay out otherwise."

"Wait, really? And nobody sees the obvious flaw in that system?"

"They see it, they just don't care. But enough about America's war on drugs. If I hear anything else, I'll pass it along. If this city does have an actual cannibal killer, I'm in agreement that that is a bad thing, as they probably won't stop at just one meal. We could have our own Albert Fish, or Jeffrey Dahmer or Andrei Chikatilo running around out there. Those guys were all white, by the way. I trust you can see yourselves out."

II

They were back in the van, stuck in traffic downtown. They were patched into a group call with Budd, Echo, and Andre, their faces showing on the monitor in split screen. Budd was at what looked like the dining room at the Fort Fortuna hotel and casino. Behind him was a massive stone fire pit with various meats dangling over a roaring flame, buxom servers slicing off fresh hunks for tired-looking tourists.

"Nobody knows squat," said Budd over a plate of charred sausages. "Tilley's body was found in the parking garage here; that was true. Looks like someone from Zoey's fan club then came and scooped it up before anyone from the city could get down here, like they'd been tipped off it was here, or already knew. Fortuna staff didn't even follow up after that, seemed like they were just relieved somebody took him off their hands. Either way, the carcass was here long enough for word to get out that it'd been found at the largest and most well-known Ashe joint in the city, which I suppose was the point." Budd noticed his sausages were in the frame and said, "Oh, and, while I was here, I decided to do some quality control on the buffet."

Andre and Echo were calling from Andre's Bentley, also stuck in traffic.

"We found Dexter Tilley's mother," said Andre, "but she did *not* want to talk to us. Showed her the ol' Ben Franklin subpoena, a whole

stack of 'em. Didn't budge. Then we decided to track down Shae La-
Vergne, but it looks like she's temporarily out of the country."

"Like she knew this was all about to go down and wanted to get
away," said Zoey. "That's weird, right? Okay, so who else is there to
talk to?"

"That's actually the problem," said Andre. "Ideally we'd be able
to talk to Tilley's friends but if they're all part of The Blowback then
they're definitely not gonna talk to us."

Echo said, "They're always in the Hub." That was a popular VR
hangout. "But I don't have an account, obviously, I'm much too cool
for that."

"Oh, god," groaned Zoey, "my ex used to have a part-time job in
the Hub, growing these power-up berries in a digital orchard that
he'd sell for Spoils. We'd be on a drive somewhere and I could see him
logged in with his glasses, harvesting his stupid berries. Who here has
a login? So we can go in and talk to them?"

"Not me," said Andre. "Why do I need a whole second life to make
a mess of?"

Will shook his head. "What happened to Tilley didn't occur in
the Hub, it occurred in reality. Megaboss Alonzo said the confession
bounty was put up by a single donor, hinted that it was someone high
up in private security. I assume he's talking about—"

"But that's not who killed Tilley," interrupted Zoey.

"Maybe not," countered Will, "but it is who wants you to go down
for it. That's who we're after, not the murderer. *That* could be anybody.
Random street crime, for all we know."

"No. I want to know who did it."

"Somebody should comb through Blink," said Will, ignoring her.
"See if Tilley had any dealings with—"

An alert popped up on Will's phone. Zoey couldn't read it from
where she was sitting, but she saw Will's forehead scrunch up.

Another alert, this one on Wu's phone.

Another, this one on the van's security system.

She heard three more tones through their conference call, Andre, Echo, and Budd all getting the same notifications.

Budd jumped up from his table. "Where are you guys? Right now?"

"Intersection of Thirty-first Street and Thirty-sixth Avenue," said Will. Note: The street naming system in Tabula Ra$a made no sense whatsoever. "Heading west."

Budd was moving now, abandoning his food. "You need to get off if you can, or you're gonna run right smack into it."

Zoey asked, "Run into what?"

Will said, "There's going to be a riot. At the Night Inn."

Wu studied the display on the windshield. "We can turn off at Park, that would likely keep us clear . . ."

Zoey said, "No. Take me there."

Wu said, "That is an extremely bad idea."

"If these are Tilley's friends showing up at the inn, they're going after the girls, right? To get revenge? These are the girls *we* convinced to go back to work after the thing last month. Wu, go. Don't make me repeat the order."

Traffic cleared as navigation systems collectively started routing other vehicles away from the disturbance. Zoey's disguised van rolled up to a spot about a block away from the Night Inn, close enough to see the front of the building had been repaired from the hostage crisis (in reality, that'd probably been done weeks ago) and the entire front of the building was a looping video of an adorable girl's smiling face, big round cheeks and brown eyes, her fingers laced under her chin. Animated text scrolled around her face saying,

YOU'RE SAFE HERE.

Subtle, thought Zoey. Also, the situation did not look like a riot. There were a few dozen people in front of the building, just kind of yelling at it. She couldn't quite make out what they were saying. Something about ponies? Zoey had expected burning cars and clouds of tear gas, but it was just a weirdly awkward gathering of idiots. None of them seemed to know what to do. It was actually kind of disappointing.

"This is what everybody's freaking out over?"

Will studied the scene. "We didn't say there was a riot. We said there was *going* to be one. A spontaneous riot, within the next five to ten minutes."

"It's a spontaneous riot, but they scheduled it in advance? That's thoughtful."

From up front, Wu said, "It wasn't scheduled. There's an unrest algorithm that uses Blink to predict outbreaks of violence."

"So it's saying there *might* be a riot."

"No," said Will, "it's telling us there *will* be one."

And with that, a guy kicked over a trash can. Several people moved in to capture the damage on camera, getting the word out that chaos was occurring and that anyone who wanted to be famous should come join in. Breaking the seal.

"So what do we do? How do we defuse it?"

"You can't," said Will. "You have guards on the door and additional security on the way. If you step out there, they'll go nuts at the sight of you."

"Does the software tell you that, too? This is crazy!"

"It's not complicated. You have preexisting moods, multiple ringleader personalities in proximity, and a triggering event that happened about twenty minutes ago. It's like a chemical reaction, at that point we're just waiting for it to start bubbling up."

"Triggering event? What was that?"

"There's a new video, from Dexter Tilley."

"Tilley is dead," said Zoey, watching as the proto-riot overturned another trash can. "Unless someone's resurrected him again?"

"It was made two weeks ago, but it was just released while we were talking to Alonzo. Here . . ."

Will put the video on one of the van's monitors. It was a close-up of Tilley's teary, trembling, pimply face. He was sitting in what looked like a makeshift living space built out of a shipping container—ribbed white metal walls, no visible window, an open case of self-heating ramen containers in the background. The young man took some pills, then took a drink from a bottle of water. He sniffed, let out a long breath and then said,

"They call it a teaser pony. On a horse ranch, it's hard to tell when the mares are in heat. But other horses can tell. So what they have is a male pony, a little one, maybe a Shetland. And what they'll do is lead the mares past him and when he senses one is ready to breed, he'll get an erection and start thrashing around, desperate. Then they'll bring in a stallion to mount her. See, they pick a pony because he's physically too small to even do it. Even if he gets access to the mare, he can't mount her. And they know he's too small to hurt anyone when he finally lashes out. That's how he spends his life. Throbbing, desperate arousal, no relief. Rage and frustration but powerless to get revenge. Too dumb to know he's just a tool, that others count on his pathetic neediness for their own profit. That's me. My whole life. I'm the teaser pony."

Outside the van, a mobile vending machine that had been parked next to the entrance of the Night Inn raised itself up on tiny wheels and started rolling away, as if it was getting worried about the riot. Some of the kids saw it, surrounded it, and tipped it over, smashing the glass in front. Zoey felt oddly sorry for it. Bottles of soda and beer rolled out and some of the burgeoning rioters grabbed them and chucked them at the facade of the building, hooting and yelling at the sound they made when they smashed.

"So, first of all," continued Tilley on the screen, "I want to thank all my brothers out there who helped me find her. I tried to call, she blocked me. Tried to follow her on her Blink, she blocked me. Blocked me everywhere. Tried to find her at the inn, they said she was gone. Went to her mom's place, they had private security at the door, from the Suits. Finally found out they had Shae holed up at a hotel out of town. And you guys, you heroes, you got me the room number, I know it wasn't easy. But she's got security there, too, the cow funding this whole thing, and I know that I can fight through and get to the door if I want. Tear down that door, tear down the building. But I don't do it. All I wanted, *all* I wanted, was to say good-bye. To apologize. To make her understand . . ."

Tilley broke down in tears.

"I chickened out, brothers. I let you all down. Didn't even approach the building. I know what her answer would be. I have all of this love to give, and nobody wants it. So I become everybody's puppet. I have this need, like an addiction, so they use it to control me. They smile, flash some thigh, touch me on the arm to get a bigger tip. 'You want this? You want this? Well, you can't have it.' Giggling the whole time. So funny, isn't it? To watch me starve? Funny how I didn't hear laughter that day at the inn. Funny how only then, when she saw what I could do, understood what I could do to *her*, did she finally see me as a man.

"But even then, she had all the power. If she'd refused to go along, made me kill her, we all know how it'd have played out. Headlines about another pretty girl murdered by an evil brute. A martyr. A symbol. But now, I understand. *I* can be that symbol. A symbol of a system that profits from our urges and then tries to shame us for having them. You did this, Shae. And for the rest of you, you know this isn't just about her. This is about a whole system. My brothers, it's time to burn it down."

Outside the van, someone had found bricks. One was chucked up at the building's facade. It smashed into a second-floor window, through the thin video screen. Sparks flew, static rippled through the animation of the smiling girl's face, making her eyes briefly look like she was having a seizure. The rioters went wild, excited that damage had been done. Another threshold had been crossed.

Wu said, "They're here."

Ashe Security vehicles pulled up on the sidewalk, teams in armored gear spilling out. Zoey spotted Kowalski among them. The rioters erupted at the sight, throwing bottles, then bricks. They seemed to have hit another gear, everyone moving with confidence now, feeding off each other. Half of the security team tried to form a barrier in front of the door, while the rest went inside, presumably to evacuate the staff through the other exit. The screaming and chanting got louder, some spectators joining in until it wasn't clear where the riot stopped and the bystanders started. They, too, fed off each other, the growing crowd bringing with it the cruel courage of anonymity.

A bottle bounced off the van. The riot was spreading outward, engulfing them. The kid who threw it was just feet away, wearing a Halloween mask that projected a holographic skull, a design similar to the digital disguise Tilley had used the night of the hostage crisis. A security guard with a riot shield shoved him back and the kid stumbled and bumped into the side of the van. His face landed right on the window, inches away from Zoey's. The mask slipped on impact and Zoey looked right into his eyes. He couldn't see her, the windows were so tinted that it'd have been easier to see through the metal door panels. But seeing the guy's facial expression . . . that was the first time Zoey truly understood.

The trolls who occasionally showed up to yell at her, they were always smiling or at least smirking. Common bullies, having fun, members of a loose hate group who barely believed the slogans they scrawled on her buildings. What she saw on the face of this guy was something completely different: rage on a level that could only be called a kind of madness. She got the sense that if someone slid a big red button to that man and said, "If pressed, will destroy the entire planet," he'd have hammered it. All sense of consequences gone, a fury that blots out the future.

Wu said, "Look!"

He was leaning toward the windshield, pointing upward with a finger.

A drone was buzzing in toward the building, way up, at about roof level. Dangling below it was a big plastic drum, hanging from makeshift straps. Zoey's first thought was that it was a bomb, but that couldn't be right. Things hadn't progressed to the Bomb Stage, had they?

It would be much later when Zoey found out what was *supposed* to have happened here. The barrel was full of a white, hot liquid, a rubberized sealant somebody had stolen from a nearby construction site, the same place where they were finding the loose bricks. Their big, hilarious plan was to crash it into the building, spattering the white goo down the facade. See, so it would look like somebody had ejaculated all over the face of the girl in the video loop. They presumably didn't know that the material was highly flammable until it cured, or maybe they did know and didn't care. Either way, the drone and barrel crashed into the building as planned, splattering the goo down the screen and then into the sparking hole where the brick had gone through earlier. The liquid ignited immediately, a curtain of flame whipping upward.

Zoey sucked in a breath. The crowd outside went wild.

The kid outside threw a brick at the van's window, unintentionally hurling it right at Zoey's skull. The brick bounced off without leaving a scratch. They'd have gotten the same result if the brick had been a shotgun blast. This confused the kid, plus everyone who saw it happen. They didn't put together the fact that this meant the van was in fact an armored vehicle in disguise—the riot hive mind is not a genius—but rather felt the dumb frustration of a dog that can't figure out how to open the toilet lid to get a drink. Several of the rioters ran over and started pushing on the van, rocking it, having decided that it'd be fun to tip it over.

Wu didn't wait for an order from Zoey. He slammed on the accelerator, steered up onto the sidewalk, and drove right through the crowd. They hit one guy, hard, knocking him aside. Zoey felt it in her gut. They bounced down off the curb and got onto the street again, passing emergency vehicles whooshing in from the other direction. Professionals throwing themselves into danger on Zoey's behalf.

She should be back there. This was her crisis, it should be her mess to clean up. And yet, they drove away, farther and farther from the danger, and Zoey said nothing. She reassured herself that ultimately she would pay the bill, that those emergency workers were doing their jobs, that everyone would understand.

She hated herself.

Will told Wu to stop somewhere. If they were being followed, he didn't want to lead them all the way back to the estate and give up the identity of the cover vehicle. They wound up in the parking lot of a company called Life Partners, a place that rents friends you can hang out with or who'll help around the house. The building was designed so that it appeared the entire structure was being held aloft by a crowd of smiling statues, each with one hand held above their head to bear the load, the other giving a thumbs-up.

Zoey watched the feed from the inn. The fire had melted huge chunks of the facade and the blaze had spread to the interior. Smoke was billowing out of several windows. Guards and employees were draining out of the building, fleeing the fire.

She was struggling to breathe. Wu was asking her things, expressing concern. She couldn't really hear him. Will was watching her, saying nothing.

She looked at him and tried to steady her voice. "Is . . . is this my fault?"

"Why are you asking that question?"

"Why can't you just say 'no' when I ask something like that? *God.*"

"You're not a child," said Will, gently. "I won't treat you like one. You're asking me if this was your fault because you want to know what emotion you're supposed to be feeling right now. Are you supposed to be beating yourself up? Well, that's the wrong question. The world doesn't care about your emotions."

"So what question should I be asking?"

"Whether or not you would do it differently next time. Everything that happens matters only in terms of what you can learn from it going forward."

"Are you going to lecture me about how I should have had Tilley killed?"

"Would that have prevented this?"

"I don't see how it would. Even if you'd made it look like an accident, like you said, they'd have found a way to blame me. Hell, for all we know his death *was* an accident and they're still blaming me."

"I agree."

"You do?"

"Yes. You were right, I was wrong. My way would have made him a martyr, just a few weeks sooner."

"So, what in the hell am I supposed to learn from a bunch of people going nuts and torching my building?"

"Some rioters in this world have a legitimate grievance. Do these?"

"No."

"Are they rational in the demands they're making of you?"

"I can't even tell what their demands are."

"So, we couldn't have done anything to prevent this—they're doing what they were already determined to do, for their own reasons. That means we move past self-doubt and don't look back. Now the only question that matters is how do we fix it."

"All right. How?"

"Are they organized?"

"It didn't look organized."

"It can be hard to tell from the outside sometimes. Chaos can be someone else's goal."

"Oh, wait, I just thought of a joke. Say the word 'organized' again."

"Alonzo thinks a specific person is behind this. If so, we need to find out what *their* goal is."

Zoey stared at the feed from the inn. Ambulances were on the scene.

"Do you think everyone got out?"

"Probably, crews were already on the scene when the fire started. I don't have much hope for the building. I'm not saying it had no fire extinguishing systems, I'm sure it had something, but your father liked to invest in the parts of the building that boosted profits and inspectors used to be very easy to bribe." He turned to Wu. "Arrange to switch to another vehicle, get us back to the estate."

Zoey said, "What? No. We're not done out here. We haven't even solved our mystery."

Will looked at her. "Are you sure?"

This was not asked in the way that, say, your mother would ask if you're sure you don't want dessert. It was asked the way you'd ask a scrawny mover if he's sure your huge, expensive mirror isn't too heavy for him to carry alone.

"Don't ask me again."

Will patched in the rest of the team again, the split screen taking over the main monitor. Everyone was in vehicles now, en route to somewhere.

"I want to know who's behind this," said Will, "and I want to know in the next five minutes."

Budd said, "We just did a Bacon search on Blink of every unscrupulous rich asshole in the city—a list that, by the way, is longer than an elephant's cocktail party anecdote—to see if anyone connected to anyone connected to one of them had ever interacted with Tilley. We got one hit, and it's what I think you were about to say earlier, before we got interrupted. Two weeks ago, Tilley was seen speaking to an employee of Titus Chobb."

There was a silence across the call.

Zoey said, "*The* Titus Chobb?"

Budd said, "Yes, ma'am."

"I'm just kidding, I have no idea who that is."

Echo said, "He owns the Vanguard of Peace, which is now the largest private security firm in the city and is rapidly becoming the *only* one. He's continuing to buy up all of the smaller firms, one by one."

"So he has a massive personal army. Great."

"Chobb travels with a jammer," said Budd. "Any outgoing feed will get scrambled if the camera is within a hundred feet of him. All we have is this shot . . ."

Budd put a brief, looping clip of Dexter Tilley on the screen, looking sweaty and deranged, talking to a terrifying giant of a man. The giant had carefully mussed brown hair, blue eyes, and an elaborate asymmetrical beard. He was wearing armor that may or may not have been a Halloween costume.

Zoey said, "That's Titus Chobb? Why do this city's captains of industry aspire to be cartoon characters?"

Andre said, "No, Chobb is the greasy dude sitting at the table with his son way back behind them there. The giant is Chobb's personal bodyguard, Dirk Vikerness."

Will nodded. "This is what Alonzo was hinting at. He's no fan of Chobb or the VOP in general."

Zoey studied the giant, muscled bodyguard and said, "I suppose I have to go flirt with him, too."

Will seemed to actually be thinking seriously about that. "Budd, you can get through to Chobb, right? See if he'll meet me for lunch today."

"It'll just be you?"

Zoey said, "No, I'm going. If this Chobb character is trying to destroy my life, I want to look him in the eye."

Will glanced at his watch. "All right, if we take the slow, extra-discreet route, that won't leave much time." After a beat, he said, "We need to get organized."

"Otherwise we'll end up like Tilley," said Zoey. "*Dis*organized."

Echo said, "What do you need us to—"

"Because he was missing his organs!"

"What do you need us to do while you're up there?"

"Get security to the other properties," said Will. "Nothing else burns today."

"And get inside the Hub," added Zoey. "Actually, can we just buy the Hub? It's a fake world, what can it cost? We'll buy it all up and shut it down, the trolls will hate that."

Echo said, "I'll, uh, look into that."

"And what exactly do we need to be bringing to this meeting in the way of backup? This Chobb guy has an army, right?"

"He's just a businessman who happens to own a private security firm," said Will. "He's ruthless but he's not some kind of supervillain."

"All right. So, where do we find him?"

"He spends his time floating above the city in a huge black zeppelin."

12

Will had not been joking about that.

The big black blimp had once been a restaurant called Innerer Schweinehund. The passenger hold famously only had room for six tables plus a separate, tiny bar and then the kitchen. The chef, Werner Wolff, was a big deal, he'd had a popular Blink stream that was mostly just a camera looking down at the counter while he plated dishes. The man was an artist and a psychopath, working magic in his kitchen and then raging at staff and customers alike. Getting a table at his floating restaurant used to mean four years on a waiting list . . . or if you were Titus Chobb, you finally got frustrated with the wait and bought the restaurant, turning the dirigible into a company meeting space and Wolff into your personal chef.

Also, the blimp was "black" in the way a blinding spotlight is white; the surface was made of a special light-absorbing nanotube material that reflected no features or contours whatsoever. From the ground it was impossible to even grasp that it was a three-dimensional object, it just looked like a perfect hole punched in the sky. You could routinely find tourists staring up at it and blinking their eyes, thinking there was something wrong with their vision.

Zoey, Will, and Wu were told to board the restaurant from the rooftop of a building called Freya's Palace (not one of Zoey's, she'd asked) and were informed that the blimp would then take a leisurely hour-long circuit around the perimeter of the city. The airship was already perched on the roof of the sculpted marble tower when they pulled up. The building was all curves and flourishes (Zoey wondered if a woman had designed it) and from the ground, the attached blimp made it look like it was wearing a black beret. Inside, she found that Freya's Palace's interior seemed to be a gigantic spa complex for rich women, a silent space with customers shuffling around in white robes. They entered a glassed-in elevator that rose through a transparent tube surrounded by an aquarium, so that passengers could enjoy annoying exotic fish as they ascended.

Zoey put her hand into her jacket pocket and felt the tube of her mom's stupid skin cream. She pulled it out, the little animated flower dancing on the logo. Guaranteed to give you the confidence of a . . . daisy? Still, she twisted out the petals and smeared it on her hands. Maybe it would stop them from shaking so much.

The blimp docked directly to a glassed-in enclosure on the top floor. As they stepped from the elevator, the black shape loomed overhead, blotting out the sun. They entered a narrow door to the airship's passenger compartment and were met by the armored muscles of Chobb's bodyguard, Dirk Vikerness. His beard was trimmed in the shape of a snake that emerged from his left sideburn and coiled around his mouth, ending where a normal mustache would stop. He had dazzling blue eyes and the expression of a man who knew they were dazzling. He wore sculpted yellow plates around his shoulders and chest, the armor flat black the rest of the way down. The company colors.

In an accent that sounded Swedish, he said, "Ah, you are here. I hear the fire at your building is nearly out. I am sure you wish you could be there, helping your people get to safety." He focused on Wu and said, "I will need to collect your weapons, I'm afraid. Blimp rules."

Wu looked at Zoey for confirmation. She deferred to Will, who nodded. Wu turned over his katana, several blades, and a bracelet weapon he had mounted to his good wrist. Even then, Zoey was confident he hadn't given up everything. She had her augmentation-control necklace, but couldn't see Raiden scars on Vikerness. She figured he knew he could cave in somebody's skull using only what genes and steroids had given him.

The weaponry now in his hands, the giant man said, "Thank you. Now we are going to be brushing up against our max weight; are all three of you under two hundred pounds?"

Zoey said, "Yes."

Looking right at her, Dirk said, "Are you sure?"

Zoey had to crane her neck to make contact with those icy eyes.

"I don't get it, is this how you flirt? If so, will you consider it a turn-off if I keep stopping to laugh at your beard?"

Will, sounding annoyed, said, "You're keeping your boss waiting."

"Of course, everyone's time is important, I'm sure," said Vikerness. He gestured them into the passenger deck. "Life is always shorter than we think."

They were led to a table where Titus Chobb was already sitting. He was a small, oily man with dark eyes and graying hair that was shaved on the sides and swept over up top, a style designed to be combed with fingers after rolling out of bed. His outfit was khakis and a denim shirt, looking like he was ready to go out and supervise some landscaping work. His eyes said he was being interrupted from something he'd much rather be doing and Zoey guessed that he wore that expression twenty-four hours a day, even when sleeping.

Will said, "Titus."

"I got another meeting at this time, client is waiting in the bar area, getting more pissed off by the minute. Make it quick."

They took that as their cue to sit.

Before they could begin, Chobb said to Will, "And before we even start, let me make it clear that this meeting fulfills the favor I owe you. Whatever you're about to ask me for, it doesn't start from a place of me owing you a debt. Even that is being generous. The favor was owed to Arthur, not you." He turned to look at Zoey for the first time.

"Your father was a great man. Tragic the way it ended for him, but also inevitable. Men like him typically don't die in their sleep."

Zoey got the "Your father was a great man" stuff a lot, usually at functions with donors trying to get on her good side. Her father had impregnated Zoey's mother, abandoned her, then all but threatened her with death if she pursued paternity. He had made his money by crushing the desperate and vulnerable like grapes in a wine press. Still, Zoey had developed an answer that seemed to satisfy everyone.

"He was passionate about what he believed in."

The whole room jolted. As the airship pulled away from the rooftop, Zoey watched the world sink down from the side windows. Her stomach did a drunken backflip and fell flat on its face.

"When he died," said Titus, watching the city drain from their view, "his vision died with him."

Will quickly cut off any chance for Zoey to reply to this. "I know your time is valuable. And you know the context for this meeting."

"I'm actually surprised you're up here talking to me, rather than down there trying to quell the uprising. Getting big enough to make the news now. Scaring away tourists. Destabilizing our fragile paradise. Every empire is a house of cards, as you well know."

"But business must be booming for you," said Will. "Every mom and pop shop will want private security at their door."

"Only if said security ensures a steady flow of happy customers who're in the mood to spend money. If there is unrest in the streets to the point that everyone is afraid to leave their apartments, then a guy at the door with a yellow jacket and a machine gun isn't going to make a damned bit of difference. When the money dries up, so will security budgets. No, *my* perfect scenario is a completely peaceful city and a populace who appreciates that only my services can preserve that peace."

A completely nude woman with a body like an Olympic swimmer strode up. She was wearing white body paint, so that she looked like a Greek statue. Zoey wasn't taken aback—she was familiar with the chef's crew of servers, as they had also been a prominent part of Wolff's streams. The woman placed a platter on the table and Zoey glanced over at Will to see if he'd ogle her as she walked back to the kitchen. He did not. Zoey did. A bit.

The dish on the platter looked like some kind of chilled bean thing, served on a misty tray of liquid nitrogen. Yep, this was a Chef Wolff dish, all right.

Will said, "So we all have the same goal, then. We need to quell this."

"How do you intend to do that?"

"A two-pronged approach of showing force in the streets, and putting these ugly rumors to rest."

Chobb raised an eyebrow. "You think that'll do it, huh? That's making me think you don't even understand what this is about."

"We were there," Zoey interjected, "in the middle of the riot. Bricks hit the van. I'm pretty sure I get it."

Chobb laughed and looked back at Dirk Vikerness, who was looming over his shoulder.

"What was it, ninety seconds?"

The bodyguard chuckled.

Chobb turned back to Zoey. "I said to him before you got here, I've never known a woman under thirty who could go more than two minutes without talking about herself." To Will, he said, "You didn't give her the standard 'let me do all the talking' speech on the way here?" Back to Zoey, "I'd explain it, but I doubt you'd be able to stay quiet long enough."

Zoey bit her lip so hard she tasted blood. "Give it a try. I'm always eager to learn."

Chobb carefully rolled some of the bean things onto some kind of fancy cracker, sprinkled some kind of orange crumbles on top, then dabbed it with a pulpy red sauce.

As he chewed, he said, "A long time ago, a capable, strong man, perfected by millions of years of natural selection, emerged from his cave."

Zoey thought, *Oh, god. He's one of these guys.*

"Then another strong, capable man—and it was a man, not a woman—walks up and says, 'Help me build my hut and in exchange, I'll help you hunt later.' And the man said, 'Sure, but I don't trust your caveman brain to remember this favor, so write it down on a note. A piece of paper that proves that I did something great and that in exchange, someone must do something great for me.' Those transferable acts of heroism are what we call 'money.' Each and every dollar represents a bold action from a talented, competent, hardworking man somewhere in the past. When that system is functioning as intended, no one is victimized, no one is cheated. It's just an exchange of glorious acts, men trying to do the most good for others so that they can get the best in return, until the untamed wilderness is transformed into a flourishing paradise."

He paused to assemble another bite.

"Where that all falls apart," he continued, to Zoey's dismay, "is when bad actors decide they don't feel like doing the hard work of achieving greatness—learning a skill, building something. They would rather just sneak in under the cover of dark and steal someone else's heroism. Or, out of jealousy, demand the government take it and give it to them. *Or,* when lazy children inherit a stack of heroism from their hardworking father, then demand that they themselves be treated as heroes. Do you know what the name of this restaurant means? 'Innerer Schweinehund'?"

"'Inner pig-dog.' I used to watch Chef Wolff's stream, back when this was a restaurant. Though it's kind of weird he went with that when 'Cloud Nein' was out there."

"The inner pig-dog is the laziness that haunts a man's soul," said Chobb, explaining the thing that Zoey had just told him she already knew. "The voice telling him to quit, to kick back, to have a beer, that nothing is worth doing. It's the part of yourself we have to kill to accomplish greatness. Any man in the world who has built anything, or become great at something, bears a medal on his chest declaring that he's defeated the schweinehund. And we bristle when we see anyone who gives in but still gets their share of the spoils." He pointed his spoon at Zoey. "*That* is why they hate you."

"Because I inherited my money?"

"Because every man can feel when things are out of balance. We are built to be sickened by injustice."

"And here I thought people were mailing me rape threats because they're psychopaths who get turned on by spreading fear."

"Psychopaths persist in the species because women find them attractive, thus breeding more psychopaths."

Zoey felt Will shifting in his seat, sensing the annoyance building in him. He had little use for these debates that Zoey was somehow constantly getting sucked into.

"Whereas men," she said, "choose their sex partners based purely on moral virtue. Getting back to the original topic, what, in your estimation, would make all of this go away?"

"You've seen the video of when the North Korean government fell? The crowds tearing down that statue? That's when the mob will be satisfied."

"Only I'm the statue. So, what, I should retire? Take some money and go back to Colorado?"

"No, I don't think that would do it. I think they need to topple you."

"Speaking of Korea," said Will, before Zoey could open her mouth, "you built all of this off of contracts you had over there. When you were with Odin's Hammer. All that off-books work behind the border."

"You were there."

"I was. I saw the aftermath of your people's work in Kaesong. I understand they were paid very well. Deservedly so. It can't be easy to shoot a five-year-old child, they make for such small targets. Well, I guess it's easier when they're starving. And barricaded inside a school."

"And now their surviving comrades, instead of starving in the streets, can dine at one of the four Chick-fil-A locations that just opened in their city. What's your point?"

"My point is, if I were to, say, smash you through that window and feed you to the propellers—"

Zoey grabbed Will's arm. "Stop. Go. Walk away. Go outside and have a smoke." She glanced back at Wu. "You, too. I want to talk to Mr. Chobb alone."

Will stared daggers at her, but didn't move.

She repeated. "Go. There's a little bar through that door, right? Go have a drink." To Wu, "And yes, go with him. Don't make me say it again."

They both left, reluctantly. Chobb almost imperceptibly nodded to Dirk Vikerness, who stepped away, taking up a position in the corner instead of leaving the room, as Zoey would've preferred. Chobb was spooning more beans onto a cracker. Zoey grabbed a cracker and started doing the same.

"What is this? Some kind of bean salad?"

"They're all eggs. A mix of salmon roe, caviar, escamoles—that's ant larva. The orange crumbles are sugar-cured egg yolks. These are fried blinis. The sauce is a Moroccan harissa."

She chewed. The eggs were just frozen enough to kind of gently shatter in the mouth, the sauce was spicy and minty. The varying temperatures hit her tongue in waves. It was deeply unsettling and also she immediately wanted more.

Chobb nodded in the direction Will had gone and said, "You know he agrees with everything I just said, right? Don't let him tell you any different. He knows he should be at the head of the table. I can't even imagine what lies Will is telling you to make you think your interests are aligned. And I'll say this—I think it's cruel the way he's stringing you along, letting you be the public face of the operation for whatever demented purpose he's decided that serves. This summer, when I heard he'd supposedly found you like that and gotten you to a hospital, I said, 'Ah, there it is. That's how he's going to do it once he's decided he's done with her. He's set the stage.' Soon they'll find you in the tub with your wrists split open and he'll say, 'We all knew she was troubled, the poor girl. Even had to be institutionalized at one point. The burden of leadership was just more than what little Zoey could bear.'"

Instead of taking the bait, Zoey swallowed, leveled her gaze at Titus Chobb, and said, "They're right. The Blowback, I mean. I had Dexter Tilley killed."

She watched him very carefully. Anyone can suppress a reaction when the situation calls for it, but it is almost impossible to avoid that initial half-second response. It was in that fraction of a moment that Titus Chobb flashed an expression of mild amusement, the look of a man who had heard a statement he knew was a lie and was relishing the power of knowing the truth. And in that moment, Zoey knew that either Chobb had killed Tilley, or knew who had done it. It wasn't that strange of a thought; the man's empire was built on gunmen who, in a sane city, would have washed out of a police academy. If he wanted it done, he could have ordered it with a glance and a nod.

Still, Chobb's expression recovered faster than most people's, she had to admit.

"Well, that's good to know. Am I supposed to be scared?"

The nude server returned and placed in front of each of them a small wooden plank. On each was a piece of meat that was still squirming. It was a flayed eel, its head intact but body sliced open and pinned to the wood, like a dissection in biology class. Zoey suppressed her urge to recoil in disgust but, just like Chobb, knew she did not do it in time.

Chobb said, "This way, you know it's fresh."

Zoey tried not to look at it. Still, she could *hear* it. A slimy exposed wound, writhing in pain.

"I don't expect you to be scared of me, no. But if the roof blows off this city . . . it's not going to look like anything you've seen before. How many private security staff do you have on your payroll?"

"Over a thousand," he said, as he carved off a piece of eel. "And growing."

"But you don't accept anyone who has implants, and you don't use any other Raiden gadgets. No tiny blasters that can melt a whole car."

"That's because none of it works. I just heard about a man who's in the hospital, still on fire a week later."

"The *bootleg* implants don't work. They have buggy software, by design. That's because there's only one source for the real thing. And I'm not selling. Yet."

Chobb stopped chewing. Just for a second, but she caught it.

She continued, "This situation in the city *will* get fixed, and soon. I can't make them love me, but I can make them piss their pants at the sound of my name. I would prefer it not to be that way. But if they don't leave me a choice?" She shrugged.

"I believe you. After all, *you killed Dexter Tilley.*"

He cut off another chunk of the thrashing eel and took a bite. As he chewed, they locked eyes for about three seconds.

Zoey looked away first. She picked up her knife and sliced the head off her eel, putting it out of its misery, and stood.

"Where's the server? I want to leave her a tip."

13

Zoey joined Will in the cramped little bar area and they had a drink in silence. The encounter had gone more or less the way they'd planned it. They were passing a giant golden cat on their left—a Chinese casino designed as a five-hundred-foot-tall *maneki-neko*, like the "lucky cat" figurines with the left paw that waves back and forth in a beckoning motion. The building did in fact have a motorized arm, slowly tilting back and forth to their left as if at any moment it could reach over and slap them out of the air. Zoey felt a twinge of bitterness at the sight of it; this joint was the only reason she wasn't able to design her own headquarters like a giant cat, as it'd have been seen as a petty knockoff.

They finally landed back at the Freya's Palace rooftop and a few minutes later, they were back in the van, stuck in traffic. Now that she knew about the canceled subway project, Zoey would silently curse her father every time she crept through Tabula Ra$a's constipated surface streets. A few blocks from the hotel, a Threat Warning briefly popped up on the van's monitor, noting that someone up ahead was concealing an assault rifle under their clothes, but that they were alone and did not convey hostile intent from their posture. This kind of thing wasn't uncommon in the city and the van probably figured one person with one weapon didn't pose much in the way of a threat, considering how many ways the vehicle could instantly ruin any assailant's day.

They hit a stoplight and Zoey said, "Chobb isn't just stirring up the mob. He either did Tilley, or knows who did."

"Correct. And now he's happy to sit back and see how it plays out."

"Would he feel the same way if we put a bounty on him? Have Wu board his blimp via jetpack and chuck Chobb out of it, screaming?"

Wu said, "After all of these months, I feel like you still don't completely understand what a bodyguard does."

"This group, The Blowback, would just add that to their list of grievances," said Will. "Chobb did this to light a fuse, killing him doesn't stamp it out."

He said it like he'd already considered it as an option.

"So how do we stop a lit fuse?"

"That depends on how far you're willing to go."

"You can't just kill them all, Will. There are thousands of people in my personal hate group. Tens of thousands."

"Well . . . yes and no. You remember the Goldstone building fire back in the spring? All those deaths because the alarms didn't go off, and the office workers just sat there until it was too late?"

"I think so."

"The victims smelled smoke. They all wanted to get out but they didn't hear an alarm. The alarm, in that situation, wasn't there to announce there was a fire—they knew there was a fire. The alarm was there *to give them permission to get up and leave*. Nobody wanted to be first, the social pressure kept them glued to their seats. Well, mass violence works the same way. It just takes one person to be the fire alarm, to give everybody permission to go wild. But probably half of the rioters back at the inn couldn't pick you out of a lineup or even explain what they were angry about. It's a core of obsessed true believers surrounded by a cloud of fence-sitters looking for a purpose to cling to. Most of those would disperse if the core were to . . . go away."

"But taking them out would just turn them into martyrs, like Tilley."

Will thought for a moment, a pause Zoey had come to recognize as Will deciding whether or not to share a piece of potentially upsetting history with her. Or, having decided, trying to figure out exactly how to frame it in the best light possible.

"There was a fundamentalist Christian group," he began, "who was giving your father trouble, this would have been more than ten years ago. It was led by a guy who called himself Phinehas and when I say fundamentalists, I'm talking polygamy, child brides, didn't believe in money or the right to own property because it all belongs to God . . . the whole thing. Maybe a hundred members altogether. So, first they started squatting in one of the under-construction hotels, claiming that a message from the Lord had told them it was their holy site and destined to be a temple. Then they started harassing sex workers and customers at nearby brothels, calling them sinners, filming them and saying they would tell their families back home, yelling to passing tourists about how we were spreading pestilence. One time, one of the girls started yelling back and some of these guys beat her up pretty badly. You know, to save her soul."

Zoey braced herself. Will always played up the badness of Arthur's enemies in stories like this, to make what they did in response go down easier.

She sighed and said, "And to deal with them, you did . . . what?"

The Threat Warning briefly popped up on the monitor again. Same guy with a gun, somewhere in the vicinity. Zoey noted that Wu was tapping his screen up front, tracking the guy. Just to be safe.

Will flicked his eyes over to the monitor before saying, "Now, in PSYOPS training they taught us that social norms exist to keep societies running smoothly over the long term. So if you have a splinter group with a belief system based on rejecting social norms—a cult, a gang—they're usually destined to self-destruct because there's a reason society has those rules, right? It's like starting a motorcycle gang that doesn't believe in traffic lights, you're just counting down until the crash happens. That means that within those groups there are already fractures or contradictions ready to be exploited. Somebody in there is a hypocrite.

"Well, Budd did a little digging and found that the group's second in command, a guy who called himself Malachai, had lost a daughter a couple of years before, when she was just nine. See, the group didn't believe in modern Western medicine, they said all ailments could be cured by prayer or whatever weird purification ceremonies they were doing. It turned out those were ineffective at treating a respiratory infection in a child already suffering from asthma. Malachai and the girl's mother begged the leader, this Phinehas, to take her to a doctor. Absolutely not, he says. So they all stand there and watch this girl suffocate and as a reward for this show of faith, Malachai gets elevated to his current role as Vice Messiah."

"Okay, just how dark is this story going to get, Will?"

"So, there's a device called a hypersonic projector, that can beam an audio signal like a laser, you can aim it at a person in a crowd and only they'll hear it. Do it to a person who is alone, and they'll perceive it as a voice in their head. As it happens, one day Phinehas's favorite wife comes down with a terrible and mysterious illness. Something very much treatable in a modern medical setting, but impossible to treat at home. Her condition goes downhill very quickly, so much vomiting that she's becoming dehydrated and has lost consciousness. The entire group is constantly praying for her recovery and, sure enough, they get an answer. Or, rather, one of them does. Phinehas, alone in his room, hears a voice as plain as day, telling him to take his wife to a nearby clinic, that the Lord is going to work through the doctors to see her back to health, that this exception is being made due to the important role said wife is going to play in fulfilling the prophecy and the building of the temple. Later that night, without telling anyone else about this divine message he's received, Phinehas sneaks her off to the clinic and they immediately hook her up to an IV."

"Who was operating the magic voice thing, to beam the message into his head?"

"Andre. So, just moments later, Malachai, the second in command, is awoken in his room by a vision of his deceased daughter, floating outside his window—"

"Oh my god. That was, what, a hologram?"

"And a replication of her actual voice, both constructed from what few videos we could find from when she was alive. The spirit directs him to leave the construction site he's squatting in and to go down to the sidewalk. There, his daughter's spirit points him toward the clinic, tells him to go to a certain room if he wants to see a false prophet in action, saying the man who sentenced her to a horrible death is now indulging his own wife with the very care the daughter was denied. Malachai bursts into the room with Phinehas and his wife, a fight breaks out, Phinehas winds up dead via a scalpel to the jugular. The next week, Phinehas's inner circle murders Malachai and five of his most loyal followers in retaliation. The rest of the group takes sides and either kill each other, or flee the city to go find some other movement to get brainwashed into. Problem solved."

"And what was the wife's name?" asked Zoey. "The one who almost died?"

"I don't remember. Something biblical."

"And she just happened to get sick right when you needed her to, for the plan to work? You didn't make that happen?"

"When did I say that?"

"Wow."

"I asked you how far you were willing to go."

The light had turned green at the intersection, but the pedestrians in the crosswalk kept coming, ignoring the signal. Wu edged the van forward slightly and tapped the horn. In this city, it just made the people walk slower.

Zoey said, "Well, the good news is Stench Machine got twelve new followers on Blink today." He had a camera attached to his collar, people could watch him stalk the courtyard at the Casa de Zoey.

"Have you ever watched him try to hunt a bird? It's hilarious. One time he lunged after one that was already dead and still missed it."

The pedestrians had parted and Wu was finally allowed to pull into the intersection, then as he crossed the lanes and reached the opposite crosswalk, a single figure strode out and stopped right in front of the van. The vehicle automatically detected the pedestrian and slammed on its brakes, leaving the van in the middle of the intersection where it would be blocking cross traffic once the light turned. The person standing there, Zoey noted, was the one who had already been highlighted on the Threat Monitor. The man, a small, muscular guy with a mass of red hair, looked right at them.

Zoey had found that Halloween month was fraught with awkward social situations in Tabula Ra$a, as it was never clear when exactly someone was or was not in costume. This was a city in which you could stand in line at a taco truck in April and end up behind a guy wearing a cape and a sword and in front of a woman wearing nothing but thin strips of gauze and a flamboyant wig. In late October, complimenting someone on their "costume" was dangerous business, if in reality they had just come back from the dentist. Zoey was pretty sure, however, that the man standing in front of the car giving them the stink eye was not dressed for Halloween.

He had long, red braids that made Zoey think of a Viking, which spilled over enormous metal shoulder pads. Below that was a bare torso covered in tribal tattoos. Below that, a codpiece that was flickering with animated flames. Belts of ammunition crossed his torso. Hovering on either side of his head were plastic skulls with blazing red eyes, whizzing softly as tiny propellers held them aloft.

The ginger Viking reached behind him, his hand vanishing under an emerald cape, then brought out an exotic-looking machine gun that the van, of course, already had noted. Some of the pedestrians in the crosswalk fled at the sight of it.

Some of them.

"They've made the van," said Will, stating the obvious.

Wu tapped an icon on the dash. A booming electronic voice said, "YOU ARE OBSTRUCTING THE VEHICLE. IF YOU DO NOT MOVE AWAY IMMEDIATELY, EXTREMELY PAIN-FUL COUNTERMEASURES WILL BE DEPLOYED. IF YOU IGNORE THIS WARNING, ANY FURTHER ACTIONS WILL BE CONSIDERED SELF-DEFENSE."

The man glanced to his left and right, then smirked. About a dozen pedestrians in the crosswalk fanned out in formation. They weren't armed, they weren't in combat gear. At least two of them were boys no older than thirteen. They just stood there, eyes fixed forward. A human wall, blocking the street.

The Viking sneered, pulled up the machine gun, and thunder-ous orange fire erupted from two different barrels. A cluster of white pock marks appeared in the glass in front of Wu. Zoey ducked and screamed, joining a chorus of pedestrians outside doing the same. Wu, however, remained calm—there was a reason the vehicle's secu-rity protocols didn't see this as a lethal threat. The bullet marks in the windshield quickly healed themselves.

But the dozen people who blocked the road also didn't flinch. The protocol here was to just run the threat right over, but they couldn't do that, or go around him, without flattening three or four noncom-batants, including some minors. The man had brought human shields and was no doubt streaming their plight to the world. Zoey turned and saw that there were more human shields behind them and there was stalled traffic on both sides. They were boxed in, and would re-main so until or unless Wu decided to call their bluff.

As the Viking reloaded, he yelled, "CONFESS!" Then one of the hovering plastic skulls opened its plastic jaw and in a cartoonish skel-eton voice repeated, "CONFESS!"

Will said, "Just go! They'll move."

Zoey was not so sure of this. Before Wu could act, the Viking reached behind him and pulled something else out from under the cape. He flung the object toward the van—it was a little black disc, like a hockey puck. It hit the windshield and stuck there, attached by three prongs. The van's threat software was rapidly scanning the device and immediately flashed,

UNKNOWN OBJECT

The three prongs on the puck glowed orange and acrid smoke hit Zoey's nostrils. Liquid glass dripped down from the spot like candlewax . . .

Then the windshield shattered.

Molten glass splattered the interior of the van, bits landing in Zoey's hair and on her jacket. She smelled herself burning and suddenly had a vivid flashback to a teenage encounter with an abusive scumbag and an electric stovetop.

Wu sat back up in the driver's seat in time to see the Viking aim his gun again, now with no barrier between them.

The man, grinning broadly, yelled, "CONFESS!"

The human shields stood fast, but Wu made his decision: his job was to protect Zoey. He punched the automated override on the dash, then—

Everything went flying.

The world was spinning, crashing.

Zoey found herself on the ceiling of the van. They were upside down, junk tumbling all around her. A cup of coffee splashed next to her shoulder, soaking her jacket. Monitors exploded next to her. Bullet impacts, the Viking spraying into the vehicle.

The van's female electronic voice said, "BYSTANDERS IN PROXIMITY—AWAITING COUNTERMEASURES AUTHORIZATION."

The rear doors opened. It was Will, kicking his way out. Zoey looked back toward the driver's seat and saw Wu roll away from the windshield, away from the gunfire.

He pointed. "Follow Will!"

This seemed like the slightly less bad of two horrible options. The van was now an immobile death trap.

Zoey crawled out onto the pavement and the surrounding crowd immediately started alerting the Viking to where she was. ("She's going out the back! Hey!") Will took cover behind one of the open van doors.

The Viking yelled, "Confess, and this can all be over!"

The van, as if in reply, said, "BYSTANDERS IN PROXIMITY—AWAITING COUNTERMEASURES AUTHORIZATION."

Zoey said, "Van! You are authorized!"

Compartments on each side of the vehicle slid open. Out from them poured what looked like a swarm of thousands of insects. They circled above the overturned van for a few seconds and then dispersed in every direction.

They were tiny pea-sized riot control drones programmed to launch themselves at aggressors, anyone in the crowd who was taking any kind of hostile posture. They would then swarm their faces, pushing into nostrils and ear canals and eyes, emitting a high-pitched shriek that smashed around inside the target's skull. The frequencies were carefully crafted to trigger a primal panic response in the brain, creating the impression that the howling, mortal threat was coming from a specific direction—in this case, the van. In virtually every human, this would instantly trigger an irresistible urge to run at full sprint in the opposite direction.

Zoey stepped out from behind the cover of the van door and watched the crowds flee from her like a puddle from a dropped stone. The buzzing drones swirled around her, brushing strands of Zoey's hair as they whipped past to go overwhelm some stubborn target.

She looked to her left. A semi was there, towing a huge stainless-steel cylinder. That's what had rolled the van, presumably having been hijacked/stolen by the bad guys who had been lying in wait at the intersection. The driver of the vehicle was isolated from the drone swarm, the black specks bouncing off his windshield like bees, trying to get at him.

Zoey looked for the Viking. About ten feet in front of the over-turned van was now a clump of six people, their heads together, arms locked, forming a human dome around the Viking who was kneeling in the center, shielding him from the swarm. The barrel of his gun poked out between two torsos.

All of this had been planned and practiced. This infuriated Zoey.

Will said, "Zoey! Get to cover!"

Nah.

Maybe it was her mom's stupid confidence-building hand cream. Maybe her sanity had finally just snapped. Or maybe she was just get-ting sick of this shit. Zoey strode through her insect swarm and dug into her jacket pocket for a band to tie her hair back.

One of the kids she'd thought was no older than thirteen was standing next to the igloo of human shields, holding his ears, crying, the drones crawling around his face.

"Stop!" he cried. "Make them stop!"

Zoey stopped near the bullet-riddled front of the van. "Get out of here! All of you! If you get a couple of blocks away, they'll leave you alone!"

The kid didn't move. No one did. These people were *nuts*.

"Please!" cried the kid. "Make them stop! Please!"

Camera drones above, bystanders with their own cameras on all sides. These people were creating a propaganda clip they could snip out of context and use against her forever.

Zoey said, "Van, turn off the countermeasures. Drones, uh, go back home. To the van or whatever."

It was never totally clear to Zoey what voice commands would or wouldn't be understood, but the swarm of tiny drones swirled their way back to her, landing on the pavement around her feet. They actu-ally set themselves on the ground in formation, in perfect rows. Ready to take off again if asked.

To the Viking, she said, "I know this is probably too complicated for you to grasp, but if you kill me, *you don't get the money.* You need a confession. If you just wiggle my dead jaw and try to imitate my voice on camera, they're probably going to notice."

The people forming the human igloo around the Viking stepped away from him. He stood there, working a lever on his machine gun, looking smug.

"And I am not leaving here without that confession," he shouted back. He didn't need to shout for Zoey's benefit, they were at casual conversation distance now. This was all for the benefit of the witnesses.

Zoey put her hands on her hips. "Dude, the vehicle behind me has a dozen other countermeasures I can order, including one that will turn your body into a roman candle. But I'd prefer to talk it out. So to you, to everybody watching the streams, I'm telling you that *we didn't kill that guy.*"

The Viking smirked. "We have witnesses, cow. Anonymous staff from Salt Lake Wellness." That was the upscale mental health facility Zoey had done her time in over the summer. "We have copies of the report from the doctor. Your admission was not due to a nervous breakdown, but from a neurological side effect from eating human flesh."

"*What?* Holy crap, you people have made up a whole mythology here."

"Look. Your left hand is trembling! Another side effect of the disease."

"I just crawled out of a car wreck! I have burns!"

"We have anonymous experts who say you would have had to have eaten over a hundred human livers to show these kinds of symptoms. More, if they were the livers of children, which we all know is your preference."

"Will you listen to yourself? You just keep adding things! You know, it's almost a compliment to how clean of an operation I run now, that you've had to make up something that sounds like it came from a B-horror screenwriter just before his heart exploded from a coke overdose."

"Stay back, Blackwater," shouted the Viking.

Will had circled around to the other side of the van. He was carrying something.

The Viking aimed his gun at him and barked, "Drop whatever that is."

It was a black object the size of a lantern. Will set it at his feet.

The bystanders had been pushed back about a hundred feet, but were creeping in again, curiosity drawing them like sharks to a shipwreck. The passengers in the stopped vehicles had gotten out to spectate. This included the Viking's accomplice who'd been driving the semi. He was now standing by the vehicle holding a black club—one of the shock-sticks you could see all over the city these days. They could stun you, or turn your chest cavity into a smoking hole, depending on where the wielder had set the dial. The guy was close enough that he could be on top of Zoey in about three steps.

The Viking shifted his aim slightly and said, "You, too. Stop right there."

This time he was talking to Wu, who had shambled up from behind Will, like a zombie. In addition to the arm that was already in a cast, he was now also bleeding badly from his scalp and dragging one leg behind him, as if he couldn't bend the knee.

Zoey said, "Well, it looks like we're at an impasse. I'm not declaring myself to be a man-eating liver addict just because you're pointing a gun at me. If we start allowing truth and lies to be decided that way, society will . . . well, keep being exactly like it is."

"If you don't confess here, we'll take you to a place where you'll have more time—*and incentive*—to reconsider. Enoch, stun the cow and bind her hands."

The guy from the semi approached and a crackle of blue sparks flickered from the end of his baton. He took two steps forward—

In a blur, Wu flew toward the man, chopped his throat, punched him in the balls, grabbed the baton, smashed it, and twirled the guy around so that Wu was now using him as a human shield. It took about four seconds from beginning to end.

The Viking said, "Let him go! You think his life is worth a million bucks to me?"

The guy said, "Hey!"

To the Viking, Will said, "You're new in town, aren't you?"

"What?"

"You're new in town. Maybe you came here for this particular bounty?"

"Shut up!" To Wu, "You've got five seconds to let him go!"

"I can tell, because you're using a firearm. The device at my feet is a propellant cooker. They're well known around here. When activated, it will send out a pulse that will detonate every live cartridge in the vicinity. Including your spare magazines and the ammo belts you have draped over your torso for decoration, assuming they're real. Please take a moment to visualize it."

"Shut up!"

Zoey said, "It's an objectively stupid invention, but we didn't design it, so don't blame us. The last time somebody set one off in public the hospitals had to treat over three hundred accidental bullet wounds. We are, after all, in America and, also, Utah. There's also the fact that all of those bullets would be firing wildly just feet away from the tanker truck over there. I don't think any of us, including the bystanders and the people working in these buildings, want that thing going up."

Will said, "And as of . . . now, the device is armed for sound activation. You pull that trigger, soon the news will be recapping a spectacular tragedy over a montage of our last-known photos."

It looked to Zoey like the Viking was, in fact, considering it.

His accomplice, still standing upright with Wu's arm around his neck from behind, said, "They're tellin' the truth, man. I tried to tell you, that's why I brought the Thor club instead."

Will said, "Wu, let him go, get in the semi." To the Viking, he said, "Since I assume you stole this, I also assume you won't mind if we take it home."

Wu tossed the Viking's partner aside and pulled himself into the tanker truck. Zoey thought it was odd that they were going to escape in the most flammable mobile object in the city, but maybe that was Will's plan. A sort of mutually assured destruction.

Will looked toward Zoey and nodded to the truck. She took the long way around the back of the wrecked van to avoid the Viking's partner and climbed into the cab of the semi next to Wu. The cab smelled like old sweat and cigarettes. Will picked up the cooker device and followed, squeezing in next to Zoey. The Viking made no move to stop them.

Will said, "Go."

Wu had to back up, then turn slightly to scoot the toppled van out of the way. The lane ahead was clear of traffic, since by now they'd been blocking everything behind them for several minutes, and this time the human shields let them pass. Zoey nervously studied the monitor on the dash that displayed their surroundings, watching the Viking shrink into the distance. They got a block away. Two. The truck was as fast as a very stubborn mule that had died and was now being carried up a hill by a swarm of ants.

Will said, "I messaged Carlton to dispatch the sedan, with drone cover. We're creating a secure vehicle switch location at—"

Wu said, "What is that?"

In the sky ahead was what looked like a giant white bird, diving directly toward them.

"Is it a plane?"

They didn't need any special sensors to find out. A monitor on the semi's dash was already tuned in to Blink coverage of the event (currently trending as "ASHE ARMORED VAN REK'D BY REDD GUNN—#COWFESSION!"). The star of the feed at the moment was a man in a flying apparatus with gleaming white fold-out wings and twin jets of blue fire pulsing from the back, swooping down from the sky, Zoey's rumbling tanker truck ahead. According to the feed, this guy was named the Human Tank, which was presumably a name he'd picked before he'd bought the wings.

Zoey breathed, "What do we do, what do we do?"

Will said, "Keep driving, and pray that he's not carrying an explosive to do a suicide run."

Wu stepped on the accelerator. They rolled along, passing sidewalks full of bystanders who now had turned their eyes skyward, anticipating the conflict, as usual grossly underestimating what constituted a safe distance.

Will turned his attention back to the rearview monitor and said, "He's following us."

On the screen, the Viking—who according to the feed was named, *sigh*, Redd Gunn—had commandeered a motorcycle and was gaining on them fast.

From the front, the Human Tank drew lower and closer. He tilted his wings back to decelerate and the blue jets shifted as he began his descent, apparently intending to land right in front of the semi. The wings, which weren't only white but were glowing, as if to appear angelic, were as wide as the entire street. The pilot was draped in white cloth and gold belts, topped by a platinum wig. Was this his Halloween costume? His superhero branding? His everyday dress? Zoey had only a few seconds to speculate before he quickly descended to the street in front of them.

Too quickly.

As far as Zoey could tell, the flying apparatus was supposed to have used its thrusters to gently lower its pilot to a spot just above the pavement. But if so, the mechanism failed, as bootleg Raiden technology frequently did. As such, the Human Tank landed hard in front of them and Zoey was sure she could hear both of the man's legs break with an audible *snap* when they hit the pavement.

He collapsed, screaming. A glowing, golden sword he'd been carrying clattered to the pavement.

To be fair to Wu, he did try to stop. But the most advanced brakes in the world still have to adhere to the laws of physics and they were currently towing several tons of liquid cargo. Wu braked and cranked the wheel, the tanker behind them jackknifing around behind them. None of it was enough to save the Human Tank. Their wheels ran right over the guy and his stupid wings, all of it crunching and tangling under them.

Both front tires popped. Wu stayed on the accelerator, but they were now dragging the equivalent of a light aircraft across the pavement beneath them, rolling up a mangled corpse in the wreckage. The semi skidded to a stop, the gleaming cylinder skidding around and banging into a utility pole on the sidewalk.

Zoey expected an explosion. None came. She let out a breath.

Will said, "Get out!"

The moment Zoey opened the door, she heard more tires squealing. The Viking Redd Gunn had apparently been going full speed on his motorcycle when the tanker truck had stopped abruptly in front of him, the trailer now angled to block the road entirely. The guy tried to brake, then the wheels wobbled under him until the bike tumbled over and skidded away, the man himself rolling to a stop under the trailer.

Zoey jumped out of the cab. There were a few seconds of peace, during which she still expected the tanker to randomly choose that moment to explode and engulf all she surveyed. Then she glanced to her right and saw the tanker had come to a stop right in front of a sign that said BUDDING MINDS DAY CARE.

Redd Gunn was still lying under the tanker, moaning.

Zoey yelled to him, "You're going to feel incredibly dumb once you realize I'm not guilty of anything. Stay there and we'll get you an ambulance. You lost this one."

Once again, Zoey had stumbled across the exact wrong thing to say. Redd growled, rolled over, and looked around for his gun. He found it. From a prone position under the tanker, he aimed at Zoey. And then many things happened at once.

She screamed for him to stop.

Redd squeezed the trigger.

Zoey saw an orange flash. She felt a puff of air caress her temple.

Then the cooker activated from inside the cab of the truck. There was a blue flash and a fleeting wave of static in the air that made the hair on Zoey's arms stand on end. And then, fireworks.

A rattle of explosions, little bursts of flame up and down Redd's body, bullets from his draped belts firing and puncturing him from every angle. Above him, sparks erupted as one shot after the other impacted the tanker truck.

Zoey was being tackled, Wu throwing her to the ground and getting on top of her, rolling to get his body between her and the dozens of detonating cartridges Redd Gunn had strapped to his person.

Screams and chaos from all around. Zoey wanted up, to run, to get away from the fireball she knew was coming. She could see the day care from the ground, saw little curious faces pressed to the window and a frantic elderly woman screaming at them to get away.

The last bullet went off.

There was silence.

Then, trickling liquid.

Zoey risked a look over. The tanker was leaking from a dozen holes, drenching the corpse of Redd Gunn, pooling around the wrecked motorcycle nearby. A pale, milky liquid, swirling and mixing with the blood on the pavement.

Wu let Zoey up and she took a cautious step forward, noting the logo on the side of the tanker. It was a dancing cartoon cow over the words, REAL MILK, FROM REAL COWS!

Will walked up and the three of them stared at it.

Finally, Zoey said, "Oh, right. They were playing off the whole cow thing. That makes sense."

A fast-talking man was approaching from behind. Zoey thought she recognized the voice. She turned to see Charlie Chopra and his entourage, his eyes wide, a big smile on his face, Cammy the camera drone hovering in front of him.

"Incredible turn of events, my lovely disciples. And I want to reiterate, if someone tries to sell you a personal flying apparatus, it's not the flying part that's hard. It's the landing. Gravity is what keeps our children and pets from flying off into space, but it is a jealous, jealous mistress."

Will walked calmly over to a stopped Mercedes being driven by a middle-aged man who looked like a stockbroker. Will opened the door and stared wordlessly at the driver for five seconds. The driver, also never saying a word, exited the vehicle.

Will got behind the wheel and said to him, "Buy any model you want, send us the bill."

Wu was talking to Zoey, urging her toward the car. Her head felt like it was full of bees. There were faces everywhere, bystanders, people recording, pointing, muttering. Charlie Chopra moved toward her, smiling over his braided beard, clearly hoping to get a comment from her. He was saying something. She wasn't able to process the sounds. He stopped talking and seemed to be waiting for a response. Zoey stared at him, then felt something in her jacket pocket, the plastic tube.

She pulled it out and said, "Hey, everybody, buy this . . . daisy-flavored skin cream. Thanks."

Then she vomited tiny eggs onto the pavement.

14

Drones tracked the borrowed Mercedes back to their neighborhood, but no one was making an effort to stop them. Zoey told herself not to watch the feeds about the incident on the way back, that she could get more actually useful information in other ways. She made it less than five minutes before pulling out her phone. From the back seat, she watched the string of live camera feeds, blinking from one to the next as the software detected new developments, mostly about crews rushing to the aftermath. The chat streams flowed alongside the feed and a single message was getting reposted thousands of times:

TOMORROW NIGHT, WE STORM THE WALLS

They made it back to the estate and pulled into the underground garage. Echo and Andre were standing there waiting next to Andre's Bentley, rushing to greet them as they exited the car.

Andre said, "We watched the whole thing. So now they have to throw out all that milk, right? Got bullets in it."

"He had all of these people," muttered Zoey. "These regular people. Just . . . acting like human shields. Ready to die. Just to screw me. Kids. Some of them. Just kids . . ."

She was shaking all over. Cold.

Wu was behind her, now clutching a towel to his bleeding scalp with the hand that wasn't in a cast.

"Wu, go to the hospital again."

"It is fine, cuts to the scalp always look worse than they are. The leg hurts but I have full range of movement and an elaborate collection of painkillers in my room."

Echo said, "The city's Unrest Index is at six point five."

Zoey said, "The what?"

"It's the index that measure's the city's unrest," elaborated Andre.

"Same system that predicted the riot," said Echo. "You go over seven and you get multiple riots across the city in specific hot spots. An eight is general chaos that shuts down entire neighborhoods, a ten means all social norms are gone and your city is no longer a city."

Zoey tried to keep it together. "But *why*? Who was Tilley to them? Was he like their president?"

Will shook his head. "It's not about him. These things take on a life of their own. It's a self-sustaining reaction."

Echo said, "And they can always find fuel to keep it going. This morning, a homeless man was found dead around the encampment in the park. Natural causes, he was sixty years old and sleeping outdoors. But the city has the stray dogs problem . . ." She apparently grew alarmed at Zoey's appearance and stopped herself. "Hey? Are you okay?"

"Yes. Great." Zoey didn't feel like she had complete control over any part of her body at the moment.

"Anyway," said Andre, picking up the story, "corpse lays out long enough, dogs will get at it. Chew off parts. Well, somehow through the grapevine, by noon the chunks bitten off by canines became 'all organs missing' and 'lifelong homeless dude' became 'valued member of The Blowback community.' Guess he got kicked out of a Livingston Foundation shelter last month and—"

"Why would we kick out a homeless person?"

"Bit a member of the staff. Anyway, that was enough of a connection for the conspiracy crowd. Counting the two dead from the situation you just came from, the narrative is that you're on a rampage. Just eating enemies left and right."

Zoey had a sudden, vivid memory of a bullet brushing past her right ear and found her legs would not support her any longer. She decided to sit down on the concrete floor, and then lie down. It was nice down there. Cool. She curled up. She could not stop shivering.

She vaguely sensed everyone above her going nuts, running to her. She felt Echo's hand on her arm. Even with her eyes squeezed closed, she knew it was hers.

"I'm okay. I'm okay. I just need a minute. Just . . . continue the meeting. I'll listen from down here."

Will, amazingly, did just that. "All right, the good news is we're much better informed now than when we left this morning. We know everything we need to know aside from the exact manner of Tilley's death, and that was always irrelevant. We need to map the anatomy of this group and find where it's weak."

A pair of cowboy boots approached. Budd had arrived. From the floor, Zoey said, "Hey, Budd."

Echo said, "She's in shock."

Andre said, "What's the thing they're all saying in the chat? About storming the walls? They think they're comin' here?"

Zoey decided she was done with this meeting. She got up and shuffled away, muttering something about needing the bathroom, saying not to follow her, that she'd be right back.

15

Zoey took the elevator up to the library, emerged from a hidden door behind a sliding bookshelf, and made her way to her room. She stumbled into the bathroom, splashed water on her face, and concentrated on her breathing. She stared into the vanity mirror. There was something hard and lumpy in her hair, a splatter of molten glass or plastic that had landed there and solidified. She cut it out with scissors. Her jacket and both shirts had burn holes around the shoulder. She took them off and tossed the shirts in the trash. This revealed pink burns on her shoulder and arm, overlapping with the rainbow-shaped scar on her back left by that stovetop all those years ago.

There was a chair in front of her vanity. Before she knew she was doing it, Zoey picked it up and swung it at the mirror, shattering it. Stench Machine went sprinting away. She hadn't even known he was in the room. She found him crouched in a corner, his hackles raised. She got down on the floor with him, put him in her lap, apologized.

Wu knocked on her door—Zoey knew his knock—and she yelled that she was fine. A couple of minutes later, this was followed by a different knock. Her mother's.

"Come in."

Zoey's mother rushed in, got down on the floor with her, put her arm around her.

"Oh, honey, oh my god. Z . . ."

"I'm fine. Fine. I'm . . . I'm fine."

"Talk to me, Z."

"It's nothing. It's everything. Things are bad, Mom. In the city. Those people who hate me—"

"Your trolls?"

"It's not just that. Not anymore. It's all turning toxic. It's in the air. People are dying. Because of me. Because they hate me that much. Everyone. They all hate me. I can't . . . I can't fit it in my head. All that hate."

"Honey, look at you! This place, these people. This is making you miserable. How loud does the universe have to scream a message at you before you hear it? Let's get out of here. You and me. Let's just go."

"I . . . don't completely disagree with you."

"You never once, in all of your years, said you wanted something like this. The money, I mean. The businesses. And I was there for every one of your phases. When you were eight years old and said you wanted to be the first girl to play in the NBA, I bought you that basketball goal, the one the neighbor boys broke. Later on, you wanted to be a pilot. Then a standup comedian. In your time with Caleb, all I heard about was how you wanted a family. You wanted to be a cool mom, one who travels, takes her kids all over the world. *That's* your real life. This, all the money and endless meetings with these . . . *lizards,* these reptiles in suits. It isn't real."

"Whatever I do, I have to clean up this mess first. Otherwise I'm no better than Arthur. Running away."

"Who told you that? Will? I swear, sometimes it seems like that guy has this hold over us, like he's a cult leader or something. Honey, *this isn't our mess.* And I'm telling you, when this fiasco is over there'll be another one right behind it. Say the word and we'll go find Will and tell him off together. What do you think?"

Zoey didn't answer. She kissed Stench Machine on the head. He hated it.

Her mom said, "Can I run you a bath?"

"No." The bath would actually run itself just with a verbal command from where they were sitting, but still it was a nice gesture. "This is a mood that not even *that* tub can fix."

Zoey stood, setting Stench Machine aside. "Can you do something for me? Go find Will and just . . . tell him I need some time. I have to think."

Zoey actually didn't care in the least if Will got this message or not. She wanted to be alone, to give her mother an errand to run. "Can you do that?"

"Of course."

Her mother left and Zoey started to leave after her, then remembered she was still in her bra. She grabbed a T-shirt bearing the logo of a band called Monkey Sheriff, and was still pulling it down as she stormed toward the door, almost knocking Wu over. He'd been in there the whole time, apparently having followed her mother inside.

Down the hall. Down the stairs. Down the west wing hallway. She kept walking until it ended at the ballroom. She went straight for the tarp covering the giant, humming school bus–sized machine. She peeled it back.

The machine was black, segmented into rings in a way that made Zoey think of an alien robot caterpillar. She guessed it didn't have to be an *alien* robot, but it definitely looked weird. They referred to it as Santa's Workshop, because it spat out toys. It was the Raiden device fabricator that they believed/hoped was the only one capable of making real, reliable gear. Right now it was hard at work on something harmless: Zoey's Halloween costume, finished parts of which were leaning against the wall nearby. Zoey took Halloween seriously and she had been telling the truth when she told Alonzo her costume wouldn't fit through the door.

But at any moment, she could load up a new task and out the end would fall something small enough to hold in your hand, or that could be implanted *inside* your hand, with enough power to tear a car in half or turn a crowd of enemies into a scattered field of black, smoking bones. The gadgetry that came out of the machine was intended to transform a human into a conduit of terror, to destroy and kill in spectacular ways. All of it had been designed by a madman who was now dead, and investing in it had cost her father his life.

If what Will said was true, if all of this chaos was coming from a few ringleaders who themselves were following the prompt of Titus Chobb, she could use this machine to unleash hell upon them. *All* of them. Put out a call for a group of the most sadistic bastards in the city, give them the powers of demigods, and turn them loose on her tormenters. Become the monster they claimed she was.

Zoey turned on Santa's monitor and flicked through menus looking for schematics. What she was seeing was incomprehensible to her, she'd need Echo's help to accomplish anything. She tapped some buttons at random and at one point it made a scary beeping noise, so she quickly exited out of the menu before the machine could explode or melt down or whatever.

Then she remembered something her mother had said, and went through a small door into the courtyard. Shoved between some bushes was the rolling basketball goal she'd forgotten she'd bought in early September. Her therapist had recommended it, said repetitive tasks were good stress relief. Well, her city was burning down and enemies were coming to storm her home and rip her to pieces, so this would be a good time for that. She dragged the goal out to a mostly open section of grass, about ten feet away from a sidewalk that would be her free-throw line. A folding banquet table was somewhat in the way, stacked with Halloween party supplies—the stuff was piled all over the courtyard. She grabbed the lip of the table and flipped it over, sending everything crashing to the ground. It took some time to find the ball under some shrubs nearby. It was a little underinflated, she had to slam it to make it bounce off the sidewalk. It would do.

She shot, the ball bumped the front of the rim, then the backboard, then rolled in. That was a miss. Anything that hit the rim was counted as a miss. Anything that banked in was counted as a miss.

That was bad form, the fact that it fell through was irrelevant. Process was all that mattered, her high school coach had drilled that into them. Master the process, and the outcome eventually works out.

She had become a starter her sophomore year, after four other girls had gotten suspended for drugs. That was on the varsity team, too. Granted, they were too small of a school to have a JV team, but still. She was good, had been even better back in middle school before she started smoking, before the hormones went to work on her body. She loved the contact, setting a screen that knocked another girl on her ass, running through sweaty elbows to get to the rim, standing in among three girls taller than her and boxing out, tipping the rebound to herself. Talking trash. Nobody came to the games. It didn't matter.

She shot. The ball bounced off the front of the rim, came right back to her. She shot again, knew it was a bad one before it fully left her fingertips, watched it clang off the right side of the rim and go flying. She went to go chase down her own rebound but Andre caught it and bounced it back to her. He had been standing out there the whole time, waiting for her.

She shot. Nothing but net.

She said, "You're like Budd, following from in front. So, do you people take a vote every time to see who has to come talk me down?"

"Eh, somebody usually volunteers."

"Last time it was Echo. When I got mad about the air conditioner?"

"That's because you specifically said that if any of us came after you, that you'd stab us. Had a kitchen knife in your hand. She was the only one who thought you wouldn't follow through."

Ah, the infamous Air Conditioner Tantrum. Growing up, airconditioning was an expensive luxury reserved for days when it was so hot that a normal life was not possible. Summer nights were about fans, an open window, and partial nudity, the sticky clamminess acting as your alarm clock. When she'd moved in with Caleb for those couple of years, his rental house in Lafayette had central air and Zoey freaked out anytime it was turned on before July or after August. She always imagined money flying out of the window. The Casa de Zoey, on the other hand, ran off of a geothermal system and solar panels. She had no power bill, according to Will. So, she got to where she was okay with leaving the air on, but it made a weird noise, an almost imperceptible whine that gave her a headache. She mentioned it one day and somebody guessed it was some squeaky bearings, or some other tiny flaw deep in the system. Crews were there the next day, and the day after. When they left, the noise was gone.

Then, by sheer chance, Zoey happened to see the invoice for the HVAC repair: $26,423.

Enough to feed a family for months. Enough to get a homeless person off the streets for a year. Money she'd burned to solve a minor annoyance.

She had thrown a fit, made a fool of herself, demanded they undo the repairs (which of course was dumb, they'd just charge that much again to put the broken parts back on), demanded she be consulted on every expense in the future (also dumb, unless she wanted to start scheduling panic attacks every hour). Then she had stormed out of the room and Echo eventually came after her and brought her a cupcake, which was incredibly demeaning and also worked.

Zoey shot. Again, nothing but net.

She said, "Want to play a game of horse?"

"Nah, don't think your back could support my weight."

She gathered the ball, and just held it this time. "They know we didn't kill Tilley. Or do any of the other stuff. They *have* to know, deep down. The whole thing about us being cannibals, or whatever. They don't even believe it, they're not even trying all that hard to make the story consistent."

"There are things people actually believe," said Andre, "and things they only pretend to believe because it's convenient. But over time it don't matter which is which, it all just blurs together. People are like that."

"Okay, so why would they choose to believe this particular awful thing?"

"Because they hate you, Zoey. And because they hate you, they need to come up with a reason to hate you. See, because otherwise, they're just bad people."

"What? That doesn't even—why do they hate me in the first place?"

"When you played ball, were you best buddies with all the other girls on the team? Did you all hang out together in the off-season?"

"No."

"But when you were together on the court, when you won, you felt something. Maybe any other time you couldn't carry on a conversation with any one of them without wanting to blow your brains out, but on the court, you suddenly had a bond. All of them differences fell away. That's why we have sports, the game is just a pretext to let you go out there and feel that."

"So it's just a game to them? Is that it?"

"Well, that feeling, you get that in a war zone, too, only a hundred times stronger. So call it a game or a war or whatever, ultimately it's just about that bond. So, yeah, the thing they hate isn't even you, it's a fictional version of you they've crafted to be as hateable as possible. The more they hate you, the more they love each other."

"So they turn me into a cow monster."

"You understand the origin of the cow thing, right? They're not calling you fat. Well, they're not *just* calling you fat. Among these groups, 'cow' is slang for a harassment target. Your reactions are entertainment to them, they milk you for tears, for pain. But they're humans, so at some point they'll feel guilt over it. That's when they need to manufacture some new reason to justify it, a shared fiction that lets the game continue."

"Okay, so how long can that go on? At some point that hate has to dry up. I mean, *it's been months.*"

There was no answer, and she could tell Andre was straining not to say something.

She threw out her hands. "What?"

"I want you to replay what you just said, and think about who you just said it to."

"Okay. I get it. Racism has been going on for millions of years. I got a whole speech about that this morning, from the heart-eating guy."

"Yeah, sounds like Alonzo."

"I'm sick of being lectured to. I've done nothing but try to go legit since I got here. I'm surrounded by corporate sharks, people who got their power specifically *so* they could abuse it. And because I'm out here *not* doing that, because I'm actually trying to be a good person, they all see it as weakness."

Andre again suppressed a response.

"You obviously want to say something."

He hesitated. "Zoey . . . you don't deserve the hate you're getting. Not you, not anybody."

"But?"

"But . . . you've *never* abused your power? Never ever?"

"No. Not on purpose."

"You never pressured a subordinate into having sex with you?"

"*What?* Are you talking about Armando? That was . . . he was into it. All I did was suggest we go swimming, because we were hot, and we didn't have bathing suits. He initiated almost everything after that! As fast as he could! Nobody put a gun to his head."

"He was a subordinate, somebody you employed, who took orders from you. Same as with that personal trainer."

"Now the personal trainer, that was absolutely his idea. I don't even think he was a real trainer. Will found him, and I swear to god he knew what he was doing. I think that was Will trying to relieve my anxiety."

It actually wasn't the worst thing she'd tried, but this conversation was not the place to mention that. She bounced the ball. Shot. Missed.

"There's power in how other people see you," said Andre, "and I don't think you get how scary you are to people now. In those parties you go to with all them captains of industry, you can think of it like a spiderweb, all these crisscrossing vectors of power. This one is afraid of that one, who answers to this other guy over here. Sure, nobody's putting an actual gun to anybody's head, but it's because they don't have to. It's just understood. If you don't want to become a monster, if you don't want to become like Chobb or even your daddy, you've got to start paying attention to that stuff. Otherwise, you'll become one of them and you won't even notice the change."

"If all that's true, if I'm *sooo* powerful, why do I feel like nothing I do matters? I march right into Alonzo's lair, I march right into Chobb's stupid Blimp of Evil, I march right up to a brainwashed hate mob with a gun in my face, and for what? My mom was right, behind every monster there's just another monster, forever. If I'm so scary to everyone, then why can't I actually change anything?"

"It's frustrating, isn't it? Makes you want to lash out. Find one tangible bad guy and just unleash all that rage on him."

"Sure does. Go over to the Workshop, tell it to make me a big death ray that will fry everybody."

Andre said nothing.

Zoey faced him. *"What?"*

He still said nothing.

"Oh. You're saying that's why this group decided to hate me. They feel powerless."

"I knew you'd get there. Why do you think they're targeting you, and not any of the giant multinational corporations who screw them over on a daily basis? Or somebody like Chobb? It's because they think they can get to you, that they'll see some kind of victory, feel strong again. That's why half the time they talk like you're an all-powerful, all-knowing mastermind and half the time act like you're Trailer Park Barbie. To serve their purposes, they need you to be both."

"They said they're 'storming the walls' tomorrow night. You think they're coming here."

"Doesn't it sound like it?"

"But if they show up here and we defend ourselves, then I'm the bad guy. I can't win. Well, I'm not just going to sit here and wait. Will said in any situation like this, it all comes down to a core of ringleaders. These people want to make me think they're infinite and anonymous, an unstoppable swarm. But they're just people, a specific number of flesh-and-blood human beings. I want to find out who they are."

"Will's already got Budd on that."

Andre picked up the ball. He spun it around in his hands, assumed a shooting posture, eyeballed the rim. He shot. The ball missed so badly that it hit off the top of the backboard, bouncing up and back, flying into a second-floor balcony where it shattered a potted plant.

Andre squinted at it and said, "Are you sure that hoop's regulation?"

"I want to talk to these guys," said Zoey. "Face-to-face. We have to give sanity one more chance."

"And if that don't work?"

She didn't answer.

16

Budd had a list of names by dinnertime.

They were eating their evening meal in the courtyard, in a gazebo surrounded by goofy-looking skeletons and witches and faux stone walls. The whole courtyard would be turned into the haunted maze by Monday, Halloween Day, for kids to be chased around by not-too-scary holographic ghosts, mechanical zombies, and drone gargoyles buzzing overhead. At the moment it was just a mess, displays piled in corners, animatronic vampires leaning drunkenly against trees.

Budd was projecting onto the table a paused video clip from the riot at the Night Inn. Next to it, in another window, was a paused clip from the hostage standoff a month ago, a view of the mooing dudes in the crowd. A series of lines and labels identified the men who had appeared at both. Her trolls lived all over the world, but the concern right now were the ones who were local, who could plausibly show up at her door tomorrow and maybe recruit others to do the same. Lots of the guys were wearing some version of those digital skull masks she kept seeing, but they were still able to put together a handful of names.

Andre said, "Just a bunch of nobodies. Most unemployed, collecting federal PDR checks. The rest work part-time, spend hours a day in the Hub."

Zoey said, "Hey, you're talking to a former PDR girl." The federal basic income payments were derisively called "Please Don't Riot" checks by those lucky enough to not need them. "So if these are our ringleaders, the ones who'll 'storm the walls' of the estate, what would that even look like?"

Echo said, "If these guys show up at the gates with rocks and bottles, they will be . . . *repelled*. The grounds' automated security would turn that into a sad spectacle. If they show up with firearms, that will go even worse for them. Ask Redd Gunn."

Echo was eating some kind of kelp noodle ramen dish. Will was having a glass of scotch. Everyone else was having smoked short ribs glazed in hoisin sauce, pulled and stuffed into steamed bao buns with some shredded carrots, cucumber, and green onions on top to make it healthy. Hell, it was practically a salad.

"The true threat," said Will, "is if their benefactor funds something more serious."

Zoey said, "Wait, are we talking about Chobb showing up here with his personal army? The VOP?"

"What would he gain by losing half of his staff and equipment invading the home of a local real estate developer? No, if he involves himself, it would be by proxy. Putting up money or . . . something."

Budd said, "There are no serious bids out to hired guns, muscle, or souped-up vigilantes. Lots of talk, a lot of it in jargon I can't unravel, but I can't find where it's being put into action at all."

Zoey said, "Right, because as you keep saying, they spend all their time in the Hub. That's where they're doing their planning. So who here has gone into the Hub to see what's what?"

No one answered.

Zoey said, "What, are you *all* too cool to put on a VR headset? Jesus, hire a teenager to do it. This is where the bad guys are, right? Echo, did you get a price on buying the Hub?"

"It's a decentralized platform that every VR network and game uses, it's like trying to buy the internet. I did find an investment opportunity in authenticating the purchases of persistent digital goods. Looks like there's a massive upside there—"

Will said, "Focus, people. They're planning something for the actual world, we don't care what they fantasize about inside their imaginary clubhouse, we care about how they implement it out here."

"To that end," said Budd, "all I've found is one guy who's rented a moving truck, another group has put together money to buy a drone. A big one, the kind that can carry some cargo. That's about it."

"What could they do with that?" asked Zoey. "The drone could drop a bomb on us, right?"

Budd said, "If they were buying a bomb big enough to matter, I'd know about it."

"Maybe they're going to try to use the truck to ram the gates?"

Will made a dismissive gesture. "There are pillars that pop out of the ground that will not only stop it cold, but turn it into a shattered wreck. Those gates don't look like much because they're purely decorative. The real defenses are buried, all around. You've got to remember, Arthur wasn't just paranoid about rival mobsters trying to take him out. He was anticipating a SWAT team from the feds or North Korean infiltrators."

"He was paranoid about the North Koreans coming to Utah? My father sounds a little bit crazier every time you talk about him."

"Oh, that wasn't crazy at all," said Andre. "One tactic that came up in the war, they'd grab body cam footage during raids, run facial recognition of ground troops through social media. Get their names, send squads to go kill their families back home. Both sides did it. There were dozens of murders in the states that the government thinks were retaliation against the spouses and kids of operatives. Kept it quiet, so as not to cause panic."

"Jesus."

"The point is," said Will, "that the only people who've ever gotten in here did it because they were let in."

"But if they're coming from the sky . . ."

Echo said, "The defenses actually extend upward several thousand feet. They fire high-velocity projectiles straight up. Even if they stole a military helicopter and tried to land it on the lawn, the defenses would tear the rotors off. I mean, you wouldn't want to be standing right under it when it happened, but . . ."

Will said, "Zoey, this place is a fortress."

"But these people would know that, right? And they're coming anyway?"

"Exactly," said Echo. "The fact that nothing is turning up is . . . alarming."

Zoey studied the paused video on the table and said, "I want to talk to them, the ringleaders here. Face-to-face, in real life. Where do we find them?"

"The biggest concentration of them lives in the Screw."

"Let me guess, that's a brothel?"

Andre said, "You think they all live in a brothel? Wouldn't be a very profitable one."

"It's a sort of spiral-shaped building," said Echo. "It's not residential, it was built as storage lockers. The storage operation went belly-up and, like every conceivable structure in the city with a roof and walls, it quickly filled with squatters."

Andre added, "You can imagine how it smells."

"Well, I'm going out there," said Zoey.

"To the Screw?" Echo clearly hated the idea. "Why? To let them know you're not scared?"

"No. To let them see that I *am* scared. Let them and everyone on Blink see me as a person, not a monster they've constructed in their head. You want to go?"

"Better to be there than stay behind and worry myself to death."

"So how do I get out there without my vehicle getting swarmed by angry mobs on the way?"

Andre perked up. "Ooh, you want an aircraft?"

"Do we still have a company helicopter?"

"Nah, I'll get you somethin' better."

Will said, "I'm going to urge you not to do this, but I realize that will accomplish nothing so I'm going to proceed to the next part of the conversation where I compromise and say the rest of us will work out an extraction in case things go sour. Set up far enough away that—"

"No," Zoey said. "You're staying away from this one. Remember the goal is to *not* terrify them. It'll just be me, Echo, and Wu. I've got something else for you to work on."

Choosing his words carefully, Will said, "Zoey, you are underestimating your opponent. I don't care what their equipment or training is like. This is a bunch of people who have turned hatred of you into their religion and they have *nothing to lose*. You are dealing with zealots and if they get their hands on you, we have no idea what they'll do because *they* don't know. Regardless of the mindset of any individual in that building, the twentysomething hive mind is a psychopath. I'm telling you—don't go in there without backup standing by."

"Here's what I need you to do while the three of us are at the Screw. All of you. Budd, Andre, you, too. If we had to get to Titus Chobb, like personally get to him, I want you to find out how that could be done."

Andre said, "The man commands a personal army, Zoey. Problem isn't getting to Chobb, it's what happens to you after."

"That's part of what you're figuring out, how to avoid that. If it turns out there's no way to do it, then come back and say so. Then I'll hire somebody who can."

Will fixed her with his gaze and said, "Like I said earlier, there's always a way. Assuming this plan would allow us to incorporate whatever means are available."

"Yep, whatever it takes. And then our goal from here on is to make sure we don't have to actually do it. I know you like using ghost holograms to torment people, maybe have him visited in the night by three spirits to remind him about the true meaning of Christmas. Then tell him it also applies to Halloween, I guess."

Will, apparently taking this suggestion seriously, said, "I don't think he would fall for that. Remember how he got his start, this man knows almost as much about psychological warfare as anyone at this table. Still, everyone has a blind spot that they avoid so strongly that they don't even feel the blade slipping into it. Just have to find it."

"All right, let's move before Will says anything else that makes him sound like a Bond villain. Unless there's dessert."

"You banned dessert from the menu," said Carlton, who it turned out was standing behind her. "Out of concern for your weight, I believe."

"Yes. Right. That was, uh, a test. You passed. Let's move."

17

Andre's friend who had access to high-end, Special Forces–grade gear was apparently happy to do business at seven P.M. on a Saturday night. After a couple of calls, Zoey, Andre, and Wu watched as a surprisingly huge helicopter slowly descended toward the roof. It was quiet for a helicopter, the twin angled rotors making a low, pulsing noise that seemed weirdly ominous to Zoey, like a distant stampede felt through the ground. As it landed, she had to shield her eyes as they were buffeted by wind and debris.

"They use these for night raids," said Andre, over the noise. "Engines are electric, everything built to minimize sound, even the heat signature is almost impossible to track. Now watch this!"

Andre swiped some things on his phone and the skin of the helicopter turned transparent. It wasn't *invisible*, you weren't going to accidentally bonk your head on it when walking past, but if it was airborne and you were trying to spot it from the ground at night, you'd have no chance. It settled on the roof and the rotors slowed to a stop.

Zoey asked, "So, who flies it?"

"Flies itself. I'll show Wu and Echo the commands, it has all sorts of emergency evacuation protocols, can create a secure LZ all on its own. All automated."

"Why are you showing them the controls and not me? You don't think I could handle it?"

"Do you want me to show you?"

"No."

Wu said, "If this goes awry, if it turns into a riot, my job is to get you back to the aircraft and to suppress pursuit. If that occurs, it is very important that you follow my instructions."

"Sure, as always."

"No, not as always. You seldom do as I say. If we have to evacuate, I will be working in conjunction with the helicopter's countermeasures; there is a specific extraction protocol. Do you understand?"

"Yes, I do. I also think we're going to go talk to a bunch of cowards who'll be shocked that we're even there. I doubt they'll even come out to talk to us. But this isn't for them, we're not trying to charm their pants off, we're trying to charm the pants off the audiences watching at home. All of the hangers-on who could maybe be swayed."

Will had walked up at some point, clearly wanting to make one last argument to call the whole thing off.

"If they agree to meet," he said, not even glancing at the giant helicopter on the roof, "don't let them take you to another location."

"Thank you, Will. And when you use the bathroom, don't get your head stuck in the toilet."

"It's a mistake we've made before, they may try to do it by force."

"It happened once! A long time ago! I promise we won't get trapped in a vehicle of any kind. They'd have to kill us first. Also, I'm going to need several drinks before I do this. I think we're exceeding the limits of my mom's hand cream here."

Andre said, "There's a wet bar on the helicopter."

He wasn't joking. A few minutes later, they were on board and Zoey found that the helicopter, like much of the gear they used, was military grade but tricked out for ultrawealthy executives who need to be dropped into hostile countries without risk of kidnapping. Leather seats, woodgrain paneling, and monitors all over to simultaneously check stock prices and track any antiaircraft missiles that might be heading their way.

They all strapped themselves in and as the three of them lifted off from the roof, Zoey found the interior was exceptionally well-insulated against even the reduced engine noise and vibration. It was the pinnacle of the kind of luxurious paranoia that Zoey never wanted to get used to. When several drones tried to follow them off the property, the aircraft automatically dispersed a shimmering cloud of something that caused each one of them to abruptly drop out of the sky. She *could* get used to that.

The residents of "the Screw" couldn't really claim a neighborhood, as none of the area was supposed to be residential. The building was perched between a huge, nondescript hangar that Echo said was a *chapulín* farm, a place where they were raising tens of millions of grasshoppers that would be ground up as cheap protein filler for poor people and also packaged as an expensive, healthy superfood for rich people, depending on which vat any particular bug happened to land in. On the other side was a structure made of steel tubes and cylinders that, according to Echo, was a "Piss Plant." It harvested human urine and extracted the phosphorus to turn into fertilizer.

In between them was a building that, from the air, really did look like a gigantic screw or a drill bit being driven into the earth. About thirty stories tall, it had been a festive orange and white at some point, but had long ago faded in the sun. There were metal railings and stairs that spiraled up the exterior. Echo explained that the whole structure was made up of detachable storage and if you wanted to put stuff in your locker, they'd actually run it out to your house on the back of a truck. You'd throw your crap in there, then they'd take it back and run it up the spiral of rails, to slot itself back into the stacks. The whole operation had gone broke years ago and every one of those boxes had since been turned into a living space. There were bibs and bobs stuck all over the building's exterior—air conditioners, water recycling units, trash and feces incinerators, many emitting little tendrils of smoke or steam into the night air.

As they started their descent, Zoey could make out people hanging out on the stairs all the way up, watching. The aircraft lowered itself gently into a spacious patch of weeds that had been the parking lot at some point (it seemed like none of these people owned cars).

Echo glanced at a monitor and said, "Their Blink chat is going wild. You've kicked the nerd nest."

"Good." Zoey unbuckled herself and took a deep breath. The rotors went silent and that silence allowed the nervousness to creep in. She'd forgotten all about getting that drink as soon as they were in the air. "Everybody ready?"

Wu slid open the door. A little set of stairs lowered itself to the grass and he stepped out, scanning the landscape while Zoey descended behind him. She studied the people looking down at her. Some were playing it calm, legs dangling over the railing, smoking cigarettes or puffing steam from vaporizers. She was, no doubt, face-to-face with her tormenters, or at least some of them. Then again, at least some of the people living here probably had no idea what the hell was going on. Zoey's heart was slowly revving up. She took a deep breath, trying to settle herself down. Using the technique she'd been taught: breathe in slowly for a few seconds, hold it for a few seconds, let it out slowly through pursed lips. She had no idea if it actually worked or not, but it always gave her something to do.

The three of them headed across the lawn and Zoey turned and scanned the sky for her drones. With the helicopter having shut down, she was certain she'd be able to hear them before she saw them. No sign yet.

Zoey got within shouting distance of the building and said, "Hey, it's Zoey. I want to talk."

No response. Some of the guys on the rails looked at each other, muttered things she couldn't hear. She then heard the faint buzz from behind her and turned to find tiny running lights flying in formation. Six red, white, and green drones landed gently around her, each designed to look like an Italian man in a chef's outfit flapping his arms like wings. Below each was a cargo hold the size of a small oven.

"I brought pizza."

Zoey had been curious to see who, if anyone, would emerge to meet her. More people were popping out of various doors, but it was presumably just to get her on camera. Word spread fast on Blink, the watch counts would be skyrocketing. Echo helped her stack the pizzas on some circular metal tables nearby that looked like they'd been stolen from an outdoor restaurant somewhere. Zoey opened one of the boxes, pulled off a slice, and took a bite.

"See? Not poison."

She waited. She looked back at Echo.

"Anything?"

Echo had her phone out, monitoring the Blink feeds. "Inside, it's chaos. I think they're trying to throw a plan together."

Finally, a guy walked out from a unit three floors up. The setup of the stairs meant he'd have needed to walk all the way around the building to get down, but instead he climbed over the railing, dropped to where the path ran back around below him, then dropped down again to the pavement. It was the least handicapped-accessible building Zoey had ever seen.

The guy was a scruffy, thin twentysomething with a knit cap pulled down over his ears. Maybe he was one of the guys they'd pegged from the videos, maybe not. They all kind of looked the same to Zoey.

As he approached, Zoey said, "Hey, what's your name?"

"He wants to talk to you."

"Who?"

"The Blowback."

"So that's one specific guy? And who are you?"

"I'm also The Blowback."

"O . . . kay. Do you want some pizza?"

"Come with me."

"He can't come out here? It's a nice night."

The guy was already walking back toward the building. "This way."

Zoey now had a choice to make. The helicopter was probably a hundred feet from the building, but that actually meant they would still be well within range of the aircraft's many dirty tricks should things go wrong. But if they went *inside* the building, they would be cut off, at least to a degree. It would just be her, Wu, Echo, and whatever they brought with them. For the thirtieth time, Zoey touched her necklace to make sure it hadn't fallen off at some point. She had seen Echo packing at least one exotic bladed weapon. Wu, of course, had various devices hidden all over his body that could do everything from temporarily blinding assailants to vaporizing entire limbs.

Zoey asked him, "What do you think?"

"You know my thoughts already. But this is why you're here, is it not? Only you can decide."

So, up the clangy metal stairs they went, rounding the exterior of the building, past one storage unit after another. Some had music wafting out from behind the closed doors, some were blasting old TV shows or Blink feeds. Some doors were propped open and the tenants stood in the doorways to get a look. Zoey said hello when she passed. Most couldn't maintain eye contact. From way below them, a couple of people mooed and giggled. They finally arrived at a cramped living space that was much deeper than it was wide. A pair of narrow beds were suspended from the ceiling and below them was a kitchenette on one side, a pair of gaming chairs on the other. At the end was a makeshift door that hopefully led to a bathroom. Zoey had lived in seven places in her life; she judged that this was better than maybe three of them.

There was a chubby kid with a round face sitting on the floor, typing on a laptop. He looked startled to see Zoey come in.

He said, "Oh! Hi."

To the scruffy kid who still hadn't given her a name, Zoey asked, "Is . . . this him? The ringleader?"

The kid on the floor looked terrified. "Oh, no! I'm just here to get you logged in."

He pointed to the gaming chairs. Each had a pair of goggles

dangling off one armrest. Ah. They wanted her to go meet them in their VR hangout, in the Hub. A situation Zoey was totally unfamiliar with, because the Suits had refused to take it seriously enough to go scope it out in advance. She should have pressed the issue, damn it.

The scruffy guy in the knit cap nodded toward Echo. "Her, too."

Zoey gave her the choice. "You want to plug into this thing with me? Or stay here and keep watch with Wu?"

"You wanted me to come to the meeting, the meeting is in there. Apparently."

Zoey eyed the googles warily. "Wait, this doesn't count as following them to another location does it? If somebody wanted to booby-trap a Hub interface thing, what's the worst they could do?"

"From the software end? Show you flashing lights to try to trigger a seizure, but only until you closed your eyes. Blast a loud noise through the earbuds, make your ears ring for a while. I suppose the device itself could be booby-trapped. Set your eyeballs on fire or something."

The scruffy kid said, "No trap. But you can exchange the goggles for any you can get your hands on, if you're scared. I don't give a shit."

Wu actually took him up on that offer. A few minutes later, the headsets were exchanged for two that had been gathered from two different sets of randomly chosen neighbors. Zoey and Echo sat and both the scruffy kid and the kid on the floor with the laptop vacated, at Wu's instructions. They were to be left alone in the room, Wu would watch the door. He checked the makeshift bathroom to confirm nobody was waiting to ambush them. The whole storage unit smelled vaguely of the human waste incinerator back there. Like turd toast.

Zoey sat and put on the glasses, the attached speaker buds automatically lowering themselves into her ears so that her sight and sound went away in unison. In that moment, yes, it absolutely did feel like she had in fact just followed strangers to another, unfamiliar place.

Breathe in slowly, hold it, breathe out.

A series of login screens appeared and went away without any action from Zoey. Once those screens dissolved, she found herself in a vast marble room that was set up kind of like a courtroom, or some kind of royal judgment council. The walls on either side were white with waterfalls every ten feet running deep crimson, as if the room was gushing blood. In front of her was a massive golden throne that appeared to be built out of hundreds of severed heads, as if each had been gilded after the beheading, all bound together by barbed wire. Zoey moved forward to get a closer look and a line of text popped into her view:

GOLDEN SEVERED HEAD THRONE—
UNLOCKABLE AT 25,000S!

She heard muttering and became aware of a couple dozen figures standing around her. Some looked like people but most were humanoid animals, all were wearing some kind of armor, none wearing the same outfit. Some had flames roiling from their shoulders, or tendrils of some kind of green energy. Their faces were all bare skulls of various types.

A moment later, a shimmering figure materialized next to her, a golden goddess of pure light. She wore a wispy shroud of undulating mist but was otherwise naked. She had Echo's face, but the boobs of a much bustier woman.

Zoey said, "Why do you look like that?"

Echo looked down at herself and grunted in annoyance. "Ask whoever created the accounts for us. Or better yet, don't."

A man suddenly materialized on the golden head throne. Zoey knew the face, the chiseled features, and pompadour of plastic jet-black hair. Instead of fanciful armor, he wore a gleaming white tuxedo.

"Can we not meet in real life?" asked Zoey. "I showed up here myself, despite the threats and everything that's happened. I'm not here to hurt you, I just want to talk."

"We can talk here," said the man who apparently called himself

The Blowback. Or one of the men? The head man? He spoke with a deep, booming voice. Artificial.

"But we're not having a conversation," she said, "we're operating puppets. You don't really look like that, and I probably don't—"

Zoey gestured with her right hand, and a hoof came into view. "Wait, am I a cow?"

She looked down and around at herself, and saw seven more hooves on the ground. She was inhabiting the body of a giant spider-cow hybrid, slick black skin like the terrifying drone they'd used the night of the hostage crisis. The only clothing it was wearing was a huge black pair of panties, with white skull polka dots.

She sighed and said, "Is there a point in me asking your name? Your real-life name, the one you were born with?"

"You may call me The Blowback."

"Of course."

"And while you and your savages may rule the Badlands, there is justice here. Equality."

"It looks like a nice place, I see why you like it. You can't have a severed head throne in real life without people asking all sorts of questions. But I don't know what the Badlands are and I certainly didn't know I ruled them."

"When you take off your headset, that's where you'll be."

Echo said, "The Badlands are what they call the rea—the, uh, physical world. The world outside the Hub."

"Okay. Well, I still don't really rule it but we're not here to argue. What I'm here to say is that I think we're all being played."

"Oh, well, that's good to hear," said The Blowback, though in a completely different tone and cadence. "I take it you mean you have Dexter Tilley with you? That he is in fact alive?"

"No, he's—"

"Or that his organs ain't missing?" Yet a different voice, coming from The Blowback's mouth. "Can you show us his organs? You got 'em with you?"

"He's really dead, but I didn't— Here, let me ask you this. Where do you think the bounty funds came from? You hate that I've got all this money, but somebody on your side has millions they can throw around. *Or,* and here's what I think, somebody rich is jerking you around. And all of us, really."

In the original deep, booming voice, The Blowback said, "That money was collected by true believers, who stand for justice—"

Then another voice, nearly overlapping, said, "A loyal member donated his winnings from an injury settlement."

Then a third, slightly accented voice, said, "It's none of your business where the money came from, bitch."

All from the same digital mouth. Zoey finally pieced together that she couldn't meet with the real-life version of this person because there was no single individual. A bunch of them were just taking turns. Were they all even in this building?

Echo said, "Is there any way we can talk to just one of you? Can you designate a representative, here in the city?"

"When you speak the truth, you speak with one voice."

They clearly weren't able to talk simultaneously, so it apparently came down to whoever keyed in first. Zoey imagined a bunch of guys with their fingers hovering over their respective "talk" buttons. The direction of this negotiation would be determined largely by whoever had the quickest reaction time. She wondered how Will would deal with a situation like that and decided that he had already given his answer: he'd bring an army, or stay home.

"You guys have access to my whole life history. You know that a year ago I was poorer than any of you. So my question is, do you think I was a cannibal back then?"

In various tones of voice, The Blowback said,

"You were indoctrinated into the cult when Arthur Livingston died."

"You're the one who killed Arthur and dined on his liver."

"I don't know what you did back then, bitch."

Zoey sighed. "Did you hear that I brought pizza?"

The original, booming voice said, "It is scientific fact that substantial wealth makes it physically impossible to feel empathy on a human level. Empathy comes from needing other people. Take that away, and the brain mutates, until it is indistinguishable from that of a serial killer. It becomes unable to perceive the consequences of its actions. The Blowback is here to show you those consequences."

"So, Echo, too? She won't eat any animal capable of feeling sadness but you think she dines on human livers?"

The Blowback looked down at Echo and asked in the booming voice, "Do they make you eat the flesh? Are you allowed to answer?"

Zoey threw her hooves into the air. "Wait, you think she's our hostage?"

Echo said, "I'm really not. I work for her willingly. Whatever you accuse her of, throw me right in. We're both innocent or we're both guilty."

The Blowback came down from the throne, using several golden faces as steps on the way to the floor. He put a hand on "Echo's" shoulder.

"We know Arthur kidnapped you at a young age," he said. "If you're still in there, the real you, tell us. Send us a signal, and we'll come get you. We can protect you."

Echo said, "That will absolutely not be necessary."

Zoey said, "What about Wu? Is he a cannibal? I'm sorry but I'm fascinated by the lore."

"Wu does the killing and the cutting. These rituals originated with Chinese Mafia."

"He's from the suburbs of Oakland."

Echo asked, "Do you know Titus Chobb?"

A member of the armored crowd behind them shouted, "Dirk!" Then this started a chant of that name.

Zoey said, "So, you do. Or apparently you know his bodyguard."

The Blowback, in a new voice Zoey hadn't heard before, said,

"Dirk Vikerness is a supreme god among men. Someone send up the DV signal! See if he's on!"

A short time later, a new figure popped into existence next to The Blowback. Dirk Vikerness looked exactly the same in the game as he did in real life, down to the finest detail. He'd even scanned in his patented yellow-and-black armor. Or had he started with the Hub version of himself and carefully re-created it in the flesh?

Zoey shot a meaningful look at the Echo avatar, then remembered Echo probably couldn't read the expression of the cow monster standing next to her. What she was trying to communicate was that their situation suddenly seemed much clearer, if not better. Out in the real world, someone like Chobb and his henchmen would have no reason to come within a thousand yards of a place like this, or talk to societal dropouts like these. In the Hub, though, all of the rungs on the ladder were rearranged, Andre's vectors of power all redrawn. And it had all been invisible to them, because all of it occurred here, in this other world.

Vikerness, whose smirk came through on his avatar perfectly, said, "What is so urgent?"

"The cow came here to scare us into abandoning the quest for justice," said The Blowback, "after she and her friends tied a man down, still alive, and had a chef make sushi out of his organs as he screamed. Making him watch his own mutilation."

Zoey threw up her hooves again. *You just keep adding things.*

"Eating him, while he pled for mercy. Then came the orgy, afterward, around his corpse."

"Oh, my god."

Dirk Vikerness seemed mildly amused by this. "Is this true? That was very foolish."

"I just came here to talk, but I'm getting an education." Zoey looked at The Blowback and said, "Let me guess—our Swedish friend here is the one who keeps turning up with brand-new scandalous information about me. And his boss has mountains of money and profits from this conspiracy theory. But none of you are smart enough to put two and two together?"

Vikerness just smirked harder. "I come to socialize when I am off work. Do you ever let Wu go home to his family?"

"We have a schedule worked out! But, see, it's harder when I'm being bombarded by nonsensical death threats twenty-four hours a day."

"If you do not want a negative reputation among this community, perhaps you should stop eating its members, hmm?"

"Tomorrow," said The Blowback, "we will come for you, and we shall have a feast of our own."

"That is . . . *not* going to go well for you," said Zoey. "I don't mean that as a threat. Even now, I don't want that outcome."

Vikerness stepped forward and said, "That sounded like a threat to me. Did it sound like a threat to you, boys?"

Zoey shook her head. A cowbell softly jangled.

"You're such a tough guy. All your muscles. Your boss, too, his personal army . . . why do you have to fight this cowardly proxy war? You're using these idiots as your foot soldiers; if you and Chobb have a problem with me, why not face me directly?"

He moved even closer to Zoey and she felt the urge to back up, even though she wasn't actually in any kind of danger. "We have more than twenty witnesses who can attest that you threatened the residents of this building."

Echo's shimmering goddess avatar stepped forward, as if to get between Dirk and Zoey. "We know you knew Dexter Tilley. You were caught on camera together. Did you kill him just for this? To stir up a bunch of broke kids?"

"How many people could have been hurt or killed in the fire at the inn today?" added Zoey. "Do you even care?"

Vikerness was looming over her now. "Out there, you can threaten people, kill them, get them to do what you want. In here, *we* rule."

"Great, I'm happy for you. This is your last warning. If you show up at my gates—"

The world was ripped away from her. Echo—the real one—was standing there, the goggles in her hand, looking frantic.

"They're locking us in."

The door to the storage unit had been closed and Wu was not in the room with them. There were muffled yells and clanging noises from outside.

Zoey screamed, "Wu!"

She reached for the latch on the door, then yanked her hand back. The handle had burned her. A shower of sparks poured through, the metal around the latch glowing orange. The room filled with acrid smoke.

They were welding it shut.

Zoey kicked at the door, then almost fell down when the entire room jolted, and then rumbled. Momentum threw her backward.

They were moving.

18

It felt like they were going down. The building's storage container mechanism had apparently been kicked to life, lowering them along the rails to ground level.

Zoey spun to face Echo. "Don't panic!"

"I'm not panicking."

"You should be! What if we run out of air?!?"

"That would take several days, even if the container were airtight, which it's not. For now, sit down and hold onto something."

"Why?"

"Because for all we know they're going to tip this thing right off the side of the building."

Zoey sat on the floor and grabbed hold of a bed frame. The room rumbled and descended, then jolted to a stop. Shouts from outside. Zoey braced herself for whatever might come cutting its way through the sealed door. She'd worn her action shoes.

Instead, there were more clunking and clinking sounds from outside, and then they were moving again.

Echo said, "All right, that's what I was afraid of. They've loaded us onto a truck."

"Where did they get a truck?!?"

"They're going to take us to another—"

"Location, yes, oh my god. Will is going to have 'I told you so' etched onto my tombstone."

"Stay calm. There's nowhere we can go that we can't be tracked. We'll arrive, we'll figure out their intentions, and decide what to do next."

"This is my fault. If they kill you, it'll be because of me. And Wu, he could already be dead. Oh my god."

"No, if they kill us, it'll be *their* fault."

"What if they dump us in the lake? And this slowly fills with water? And we drown, trying to claw our way out?"

"Then we will die knowing that we kept our cool right up until the end. Right?"

The vehicle was turning, then driving again. They were now on a road to . . . somewhere.

After a few minutes, Zoey started muttering, "I'm so stupid. I'm sorry I'm so stupid."

"Zoey, I wouldn't be working here if I thought you were stupid."

"Why *are* you working here? Like, at all?"

"Honestly? You're asking *now*?"

"No. I don't know."

Clearly thinking the conversation would distract Zoey from her meltdown, Echo sighed and, speaking as rapidly as possible, said, "I got caught cheating at one of your father's casinos. Blackjack. Me and my partner at the time. My partner told them I was the mastermind. They let her go, Arthur came in the room and offered me a job. See, because he thought I was the mastermind, which I wasn't. My parents still live in Honolulu and think I'm a high-end concierge."

"Must have been awkward with the partner later."

"The relationship grew cold after that, yes. That, by the way, is the face I imagine on my punching bag."

The truck was humming along, but didn't sound like they were doing highway speeds. Still somewhere within the industrial park. So far, at least.

Zoey sighed. "Everyone has a cooler backstory than me. I can't believe she sold you out. I wouldn't do that."

"I know you wouldn't."

"Great. Nice talk. We should hang out sometime. Why don't we hang out?"

"I invited you to go on a hike with me. Remember? You said you'd rather snort bees through a straw?"

"I guess I meant something more . . . stationary. Wait, did you say you're from Honolulu? I thought you were from the Philippines. Are the Philippines part of Hawaii?"

"Parents came from there. And no."

"I don't think I could find the Philippines on a map."

"Yes you could, the maps have all of the countries labeled. That's literally what a map is for."

"I just mean, is it weird that I never asked—"

Echo motioned for silence. The room was rolling to a stop. There were voices from outside the sealed door.

Echo said, "Close your eyes."

Zoey didn't understand the command until a piercing blue light flashed through the door frame, sizzling through the metal of the weld. The door was kicked open and men were yelling for her to lie flat. Zoey was thrown to the floor by rough, gloved hands and her wrists were bound behind her back. She was dragged out of the room and as she passed through the doorway, she could hear men inside talking to Echo, saying, "It's okay, we've got you, we've got you. You're free!"

Zoey was dragged down a ramp to the ground. There were people everywhere outside, all of them wearing the yellow-and-black armor the Vanguard of Peace goons wore when they were expecting battle. They were all inside a vast, dark space that for a confusing moment Zoey thought was an ice cave—there were transparent lumps and misshapen pillars all around her. Then she was dragged past a glass stalactite with strips of green frozen inside it—leaves of a cannabis plant, encased as if trapped in amber. Zoey suddenly knew where she was. The huge building had been a hydroponic weed-growing greenhouse, but the overhead lighting system had caught fire a few months ago, melting the clear plastic walls and ceiling for several floors above it, trapping much of the crop below when the material cooled back to a solid. It turned the whole interior into a sprawling, weed-themed abstract art installation. Zoey had watched the fire and rescue operation live on Blink back when it had happened (Tabula Ra$a was also a prolific producer of Large Structure Fire streaming content).

A set of headlights clicked on nearby, then another, revealing that multiple black VOP vehicles were parked around her inside the building, including an armored vehicle the size and shape of an RV. That's where they were taking her. Outside the door of the RV was a stern-looking middle-aged woman, waiting with a tool that looked like a handheld vacuum cleaner. Zoey's escorts stopped and let the woman run the machine up and down her body. It emitted a warning squeal and the woman nodded toward the RV. The door was opened and Zoey was tossed inside. She tumbled to the floor, unable to catch herself with her hands tied back. She was followed in by the stern woman. A monitor on the wall displayed the interior of the vehicle— the room had its own camera feed.

Then, just behind the woman, came a familiar hulking figure with mussed hair and a ridiculous snake-beard: Dirk Vikerness, suddenly here in the flesh as if he'd crawled out of the VR headset and into the real world. Of course, he'd been actually lying in wait for this. All of them had.

"Where's Wu? Is he okay?"

"You are harassing clients of the Vanguard of Peace," said Vikerness. "They have the legal right to protect themselves and their property from aggressors and we have been employed to exercise that right on their behalf."

"You are making a huge mistake. My people can get to you. To Chobb, too. Any of you. You don't want a war here."

"Let the record reflect that our scans detected that you have one or more lethal devices hidden on or in your body."

From the floor, Zoey said, "I do not, *and you know it*."

"As such, we are authorized to perform a thorough search of your person. I have brought a female staff member to conduct the search itself. I will be present to guarantee her safety."

Zoey tried to scoot her way backward, away from them, not that there was anywhere to go. She looked up to see herself doing it on the monitor.

"You're streaming this."

"The exam must be recorded on video to protect ourselves from liability," said Vikerness. "We of course do everything possible to guarantee the privacy of all suspects, but cannot be held liable if security protocols are breached and the stream becomes public." He smirked his way through the recitation of the disclaimer.

The stern woman made a move toward Zoey. She kicked at her, warding her off with her feet.

"Don't."

Dirk Vikerness pulled out one of those electrified clubs and a little fist of blue lightning popped from the end.

"If you continue to resist, I will be forced to stun you."

To the woman, Zoey said, "How can *you* not see what's going on here? Even if Chobb and Dirk here are in on the setup, why can't you see it? There *are other jobs you can get*."

The woman, sounding bored, said, "Miss, I'm going to untie your hands long enough for you to disrobe."

"She is too volatile to have the restraints removed," interjected Dirk. "I am authorizing you to cut off her clothes."

The woman, still bored, pulled a pair of scissors from a pocket. "Miss, I am going to cut your clothing off of you. If you thrash around, you're going to get cut. We'll have a hospital gown for you to put on."

Vikerness smiled and said, "If she behaves. Good girls get gowns. Are you a good girl?"

Zoey shoved her way backward along the floor with her feet, until she was pressed against a wall. The woman closed in. Zoey put her feet up again.

Through gritted teeth, Zoey growled, *"Don't."*

The woman grabbed Zoey's left foot and yanked off the shoe and sock, tossing them aside.

She grabbed the other shoe, and Zoey reached up with the other bare foot and pressed her toes into the heel.

There was a soft *sshink* and a pale, orange blur whooshed out from the toe of the shoe. A blade the shape of a chevron was now embedded in the ceiling, glowing orange, tendrils of smoke wafting off it.

The woman yanked her hands away and stood confused for a moment. Then she looked at her hand, then down at the floor, then at her hand again. Three of her fingers were now lying at her feet. There was a faint smell of cooked flesh, the projectile having seared its way right through tendon and bone. The woman started screaming and backed away, directly into the huge, muscular, thoroughly confused man behind her.

Zoey quickly folded up her legs and pulled her bound hands over her feet, getting them in front of her. The binding was a thick black strap that looked like plastic but felt like steel. On the floor in front of her was the pair of scissors the woman had been about to cut off Zoey's pants with, lying there among the fingers. They looked like they'd be useless against her restraints . . .

Dirk Vikerness rolled the screaming woman aside and lunged at Zoey. She aimed her foot at him and he stopped cold, unsure if her Action Shoe had another shot in it.

It didn't.

He then abruptly ducked and snatched at her foot. Zoey tried to pull away but he clamped a hand around her ankle and ripped the shoe off with the other. She kicked at him with her bare feet, having little effect. Vikerness grabbed the Thor club, the end crackling and sizzling the air as he brought it toward her—

There was a blast from right outside the RV's door and Vikerness whipped his head around to face it. Where the latch had been, there was now a smoking hole. Vikerness pushed away from Zoey to face the door just in time to see Echo Ling appear, her cheeks and shirt splattered with blood. The stern-looking woman was still screaming on the floor nearby, clutching her mutilated hand.

Dirk Vikerness decided that of the three woman problems he was juggling, Echo was the most pressing. He stepped toward her, then swung the lightning club in a downward arc as if to simultaneously cave in Echo's skull and electrocute her brain. She stepped aside, let the club's own momentum carry it downward, then reached out and directed the club right into the man's own foot.

He growled and fell to his knees.

Zoey scrambled to her feet, snatched up the scissors in her bound hands, and said, "HEY!"

Dirk Vikerness turned and as he did so, received a pair of scissors in his right eye socket.

He screamed and collapsed against the wall. He felt around his face, frantically trying to figure out what had just happened to him. Echo was yelling for Zoey to come with her, to get to the helicopter.

Zoey started in that direction, then on the way she stopped, gathered herself, and kicked Dirk Vikerness right in the stabbed eyeball with her bare foot, slamming the butt of the scissors, shoving the blades deep into the man's skull.

He slumped over. His hands went limp.

Echo was pulling at Zoey's sleeve. Zoey yanked away from her, then turned to look for the stern woman, and to see if there was another sharp object for her. The woman, however, was on her hands and knees trying to gather up her stray fingers. Echo was urging Zoey along and this time, she obeyed.

Outside the RV was utter chaos. Someone said, "Are you all right?"

It was Wu, holding his katana above three writhing men in VOP armor who were clutching various parts of their bleeding bodies. Two of them were missing their right hands, the hands themselves still wrapped around the grips of the guns that were lying on the molten-glass floor nearby.

Wind howled through the open space and Zoey found the big open doors of the greenhouse. Outside was a typhoon that was whipping around dust and debris, generated by Zoey's helicopter, which was now perched out there. A ring of blinding lights had kicked on from all sides of the aircraft and a booming electronic voice was telling everyone to stay back. Behind the helicopter, in the distance, were more headlights. Backup was coming down one of the industrial park roads, and presumably not from Zoey's side. Wu whipped out a blade that quickly melted its way through Zoey's restraints. The three of them ran for the exit, Zoey acutely aware that her bare feet were becoming sticky with other people's blood.

A VOP guard intercepted them on the way to the door, rifle raised. There was a buzz from above them, then a projectile zipped down through the air and hit the guy right in a patch of exposed neck between his helmet and shoulder pads. The projectile popped and crackled and the man screamed, clutching his neck, smoke wafting out of the wound.

The shot had come from a drone hovering overhead. It followed as they ran to the door, escorting them to the aircraft. Wu was bringing up the rear, covering their retreat. Zoey tumbled into the helicopter after Echo. As Wu was closing the door, Zoey took one look back into the greenhouse, at the RV. A VOP guard was looking into the vehicle, trying to make sense of what he was seeing. He had pulled off his helmet and just before the helicopter's door slammed shut, the guard turned and looked right at Zoey, an expression on his face that said, *"My god, what did you do?"*

19

Will was waiting for them on the roof of the estate, the air from the rotors whipping around his overcoat. His hand was wrapped in a bloody bandage, like he'd seen some action of his own. Zoey had decided on the ride over that if Will gave her any version of "I told you so" that she would just start clawing at his face like a rabid raccoon.

Three of them stumbled out of the helicopter, everyone splattered with crimson.

Will looked over at Zoey and said, "Are you okay?"

"Yeah. They didn't have time to do anything."

"That's not true."

"I stabbed Chobb's henchman's brain with scissors. Someone needs to find my mother. If Chobb is on the warpath after this, then—"

"She's been secured and is en route. Budd and Andre are on it."

"Oh. Okay. Good."

From behind her, Echo said, "I'm fine, by the way."

Will's mouth made it about 5 percent of the way to a smile. "I watched your escape on Blink, I *knew* you were fine. I've never seen eight men get stabbed before."

Echo said, "Wu fell off a ten-story railing, nobody's going to ask how he is?"

Zoey turned to face him. "You did?"

Echo said, "He was hit with a stun round from above. There was a team waiting on the top floor. It was an ambush."

Wu waved it off. "I didn't fall all of the way down, I was able to catch myself and swing back onto the railing one level below. Then, many armed men appeared."

"Holy crap. How did you get away?"

"I allowed them to abduct me, then secretly commanded the helicopter to follow. Then I incapacitated the guards and commandeered their vehicle."

Zoey said, "With one arm."

"The cast allows me to move my fingers a little."

They walked along the flat rooftop until they reached a circular iris door that opened to reveal the stairs down to the third floor. Arthur's old bedroom was nearby, the setup apparently arranged so that he could get to a waiting aircraft if the estate were ever overrun by Koreans and all of his many downward escape routes were blocked (his bed literally had been built with a chute that would take him to the garage at the press of a button). Zoey wasn't in the mood to point out that the style of door made it seem like they were walking into the house's butthole. That was okay, as she'd pointed it out every single other time they'd been up there.

Zoey got halfway down the stairs and found her legs would not support her any longer. She kind of awkwardly sat/fell on the steps.

"Hey, uh, let's stop here for a moment. On the stairs. I like to just sit on the stairs sometimes."

Echo said, "It's okay to fall apart a little. Now that it's safe." She looked over at Will. "When they sealed up the room, trapped us in there, I panicked, my claustrophobia kicking in. Zoey had to calm me down."

Zoey muttered, "That's not how I remember it. Why is everybody else calm but me?"

Will said, "Wu is a trained soldier, Echo is, let's say, built for this kind of thing."

"Right, and you're drunk. Say what you want to say. Say 'I told you so.'"

"What would be the point? Either you'll learn to trust my advice or you won't."

"Did my father do that? Just go along with whatever you said?"

"Arthur once chased me around this house with a gun because he didn't like the advice I gave him. I had to put him in a headlock to calm him down."

"Do I even want to hear the rest of that story?"

"Not much to it. Arthur developed a crush on a local Mob boss's daughter. Mob boss said he'd have us all killed if Arthur touched her. Arthur persisted, the girl started to act interested—the guy could really turn on the charm. I warned him, he ignored me. So, I had Echo go out in disguise and bump into the girl at a bar, do some snooping. She found out the girl was still in love with her college boyfriend who lived in New York. We arranged for the guy to hear about a job opportunity here in the city that he couldn't refuse, then arranged for the girl to run into him once he arrived. They fell into each other's arms, they're married now. Did everything we could to make it all seem like coincidence to Arthur, but he saw right through it. Got drunk and tried to shoot me, a year later he cried his eyes out while apologizing. Said I was right all along."

"How did I know your story was going to end that way? It must be hard being the smartest person in the universe and seeing the rest of us mortals bumbling around like idiots."

"You've worked in restaurants, right? As a server? It's like that customer who comes in and says 'I want the grilled cheese, but I'm allergic to cheese so leave it off.' And you want to say, 'Now, you realize that's just buttered toast?' but the customer is always right and so you do the order exactly like they said. Then when you bring it out they say, 'What's this? I ordered the grilled cheese without cheese, you brought me toast.' There's a point where you realize doing your job isn't enough, that you should have gone further, refused to take the order and tricked them into thinking it was their own idea. Saved them from themselves."

"Wait, am I the customer ordering the cheeseless grilled cheese in that scenario? Or was it Arthur?"

"You're the customer who comes in the day after that, saying, 'I'll have the BLT, hold the bacon, lettuce, and tomato.' I'm not claiming to be a genius, Zoey. I'm just saying I remember what happened last time."

"And last time, Arthur's enemies caught him alone, tore his guts out, and he died so hard that they barely found enough bones to fit in a jar. Got it. And just so we're clear, this is war now, right? I killed Chobb's right-hand man. There's no going back. Whatever is coming tomorrow night, there's no negotiating our way out of it now."

"Are we sure they're waiting for tomorrow?" asked Echo. "There's not a convoy headed this way right now?"

Will said, "No, there isn't."

Zoey shook her head. "Of course not. They said they're coming tomorrow, that's when they'll come. It's a huge Blink event, appointment viewing. They want the audience to be tuned in and waiting. That's their Devil's Night party. Somebody help me up."

Wu did. Her bones were jelly, but she thought she could make it down. They continued down to the second-floor hallway and Zoey said, "I'm taking a bath. Echo, I suggest you do the same, you have the blood of eight men on you. Wu, get some rest. Or go to the hospital and get the five or six surgeries you probably need by now."

Will and Echo started walking away, toward the elevator to the parking garage.

"Wait," said Zoey, "you're staying here, right? On the grounds, where it's safe? Echo, I've got lots of showers. Or you can use mine."

"No, thank you. I have to go feed my dogs. These people aren't running me out of my home."

"Okay. Will? I know you don't sleep but this whole house was designed for cranky men to drink and brood in."

"No, there's a card game that I'm late for."

She had no idea if he was joking, but he turned to walk away just the same. The pair were fully just going to leave, punching out at the end of their shift. This was, in fact, just their job.

"Okay then," she said to their backs. "We'll, uh, resume the war in the morning. Oh, Will . . ."

He turned.

"For your assignment tonight. Did you . . . do it? If we had to go after Chobb, is there a way to—"

He said, "There's a way. If it comes to that."

There was something funny in the way he said it, but Zoey didn't have the energy to pursue it.

"Good. Okay. Go home, yeah. Get some sleep."

She watched him go, muttering something to Echo as they walked. She'd never asked how he'd hurt his hand.

Zoey shambled her way toward her room, using the wall to steady herself. Wu followed her, despite him being the one person she'd actually asked to leave. On her way, she brought up Stench Machine's Blink feed to see if she could pinpoint his location in the yard, only to find that it was offline. This was not immediate cause for alarm, as it went off automatically when he entered the house so strangers couldn't use his feed to spy on their operation.

"Do you know where—" She opened the bedroom door and saw her cat sitting grumpily on her bed. "Oh. Found him."

Zoey patted him on the way through to the bathroom, then stopped cold at the doorway. The mirror, the one she'd smashed with a chair earlier in the day, was fixed. Like it'd never happened.

"Get Carlton."

Wu said, "Carlton, can you come to Zoey's bathroom?" a phrase that would trigger an alert on Carlton's phone. Zoey supposed she could just as easily have done that. The man appeared ninety seconds later.

Zoey asked, "Who fixed this?"

"The usual maintenance man, Russo. He has been thoroughly vetted—"

"Yeah, but who ordered it fixed?"

"I took the liberty, there were sharp pieces on the floor . . ."

"Hold on."

Zoey calmly walked over, picked up the chair, and swung it into the mirror again. She squeezed her eyes shut as shards bounced off of her face.

She tossed the chair on the floor, breathing heavily. "I'm not mad, but in the future, *ask me.* I'll clean this up. When I'm ready."

Carlton had been in his business for a very, very, very long time, and showed not even the slightest sign of confusion or alarm.

"Very good. Will you be needing anything else?"

"No, thank you."

He left but Wu stayed and he did, in fact, look alarmed. Zoey kicked some shards with her bare toes, her own fragmented reflection staring back at her.

"Are you . . . all right?"

"Yes. I'm perfect."

"I was going to head downstairs, unless you needed me for something."

His quarters were on the first floor, where he stayed when there was some kind of elevated threat level.

"Back home," said Zoey, "we always stayed in places that weren't intended to last. It was all stuff you couldn't repair, like paneling, where cracks and scratches and stains just accumulated until somebody would come rip it all out and start over."

She walked out of the bathroom, stepping carefully across daggers of broken mirror. She sat on her bed.

"But," she continued, "all of that damage, it has a story. Good and bad, you remember the crack in the closet door from wrestling with your boyfriend, you see the little rip in the screen door and remember when you got drunk and fell into it. All those scars, they're yours, they're the history of a time spent in a place."

"Like *Kintsugi*," said Wu. "Your Japanese vase, with the golden cracks. Making the damage a part of who you are." That vase was in fact in the corner, behind him.

"Yeah. Right. But this place, since I've fixed it up, it's all so *clean*. It's like in a movie, where the main character lives in a huge mansion but you can tell it's a sound stage, you know what I mean? Never any sign that it's a place where people lived, no scuffs on the floor tiles, no rings where people have set down coffee mugs. No damage. It's like it's not meant for people, like I'm an unwanted guest here. I hate it."

"I can bring my three teenagers. The place will be a suitable disaster area within half an hour."

Zoey started to smile, but it made her face hurt. She had bruises everywhere. "Do you want a beer?"

"No, thank you." He clearly wanted to leave. Probably needed to call his family, explain that work was going to keep him overnight. Again.

"When I first showed up here, right after my father died, when it was all of his stuff still here, I went down to that glass room at the end of the estate, with the hot tub. When I first saw it, there was a woman's bikini top draped over a rail. And I remember thinking, hey, a party happened here. It kind of put me at ease, a little bit. Then later, Carlton told me that bikini top was always there, he was told not to move it. My father left it as a little hint to any girls who showed up that taking their tops off was both customary and expected."

Wu said, "He was passionate about what he believed in."

Zoey got a beer for herself from the mini-fridge. She sat back on the bed and rubbed her forehead.

"Why are they going to make me do this? Why do they want to turn me into a monster? Everything was *fine*. Why couldn't they leave it that way?"

"How many people do you intend to ask that question?"

"I figure I'll keep at it until I get an answer that makes sense to me. Will says it's a core of psychopaths surrounded by a much larger group of bored idiots."

Wu gave it some thought. "I suppose. I would take it one step further and say that a psychopath is nothing but someone who is pathologically bored, to the point that they would burn the world just to break up the routine."

Zoey fell back onto the bed. "I'm exhausted."

"Get some sleep."

"No, I mean . . . in general. I wake up exhausted. Every day."

"You are twenty-three. If you can stick this out and push through, you will find it gets a lot worse."

She laughed, a little, then groaned with the pain.

He started to leave, but she said, "Is it weird that I don't know anything about you?"

"I am not offended that you do not ask about my personal life, if that's what you mean."

He was still standing with one foot out of the door. Politely answering questions from his weird boss, probably hating it more than the mortal danger he'd just been in. But the thought of being alone was killing Zoey.

"Wait, it just occurred to me that you said you had three teenagers at home. Were you serious?"

"Yes. One is in college, actually."

"Really? Wait, how old are you?"

"How old would you guess?"

"Thirty? Somewhere around there."

"I am forty-six. As of last month."

"Wow. I missed your birthday. And you never get to see your kids, you're always here."

"You are putting all three through very good schools. All destined to work very long hours to make sure their children have the same. Good night."

He started to leave again. Zoey rushed to think of something else to say.

"Do you like working for me? Am I a good boss?"

Wu, clearly now wishing he'd missed that railing and fallen to his death, said, "You are fine."

Zoey covered her eyes with a hand. "Oh, my god. You hate me, don't you?"

"Not at all. But you and I have, let's say, very different values. That is not a reason to hate a person. In fact, I would say you should beware of any men my age who too easily relate to women your age. We are from different worlds."

"Well. I'm sorry I missed your birthday."

"Will there be anything else?"

After a torturous pause she said, "No, thank you."

He closed the door. Zoey curled up on her bed, sticky dried blood on her hands and feet, pain settling over her like a cloud.

The monitor above the bed was on, and she hadn't even noticed. It showed her what was, according to the ranking tag in the corner, by far the most popular feed at the moment: a group of guys huddled around a tiny table inside one of the storage apartments at the Screw. A single piece of pizza sat on a paper plate and they prodded it with a plastic knife, as if they were afraid to touch it.

"And you see these bits of meat on here? That's not sausage," said the scruffy kid from earlier. "We got a sample to a friend for analysis. That's human flesh right there. This backs up the rumors we've heard from the VOP evidence team, that at least one of the pizzas the cow brought to us had part of a human finger in it. We'll try to get DNA and see if we can match it up with any missing pers—"

Zoey said, "Turn that shit off," and the house understood.

20

Zoey woke up in the usual way, with Stench Machine batting at her face with his paw, demanding to be fed. She fought a war against her stiffened limbs to sit upright and almost jumped out of her skin when she saw that she wasn't alone.

A figure was sitting in the chair in the corner.

A light automatically clicked on, revealing Zoey's mother, curled up in the chair, asleep.

"Mom?"

She stirred and stretched. "Heeeey."

"What's going on?"

"Got in last night, they said you were in bed already. I didn't want to wake you. I snuck in, wanted to make sure you didn't have nightmares. You always mumble when you're dreaming. Remember that, when you were little? When I used to come in and crawl into bed with you?"

"How much do you know? About what happened last night?"

"I was given a carefully edited version of events by your *friend* Will."

"I think we're at war."

"Aren't you always?"

"No, it's different this time. They, uh, are apparently coming after us, somehow. Tonight. If you stay here today, behind the walls, you should be safe."

She was shaking her head. "No. I have work, then we're all going to the Black Parade. Got to get to the good spots early."

"No, Mom, that's a terrible idea—"

"The bad people can hurt me or not hurt me, but I'm not going to imprison myself. That's doing their job for them."

"Will you do it, as a favor to me? So I won't worry?"

"Will you step away from *your* life? So *I* don't worry?"

"Come on, Mom . . ."

"I mean it, Z. You could do it anytime you want. Take what you can get away with, an amount they won't come after you for, and we'll go away together. Go back home if you want. Could go take a trip to Estes like we used to, see the elk."

"You know I can't."

"I know you *think* you can't. Honey, you're not happy here. What's here? The money? What's the money doing for you?"

"Other than allow me to get the absolute best medicine, food, housing, and transportation? Plus warmth in the winter and AC in the summer? And total freedom to go anywhere, anytime, plus power and influence and protection from anyone who would do me harm? Plus a whole world of men who actually have to take my opinions seriously? Other than that, you're right, it's just numbers in a bank account."

Zoey saw the look on her mother's face and said, "Sorry. But I have to stick this out. I just do."

Her mother shrugged. "So do I."

"You know, whenever I'm being stubborn you always say I get it from my father. But I think I get it from you."

Her mother came over and kissed her on the forehead, for probably the ten thousandth time in her life.

"Love you, Z."

"I just ask one thing. Will you at least turn your phone on? And answer it if I call?"

"Will do. And I'll be with friends."

"With that guy? Clarity?"

"Uh, no, he hasn't been returning my calls. As soon as he got payment for the skin cream stock, he suddenly canceled our weekend plans."

"I'll buy it. The remaining stock, I mean. I don't want you to get stuck with it."

"You don't have to do that."

"It's fine. I'll . . . give it away at parties. It'll be fine."

"Honey, *you don't have to take care of me.* I've always done okay. *We've* always done okay. You don't need to worry about me. I'm a survivor!"

"I know, Mom."

She left and soon Zoey was wincing her way through a shower, the pulsing water discovering new wounds for her. Then she got dressed in a battle-ready outfit: black jeans and a black denim jacket (she figured it'd make it harder to hit her in the dark) and a dark gray T-shirt that in big yellow letters said HOW ABOUT I SLAP YOUR SHIT?

Zoey found everyone had congregated in the enormous kitchen for brunch. She made a beeline for the coffee bar (situated next to an actual bar complete with a mirrored wall full of liquor bottles) and its professional-grade espresso machine. She could hear Carlton working the deep fryers across the room, while Budd and Andre waited at the counter like a pair of dogs who'd come running at the sound of a can opener. Carlton was plating karaage chicken, a Japanese junk food staple—little hunks of dark meat marinated in soy sauce, rice wine, and sake, then coated in potato starch and fried, served with a creamy mayo lemon sauce. Carlton said probably half of her father's menu requests were simply the result of him running into a street food truck somewhere in Asia and commanding Carlton to re-create it.

Will was over by a wall of fresh herbs growing in rows of hydroponic pots, on the phone with someone, sipping something clear from a glass. It was only ten in the morning and it took a moment for Zoey to realize that the mysterious clear beverage was probably water. The bandage on his hand had been replaced by a large Band-Aid.

Echo came over to the bar, carrying a refrigerated thermos that probably contained a ground-up seaweed milkshake or something. Her battle outfit was tan leather jacket over a sweatshirt and leggings, which made Zoey think she wasn't taking the battle seriously considering that was the same thing she'd worn when they'd gone to an Oktoberfest thing in Snowbird a few weeks ago. Despite everything that'd happened the night before, Echo looked like a collector had kept her in her original box until just now.

Zoey said, "My god, were you in an accident on the way home? Did your face hit a truck carrying some kind of horrible toxic waste?"

Echo said, "Funny you should say that, because on the way home I waved to you on the sidewalk, but it turned out it wasn't you, it was a dumpster full of butts. There was a hospital there. And that's where they throw away their old butts."

"I *feel* like a pile of trash butts."

"How many bruises do you have?" Echo pulled her shirt away from her neck, showing off a splash of purple. "All over my back, too."

Zoey showed a blotchy arm. "We look like we've been playing rugby. What happened to Will's hand?"

"He won't say."

"Probably bit himself in the frenzy of a hot dog eating contest."

On cue, Will approached and said, "One of you needs to put a cancellation notice together. Keep the reasoning vague."

"Cancellation? For what?"

"The Halloween party tomorrow?"

"Oh, we're not canceling the party," said Zoey. "Screw that. We have like five hundred kids coming."

"Zoey, we can't have the setup crew coming in and out today while we're preparing for the . . . siege, or whatever is happening tonight. We have a guy out there calibrating sensors and adding extra shots to the antipersonnel array. Not only would the work crews be in the way, but if these people wanted to get someone inside the barriers, by far the easiest way to do that would be to pay off one of the workers. Then you could forget about exotic tech or a VOP entry team. All it would take is one contractor putting a nail gun to your temple."

"Well, then we'd better get busy then."

"Doing . . . ?"

"Setting up the haunted maze in the courtyard. There's seven people in this room right now. The walls are all prefabricated, they just snap together. Echo has the schematics on her phone. Right?"

Echo looked to Will, hoping for a rescue.

Zoey said, "Do I own this business, or not? We're not letting these people run my life and we're not letting them ruin Halloween for those kids."

Will said, "How is it going to be safe to have children on the grounds when you're under this kind of threat?"

"Then that means we have today to resolve the threat, don't we? If the estate isn't still standing after that, then I guess somebody can let the kids tour the charred wreckage. Look, kids, it's real skeletons! Budd, is there any more information about what's coming?"

She had caught Budd in the middle of chewing some chicken.

"Uh, Blink caught a couple of ringleaders talking about a device, made to break the gates. Maybe a battering ram, I guess. They even named it."

"Do I want to know what they named it?"

"Molech."

"Ugh, these people. Will, what do we have to counter a battering ram?"

"If they break down the decorative gates and also the titanium pillars that pop up to replace it? If people come charging through, they will be cut down."

"But what if they're wearing armor, or are in armored VOP vehicles?"

"Then *they will be cut down.*"

"But if Titus Chobb is running the operation, he knows how sophisticated the system is, right? Maybe he knows a weakness, to defeat the system's artificial intelligence or whatever. Then again, he now knows we know he's involved, so knows that we know he'll be looking for a weakn—"

"Stop, the solution is the same no matter how far you go down that rabbit hole. We need more humans. The AI is nice, but to counter people you need people. That'll probably always be true."

"The problem," Budd said, "is that every sizable security outfit in the city is either owned by Chobb or could potentially get a buyout soon, so they have reason to sit it out. Our own security is stretched thin guarding the other properties. We could call them in—"

"But we'd be leaving those workers vulnerable," said Zoey. "We're not doing that."

"Yep, we knew you'd say that. But that did limit our options, you understand."

"All right. So what do we do?"

Andre said, "Get someone who hates Chobb as much as we do."

"And who is that?"

Andre, Budd, and Will looked at Zoey in dead silence. Like they were waiting for something.

"What are you doing?"

Finally Andre turned around and looked back at the door. "Sorry, Megaboss Alonzo was supposed to walk through the door at that moment. Is . . . is he not out there?"

Echo went into the hall. "No? Did anyone see him leave?"

"Anyway," said Andre. "We made a deal with Alonzo. Would have been a really cool reveal, we had it all worked out but . . ."

"Wait, the heart-eating guy? That's who we're entrusting our safety to?"

Will said, "Trust isn't necessary when everyone has the same goals, that's how society functions in general. As for the heart-eating thing, that works in our favor. If, as I suspect, our enemies are amateurs, that fear factor may turn out to be an advantage."

Zoey saw a quarter of Alonzo's face peeking around the door frame from the hall.

Andre noticed and said, "Come on in, we told her. You missed your cue."

Alonzo stepped in alongside a wiry woman with a chiseled jaw—Zoey remembered her from the counter at Alonzo's store. Both wore tailored business suits. Alonzo's was pumpkin orange, with a black shirt and no tie. Zoey was intensely curious about whether or not he'd chosen that suit for the holiday.

"Sorry, Deedee needed a bathroom and I incorrectly thought I knew where one was. It took us a while to find our way back. Oh, Zoey, there you are. This is Deedee. She's my bodyguard. Deedee, this is Zoey. You know how we did that thing with the pig heart yesterday? Well, Zoey eats people for real."

Deedee seemed unimpressed. "It's a free country. This ain't Idaho."

Zoey said, "Is it just the two of you, or are you bringing foot soldiers?"

"I can get you, I'd say, fourteen capable people on the grounds within the hour."

"All right. And will they be insulted if I ask them to help put up some Halloween decorations?"

"Not if you provide lunch." He rubbed his hands together. "So, can I see it?"

21

Several hushed and tense conversations ensued between Zoey and Will on the subject of letting Alonzo see "it" and whether or not such an offer should have been extended without Zoey's permission. Her compromise was that she would show Megaboss Alonzo "it" once she saw that his people had arrived and were in the act of assembling the haunted maze for tomorrow's possibly posthumous Halloween party.

An hour later, she led Alonzo toward the ballroom and Santa's Workshop. They entered to find the tarp was still piled into a corner from where Zoey had yanked it off the day before. The machine was still working nonstop on her costume and, at the moment, was in the process of spitting out a curved hunk of white carbon fiber the size of a car fender. Dozens of other such parts were piled in the corner for assembly. As they passed the big monitor on the opposite wall of the ballroom, Alonzo noticed it was displaying a low, wobbly camera feed that was weaving among the feet of the workers in the courtyard.

"Whose Blink is that? Someone have a camera tied to their boot?"

"My cat. He's hunting for shoelaces."

"Never had any use for cats myself. Tell you what, when you watch his feed, notice that cats don't meow when there are no people around, not even to each other. They only do it to us, that's a sound they make to mimic a human baby's cry, to get us to pay attention to them. I have enough people like that in my life already."

"What are you, a dog person?"

"I have a few I keep around."

"Dogs are too easy, they love anybody. A dog will love a stranger. A dog will love a log that sort of smells like a person. Cats make you earn it, it means something when they finally come around. Did Will tell you to dress up for this?"

Alonzo looked down at his suspiciously pumpkin-like outfit as he walked. "I always suit up. Everything straight from the store; Deedee, too. See anything you like, something similar can be on your frame within the hour."

"First time I saw you," said Zoey, "you weren't even wearing a shirt."

They had arrived at the machine, which stank of chemicals and fire and other things you probably did not want in your lungs. It ventilated to the outside, but never quite enough.

"See, funny story, the shirt I was wearing got a cranberry juice stain on it, but I thought it looked like blood and I imagined you guys walking in and I'm sitting there with a bloody shirt. Then I'd have to admit it was juice and Will would make fun of me in front of everyone. So I decided to just strip it off. I don't normally hang around my office shirtless. Funny how those first impressions get frozen in your mind like that. Kind of like how everyone decided 'Winter Wonderland' is a Christmas song, even though it never even mentions Christmas. Song could take place in February for all we know." He looked over Santa's Workshop. "So this is it, huh?"

Zoey said, "Well, the machine is just a parts fabricator, you can get one off the shelf if you have several million dollars. Andre says the Navy puts one on every aircraft carrier, it can spit out a new circuit board for the ship's navigation computer or a replacement knob for its stereo, any part from the ship's bow to the, uh, butt."

"You steal this one off a Navy ship?"

"Nah, bought it from a tech company that used it to make prototypes. That would have made for a cooler story though, I'll tell everybody that from now on."

"So it's the designs in its memory that make it special."

"Also, the raw materials have to be sourced from all over the world and they're not cheap, I'm told. Some of it comes in little barrels with radioactive symbols on them. Sorry about the smell."

He glanced into the corner, at the large pile of white and pink components the machine had been churning out. "What are you making right now? Or is that classified?"

"My Halloween costume."

"Classified, then. You know this is the most valuable machine in the world, right?"

"You can get Raiden gadgets elsewhere. You've probably run into implanted freaks yourself."

"No. You can't. You can get bootleg, janky gear from exactly two locations working off shoddy hardware and glitchy software. Only one place to get the real thing, the stuff that actually works. Right here. Or so they say."

Zoey shrugged. "If they say so."

"What's to stop someone from stealing it? You know this is worth billions, right? But look at this, Will gave me unfettered access, totally confident I'm not going to sneak my crew in to take the thing."

"Well, it's really heavy, for one."

"I'm serious, now. What's to stop the CIA from sending an actual army to seize it for the government?"

"There are so many layers of security I don't think even *we* could undo them all. I can tell you that part of it is tied to GPS, just moving the machine off the premises will cause the hard drives to melt. Like, physically melt. Logging in to it requires a brain scan from two members of the team and no, you can't just chop off our heads and use them. It not only knows if the brain is alive, but if it detects we're under duress, it automatically locks itself—we borrowed those parts off the vault downstairs. Also, it's not connected to any kind of network at all, a hacker would have to be physically in front of the machine to try to get in and Echo says the encryption would take two million years to break. That's really all you wanted? Just to see it?"

"To be in its presence. You feel that hum? That's the power to turn a man into a god. I feel like I'm in a holy place."

"I'm counting down the seconds until you ask for implants. Or at least a fancy gun."

"Ah, it's a solid life rule that if Will Blackwater hands you a weapon, it either isn't loaded or there is a much larger one pointed at your back. I wouldn't let that man implant anything in my body. You shouldn't, either. If you take my meaning."

Zoey fiercely pretended she hadn't heard that last part. "Then how did he get you to do this, to act as a garrison for the estate? Did he just offer you a bunch of money? Something for your businesses?"

"Will will insist that I'm here because I lost to him in a card game last night and now owe him, but that is not entirely true. He made me an offer and I took it."

"He didn't, uh, promise anything he should have consulted with me about first, did he?"

"Don't think I don't hear your tone, young lady. Get your head out of the gutter. Or into the gutter, I guess, since this is about politics. You probably heard, it looks like Tabula Rasa isn't going to be an unincorporated place much longer. It's getting worked out behind the scenes, with the county and the state. Going to be a real city, by next summer at the latest. Gonna recognize the charter and everything."

"Yeah, I think I fell asleep at a meeting about that."

"Oh, you shouldn't sleep on this. It means the city is going to need a mayor."

"Okay?"

"Will promised to back my play. He has pull with everyone else who'd even consider it and by pull I mean he has dirt. The way we have it worked out, I'll be pretty much unopposed." He gave her a "let's get serious for a moment" look and said, "I'm sure you know this because you work with him every day, but if you should ever decide to cut ties with Will and make him your enemy, your best strategy will be to find a time machine and transport yourself back to a point where you can undo that decision."

"So, the fact that you're on video claiming to eat a human heart, you don't feel like that will hurt you during the campaign?"

Alonzo seemed genuinely surprised. "Why would it?"

"Also, you run an organized crime operation. Why would you want an actual government here? People like you have made out like bandits. And before you jump on me for that 'people like you' phrasing, we're standing in a mansion built by someone much worse."

"The fact that you don't know why I'd run is the reason I need to run. My people are being gunned down in the streets. Beaten and harassed by private security who don't answer to anyone but the property owners. I want real police, but to do it right this time. No sadists or bullies, no guns, no quotas, no arrests for victimless vices. A system that focuses on the real problems, not just drumming up reasons to keep poor people poor. And no prisons. It'll be rehabilitation, education, reform. We'll tax the tourists to death to pay for it all."

"Trust me, I'm well aware of what the private security is doing to this city."

"Because of what Chobb's people tried to do to you last night? Do you have any idea how many of my people the VOP have done that to? My niece, she was stopped by Van of Piss security leaving the Sibal-Biyong Mall, insisted they saw her steal jewelry. Held her down, did a search right there by the door. A *deep* search. People, cameras all over. Making sure it gets recorded, see. Making an example of her."

"Chobb's people did that to send a message to you?"

"Oh, no, they had no idea who she was. That's my point. They did that because that's what they do. Because they can. Or at least, they *thought* they could. The two guards who did that, they didn't show up to work the next day."

"If my people ever did that, I'd have them fired and probably beaten."

"I think you mean what you're saying. But that's part of it, too. The rich owners of those businesses, they'll condemn the abuses but profit from the end result just the same."

"Why in the hell would they be okay with their own customers getting assaulted? Even if they *are* racists, money is money, right?"

Alonzo looked at her like she'd just asked why they can't just find a kind wizard to magic their problems away.

He seemed to be thinking about how to approach it, then said, "My mother and father moved me here from Chicago when I was sixteen. Rent was already sky-high but there were jobs and word was you could get a fresh start. No background checks in Tabula Rasa, they said. My father, he needed one of those fresh starts. See, because they'd set the rules so that if you commit a felony at nineteen, you're locked out of the good jobs for the rest of your life. So, the plan was to move with friends, a white couple who had the same idea. We were all going to get a place together, in a safe neighborhood. Combined, the four of them could afford that, just barely. So my mother, she spends the whole day here, looking at places to rent. Goes to three different buildings, all three tell her they're full up, got a waiting list a mile long. But then the very next day, one of the white friends goes to those very same buildings. *All three* had vacancies."

"That sucks."

"All three buildings were owned by your father."

This time it was Zoey who was genuinely confused. "You're saying he was so racist he just preferred the units sit empty?"

"It's not about personal feelings, not from where the owners sit. That's what you people always get wrong. It was a brand-new city, see. The landlords knew you could only have about twenty percent minority tenants before the upper-class renters decided it was destined to be ghetto and started steering clear. So, those landlords were telling the truth. There were, in fact, no more slots for *non-white* renters. And if you call them on it, they'll insist they harbor no animosity, that they're just doing what the customers want, same as the VOP, same as everyone else. And on and on it goes."

"I get it."

"Do you?"

"I get that I don't get it, how's that? But either way, you're here because we both agree that Titus Chobb is worse."

"That's true, but also we shouldn't let him set the bar. All right, I'm bored with the machine now. What time is lunch?"

22

Zoey's secret plan to give herself and the team a menial task so that the anxiety wouldn't tear her apart had *kind* of worked.

Putting the haunted maze together turned out to be a nightmare. Entire sections were missing and they couldn't get power to a whole corner of it. In one spot there was an animatronic skeleton that was supposed to pop out of the ground and chase the kids to the next area, but the thing just stayed dead no matter what. Zoey, Echo, and a huge muscular guy with tribal tattoos and a scimitar on his back had to trace hundreds of feet of wiring until 2-Bladez (that was the guy's name, though he only seemed to have one blade today) found a single spot where a tiny speck of missing insulation was causing the whole thing to short out. Something so small, and the whole system fails . . .

According to the chatter on Blink, the supposed attack on the estate was scheduled for sundown, which would be in the neighborhood of six P.M. At three, Zoey's people and Alonzo met in the Buffalo Room, so-named because of the giant stuffed buffalo head over a fireplace that itself was large enough to roast the rest of a buffalo in, should someone ever feel the need.

Alonzo was moving casually around the room, admiring details of its construction. Budd stood near the fireplace, Will paced around with a drink in his hand, and Andre and Echo sat in a pair of antique leather chairs. Zoey was buried in an enormous, eight-foot-wide leather beanbag she'd had added to the room over the summer. She sank so far down into it that she was actually invisible to anyone else; the crater in the bag was like her own private little office.

Budd said, "I have the location of every single employee of the Vanguard of Peace, updating in real time. All of them are exactly where they're supposed to be, corralling early parade crowds, watching doors and warehouses, escorting rich folk. The ones who are off duty are at home, or in bars, or running errands. Six of them exchanged a lot of chatter about throwing a 'surprise party,' which I thought might be code for an attack, but if so, they're bringing a lot of beer and hamburger and are taking the time to decorate a local bar they've rented out for the evening. One of their coworkers is retiring, it appears."

From down in her beanbag well, Zoey said, "So The Blowback and/or Chobb has hired somebody else to attack the house?"

With audible frustration, Budd said, "If they have, it has officially escaped my notice."

"What about the supplies we found out they bought? The truck? Big drone?"

"Both sitting in a garage, unattended."

"And when one of you bought a headset and went into the Hub to infiltrate their group in there, what did you find out? And you know I'm going to throw a fit if you say you haven't tried."

"I did," said Andre, sounding proud. "Logged in, found myself in a big virtual lobby with a bunch of naked people. I asked around to try to get the lay of the land, was greeted with a torrent of racial slurs, even though my avatar was a flamboyant talking unicorn. I responded in a way that I believed was reasonable, only to find I'd been bounced from that lobby and put into a different one, full of people who were all speaking Chinese."

Echo said, "If you're not acclimated to it, it's pretty much like an American from Wisconsin trying to infiltrate a terror cell in Sudan—they see you coming a mile away. Meanwhile, out in the physical world, five different properties of ours were vandalized this morning, all with the same phrase, all done simultaneously by different vandals in skull masks."

"Do I want to know what the phrase is?"

"'Tonight We Feast.'"

Zoey stared at the ceiling from within the beanbag crater. "Here's what I think. I think their 'invasion' or 'siege' or whatever amounts to nothing more than a threat intended to keep me in the house, to ruin my Devil's Night. Well, if nobody shows up, I'm going to that parade. If they do show up and try to kill me, I'm *still* going to that parade."

Echo said, "Wait, I thought you'd spent the last month saying you weren't going? Because parades are stupid and you get nervous in crowds where there aren't bathrooms nearby? You went on a twenty-minute rant about it two weeks ago. I think the phrase you used was 'I'd rather poop a sun.'"

"Well, I've changed my mind. I'm going. Will, did you find out who killed Dexter Tilley? Everybody remembers him, right?"

"There is something," said Echo, "but it's nothing."

"What the hell does that mean?"

"It's . . . weird."

Zoey tried to sit up, but struggled as the bag shifted under her. Everyone seemed to wait patiently for the sounds of Zoey's thrashing to stop.

Finally she just gave up and said, "I'm listening."

"When a conspiracy theory becomes mainstream," said Echo, "the early adopters have to latch onto a different, even more niche conspiracy, since their identity is tied to going against the grain. Since everyone has come around to the idea that Tilley died because you ate him during a ritualistic cannibal orgy, there's now an alternate theory that he died while playing a game. A specific mission in a fantasy game called *Crimson Day* that they've decided has some kind of symbolic importance."

"Okay? Why would that even matter?"

"Well," Echo continued, "the thing is, we *do* have his account logs from the Hub, and his logout approximately matches our best estimate for time of death, based on when he was last seen alive and when he turned up at Fort Fortuna."

"And you're one hundred percent sure that one of those VR headsets can't malfunction in a way that makes all of your important organs dissolve?"

"I think what you meant to ask is, can we pinpoint the login location and figure out *where* exactly he was when he died, thus narrowing down both the cause and suspects. The answer, so far, is no. He was using an incredibly encrypted VPN. Like he didn't want anyone to know where he was logging in from."

"Right, that's what I was really asking."

"And . . ." Echo paused, as if getting a "stop talking" signal from someone. "Never mind."

"What?"

Will said, "We don't want to introduce a bad theory without information to back it up. It just clouds our thinking."

"You know I'm going to make you tell me."

Zoey heard only silence from within the indentation of the beanbag. She made the enormous effort to sit up and then crawl over to where she could see, her bruises aching all the way.

"Well?"

Echo finally said, "That chef that Chobb uses, Werner Wolff, his specialty is exotic meats, he boasts he can prepare anything as cuisine, even roadkill and all the parts of the animal not meant to be eaten. He has this whole thing about tasting nature, not factory-farmed animals that he says have had the flavor bred out of them. Says they're no better than the vat-grown stuff—"

"Yeah, yeah, he's famous for that." Zoey could feel where this was going, and was mentally urging Echo to talk faster.

"Well, there's a fledgling theory that after Titus Chobb's wife died of cancer a couple of years ago, that he came to believe that in order to stave off disease and achieve immortality himself, he needed to regularly eat the organs of a young male. And the rumor is that his chef saw this as the ultimate culinary challenge."

Zoey tried to jump down off the beanbag, but stumbled and kind of rolled off onto the floor. She scrambled to her feet, breathing heavily, pushing her hair back from her face.

"Okay . . . but why pick Tilley for that?"

Will said, "Zoey, there is no evidence for this whatsoever. The nonsense about thinking he can gain immortality, Chobb is not crazy or even superstitious, he doesn't think that way."

"Grief does weird things to people."

Alonzo said, "Ooh, I got it! He chose Tilley because the ritual needed a virgin."

Echo said, *What ritual?*"

"Come on, you can't eat a person without a ritual. You're not just going to treat it like making a pot roast."

"Good," said Zoey. "Let's follow up on that. If nothing else, maybe it's significant that there are rumors going around that point somewhere other than me."

Will said, "We will . . . follow up to the fullest degree that it deserves."

"Final point of order. I know where Stench Machine is, he's currently in the courtyard stalking a discarded glove he apparently thinks is a bird. Where's my mom?"

"At work at the clinic," said Budd, "being monitored. If someone comes after her, we will know long before they get there."

Andre said, "Hey, look at that! I got a message in my Hub inbox. One of the naked avatars I yelled questions at apparently decided to follow up after I got booted. It says . . ."

Andre messed with his phone, apparently unclear on how to actually see the contents of the message.

"Here. It says The Blowback has a thousand officers commanding a million foot soldiers. And they intend to raze the estate, seize the objective, and eat it—I assume they mean you—at a ceremonial feast at midnight."

Alonzo perked up. "You didn't tell me a *million* nerds were coming. I'd have brought a fifteenth man."

Zoey scoffed. "Well that's just—I mean, now we know it's a bluff. Ha. A million soldiers? There's no way. Right?"

23

The sun was setting and there was still no indication that, say, the entire North Korean military was amassing somewhere nearby—*someone* would have noticed. Still, Alonzo's team had been dispersed to various points along the walls that Will had determined were tactically the most likely places to attempt a breach, with two shooters placed on the roof with a clear view of the gates. Guns were a no-go on Zoey's side, as the grounds were dotted with the propellant cookers that had ignited Redd Gunn the day before. Anyone who showed up with firearms would have a very bad time and the bigger the guns, the worse time they'd have. As such, Alonzo's men had been supplied with railguns from the Suits' arsenal, rifles that could send a pulse of electricity down the length of the barrel, carrying with it a tiny object that flew so fast that the impact alone would splatter a human body like a ketchup packet under a car tire.

Echo was inside in the conference room, monitoring all of the security camera feeds. Budd was working the phones, trying to get a line on anything that might be occurring, anywhere. Andre had been piloting a drone to monitor everything from the sky, until he crashed it into a tree and now he was wandering around the grounds with nothing to do.

Will stood in the front yard in the orange glow of the huge house-sized jack-o'-lantern, drinking scotch next to Andre. Zoey and Wu approached and a moment later they were joined by Megaboss Alonzo and his bodyguard, Deedee.

Zoey made eye contact with Deedee. "You don't say much."

"People don't ask me much." She did not smile when she said it.

"Are you missing big Devil's Night plans for this? Were you supposed to be staking out a spot along the parade route?"

"If I want to watch a string of noisy eyesores driving along at walking speed, I can just look out the window of my apartment any day of the week. I'm *supposed* to be getting the winter collections up on our racks. Some of us don't just get to take off from work when something more fun comes along."

Alonzo, forcing a jocular tone, said, "Don't let her fool you with that, she's got girls to do that work. The store's the job she puts on her taxes, this is her real job, being the eyes in the back of my head."

"I stand corrected," said Deedee. "What I meant to say was I should be at the store explaining to those girls why they did the whole thing wrong and making sure they fix it the right way." Alonzo started to reply, but Deedee cut him off. "And go right ahead and swallow your speech about how I need to learn to delegate. Not in the mood."

Zoey glanced around. "Well, I don't see a million people. Unless they're tiny. Wait, I'm freaking myself out with the thought of a million little elves pouring over the walls."

Andre gave her an ugly look. "Ew. Now I'm gonna have bad dreams. Why'd you have to say that?"

Budd's voice came through Zoey's earpiece. "They just announced the battering ram was at the gates."

"I can see the gates from here," said Will, "and there's no battering ram there."

"Unless it's tiny," muttered Andre. "Got a little rat driving it or something."

Alonzo said, "Let's get serious now. This is what we've been waiting all day for."

"A white moving truck just turned onto the inlet road," said Echo's voice in Zoey's ear. "It's the one Budd's been tracking since they rented it. Will arrive at the property in a few minutes."

Everyone exchanged serious looks. *Here it comes,* thought Zoey. The "million foot soldiers," be they real or metaphorical.

Will asked, "Can you get a scan of the truck's interior?"

"Just a moment," replied Echo. "All right . . . there are people in the back with . . . something. Oh, it's the drone. The one Budd said they'd bought, consumer model."

Will said, "How many people?"

"Two."

"What if they're going to use the drone to drop a bioweapon on us?" asked Zoey. "Like the million foot soldiers are viruses? Or bacteria?"

Will said, "They don't have a bioweapon. If there was a place making or selling such a thing we'd already know about it."

"Nanobots? Oh god, I didn't think about nanobots."

"If they managed to build an army of microscopic attack robots without us hearing anything about it, then they deserve to win."

"The truck is stopping," said Echo. "They got right up to the property line, parked."

Will nodded. "They knew exactly where the countermeasures kick in. Zoey, get inside."

"Don't tell me what to do."

"I'm *suggesting,* as your *employee,* that you get inside. Wu?"

Wu said, "There really is no reason to stay out here."

"There is a reason, which is that it's my house and my yard and I can stand in it if I want to. They don't get to decide that."

Alonzo said, "Damn right!"

"They're pulling out the drone," said Echo, sounding a little excited.

Will nodded, also relieved that something was actually happening. "Alonzo, make sure your people are watching all of their stations, this could be a distraction for whatever they're actually about to do. I don't want every pair of eyes on this thing, no matter what it is."

Alonzo said, "Sure," but made no move to tell anyone anything.

Soon the drone took to the sky. From their position it was almost invisible in the evening gloom, just a couple of tiny running lights. Alonzo pulled the rail rifle from his back so he could get a look at the thing through its scope.

Echo's voice said, "It's heading your way."

Alonzo peered through his scope. "It has a little box attached to the bottom that looks like an add-on. About the size of a hamster cage. No too big. Like a middle-class hamster."

Will said, "In about ten seconds it will be in range of the grounds' anti-air security. It's set to automatically blow it out of the sky, unless I tell the system not to, and I can't think of a single reason to do that unless just out of sheer, morbid curiosity."

The drone flew for about nine more seconds, then stopped, hovering in place.

Will shook his head. "Knew right where to stop."

The drone continued to hover. Everyone waited.

A tiny, piercing light appeared below it. The light split into thousands of tiny points, fanning out, forming a hologram a hundred feet across. It took the shape of a Spider Cow Zoey cartoon, fully rendered in three dimensions, complete with the black polka-dot underpants. It had a huge stupid grin, purely to show off its version of Zoey's messed-up teeth. Then, below it in huge, hovering red letters, was the phrase:

FARTBURGER COOKS BALLS WITH BALLS!!

This, Zoey would find out later, was intended to be the sickest of burns in the anti-Zoey community. Like most of their insults, catchphrases, and memes, it required quite a bit of unpacking.

Untangling this particular one required rewinding several decades to when it was first determined that one of the greatest contributors to global climate change was the production of beef, due to the sheer amount of methane cows expel into the air while digesting their feed. In order to discourage and stigmatize beef consumption, an animal rights group had launched an infamous campaign called "Skip the

Fartburger." Since Zoey's personal hate group had decided she was a cow, some had thus started referring to her as "Fartburger." Separately, it was a popular phrase among the youth to say that a particular hot summer day was "cooking balls." Once the group decided Zoey was also a cannibal and added in the detail that Tilley's testicles were missing (along with many other parts), it was decided that she was farting out all of the balls she had eaten, so much so that it was warming the city. Thus, "Fartburger cooks balls with balls." It really made perfect sense when you sat down and diagrammed it out.

Everyone stared at the hologram, took it in, then flew into action. Will shouted commands, ready for the next shoe to drop. This was, Will was sure, the exact kind of distraction the enemy would use to draw their focus in one direction while attacking from another angle. And yet, there were no signs of that attack.

Finally, Deedee rolled her eyes and took the railgun from Alonzo. She aimed, fired, and turned the drone into a cloud of whirling fragments. On the ground below, the pair of twentysomething males who had been watching the whole thing play out were now speeding away in the moving truck.

Then, there was only silence.

"No other activity, not for a mile in any direction," said Echo.

Budd's voice chimed in again. "Zoey, I called your momma, she says she's fine, off work, and drinking with friends along the parade route. No one's bothering her."

Echo again: "The Blowback put out a statement that's just four words long. 'That Was For Dexter.'"

"Hey! Everybody look," said Andre. "Over there."

Zoey spun to face him. *"What?"*

"I got the drone out of the tree!"

Zoey threw up her hands. "Oh my god. So, the 'battering ram,' the million men, all of that was just code for whatever *that* was?"

Budd's voice said, "They're still saying the feast is at midnight. Whatever that means."

Will sipped his drink. "I'm starting to think that our adversary is not speaking the same language we are."

Zoey put her hands on her hips and puffed out an angry breath. "This is so stupid. We're all idiots for falling for this. We wasted our entire day, had people running around all over the city, we're going to have Megaboss Alonzo *as our mayor*—"

Andre said, "As our *what?*"

"—over vague, totally unrealistic threats made by people who would have probably found a way to trip over their inch-long dicks on the way here. Fine. That plan you guys came up with yesterday, the 'Get Chobb' plan? We're putting it in motion. Do your thing."

Zoey walked back toward the front doors and sensed everyone was following her.

Behind her, Alonzo said, "You know, I'll be even madder if I find out this was all arranged by you guys just so my crew would help set up your Halloween maze."

Zoey took a bite of the brownie ice cream ball that had appeared in her hand and said, "We're going to hold Chobb at gunpoint and make him come clean about all of this. Then I'm going to come back here and get dressed up and I'm going to go to that stupid parade and I'm going to hate every minute of it because parades are dumb and there are always lines at the toilets a mile long—"

Zoey's shoe kicked something that had been lying on the floor of the foyer. It skidded away.

It was Stench Machine's collar, and his Blink camera.

The cat himself was nowhere to be found.

Zoey told herself that this was nothing, that it had just fallen off. Then she thought about what Will had said, about the distraction. Then she thought about The Blowback boasting that they would have a feast at midnight.

Zoey balled up her fists, bent over, and screamed as loud as she could.

24

Everyone was dispatched to look for the cat. After half an hour, Zoey made them stop.

They were all in the courtyard now, Zoey carrying a saucer of smelly homemade cat food she'd been using to try to lure him out. She set it in the grass and tried to gather herself. Everyone was watching.

"They took him," she said, keeping her voice steady. "We're just wasting time. That's what all of this was about. This is what they worked out in their stupid chat rooms."

"Zoey," said Echo, softly, "nothing breached those walls. Nothing."

"Who else was here?"

"Nobody, we canceled the work crews, normal house staff were all told to stay home today. No one was here but us."

Zoey stared at Alonzo, but said nothing.

Alonzo cocked his head. "Don't even look at me like that. I understand you're distraught about your missing animal but you will not accuse me and my crew. Not after we spent all day setting up your damned skeletons."

"What if one of your people went rogue? What if Chobb got to one of them?"

"Don't you see how that's even *worse*? You know what, I'm out. My obligation is fulfilled. Everyone be sure to vote next year."

Zoey gestured to Wu. "Search his people on the way out."

Alonzo looked back over his shoulder at her. "Which of us is wearing clothes that could conceal a feline?"

Echo said, "Zoey, let them go. Stench went into the house, through the back door when Carlton was bringing in a bag of empty beer bottles. The camera shut itself off the moment he entered, just as intended. That was ninety minutes ago. *None* of Alonzo's people have been in the house since then. Even Carlton came right back out to join us, in case you were about to suggest they turned him."

"Then we now know there's a way to sneak into the house and we have to find that hole in the security and close it. Later, I mean. Right now, the immediate problem is that *they are holding a member of my family*. And I'm telling you, if they hurt him, they die. I don't care if we don't have any staff willing to do it, this city is full of psychopaths who'll do it for a sandwich."

"Zoey," said Will, "I want you to think. We're saying that these people, these social dropouts with rich backers, they spend weeks or months developing a plan to get in and out of the estate unnoticed. In a city—a *country*—full of people who would love to do the same. They know they have one chance at it before we discover the security hole and close it. Why wouldn't they take the opportunity to abduct *you*? Get you in a room and make you confess to the Tilley thing, or even better, ignore all that and ransom you to the company for nine figures? Or, if they decide that's too risky, just try to get data off of Santa's Workshop? Or plant a bomb? Or literally *anything else* but steal your pet cat?"

"*That* is why." Zoey stabbed a finger at him. "Right there. Because they knew it was the one way to destroy me that would leave me on an island because no one else would understand, because to everyone else they've 'just' taken my dumb pet cat. I can always just go grab a new one, right? This is just another one of my little girl tantrums?"

Echo said, "Can I show you something?"

"Okay?"

"In private. Away from"—she shot a look toward Will—"everyone."

This was a strange request and in fact Zoey couldn't ever remember Echo ever having made it before. Rather than argue, she walked into the finished Halloween maze, turning a corner to get somewhat out of range of everyone else. The walls were only six feet high but that was plenty to hide both Zoey and Echo from view.

"Well?"

"Zoey," Echo began, "you're extremely upset. When you are upset, sometimes you don't see things clearly. That's not a failing on your part, it's just brain biology. But if you want to deal with this situation, you need to open your eyes to a truth that is right in front of you."

"Okay. How about you just tell me what it is."

"The fact that you *have* to trust us. Will, me, all the rest."

"How convenient for Will."

"See, you heard the words but you didn't listen. There are things we don't tell you because we know you won't hear them. Not just me, the whole team. You hate that and you want to prove us wrong, right? So here's how you can do it. Let me say this again, more blunt this time, and show me that you understand."

Zoey set her jaw and said, "Alright."

"Your ability to ever have a normal human relationship ended the day you inherited your father's money and power. You will never have that again, for the rest of your life, no matter what happens."

"You think I don't know that? You think every time I get a call from somebody back home that I don't know they're trying to get me to pay their tax bill or their cousin's bail money?"

"But you're still closing yourself off when things get rough, like you're waiting for a friend to come along who you can trust, somebody you can confide in about all these terrible choices you're forced to make. What I'm telling you is *that friend isn't coming.* Ever. Instead, you have to surround yourself with people whose instincts you trust, whether they're your friends or not. And Zoey, if the people currently surrounding you aren't trustworthy, get rid of us and get new people in here. You inherited your father's gang and if you still don't trust us, I understand, I may even agree. But I am telling you, from a position of having been there—if you can't trust us, you need to fire us. But if you can trust us then *listen to what we're saying.*"

"And what you're saying is that I need to forget about Stench Machine because there's some other, more important objective. One that I can never understand because you people are playing your billion-dollar game and I'm still over here alone on Zoey Island fretting about my dumb cat."

"Do you know how Will got the bandage on his hand?"

"Cut himself on his bedside scotch glass?"

"Underneath the bandages are scratches. Deep ones. From cat claws. He got them because when the situation went to hell out at the Screw last night, he got your mother to safety and then he came back here and *secured your cat.* Carlton told me the whole story. He was in the front yard, Will chased him down, and got him into your bedroom. There's a little trail of blood out there on the cobblestones, you can still see it. Go look."

Zoey stared at Echo. *Through* her. Trying to imagine Will chasing a cat. She couldn't.

Echo said, "You may not have friends in the traditional sense, people you can drink with and share your secrets with. All the friends you had back home, they wouldn't even recognize you as the same person now. But Zoey—hey, look at me."

She did, with great effort.

Echo fixed her gaze on her and said, "You are, in fact, on an island. But *we are on here with you.*"

Zoey burst into tears.

Echo paused for several seconds, letting her catch her breath. She put a hand on her shoulder.

"They want you to fall apart. Don't. If they've taken him, we'll get him back. But we also can't lose track of the bigger picture, that's all."

"What if . . . what if they're hurting him?"

"Then the faster we find him, the better, and the more methodical and logical we are in our approach, the faster we'll find him."

Zoey nodded and wiped her eyes. "We need a plan. A good one."

"If you're right, we're facing a hive mind of obsessive nerds backed by a billionaire with access to an army and an arsenal, who knows we're coming, and in fact wants us to come."

"You're right. We don't need a good plan. We need a *stupid* plan."

25

It was after seven P.M. on Devil's Night, which meant hundreds of thousands of people were either at parties or lining up for the parade, many wearing costumes that could easily fit into your back pocket. Meanwhile, the Suits were having a grumpy argument around a conference table. Zoey imagined they were locked in an angst submarine floating through an ocean of drunken carousing.

"That's what I keep sayin'," said Budd. "I've dealt with actual anti-government insurgency groups that were chattier than this. There is zero talk about your kitty cat leaking out of the Hub."

"But we know where they've taken him," said Zoey, "or where they're going to take him, right? To the Screw. Wouldn't they do this where they live?"

"Maybe," said Will, "but someone posted this about fifteen minutes ago."

He brought up a poor-quality photo onto the monitor. It was a young man in a dress or, at least, the person had the build and posture one would associate with a young man. The dress had little cartoon cat faces all over it and the guy had stuffed key parts with pillows to make it bulge out. A black-and-blue wig completed the ensemble: it was, in fact, a Zoey Ashe costume. The possibility of someone dressing like her for Halloween hadn't occurred to Zoey until just now, but she guessed she should have expected it. People here went for darkly funny costumes above all else, and to these guys, her mere existence was both horrible and hilarious.

In the fake Zoey's right hand was a plastic pet carrier. Its rear was to the camera, but the slits in the plastic showed tufts of white fur. The caption on the photo was OFF TO GO WIN THE 10K AT THE ICC. DIDNT THINK I'D FIND A CAT BUT WE MANAGED LOL

Zoey first went cold, then felt a wave of relief. The carrier was proof they'd kept Stench Machine alive and from what she could sort of make out from the slots, he was standing up. So his legs worked.

"What's the 10K ICC bit about?"

"The $10,000 Inappropriate Costume Contest," said Echo. "It's being held in the park at ten."

Zoey studied the photo. "What's his name? It is a guy, right?"

Budd sat up. "Ah, we don't know yet. Will only spotted this picture because it was tagged by several of the ringleaders."

Zoey gave him a brutal look. "*Why* don't you know?"

Echo said, "The framing, the angle, and the costume make it impossible do anything other than estimate height and build. And see how blurry it is? That's a filter, intended to hide details in the background. Whoever took this is very aware of the identification techniques we'd be using."

"Remember, this isn't a leak," said Will. "It's a public post, one they knew we'd see. That would suggest that they want you to know, or at least to think, that your cat is going to be at the costume contest in the park."

"So they can do, what? Let me snatch the crate from the guy and find out it's empty? Then they all get me on Blink while I start crying?"

"That's the best-case scenario, that this is just The Blowback doing whatever they can to milk the game a little bit longer."

"Milk? Did you intend to use that phrasing?"

"*Yes.*"

ZOEY PUNCHES THE FUTURE IN THE DICK 217

"Nice."

"Worst-case scenario, they did this on Chobb's direction and he'll have an army waiting to get even for Dirk Vikerness."

"Well, the plan's the same either way. We go to the park and snatch this guy up. If he's got my cat, great; if he doesn't, well, then we'll have the guy and I bet he won't hold out long under interrogation. At the same time, we need a second team at the Screw. If this dickhead turns out to be a diversion or bait, then that's where my cat will most likely be. We'll just be ready to extract him from either place."

Andre said, "Chobb and his puppet mob will be anticipating both moves."

Zoey nodded. "And we are anticipating their anticipation. I'm on the costume contest team. If this is our guy, I want to be there, handle it personally."

Andre looked to Budd. "What do you say you and I go out to the Screw, try to stealth the cat out of there, if it turns out that's where he is? We're not gonna outnumber 'em anyway, might as well see if we can finesse it."

Zoey turned to Will. "Do you want to say some perfunctory thing about how I should stay here and let you people do the dangerous part?"

"Well, if they've found a hole in the estate's security then it's not safe here, either. If they can get your cat, they can get you."

"Right, everything is terrible. I'm getting discouraged, Budd, tell me a joke."

Without hesitation, Budd said, "A pirate walks into a bar. He's got a steering wheel sticking out of his fly. Bartender says, 'That looks uncomfortable' and the pirate says, 'Yarrgh, it's driving me nuts!'"

"I don't get it."

"There's one more thing," said Echo. "I'll, uh, let Andre explain."

Andre looked up. "What? Why do I have to do it?"

"It will sound better coming from you."

Zoey said, *"What?"*

Andre, in a strangely apologetic tone, said, "Shae LaVergne, the hostage girl? She just bought a house for her and her momma in Salt Lake. Put half a million in cash on a down payment. She's moving her momma in from Tampa, where they're from. But right now they're both on vacation in Ixtapa, at the Cala de Mar. For two weeks."

"So what? She's spending our payoff money."

"Well," chimed in Budd, again looking uncomfortable. "That's the thing. We didn't give her any cash. She agreed to reimbursement for moving and that we'd cover some to-be-determined education or job training, but that's it. This is new cash that we are unable to trace."

"It seems like we're unable to trace a lot of things these days."

"And whatever the source," said Echo, having judged it safe to join the bad news delivery, "she's covering it up. Budd has talked to everyone in Shae's social circle, plus three of her extended family back in Florida. The mother is telling everyone Shae won the money in a lawsuit against the owners of the Night Inn, because of the hostage situation."

"But that's not true, right? I feel like I'd know, since I am said owner."

Will said, "Not only is it not true, but Shae waived the right to sue when we made our deal."

"Okay? Somebody is paying her off, and it isn't us. Why is everyone acting like it's a funeral?"

Zoey noticed that Will looked genuinely puzzled, which on his face was an expression like he'd put cash into a vending machine that refused to dispense his drink. It always chilled her when Will looked like that. Both times.

"If it was Chobb who paid her off," said Will, "and I can't think of who else it would be, that would almost imply that it's to shut her up. Like maybe she had detailed knowledge of the Tilley situation that he didn't want getting out."

"How would she know anything?" asked Zoey. "*We* don't even freaking know and we're supposedly experts at knowing things. And not just knowledge of Tilley's murder, but detailed knowledge that Chobb is willing to pay seven figures to keep quiet?"

No one wanted to say it, so Zoey finally said it for them. "Wait. Are we seriously back to Shae LaVergne having had Tilley murdered out of vengeance? I mean, under what other circumstances would she have this information, unless she hired Chobb's people to do it?"

"Maybe she didn't do it out of vengeance," offered Echo. "Maybe just to ensure her own safety."

Andre said, "So, hypothetically, let's say a few weeks after her hostage ordeal Shae decides screw it, I want Tilley taken out. So she reaches out to somebody, and somehow Titus Chobb gets involved. Chobb sees this as a prime chance to screw with us, so he has his henchman Vikerness spend hours cuttin' out Tilley's organs. Then he starts spreading the rumor that Zoey was behind it, backed up with a large amount of anonymous money put up as a bounty. So then Shae gets a guilty conscience, maybe she sees all the mess it's created for Zoey, and she says she's going to confess the whole thing. So then Chobb pays her some equally large amount of money to not do that."

Echo said, "It's . . . not implausible."

Will said, "In the grand scheme of things, does it actually matter?"

Zoey looked at him, incredulous. "It matters because *it would mean Shae LaVergne is the murderer.* Regardless of who took the contract, she'd be the one who ordered it done. She did the crime that a hate group then pinned on me, and she is apparently fine with the city descending into open war over it. Yes, it matters." To Budd, "Can we reach Shae in—where did you say she was?"

"A resort in Ixtapa. Mexico."

"We need to talk to her. Oh, and what about the other theory?"

Echo said, "Other theory?"

"That Titus Chobb is a cannibal who eats the young to preserve his youth."

"Zoey . . ."

"I actually did follow up on that," said Budd. "Asked a lot of my sources, people who've got their pulse on the streets, plus some influencer types on Blink, like Chopra. They hadn't heard it. I instructed them to ask around, and to have others ask around, too. It's curious, I came back an hour later and suddenly you could find quite a few people who'd heard the rumor, and some were citing it as gospel. Everybody'd been asked about it enough that they just assumed there was fire under the smoke. Curious how that works."

"But you got no actual information. Fine. All right, we're wasting time. We need to stage a cat rescue operation and, on very short notice, I need a Devil's Night outfit that hides my face. How quickly could we get a convincing costume-slash-disguise together, complete with some kind of makeup or mask that'll let me walk through a crowd without getting abducted or pelted with rocks?"

Will said, "The amount of time it takes you to pick something out from the disguise closet."

"The what?"

26

Arthur Livingston's old quarters on the third floor were untouched, aside from the man's personal effects having been cleaned out and the clothes donated (the man had owned *a lot* of suits). Zoey had never claimed the room for herself, she just found it creepy. That's why she didn't know that if you passed through Arthur's five-hundred-square-foot walk-in closet, once full of hundreds of tailored suits, you'd find a slim, hidden door that led to a room full of wigs, fake facial hair, and shelves full of latex makeup appliances. The man had led a ridiculous life.

Zoey sat in front of a vanity in said room, having Echo apply thin sections of latex to her cheeks. There was still a smelly ashtray on the counter where Arthur would apparently puff away at a cigar while he was getting his disguises applied.

"There should be a lot of blood and swelling around my nose. My whole face should be a mess, really. What time is it?"

"Quarter to nine. We're almost done."

In the mirror, Zoey saw a mass of fake fur pass behind her. Wu, in costume.

Zoey said, "You're going to be hot in there."

"I once took part in a firefight on a one-hundred-degree day wearing a full biohazard suit," he said. "It will be fine."

Will walked up, glancing at Zoey's reflection.

"They're almost done in the garage."

Santa's Workshop had spat out the last of the components of Zoey's Halloween costume, but a lot of assembly was still required. Andre and Carlton were snapping it together.

"Also," he continued, "Andre has secured an infrared scanner that can penetrate walls, they'll be able to get an analysis of the Screw's occupants from about a hundred feet away. They just have to come up with a plan to get close enough to scan the building without drawing the notice of the dozen yellow jackets patrolling the grounds. No ambush this time, they're just there in the open. Waiting."

"Then our guys just have to find a cat-sized heat signature, right?"

"Well, lots of the people who live in the Screw presumably have pets, so they'll have to figure out how to narrow it down to your specific cat. Then there's the minor issue of extracting him without triggering a pitched battle with the VOP that leaves thirty people dead."

"Right, because that would upset Stench Machine. What you're saying is that it's way better if they actually are bringing him to the costume contest."

"You mean, if they're using him as bait in what almost certainly *is* an ambush? Think about how Redd Gunn staged his attack yesterday, drawing what looked like random bystanders from the crowd. The Blowback's people don't wear uniforms. For all we know, they actually have their thousands-strong army, only interspersed through the park."

"Yeah, that would be . . . unfortunate."

"And even if there are zero of them waiting there, there's still the bounty on your head. The moment word gets out that you're in the crowd, the same gaggle of possibly-enhanced and probably-drunk vigilantes will try to snatch you up to collect. It's very possible that Chobb's mob doesn't intend to show up with the cat at all, that they only want to draw you into a public place and then let raw financial incentive wreak havoc for them. Do you have your necklace?"

"You can see it on my neck, Will. Is my mother safe?"

"Your mother is doing exactly what she wants, same as always. You understand the plan?"

"I helped come up with it!" He had a coin out now and was making it somersault across the top of the fingers on his right hand, his fancy way of fidgeting. It was driving Zoey nuts. "Actually, why don't you go help Echo figure out how the catnapper thwarted the estate's security?"

"She has a theory, but you're not going to like it."

"As opposed to everything else I've heard today?"

"She thinks the intruder snuck into the house days ago. Or weeks ago, even. Came in with the crews that dropped off the Halloween supplies, or during some other routine maintenance, then just laid low until the right day. Then they wouldn't have had to worry about getting in when our guard was up, just getting out, which is in fact easier, if not exactly easy."

"Wait, her theory is that I had some psychopath from The Blowback secretly *living in my house with me* for who knows how long? While I slept? While I took baths? And who knows what else?"

"It's a big house. Security should have immediately detected another person but if their gear is sophisticated enough? All measures have countermeasures. Again, remember who's pulling the strings behind all of this. I said you wouldn't like it."

"Well, my mom always told me that when life is overwhelming, just pick one thing and worry about that. Block out everything else. For right now, we're getting Stench Machine back. That's our only job. Once that's done, we'll move on to the next thing. They want us to be frantic and confused. We have to respond by keeping focused. We're smarter than they are, right?"

She dug into her pocket for her tube of her mother's pyramid scheme confidence-daisy skin cream. She wondered how much you'd have to apply to get so confident that you'd just lose all awareness of your own mortality, because that's kind of what she needed right now. She actually looked for a label about dosage and instead only found a single warning in all-caps: DO NOT USE ON GENITALS.

27

The $10,000 Inappropriate Costume Contest was being held in the Arthur Livingston Memorial City Park, which meant making it through the Arthur Livingston Memorial City Gridlock. This was the part of being an action hero nobody had ever told Zoey about, that half of the problem is always just getting there. As such, her ICC team was taking three vehicles to get to the site. Of the three, Zoey's was by far the least secure, but also the most discreet.

She was on the back of one of the city's electric pay-by-the-hour Vespa scooters, Wu weaving it around stalled traffic, Zoey trying to keep the fur of his costume out of her eyes. On one hand, leaving the house in anything that wasn't a luxury-model military vehicle felt like she was cartwheeling down the street naked. On the other, after having gotten trapped inside the overturned armored van earlier, she decided she preferred the feeling of open air around her, passing through crowds as just another nobody on a scooter. She got some glances, but they were clearly reactions to the costume, not her.

Echo's voice spoke from her earpiece. "The guy in the Zoey costume just went live on Blink. He's in the back seat of a car, says he's heading to the park. The cat carrier is visible next to him."

Zoey, hoping that her attached mic could discern her voice from the wind and traffic noises *whooshing* around them, said, "Can you see Stench Machine in the vehicle with him? If so, can you detect his mood?"

"Uh . . . no, the carrier is solid plastic on the top, that's all I can see at the moment. We're nailing down the make and model of the car."

A moment later, Head of Security Hank Kowalski was patched into the line. "It's a black Geely Series X Towncar, we just grabbed it on a traffic cam on the corner of Rhoades Road and Streeter Pike. In front of and behind the sedan are armored VOP escort vehicles. Four of them, total. Who the hell is this guy? What are you people up to?"

Zoey said, "We think they have my cat."

"To make myself feel better, I'm just gonna tell myself that's code for something else."

Echo asked, "Do you know where the vehicle originated? Did they pick him up at the Screw? The old storage units on Avenue Lane?"

"It emerged from a secure vehicle switch location."

Zoey said, "Nobody else thinks it's strange that Chobb's security team is escorting this random dropout kid to the costume contest? Just openly surrounding him in armored vehicles? Wasn't the whole point of riling up the trolls that he could wreak havoc from the shadows?"

Before anyone could answer, Wu pulled onto the sidewalk and parked the scooter in the customary way, by disdainfully dumping it over right in the middle of where people were trying to walk (in this city, doing anything else would have drawn attention as aberrant behavior). He and Zoey walked the final two blocks to the park, hundreds of faces passing them on the sidewalk, every brief moment of eye contact stopping Zoey's heart for a beat. She imagined the whole crowd suddenly swarming her, burying her, tearing her to pieces. Instead, she passed through unmolested, shoulders brushing past her, Zoey feeling like a sausage rolling through a pack of hungry dogs.

They arrived to find the park was a train wreck. Literally; that was the theme of this year's decorations, a locomotive accident with hundreds of gruesome fatalities. A line of smashed, overturned, and burning train cars—real ones, brought over from an abandoned rail yard—snaked through the park, partygoers shuffling around and climbing over them. Unsettlingly realistic corpses and severed limbs littered the ground. Massive zombie buzzards the size of pterodactyls swarmed overhead and occasionally swooped down on tattered leathery wings, snatching up some body part in a jagged beak and hauling it back into the sky. Again: Devil's Night was not for kids.

Zoey jumped as the nearest corpse opened its mouth to speak. Then she saw that the mouths of all of the mangled corpses were moving in mechanical unison. In a ghostly chorus, the dead announced that the Inappropriate Costume Contest was due to start in fifteen minutes.

"The five vehicles in the Stench Machine convoy were just waved through the VOP security cordon," said Echo, in Zoey's ear. "They're parking now, looks like . . . I'm going to say eight guards."

"Where?"

"Northwest of you."

"What am I, a goddamned mountain man?"

Wu nudged her and pointed in the direction that was presumably northwest. They pushed their way through the crowd of costumes. She saw one guy dressed as Margot Greggor, a woman who made headlines for killing her two toddlers and stuffing them into an oven (the costume required two charred dolls). There was a couples costume, Congressman Whitley and the teenage girl he allegedly raped and murdered (the girl made up to look exactly like the recovered corpse as it appeared after five days in the Potomac, wrapped in garbage bags). Another couple was dressed as Jesus and Muhammad in fetish gear. She saw a man in blackface and an orange Afro dressed as pop star Latrell La'range, who had been arrested a few months ago for masturbating in public and the man wearing the costume was crudely simulating that.

Echo said, "You're almost there."

Zoey already knew. Partygoers were turning, pointing, recoiling from a team of armed guards acting like Secret Service clearing the way for the damned president. Zoey pushed through gawkers and saw the kid in the bad Zoey Ashe costume emerge, now about fifty feet away.

And it was just a kid, *maybe* eighteen. He hadn't covered his face in anything but sloppily applied makeup he'd probably borrowed from his mom or girlfriend, including mascara applied to look like it was running, as if his Zoey had been crying. He was saying something to one of the guards and Zoey noticed he'd painted three of his teeth black, to look like they were missing. The real Zoey was missing a lower canine from a skateboarding accident when she was a kid and had a chipped incisor from a hard slap administered by a stepdad wearing a bulky class ring. Her tormenters loved to exaggerate her bad teeth and that was the only reason Zoey hadn't gotten them fixed, even though she'd had a couple of unrelated oral surgeries since inheriting the money. It would feel like giving in.

Echo said, "Everyone is in position."

Zoey momentarily panicked when she saw the kid had emerged without the cat crate, but he then turned and reached back into the vehicle and pulled it out. She caught hints of movement and fur through the narrow slots in the door and sides.

Breathe.

She forced herself to focus through a rage that was crawling through her body like fire ants. She wanted to run over and rip the carrier away from him but took some pride in the fact that she knew better. The VOP team would cut her down before she took a step. Cool and methodical wins the race.

As such, they had discussed every possibility for this part. That the crate would be empty, or contain a stuffed cat, or a bomb, or some prank device that sprayed acid or diarrhea in Zoey's face. The first step was to have Wu scan for—

"There is no explosive device," he said, his voice muffled from inside his costume. Under there, he was wearing glasses that sprayed threat data across his field of vision. "I see no mechanism of any kind."

The kid walked toward them through the crowd, heading for the staging area for the contest. He was unspooling a trail of yellow-topped guards behind him and they looked ready to blaze a path back to the safety of the vehicles should he be accosted. Again, this was no ambush, this was deterrent all the way. Zoey didn't understand, too focused on her cat to put it together.

Zoey steeled herself and walked casually toward the approaching young man who was dressed like a cruel caricature of her, on a path to intercept him but acting like she hadn't seen him yet. She felt her heart knocking on her sternum.

She strode directly toward the kid, nearly bumped into him, and in her most shrill, drunk-girl voice said, "OH. MY. GOD!"

She made a big show of looking the kid's costume up and down.

"You've even brought a real cat!" Zoey grabbed Wu's furry sleeve. "Dana, look!"

The kid looked at Zoey, the recognition dawning on his face. Not that he was recognizing Zoey, but that he was recognizing her costume. As Zoey.

Specifically, she was dressed as Torture Victim Zoey Ashe. Echo's latex and makeup made her face look bloodied and beaten, her features swollen beyond recognition. She wore a cheap wig that vaguely mimicked a previous hairstyle, complete with blue streaks framing her face. She wore padding to exaggerate her figure and had loops of twisted, bloody wire around her neck and each wrist, as if she'd been bound up by a psychopath. Wu, meanwhile, was dressed in a cheap cat costume with white fur. Its markings had been quickly spray-painted to mimic Stench Machine's, a black blotch down his face and chest.

The genius in Echo's costume design was that Zoey was utterly unrecognizable under the costume of herself. Her eye color had been changed with a blue dye applied with drops that would look natural even under a microscope. Her actual breasts were taped down (well, kind of) underneath an uneven, lumpy, overstuffed bra. Her actual missing canine was replaced by a prosthetic tooth Echo had glued into the gap, then two random healthy teeth had been crudely painted black. Under the bad Zoey wig, strands of blond leaked out. Her shoes added two inches to her height. Under the pale Zoey makeup were hints of a fake tan, the skin tone of half the girls in the city. She looked like a different, prettier woman trying to make herself comically ugly.

The kid unenthusiastically said, "Cool."

"I had a friend do the wound makeup! She has a 3D printer in her house! I have to split the ten thousand with her if I win. The cat costume is rented, but we painted it, do you think we'll have to pay for it?"

"I . . . don't know."

The young man was incredibly uncomfortable with the conversation and seemed like he wanted nothing more than for it to be over.

In Zoey's ear, Echo said, "Sixty seconds out. Separate him from his detail as much as you can."

Zoey, in her drunk girl voice, said, "I'm getting all of the Zoeys together for a picture! We've got four so far. Come on!"

She grabbed his arm and pulled him along. He muttered some weak objection and glanced back at his security as he slowly walked with her.

Zoey leaned in close to his ear and said, "Who are those guys? Are they in costume or are they, like, actual gunmen?"

The kid said, "Uh . . . they're with me. I'm actually not supposed to—"

"They're with you? Are you famous or something? Come on, one picture and we'll all get drinks!"

Zoey pulled him along a little faster, making a show of casting a playful look back at the kid's escorts, like she was making a girlish game of running away from them, inviting him to break the rules. The kid sped up to a trot to keep up with her, but glanced back nervously.

"Hey . . . I'm not supposed to run. I just had—hey . . ."

She kept urging him along, to limited success. Three of the guards were jogging to close the gap, bumping through partygoers in offensive costumes, talking into their own radios, relaying instructions. Wu ran alongside Zoey, but his role was to ensure her safety. He would not, he made it clear, actively participate in an abduction.

Zoey said, "How long now?"

The kid turned as if to ask who she was talking to just as Echo answered in her ear. "Thirty seconds. Get him away from those guards."

Zoey looked back at the kid and said, "Hey, why don't you have your goons wait here while we—"

The kid dropped the cat carrier.

Zoey heard a yelp and scratching from inside.

The kid had to stop and retrieve it. He seemed to be breathing hard, like this little bit of exertion had been too much. That gave three members of his security detail time to catch up. One of them pointed a gun at Zoey. Another pointed a gun at Wu.

The first one said, "I need to see some ID."

The kid said, "It's fine. We're going to go take a pic—"

"SHOW ME ID, NOW."

The wind picked up, blowing around trash and dead leaves, whipping fake wig hair into Zoey's eyes. There was a noise from above, the sound of the air being battered to death by twin rotors. Everyone looked up. Zoey's rented stealth helicopter had arrived.

Dangling from cables below the aircraft was an object much larger than the helicopter itself, hidden under a tarp that was flapping and snapping in the breeze. The object was lowered slowly to the ground, the helicopter setting it down in a spot in between Zoey and the row of vehicles from which the kid and his entourage had emerged. The cargo, the size of a house, hit the grass and the helicopter detached the cable and flew away. The tarp fell to the ground, revealing Zoey's Halloween costume, the one that Santa's Workshop had been grinding away at for more than three weeks. It stood on four huge, pink legs. The crowd gasped and hooted and laughed. The guards started shouting commands at each other.

Like all good costumes, this one required a fair amount of explaining to the uninitiated, which of course made it that much more impressive to the initiated. The design was based on a popular anime series called *Our Hero Reo*, which was about a little girl named Naoko and the tiny toy cat she keeps in her pocket. Thanks to a series of accidents involving magic and time travel, the toy cat had the ability to transform into a gigantic, destructive mecha-cat named Reo. The central joke of the series was that the giant cat was actually not useful for combating the many colorful, monstrous enemies that plagued that universe's Tokyo, because even as an enormous mecha-kitty, Reo only wanted to cuddle and make people happy (Zoey figured that last bit was either part of the fantasy, or cats were much different in Japan). So, about once an episode, this giant robotic cat would go bounding around, wreaking havoc, demanding pets from friend and foe alike while puking up colorful gifts and farting pink clouds of floating hearts. The whole time, an exasperated Naoko would be frantically chasing after it, trying and failing to coax Reo into actually assisting their mission in some way. Zoey had always identified with Naoko, for some reason.

Zoey's Halloween costume, which was supposed to have made its debut at tomorrow's party to the delight of all of the kids in attendance, included a twenty-foot-tall mech made to look like it was part Reo and part Stench Machine. It had all of the pink-and-white highlights of the cartoon character, with the coffee-stain colorings of Zoey's missing cat around its chest and chin, plus his spiked collar. Zoey herself was to be dressed like Naoko (that is, a twenty-fifth-century schoolgirl) and would have controlled Stench Reo by remote. Echo was operating him at the moment.

From the mouth of the giant cat robot came a booming, altered version of Zoey's recorded voice, loud enough to shake the ground.

"MEOW! WHAT'S ABOUT TO HAPPEN IS *NOT* MY FAULT!"

That was a Reo catchphrase, but the Vanguard of Peace guards apparently weren't fans of the show. They opened fire with their ribbon guns, the weapons' bundle of six tiny barrels spraying holes into the torso of the cat-shaped mech. This had no effect whatsoever.

Stench Reo was not of course designed to be outfitted with real weapons, it was only rigged to do a few Reo-esque tricks and phrases to impress the kids. However, if the yellow-jacketed guards looked closely, they would note that a bulky rifle had been hastily duct taped to its chin. The cat took a few long strides toward the row of parked VOP armored vehicles and fired said rifle, launching a barrage of glowing projectiles the size of beer cans. Each landed on the hood of one of the VOP trucks with a *clunk*.

Fearing a series of explosions, both guards and bystanders quickly backed away. Instead, each canister began sparking at the base, then emitting smoke. The projectiles each cut their way through the armored hoods of the vehicles, spraying the engine compartments with a shower of thermite. A puddle of molten metal and plastic oozed out from around the front tires, like the vehicles were soiling themselves. Zoey was pretty far away from the action, but even from there the fumes were strong enough to burn her eyes.

The VOP guards went nuts. Their means of evacuation now disabled, the men rapidly tried to coordinate with each other, ready to hustle their ward out of the crowd and into some backup vehicle. The three gunmen were closing in on Zoey and the kid now, five more heading their way.

The cat, with its butt still facing Zoey's direction, crouched down and raised its haunches into the air, just like Reo in the cartoon. A compartment opened up, revealing a circular array of barrels aimed upward.

The booming electronic Zoey voice said, "MEOW! OH NO! HERE IT COMES!"

Zoey ran over and grabbed the thoroughly bewildered kid and, trying to stay in character, said, "Oh my god, that thing is going to attack us! Let's go!"

She tugged at him and he sort of followed.

Behind them, Zoey heard one of the guards say, "Hey! Stay in sight!"

The mecha cat said, "HOLD YOUR NOSE!" and from the barrels were farted dozens of canisters that landed on the lawn all around them. Upon impact, each spewed a thick pink cloud of smoke, belched forth in a series of heart shapes which then expanded and overlapped, reducing the visibility to zero. It smelled of strawberries, just like the cartoon cat's farts were said to. The children, Zoey thought, would have gone wild for this part.

Zoey grabbed the kid, made sure he still had a grip on the cat carrier, and said, "IT'S POISON! GET AWAY FROM IT! DON'T BREATHE! LOOK, A GUY BACK THERE JUST DIED! THIS WAY!"

She pulled him along and this time he followed without protest. The smoke was not poison, of course, but it did have a strong scent and to a scared and confused young mind, it'd be easy to think it was getting harder to breathe, even if it was really the panic doing that.

Zoey actually got lost in the smoke for a moment but was able to track Wu's white furry shape ahead, hoping he was heading in the direction of fresh air. As the smoke got thinner, that only encouraged the kid to run more, until he was leading the way, swinging the cat carrier around in a careless manner that infuriated Zoey.

The three of them stumbled into the clear and were immediately staring down the barrel of another gun.

It was a guard in full Vanguard of Peace riot gear—gas mask, yellow chest plates. Then there was a buzz and a large black-and-yellow drone lowered itself to aim an additional pair of barrels at Zoey.

From the drone came an electronic voice that said, "STOP OR WE WILL USE DEADLY FORCE. LAY FLAT ON THE GROUND."

Zoey's chest was heaving, her hands on her hips. The kid looked so winded that he seemed on the verge of passing out. She looked back at the roiling pink cloud of smoke, knowing the rest of the VOP team were back there, seconds away.

The kid said, "It's okay! We're okay!"

"GET DOWN OR WE WILL SHOOT. YOU HAVE THREE SECONDS."

Wu did it first, keeping his costume paws raised, quickly going flat. Zoey followed suit, now hearing men shouting from behind her. Behind the guard and drone, another VOP vehicle rolled to a stop, having plowed its way through decorations and food stands to intercept them. The rear door popped open. The guard yanked the kid over and pressed a gas mask to his face.

"WE'VE GOT YOU. BREATHE NORMALLY." The guard, presumably into a radio, said, "WE'VE SECURED HIM, EVACUATING NOW."

While the drone kept its weapons pointed down at Zoey, the guard shoved the kid—and the cat carrier—into the back of the vehicle.

The guard then returned and said, "ON YOUR FEET. BOTH OF YOU. YOU HAVE BEEN DEEMED A THREAT TO OUR CLIENT AND BY LAW AND VANGUARD OF PEACE POLICY, WE ARE DETAINING YOU. MOVE!"

Zoey stumbled to her feet and the guard roughly yanked her along, dragging her and shoving her into the vehicle with the kid. Wu climbed in and the guard slammed the door.

28

The foot soldiers of the Vanguard of Peace were not, for the most part, morons. Or at least they weren't morons about being foot soldiers. As such, they tended to know where their vehicles were at any given moment and what they were doing. They also tended to notice if a vehicle was one of theirs and not, say, a rented yellow moving van with the sunny VOP logo hastily attached to the side. They further would notice if another guard was equipped with officially issued gear, or if they were wearing an improvised uniform and carrying a wildly unofficial railgun.

The young man in the Zoey costume in the back of the vehicle could not have been expected to notice these differences, not in the middle of a heart-pounding escape from what must have seemed like a nerve gas attack from an oddly whimsical terrorist. The eight pursuing guards, however, emerged from the pink smoke and knew exactly what had occurred: their ward had been abducted into a strange vehicle and, for all they knew, was already dead.

Inside the van, Zoey peered out the rear window and saw several guards rushing toward them, screaming orders.

"Guys! We need to move!"

Their own yellow-jacketed guard climbed into the passenger seat, turned, and said to the kid, "Let me see your hands."

He did, and was confused to see they were suddenly in handcuffs. The guard ripped off the helmet to reveal Echo's face.

Trying to sound intimidating, she said, "These are pacification cuffs. If they detect you struggling, you'll get a shock. If you run, you'll get a shock so hard that it will paralyze you for the next half hour. Just sit still and we won't hurt you."

The kid said, "Wha—who are you?"

Zoey said, "Damn it! They're already here! All of them."

Wu pulled off his cat costume head, his hair matted with sweat. He peered out the window, but didn't need his fancy threat-assessment glasses to tell him the obvious. "We didn't get enough separation from the guards."

"What do we do? *Guys?*"

From the driver's seat, Will said, "Hang on."

He hit the accelerator, but while the rear wheels were still spinning in the grass, the two nearest guards fired their weapons, aiming low. The impact shook the vehicle and the van sank several inches on one side. Smoke drifted up past the windows, as if the wheels were being melted from under them. The electric engine whined, but with half the wheels disabled, the van only skidded around in a sad, wobbly donut.

Will muttered a curse.

The rest of the guards quickly encircled them. Wu unzipped the cat costume and peeled it off using his one good arm. Underneath were black fatigues and a vest that he had told Zoey could stop most bullets. She probably should have asked for one of those. He checked the projectile bracelet on his wrist, probably counting his shots.

Outside, two of the guards fired again, taking out the other two wheels. For the third time in two days, Zoey was trapped in a completely immobile metal box and surrounded by enemies. That was the kind of thing that used to almost never happen to her.

Will punched away at controls and, *almost* sounding calm, said, "Buy us more time. I don't care how."

Echo brought up her phone. "What else can the, uh, cat do?"

Zoey watched the ring of guards close around them and said, "Uh, not much? Hit the last button. The puke thing."

Echo tapped her phone.

A pair of guards approached the rear doors, tested to see if they were locked. They were. Same with the side door. Instructions were shouted back and forth and they jogged away, presumably to get equipment to cut their way in.

The nearest guard shouted, "Exit the vehicle with your hands in the air and lie flat on the ground! Leave all weapons behind. If we have to enter the vehicle, we can and will use lethal force. This is your final warning and your final opportunity to end this without bloodshed."

Zoey looked nervously back at Will. "Should we . . . say something?"

He glanced into the side mirror. "Looks like they're about to get their answer."

Moments later, Stench Reo came bounding through the pink smoke.

The guards turned to face the giant cat-bot and shot at it some more. It was now so full of holes that it would probably whistle when the wind blew. The cat opened its mechanical mouth.

Zoey's electronic voice said, "OH NO! I HOPE THIS ISN'T AN EXPENSIVE RUG! BLECH!"

Five hundred small plastic tubes came flying out, like a spray of vomit.

"MEOW! PLEASE GIVE YOUR MOMS THESE FREE TUBES OF CRAZY DAISY MOOD ENHANCING CREAM OR WHATEVER IT'S CALLED! THESE HAVE NOT BEEN TESTED BY THE FDA!"

The guards fell back and took cover behind the van, presumably thinking the tubes would explode or something. But no, they were just skin cream, that, at the moment, seemed to be doing nothing to enhance anyone's mood.

The hostage watched all this happen from inside, eyes wide. "Who *are* you people?"

The VOP team spent several minutes analyzing the projectiles before deciding it was safe to refocus their attention on the van. The guard who'd left earlier returned with a small tool.

Echo said, "We've got about thirty seconds before they cut their way in." She pulled a blade out of her boot. Zoey had no weapons.

The guy with the tool pressed it to the back door and there was a hiss and smoke. Blue light reflected off his faceplate.

Zoey looked back to Will and said, "If we just toss the kid back out there . . ."

"That won't matter. Not now."

The noise from the cutting tool stopped. The guards approached in formation. They yelled their warning again, demanded they all surrender, lie down, take the peaceful way out.

Zoey backed away from the door. "Somebody? Will, go talk to them! Do your thing!"

Will said nothing, didn't even turn to look back at her. The lead guard came up and yanked open the door.

He aimed a gun at them and said, "COME OUT AND—"

Someone shouted from behind him. He looked up.

Wind was kicking up dust around them again, the mini-hurricane that accompanied the helicopter wherever it went. Zoey couldn't see the aircraft itself from inside the vehicle, but knew what it was there to do. *Finally.*

There was a heavy metallic *thunk* above them—magnetic hooks clamping onto the roof of the van.

Will said, "Grab something."

There was a hard, upward jolt and then they were rising, hauled up and away by the helicopter. The rear doors were wide open, air rushing in. Then the van abruptly tilted backward, threatening to spill everyone out onto the ground below. Zoey grabbed the nearest rigid object she could find.

They continued to rise. Zoey happened to register something skidding along the floor and she realized with terror that it was the cat crate. She reached out, missed it—

Echo stopped it with a foot, hooking it just before it reached the open door.

Zoey stared out, watching the train wreck party falling away below them, the guards shrinking into a little circle of yellow specks, zombie vultures circling overhead.

Their hostage yelled over the howling wind. *"What is happening?"*

The helicopter lurched forward and the van tilted in the other direction, gravity sliding everyone toward the front. The door slammed shut but wouldn't latch, as that mechanism had been destroyed by the guards. Wu reached out and held the doors shut with his one good hand and used the other arm to hook a cargo strap with his elbow.

After several minutes they leveled out and in the relative calm, everyone stared at each other as if to reassure themselves that they had somehow pulled that off. Wu actually barked out a laugh and Zoey was suddenly reminded that, contrary to what he may say, the man lived for this kind of thing.

Echo surveyed the interior and said, "Everyone okay? Do we need to do a roll call, make sure nobody fell out?"

Zoey crawled back toward the plastic cat carrier. But already she knew. She sensed it, but also, she smelled it. She pulled open the latch and inside saw a random, skinny white cat. Maybe a stray they'd caught. Zoey looked back at Echo and just shook her head.

The hostage kid looked more confused than ever. Will, no longer needing to operate the now-airborne van, left the driver's seat and braced himself against the wall. The kid turned and registered who he was seeing.

Blood drained from his face. Urine pooled around his shoes.

The kid tore his gaze off of Will to look at Wu, then Zoey. Piecing it together. Zoey had never seen anyone as afraid as that teenager was in that moment. She almost felt bad for him. *Almost.* She peeled the itchy latex makeup off of her face. The helicopter apparently was turning in the air, the whole van tilting sideways. She had to reach out to brace herself once more.

She said to the hostage, "We may not have Stench Machine. But we have you. Tell me where he is."

The kid looked back and forth between Zoey and Will. "Where *who* is?"

"Fine." To Will, she said, "If someone else has him down at the park . . . I wouldn't even know where to start. Tell Budd and Andre it's on them now. They're our last hope."

She stared down the hostage.

"And *his* last hope, too."

29

The helicopter flew itself to a preprogrammed destination: the main storage lot of Move Kings, the rental service where they'd gotten the van after every option for a tactical vehicle had fallen through. They needed a place to put it now that it was surely being tracked and this was as good a spot as any. The helicopter lowered the van and its passengers onto the lot, then hovered nearby for want of a clear landing spot. Zoey left a note on the dash of the van, apologizing for changing the logo and getting the rear latch destroyed and the wheels melted and pissing in it.

Then the four of them hustled over to the helicopter itself, Zoey wondering what complex mechanism would be used to raise them up to the aircraft that was suspended about ten feet above the ground. It turned out to just be a goddamned ladder. A flimsy one that unfurled itself from the bottom of the side door. They climbed up one by one, Zoey feeling like the wind from the rotors would toss her off of it at any moment. Their hostage made no effort to escape. When push comes to shove, almost everyone complies.

Once inside, they slammed the door and the aircraft swept into the sky, coughing out shimmering airbursts that downed several drones that tried to follow.

Echo sat in the cockpit and said, "No fewer than four full-sized VOP aircraft have taken flight in search of us."

Zoey thought that seemed like a lot just to prevent her from getting her cat back. Then again, up to that moment, she hadn't known that the Vanguard of Peace had an air force at all. Will, however, seemed prepared for this and said their helicopter would enter a stealth holding pattern outside the city. Lights off, invisibility skin on, engines in quiet mode, skimming over hills in a way that would make it very hard to find. For a while, at least.

Thus, within minutes, they were flying low and slow, the glow and flicker of Tabula Ra$a's animated skyline flashing and pulsing in the distance. They needed to remain ready and undetected in order to extract the two-man Screw Team of Andre and Budd if things went off the rails, or the two-men-plus-Stench-Machine Screw Team if things went well. It was then that the kid, still in his crude Zoey costume, apparently found an opening to make his case.

"Look. You guys . . . I understand things got way out of hand. I'm really, really sorry about that. We can work something out—"

Zoey cut him off. "We can set those handcuffs to shock you if you talk. Do we have to do that, or can you just voluntarily shut up?"

That wasn't a feature of the cuffs as far as she knew, but the kid seem to buy it, or at least the sentiment behind it.

"Do we have some kind of hood or something we can put on him? I don't like him staring at me. Does this helicopter have a cabinet full of hostage-taking supplies somewhere?"

Echo gave Zoey a disapproving look, but then said, "I guess it's better if we're not keeping him in the loop on everything we're doing. Hold on."

She found a headset in the cockpit, disconnected it, and used it to cover the kid's ears. They did not in fact have a hood or a blindfold, but Zoey put the head from Wu's cat costume on the kid, turned backward so he couldn't see out. His cuffed hands were trembling. He smelled like pee. Zoey had a fleeting feeling like this was all a weird dream she was having.

They started this, she thought. If everyone had just kept to themselves, none of them would be here. She'd be at home, in her pajamas, prepared to curl up with a bottle of something and looking forward to not attending the Black Parade.

Will said, "I've got Andre."

He put the call on the monitor. Zoey thought he and Budd would both be wearing black burglar clothes and draped in grappling hooks, but they were just dressed like they always were, sitting in what looked like a bar from the old west. Visible in the background was a mechanical old-timey bartender who was frozen in place while wiping a glass—probably designed to get shot in the face by an animatronic cowboy at some point in the evening.

Zoey asked, "Are you guys drinking?"

"This place is closed," said Budd. "We let ourselves in, I'm buddies with the owner. It's just outside the industrial park. We're bein' watched from the skies, needed to get indoors. Will's text said you came up empty?"

Zoey glanced over at their hostage. "Sort of. We don't have Stench Machine. Otherwise everything went perfectly. You should've been there."

Andre said, "Well, no unusual activity so far at the Screw. Or, nothing that looks unusual to us, it is our first time watchin' the place. We've parked a jammer drone on their roof, when we turn it on, it'll kill any outgoing Blink feeds. And they'll know it, too. Or, they'll know they're blocked, but hopefully will take a while to figure out why. The idea is if they want to eat your kitty on a live broadcast, they'll hold off if they know they've gone dark. No audience."

"That'll stop them from eating him," said Zoey, "but won't stop them from killing him."

Budd said, "We're banking on them wanting the whole, uh, meat preparation process on camera. For maximum effect."

Zoey was about to answer, but choked on the words.

Andre quickly jumped in. "So, uh, the stacks of storage units weren't built to be residential, obviously, so there's no gas running to the building, everything is electric. Figure if there's no power, there's probably nothing to cook with. We're, well, assuming they're not intending to eat a raw animal."

Zoey absolutely did not want to cry in this situation, in front of these people. She made herself nod. At least the hostage couldn't see her.

"Now, you've got the piss factory next door," said Budd, "the grasshopper farm on the other side, trucks coming in and out of both at all hours. Next thing is we'll arrange a little accident. Nothing fatal, but if we do it just right, it'll knock out the power and also trigger a hazardous materials warning to evacuate the building. For the emergency crews that come, herding those people should be like trying to catch a fart with a fork. This should draw in a bunch of drones to see what's goin' on, one of which will be ours, which will be carrying our infrared scanner. If whoever is holding the cat evacuates him, we'll find him in the crowd and track him from there. If they leave him behind in the building, even better—we'll have a clear path to slip in to get 'em. We've got disguises for that part."

Andre added, "One way or the other, the whole evacuation and cleanup procedure should take hours, maybe all night. With any luck, it won't be until they all file back into the joint after the all-clear when they'll be like, 'damn, cat's gone.'"

"You've already got a rendezvous point programmed in," said Budd, "a soccer field not too far from here. You pick us up, we'll all go home and have a good laugh about it."

"Assuming the cat is there at all," grunted Will, "and they're not already set up at some third location."

Zoey flicked a hand at him. "Hush. All right, guys, when do you go in?"

Budd answered. "As soon as our truck turns down this street here. Which is right . . . now."

Absolutely nothing happened for a solid minute.

"Sorry, it looked a lot closer on the tracker. Here it comes."

The monitor switched to a drone feed, looking down on a tanker truck as it rumbled into the industrial park.

Andre's voice was still audible in the feed.

"We're already in control of this one."

The semi suddenly weaved in the road, swerving across the center line and back again. It didn't look like they had *that* much control. Still, the truck did a passable job keeping in its lane, until it was time not to.

It suddenly veered to the right, jolting off the road and bashing through a chain-link fence, rumbling through the parking lot of the Screw. It ran through the outdoor cafe tables and chairs, knocking them aside like doll furniture. The truck then careened and over-turned, the tanker skidding on its side and slamming into the base of the building, sprays of liquid flying in arcs, splashing against the walls. Then the tanker ruptured completely and several thousand gal-lons of human urine washed in waves over a junction box that the crash itself had already knocked askew.

Sparks flew. There was a flash and a sharp clap, like a tiny explosion.

Lights blinked and then, a moment later, the Screw want dark.

The feed cut back to Andre, looking relieved. He wiped his forehead. "Just like I planned."

Next to him, Budd watched the immediate aftermath on his phone. "Guards are swarming the truck, thinking it's a suicide attack. Give 'em time, they'll conclude otherwise. Even if they sense shenanigans are at hand, it don't matter. The spill's gonna send ammonia fumes up into those boxes and they've got no real ventilation. Everyone will have to be cleared out at the orders of the property owners, whether they want to go or not."

Andre said, "They don't wanna get sued after a bunch of unem-ployed nerds get piss lung." He stood. "We have to get into costume."

Echo switched the feed over to the drone, which was circling the Screw. Down in the darkness, flashlight beams were whipping around the scene of the crash and people could be heard yelling questions and accusations. The beginnings of the chaos they needed for their plan to have any hope of working.

Echo said, "Two more VOP aircraft have taken to the sky. They *will* find us."

Will glanced at some dots on his monitor, which presumably marked the location of said aircraft. "That was inevitable. Once they do, it'll just confirm that we're not heading toward the Screw. It's fine if they find us, as long as they don't find Budd and Andre."

Zoey said, "Can't they shoot us down?"

"They can, if they try hard enough. All helicopters are made to crash. But they won't try. Not as long as we have him on board." He nodded toward their hostage.

"Why would they care about . . ."

Zoey's words faded. She turned from the monitor and studied Will's face. Then she got up, went over to the kid, and pulled off his furry costume head and headphones.

The kid's face was covered in beads of sweat, either from fear or due to the costume apparently being designed to cook its wearer alive. His eyes were wide, looking like he'd spent his brief time in sensory deprivation imagining various torture scenarios he'd have to endure.

Zoey said, "You. What's your name?"

This question really confused the kid. "I don't—you know my name."

"Yes, The Blowback. Tell me your *real* name, the one you were born with."

The kid once again looked back and forth from Zoey to Will, looking like he'd been asked a question in a foreign language he didn't understand and was hoping someone would translate.

Will, looking very much like he already knew the answer, said, "Tell her."

"Marti?" said the kid, like he was now scared that he was giving the wrong answer to a trick question.

"The whole name."

"Marti Chobb."

30

Zoey stared at Will. "So we just abducted Titus Chobb's . . ."

"Son."

"And you don't seem worried or surprised by this."

Will didn't answer.

"Meaning you knew that's what we were doing."

"I strongly suspected."

Marti gestured toward the cat crate. "Did you think that was really yours? It's just part of the costume . . ."

Will said, "I know. Your father is executing a misinformation campaign to mobilize an insurrection against our organization and you are involved to some degree. Your father may not have understood how seriously we take this sort of thing, but I believe he knows now. Do *you*?"

Marti swallowed. "Are you going to kill me?"

He seemed to visualize himself being thrown from the helicopter, after having first been skinned alive and set on fire.

Zoey said, "No! I didn't even know who you were. Even if Will apparently did, and he and I will have a discussion about that shortly. We're not the villains here."

"You attacked me with a giant robot and kidnapped me into an invisible helicopter."

Will asked, "Did your father know you were going to the park tonight?"

"No. I'm supposed to be at home in bed. But that security detail follows me wherever I go, I couldn't get away from them. It sucks."

"Tell me about Dexter Tilley."

Zoey stopped him. "No, Will, how about *you* tell *me* about Marti. When did you know that's who we had?"

"I suspected it was him in the photo, had about the same build. But I didn't understand why Titus would send him out as bait. Even with the guards it's a stupid risk, so I assumed it was a ploy, that they'd swap in someone else."

"And you didn't feel the need to share any of this with me? You've just got your own agenda over there?"

On the feed, there was the sound of an explosion and shouting. She turned to the monitor—

It had gone dark.

"What happened?"

Echo, trying not to sound alarmed, said, "There was a flash, like something blew up, and then we lost the drone."

"Lost the connection or lost the actual drone?"

"I don't know."

"Because the drone has the cat scanner thing, right? The heat signature scanner?"

Will said, "We have to head out there."

"If we do that," interjected Wu, "they will detect our approach long before we arrive and intercept us at the rendezvous point. They can prevent us from landing or from taking off again. They'll have many options, once they realize where we are going."

"We, on the other hand, have just the one option," answered Will. "The VOP can close the roads in every direction leading out of the industrial park, so we're Andre and Budd's only chance for extraction. And we can't let Chobb take them into custody, not as long as we have his son. That would go badly."

"Then I recommend that Zoey and I be landed in a safe location before you do the extraction. Since, as you said, you have put her in greater danger by sealing her in a vehicle with Titus Chobb's captive son."

Zoey waved him off. "You know I'm not doing that. Budd and Andre are out there because of me, I need to be there."

Will shook his head. "He's actually right, and this isn't a sexism thing. It's bad strategy. Taking you into the teeth of whatever has happened there puts you in danger of falling into Chobb's hands. If he gets you, he gets total control over the situation."

"Then we make sure he doesn't get me. You wouldn't be saying this if it was my father sitting here instead of me."

"If I agree with that statement then you'll say I'm holding you to a different standard. If I disagree, you'll say, 'Well, I'm not my father.' So what's the point of responding at all? You've already made up your mind."

Zoey studied the monitor, the one with the map showing the six angry red dots. "If we run into one of the bad guys' helicopters, can we shoot *it* down?"

Echo said, "You want to shoot down a helicopter over a populated city? You've seen what one of those looks like when it crashes, right?"

"You know I have. So we're going?"

"Turning around now. You'll feel us banking."

They tilted, heading toward the industrial park and a situation that had apparently gone badly awry. Zoey figured that, in retrospect, they probably should have predicted that.

"Hey, Marti," said Zoey, "whose cat *is* that?"

He shrugged. "Just a stray I guess. It hangs around my dad's ranch."

"We need to get him water. When we get somewhere safe, I mean."

"Okay."

They flew for a moment. He wouldn't even look down at the cat. Just a costume prop to him.

She said, "I want to ask you a question."

"Okay."

"Why? Why all of this, why come after me?"

"I wasn't really a part of that. I—"

"Yes you were. Come on."

"I don't know. It just got out of hand, like I said."

"'Got out of hand.'"

"You wouldn't understand."

"People say that to me ten times a day. Why wouldn't I understand?"

"Because you're not a guy."

"Explain it to me, then. Tell me what it's like."

Marti looked hard at her, searching for a way to phrase it. "It's like everyone is laughing at you all the time and all you want to do is shut them up."

"I absolutely feel like that."

He scoffed. "Everyone thinks girls are God's perfect little angels. You're never in the wrong, always the innocent victims, always calm and wise and perfect. And nothing is ever your fault. If a boy cheats on a girl it's because he's scum, if a girl cheats on a boy it's because he didn't treat her right."

"Get this cat water when we get somewhere safe."

He didn't reply.

They flew in tense silence, Zoey watching out a window as the glimmering city oozed under them, white strands of streetlights and headlights crisscrossing and pulsing. A spider's web, Zoey thought, waiting for her to descend, get entangled, and be bled dry.

She jumped when the monitor suddenly blinked back on. Andre's face appeared on the screen. He was covered in sweat and appeared to be running. An ominous red glow washed over the landscape behind him.

"Can you hear me?" he grunted. "There's been a complication!"

Will rushed over. "We're just a few minutes out."

Andre stopped to swat away something that was jumping at his face, it looked like a large insect. They were swirling all around him, black specks backlit by the hellish light in the sky. It looked like a Biblical apocalypse.

"No! Abort. There's no place to land. We're gonna get snatched up, no matter what."

"That's not an option," barked Will. "Can you get on top of a—"

"No. Will, tell Zoey the cat isn't here."

"Andre, listen. Go to the—"

"They're here! Gotta go!"

There was more shouting from off-screen, and the feed went dark. Echo said, "We're four minutes out."

Will looked toward the cockpit. "Have we been detected?"

"Not that I can tell."

"Turn around."

Zoey was about to override him, tell him to go in anyway, then she heard Echo gasp at what she saw on the horizon. Zoey moved to the cockpit. They were coming up on the sprawl of low buildings that was the industrial park, from their height looking like an array of miniature models on a table. Perched in the middle of them was what looked to Zoey like a glowing Japanese lantern someone had set down among the models, casting a gently pulsing light on everything around it. The stars directly above it were shrouded behind a pillar of smoke.

It was the Screw, and it was on fire.

31

The lower half of the building was fully engulfed, the flames steadily clawing their way up through spirals of tiny boxes. It was lighting them up like pixels, the blaze sweeping up into one container apartment after another.

Echo punched the controls and the helicopter banked, hard this time.

Zoey said, "Will, we *can't.*"

"Zoey, you have to start thinking more than one move ahead. You want to help Andre and Budd, this is the direction to fly to help them. Either we'll get a call from Chobb's people wanting to do an exchange, or we'll get a call from Andre saying they got away. In either case, we can only come to their aid if we keep ourselves free."

Zoey hated the fact that she had no rebuttal for that. She grabbed her phone and started searching for Blink coverage of the fire. The camera view hopped across members of a crowd standing in a ring around the building, the heat keeping them some distance away. Those little specks were flying and buzzing and jumping around. The view panned down to see dozens of grasshoppers bouncing through the grass around everyone's shoes. Then the crowd started whooping and gasping and pointing until the view swung upward, to see what the fuss was about. Halfway up, one of the storage containers was tumbling out of its socket and rolling down to earth, trailing fire behind it like a meteor, crashing to the pavement below and scattering meager furnishings on impact. The brackets holding the living spaces in place were melting loose, the building was falling apart.

Nearby, a teenage boy yelled, "We found Foles! We found Foles! He got out!" A celebratory cheer went up.

Blink was great for showing you an event, searching "fire at the Screw" got Zoey this feed immediately, but that required the algorithm to actually know about the event or person you were looking for. What she wanted, to see if Andre and Budd were being arrested/abducted by yellow-jacketed goons, wouldn't come up for her under any combination of terms.

Echo said, "The VOP would block any feed of their arrest or transport; they wouldn't want us knowing where they were taken."

"Then what the hell do we do, keep flying stupid circles around the city?" Without waiting for an answer, Zoey walked back to their hostage. "I've already forgotten your name."

"Marti."

"Marti, I'm tired, and sore, our friends may be dead or worse, and all of this is because your people took my goddamned cat. So I am asking you, as a human being. You say you don't have him, so who does? And where are they?"

"I swear to god I don't know anything about your cat, I don't even know why you're asking. Is the cat a code word for something else?"

Will, it turned out, had been listening. "Marti, this whole city is about to combust over this. Do you understand? People will die. Bystanders. The people you're talking to right now might not survive this. Your father might not survive this. *You* might not survive this. If we find out what's going on, maybe we can defuse it."

"If you find out what's going on with . . . the cat?"

"If we find out what's going on with *your father trying to whip the city into a frenzy over Dexter Tilley's murder.*"

Zoey said, "That was your dad's bodyguard who killed him, right? Dirk Vikerness? Are you acting like you don't know that?"

"DV didn't kill Dexter Tilley. Neither did my dad, or any of us."

"But you know who did. And you know why." The look on his face made that more than clear.

"Yes."

"We're waiting."

"I'll show you. But I won't tell you."

Zoey threw up her hands. "What does that mean?"

"I'll tell you where to go, who to talk to. But I want that person to tell you what happened, because you won't believe me if I just say it. I know you won't. I'll take you there, on the condition that you let me go once you have your answers."

"Is this mysterious person your father?"

"No."

"Oh, but let me guess. This person you need us to go talk to is in some fortified location with one entrance and exit that happens to be perfect for launching ambushes."

"No. They're not. I swear."

Zoey looked at Will, who seemed to be thinking it over. But where else did they have to go?

"So this place you want us to go," asked Zoey, "will I find my cat there, too?"

"No. Not as far as I know."

Zoey looked pleadingly to Echo. "Then what are we supposed to . . . I mean . . . how much time is left?"

There was a clock in the corner of the main monitor. It was already almost eleven P.M. The "feast" of Zoey's cat was supposed to happen at midnight.

An hour. And they had absolutely nothing. No leads, no plan. Strangely enough, the possibility that they would simply fail to rescue Stench Machine hadn't ever actually entered Zoey's mind. She hadn't allowed it to. She had imagined things turning ugly in all sorts of ways, but had never thought that her trolls would just outsmart her.

That midnight would come and they would . . . do what they're going to do. The realization was hitting her in waves, like nausea.

Will said, "All right. Where is this place?"

"West Hills. The little shops there? It's in one of them."

Echo said, "That's that little area where the Ballistic Couture shop used to be. East of South Hills."

Will asked Marti, "Which shop, specifically?"

"I'll tell you when we land."

Everyone looked skeptical. An anxious warning buzzer sounded from the cockpit.

Echo leaned over it and said, "Two of the VOP aircraft are now tracking and tailing us. We flew too close to the fire."

"If we go back to the estate," Will said to Zoey, "no pursuit can get to us. We can land right on the roof and they would have to peel back at the property line. You could go inside, sleep in your own bed. Regroup."

"But then what? Nothing's been solved."

And she would be utterly alone in that bedroom.

Will nodded. Zoey wondered how often he had made these fake offers to her father, giving him the chance to verbalize making a choice that was, in reality, no choice at all. Echo went up front and punched in commands.

Zoey asked, "Wait, won't the bad guys just follow us to where we're going now?"

"It has a protocol for that situation," said Echo. "It just means it will take longer to get there."

The helicopter's "lose pursuit" system involved flying at top speed toward a tiny private airfield in the desert, but with no intention of landing there. Instead it swooped low and, from the rear, ejected a box the size of a refrigerator. The box hit the ground, bounced a few times, then expanded into a flimsy wire-frame object roughly the shape of the helicopter itself. Then, from a small compartment at the top of the frame erupted a camouflage tarp that *floofed* into the air and draped it-self over it, creating the very convincing impression that the helicopter had been landed in the field and hastily covered.

As they watched all of this unfold on the monitor, Echo said, "The decoy actually has a pair of heat generators to attract the attention of anyone scanning for infrared, it should perfectly mimic the cooling engines of this aircraft. Meanwhile, all of our own countermeasures kick in, including an exhaust capture system that eliminates our heat signature entirely. It should appear to any pursuing aircraft that we've landed in that field."

Zoey said, "It won't take them long to figure out it's not real."

"It actually will. They know this model of helicopter and they know the antipersonnel measures it comes with. No one will approach it who isn't suicidal, they'll have a whole siege strategy they'll have to put into place. Remember, they can't just blow it up, they think Titus's kid is in there."

The pursuit-losing gambit also lost them an obscene amount of time—it was now thirty minutes to midnight. No one in the vehicle said what everyone knew, which is that if the trolls' intention was to eat *cooked* cat, then Zoey's friend, the one who'd gotten her through her breakup, the one who depended entirely on Zoey for his safety and who she'd promised she'd never allow to be harmed, could al-ready be in the oven.

Zoey looked down at Marti, at his slack-jawed, stupid face, and thought carefully about exactly what would make him feel what she was feeling right now. What would make all of them feel it.

32

In Tabula Ra$a, only a handful of buildings were more than twenty years old and the vast majority had been built within the last decade. In a city in which everything is shiny and new, the hot fad was to build old.

The estate Zoey lived in, for instance, was reconstructed out of components recovered from a mansion built in 1935, transported across the country and reassembled brick by brick. Likewise, the trendy boutiques and bars selling everything from vintage clothes to hallucinogenic muffins in West Hills were often designed to look like old structures that had been renovated and gentrified. There was a candied gnocchi shop run out of a building that appeared to have once been an old-time service station that had in fact been built from scratch to look like that, complete with a new sign mounted on top of an artificially old and weathered one. Next door was a bar designed to look like it had once been a bank, including an antique vault door leading to the kitchen. The most prominent building was a decrepit granary whose roof had been partially collapsed when the neighboring silo had fallen on top of it—both structures having been in exactly that position from the design stage. It was a dance club.

None of these buildings, however, offered a strong, flat surface for the helicopter to land upon. The thing weighed eight tons, Echo noted, and would collapse most rooftops. More importantly, there was also no way for their stealth aircraft to remain stealthy as it landed. West Hills was bustling with activity (it was, in fact, along the parade route) and even the drunkest of shoppers would notice a giant semi-invisible machine chopping up the night air above them.

But, where their pursuers would be alerted by trending Blink streams about a black stealth helicopter skulking through the night, they would presumably have no reason to note the appearance of something that was, say, the opposite of that. Thus, as part of the preparations before they'd left, Andre had downloaded an alternate "disguise" for the aircraft that would let them blend rather than disappear. Echo scrolled through menus and punched it in. Instantly, the helicopter's programmable skin transformed from a night sky transparency into a bright pink wash of bouncy letters and animated women's breasts. Flashing and scrolling all around the aircraft were the words:

TITTYCOPTER

AERIAL NUDE PARTY BUS

NIGHTLY LAS VEGAS TO TABULA RA$A TOURS

BOOK NOW!!!

Dance music blasted from speakers and swirling spotlights flashed across the streets and structures below.

In the rear storage area, where in the stock version of this aircraft a Special Forces unit would have stowed their various soldiering supplies, was a second set of costumes (the original plan had required them to change at least once in the process of getting away). Andre had been tasked with finding the backup outfits and it was clear they were last-minute rentals, a bundle of seven themed costumes from the popular children's franchise *Raja's Entourage*. The five of them quickly distributed and pulled on the costumes, Zoey and Echo changing in the little storage closet.

Zoey would be dressed as Bonnie the Bonobo, Echo would be Lumpy Ninja, Wu was ShitShark, and Will was Professor Cheeselog. The hostage, Marti, was forced to take the costume of Bald Sasquatch.

Andre and Budd, had they been there, would have gone as Pizzabot and his imaginary friend, Fudgefiddle. Even though the show was called *Raja's Entourage,* there was no Raja costume, as the character had never actually appeared in the show. Every episode was about the entourage trying to frantically cover for Raja's absence from that week's adventure, a running joke being the increasingly absurd ways in which they described the absent character and his actions once they were inevitably asked, "Where's Raja?"

They each grabbed a bottle from the wet bar, to play the role of drunks in search of a Devil's Night party. It turned out one of the clubs at the periphery of West Hills had a rooftop bar (the entire structure built to look like a huge cosmopolitan glass), so the gaudy party copter hovered overhead and they all climbed down the ladder into the mass of shocked revelers below, the winds from the rotors blowing off wigs and spilling drinks. It was exactly the kind of obnoxious stunt that drunk tourists would pull on a night like this, so it was perfect for what they were trying to accomplish: none of their enemies would see that incident scroll across Blink and say, *"That sounds exactly like the kind of thing Will Blackwater would do."*

They headed downstairs, then out through the club. Once on the sidewalk, Zoey watched the helicopter take off on autopilot, leaving her feeling stranded. She adjusted her mask. It was kind of hard to see out of it, which she thought could be a problem in an emergency. She was carrying the crate with the knockoff Stench Machine inside, she hadn't wanted to leave him alone on the helicopter—she imagined him jumping up on the control console and crashing it into a skyscraper.

"So it's just going to wander around the sky until we need it?" asked Zoey. "How long until it runs out of gas?"

Echo checked something on her phone. "Uh . . . it's not gas that's the issue, it's that it's saying it has to be back to its owner by midnight? It says another customer needs it."

That got Will's attention. "Are you serious?"

"Well, it is a rental . . ."

They paused their conversation as a loud group of tourists passed.

Zoey said, "We just have to call the guy and have him extend it or whatever. I can't believe we're having this conversation."

Echo shook her head. "Nobody knows who Andre's guy is. He gets mad when you ask."

"Oh my god. Okay." Zoey turned to Marti, his face completely hidden behind the rubber Bald Sasquatch mask. "So where are we going? Time is short, for a whole bunch of stupid reasons."

"Across the street, three buildings down."

Zoey counted the buildings and found one that had been built to look like a 1950s-era storefront business with a second floor that no doubt would, at least back then, have served as an apartment for the owner. Even the brick had been made to look like it'd been painted a dozen times over the decades, as various businesses came and went. A hand-painted shingle hung from a horizontal pole that said:

PENNYFEATHER AND SONS

FUNERAL SERVICES

. . . which left Zoey more confused than ever.

They shuffled in that direction, past pedestrians, no one paying them any particular attention. Zoey's costume was a furry gray monkey wearing a pink bikini, her face completely covered by the mask of Bonnie the Bonobo. Wu's ShitShark costume was designed so that the eye holes were in the mouth of the brown shark, and she wondered how well he'd be able to see in the event of a fight. A sophisticated enough system could surely make them in their costumes, there was probably software that could spot a person by the way their heels lifted off the pavement when they walked. But they just had to make it about a hundred feet down the sidewalk, through a dense crowd of drunken people with a million other things to look at. It wouldn't even be a minute of walking. Surely they could make it that far without being spotted.

Surely.

As they walked, Echo pointed and said, "You know what's three blocks in that direction? Fort Fortuna. Where . . ."

She trailed off, as there were bystanders who could maybe overhear their conversation. She didn't need to finish—that was where Dexter Tilley's body had been found. Zoey, however, had no clue what exactly it meant.

They arrived at the funeral home to find it wasn't open. It was, of course, creeping up on midnight. There were lights on upstairs, though. Will knocked, then knocked again, forcefully. Nothing.

Will said to seemingly no one, "I know you've got a camera out here. I'm giving you one minute to get down here and open the door, or we're blowing the lock." He glanced back at the nearest group of drunk girls on the sidewalk and said, more quietly, "This is about Dexter Tilley."

Seconds before the one-minute deadline expired, the door was opened by an old man with the kind of face that probably left him few career options outside the death industry.

The creepy man said, "You could have just told me it was you, rather than playing the barbarians at the gates. Come inside before you attract any more attention."

Considering Will was in disguise, Zoey wasn't sure who the "you" was that the funeral guy was saying he'd open the door for. Did he recognize Will behind Professor Cheeselog's flashing glasses and beak? She half expected that once inside, he'd say, "My door is always open for Raja! Wait, where is he?"

Once inside, the man, who Zoey assumed was the Pennyfeather in Pennyfeather and Sons, said, "Now, how can I help you?"

"They're here to ask about Dexter Tilley," said Marti. "Same as he, uh, yelled at the door."

"I of course cannot disclose any information about customers or potential customers—"

Will stopped him. "There isn't time for that. This city is about to go to war over this."

"A privacy guarantee that dissolves under duress is no guarantee at all."

Marti pointed and said, "It's over here."

Without further explanation, he walked toward a wall display showing off various styles and finishes of caskets.

"There's a hidden door. How do you open it?"

The creepy man made no move to help. Will just stared at him. After several seconds under his gaze, the man sighed and pressed his hand to a spot on the wall and the casket display slid open. Behind it was a steel door, with a separate security system.

Zoey sighed and said, "Okay, what is this place, really? Do I need to prepare myself for what I'm going to see behind the armored secret door?"

Marti said, "You'll see."

"Is it cannibalism? A cannibalism cult? Or are you doing mad scientist experiments on cadavers? Or on people who weren't cadavers until you started doing experiments on them?"

Instead of answering, the creepy man opened the steel door with a voice command.

"Is it a torture chamber?" asked Zoey. "Ritualistic sacrifice? Corpse reanimation chamber?"

The door opened to reveal stairs. Wu went down first, as was his habit. Then everyone else shuffled past Zoey, as she stood aside and prompted them to pass. Echo was last to go down, but Zoey stopped her.

"Is the countdown still on?"

Echo showed Zoey her phone. A countdown was displayed, ten minutes left.

"This is The Blowback feed. Whether it's real or just a bluff . . ." Echo shrugged.

"Okay." Zoey breathed. "When they go live with this, it's your job to stop me from watching it. I don't want to see what they do to him, I'm not going to give them that. I need you to do that, okay? Because I'm going to try to watch it, I know I will, and you have to stop me."

"Got it."

Zoey followed everyone downstairs and found them standing in a spacious, comfy-looking lounge. There were expensive overstuffed leather sofas facing a few top-of-the-line recliners that were parked in the middle of the floor, huge monitors in every direction. A door was standing open on the opposite wall and through it was visible a bedroom that was probably fancier than any in Zoey's own estate. There was a massive circular bed, chairs, and racks of . . . devices. A sex room.

"*That's* the secret? The undertaker's got himself a sweet bone chamber under his mortuary?"

Marti said, "Through there."

He wasn't heading for the sex room. It turned out there was another door, to their left. This one was locked and, once more, required the creepy man to access it.

The door clicked open, and when Zoey saw what was inside, she went cold.

33

The Suits were standing around a state-of-the-art surgery suite: a blindingly white, sterile room, a bundle of robotic arms poised over a table.

Zoey studied the equipment and said, "Uh . . . is the mortician here a serial killer? Did he lure Tilley down here and . . . do surgery on him?"

"Everything went bad at once," said Marti, his voice trembling. "My mother died two years ago. Cancer. Just six months after the funeral, I got sick. Everything started to swell. I turned yellow."

Echo, sounding like everything had finally fallen into place, said, "Bukhari syndrome?"

Marti nodded. "I'm supposed to stay in bed for two more weeks. I snuck out anyway. I didn't even want the guards to come. I have a little pump thing in my stomach that's dripping medicine. It still hurts though."

"Is somebody going to tell me what's going on?" asked Zoey.

"You've heard about rich people paying for gene modification, to make their kids more intelligent?" asked Echo. "Well, a lot of them developed liver failure in their teens. That's Bukhari syndrome. Which meant Marti here needed—"

"A new liver," finished Zoey. "Got it."

Will nodded. "And you weren't going to make it to the top of the donor list."

"They told us that with car fatalities down so much, automated cars and all that, donor organs have dried up. They said there was less than a ten percent chance I'd survive the wait list. So, Dad went through a black market organ thing, but there were no livers. Lot of kids need them, for the same reason I did. I go to Farnsworth Academy, in my class there are four of us who needed transplants. Time was running out. My body was filling with poison. I could feel it."

Zoey picked up the story. "Sure. So your dad's henchman, Dirk, found Dexter Tilley, who was a match I guess, and knew him because they all hang around with those jerks in the Hub. Your father had him killed, brought here, had his organs taken out." Zoey studied the tangle of white robot squid arms hovering over the surgery table. "So this is an underground organ thieving place, right?" She turned to Will. "You know, the kind you assured me didn't exist during *the very first* conversation we had about this case?"

Marti said, "Oh, no. No, Tilley wanted to die. He told everyone, in Hub chat. All his trouble with that girl, he just gave up on everything. DV told him about my situation, said he could save a life on the way out. We suggested a service. He used it."

"So he came here willingly, and . . ." Zoey turned toward the creepy old guy. "What, you do an assisted suicide thing?"

The mortician looked annoyed at all of the implications that were being thrown around. He pursed his lips.

"Without disclosing any specifics about any individual who may or may not have sought our assistance, I can say that we have a number of packages for those seeking end-of-life services. One can spend the night with a paid romantic partner of their choice, or enjoy a final meal, or enjoy a selection of . . . substances that have been carefully selected to not damage the organs or remain in the bloodstream. For gaming enthusiasts, we have a custom package that caters to their lifestyle."

Marti said, "That was Tilley. He picked *Crimson Day*. The 'Children of Ares' scenario. It's a level you can't win. You're fending off this big invasion of these huge monsters, buying time for refugees to be loaded onto a transport. After the last of the survivors are safe, you stay behind and take out as many invaders as you can before you're finally overwhelmed. You detonate this bomb that takes out the last of the enemies, but sacrifices you in the process. Tilley wanted it so that when he died in the game, he would die in real life."

The mortician said, "The solution that is released into the bloodstream first induces a sense of euphoria, then extreme relaxation, then a stopping of the heart. A gentle exit. All done in strict confidence, all overseen by a representative."

Zoey said, "So people pay you to kill them."

The mortician was taken aback. "Don't be ridiculous. This is an organ harvesting enterprise; we pay above-market rates for organs one can live without, such as a single kidney. But for a package like our hypothetical customer's, in which he's offered end-of-life services with all viable organs being harvested, we pay a flat fee of two million dollars to whatever beneficiary the client chooses. The organs are then sold on the private market."

Will said, "Then Tilley left his payment to Shae. So that's where her windfall came from."

"You can designate somebody to get an organ," said Marti. "Tilley left the liver to me. That was the deal."

"Hey, guys," interrupted Echo, "the VOP have found the decoy helicopter."

She showed them a feed on her phone, an aerial view of several vehicles surrounding the camo tarp covering the wire-frame shell they'd set down at the airfield.

Zoey said, "Can you, I don't know, make it do something? To scare them away?"

"Hmm . . . hold on. Here, everybody be quiet."

Echo punched a button and then spoke words that, in turn, echoed from a sound system on the decoy aircraft.

"ALL RIGHT, EVERYBODY! WE GOT YOUR BOY IN

HERE! IF ANY OF YOU GET WITHIN A HUNDRED FEET OF THIS AIRCRAFT, WE'RE GONNA CUT OFF HIS DICK AND MAKE HIM EAT IT."

She cut the connection and said, "We'll see if that works."

Zoey said, "*Jesus.* Okay, somebody tell me how Tilley's body wound up in a box on my doorstep."

Marti's eyes went wide. "I don't know. I swear. I didn't have anything to do with that part. Really. I swear."

Everyone turned to the mortician. It was clear he was dreading this part of the story.

He took in a deep breath, then said, "If, hypothetically, morning staff should find that a client's corpse was missing, and if security footage should show that the corpse had, well, *resurrected* itself and walked out of the building under its own power, and if the existence of said corpse were to become public knowledge, it would actually be very unclear how to approach the issue without breaching the company's strict confidentiality guidelines."

Echo said, "Dirk Vikerness could have done it, if he had the right gear and copied the control codes directly off of Tilley's implants in advance. Could have just remote-walked him to the casino, then anonymously tipped off The Blowback."

"And nobody would notice an actual rotting corpse strutting down the sidewalk?" asked Zoey.

"They would, in any other city, at any other time of the year."

Zoey turned to Marti. "Okay. I get that you needed a liver, that this was life and death for you. But why pin it on me? Is it really just because your father is a dick? And I apologize if you're offended by me calling your father a dick, but please keep in mind that I'm only doing that because your father is a dick."

"Dad's been weird ever since Mom died. He's scared all the time. He's scared of the enhancements getting out, like Tilley had. He keeps saying that stuff would be the end of the world."

Echo said, "We have five minutes until the Midnight Feast. Marti, go on camera. You tell them it wasn't murder. It was suicide. If Zoey's cat isn't—if they're keeping him alive for the show then there's still time."

"Uh, no, that's where you're wrong," said Zoey. "It *was* murder."

She turned to stare down the mortician.

"If the trolls in the Hub had known, they'd have come after Marti and they'd have come after you, and they'd have been right. Tilley didn't kill himself. *You* killed him. You pushed a button and poison flowed into his veins. You paid him two million dollars for his organs, great, that's nice, but how much were livers going for on the black market, Marti?"

"Uh . . . a lot. One point five million, I think."

"Yeah, so, add in the lungs and heart and eyeballs and you've made millions in profit off this. *Millions.* By killing a man. Because instead of getting him help for his depression, you invited him to your kill suite so you could cash in on his guts."

She turned and glared at Marti.

"So your dick father was right to try to put the blame on me, to try to deflect. If they knew the truth, they'd have said the same thing I'm saying now, which is that about ninety-five percent of people who try suicide and fail, never try it again. The mood passes. It would have passed for Tilley, too, I bet. But we'll never know, because instead of helping him, you pushed him off the ledge because you needed parts."

Marti, choking up, said, *"He saved my life."*

"You could say the same if you'd stabbed a homeless guy in an alley and taken *his* liver. If you got him drunk first and tricked him into consenting to the act, would that suddenly make it okay? In Tilley's state of mind, it was the same thing. I want you to get on camera and confess. Confess to Tilley's *murder,* right now."

"I will. She, uh, took my phone, if she gives it back I'll—"

Will cut him off. "Zoey, can I have a word . . ."

"No, you can't. There's no time. Echo, give Marti his phone back. Or give him yours, whatever."

Zoey turned to the mortician again.

"What's your name? Are you Pennyfeather? Or one of the sons?"

"There is no Pennyfeather. That is just a name that was generated for the business, customers prefer their funeral parlors to sound family-owned."

"Whatever. What you're doing here? It's done. On top of the fact that you're running a murder factory that chews up the vulnerable, you knew damned well what was going on with all this, you could have defused this conflict at any time just by going public. You were happy to sit back and let that all fall on my doorstep. We're burning this operation to the ground."

The creepy man looked back and forth from Zoey to Will.

"Well . . . that is your right."

"It's my right in the sense that I can put my hands on an exotic weapon that will literally turn this into a crater, yes."

Will said, "Zoey, he means it's your right because you own this business."

34

"What? What do you . . ."

"Marti, no," said Will, "put the phone down. Zoey, this place is owned by a company called Legacy Services, which owns a chain of two dozen funeral homes, which is in turn owned by a holding company called Bold Frontier. Of which Arthur was the sole investor. And now you are."

The creepy man was now wearing a smug expression that made him look like he could be one of Satan's lieutenants. For the third time in two days, Zoey found herself unable to stand. She shakily reached back for something to hold herself up, then sat/fell hard onto the tile floor of the surgical suite. It smelled of disinfectant.

Will said, "Zoey . . . even if you'd given the order to immediately divest yourself from any businesses you find morally questionable, I don't even think this would qualif—"

"You knew. You knew this whole time."

"I didn't realize you owned it until I looked it up on the way here. It's all managed by someone else, by design. Arthur built firewalls between himself and the businesses he ran and selling organs is still very much illegal under federal law. And, while I appreciate that you take a different side in the whole assisted suicide debate, I think we can at least—"

"Shut up. You don't even get it, do you? *They were right.* The Blow-back. This whole time. They were right about everything but the eating and the orgy. But I absolutely had Tilley killed, I absolutely took his guts, I absolutely allowed his hollowed-out body to be kicked around by strangers like a beer bottle on a sidewalk."

Marti said, "And if you hadn't, I'd be dead by spring. Plus who knows how many other people, from the other organs—"

"It's seven," said the mortician. "Seven other lives, eight total, were saved due to Tilley's donations."

"*Rich people's* lives," said Zoey. "Those organs were sold, not given."

Will said, "And the proceeds from those sales were used to buy more organs, so more lives could be saved. Plus Shae and her mother have a new home—"

"Sure, sure," interrupted Zoey. "One question. What's the profit margin on this, for me? Like if they make four million dollars in profit from this deal, what's my cut, how much actually goes into my pocket? Ten percent? Four hundred thousand dollars?"

"No, it wouldn't be anything close to that. Margins are much—"

"One percent?"

"I don't know."

"Is it twenty-six thousand, four hundred and twenty-three dollars?"

"What?"

"What I'm asking you, Will, is did a poor, distraught man die, and give up his organs, *so I could get rid of an annoying noise in my air conditioner?*"

Will looked genuinely exasperated. "You can't look at it that way."

"Why not?"

Echo said, "The Midnight Feast feed is going live."

Will glanced at his phone, then walked out and brought the feed up on one of the big monitors in the comfy room. A room where, Zoey now realized, people came to party, knowing that they would never see the sun again. The last walls they'd ever set their eyes on.

Zoey jumped to her feet and was moving toward the monitor when Echo moved quickly to get in the way. "No. Turn around. Will, shut it off."

Zoey said, "No, I have to watch. I've changed my—"

"No. There's nothing to be gained. Will?"

Will studied the monitor, narrowing his eyes like he was looking for clues, trying to see the truth behind what was on the screen. Thinking. If he'd heard Echo, he showed no sign.

Echo spun Zoey around and hustled her farther back into the surgical suite. A voice on the feed welcomed everyone, announced that the slaughter was about to begin. Zoey squeezed her eyes shut and buried her face in Echo's shoulder. She smelled like sweat and fruity skin cream.

She would fix the memory of her cat in her mind, and that's what she would cling to. Curling up with him, pushing her face into his fur. Not these kids doing . . . whatever they were about to do. Holding him down, breaking his neck, skinning him, cooking him . . .

"I'm so sorry," said Marti, from somewhere behind her. "I'm so sorry."

Echo said, *"Will! Turn it off."*

She yelled it this time. Zoey had never heard that tone from her before.

Will said, "All right, all right," but before he could cut the feed, Zoey heard a scream.

A human scream.

Zoey's scream. Her own voice, coming from the monitor, begging them to stop.

She said, "Wait," and pushed away from Echo. She moved into the lounge and saw on the monitor a video feed that was clear and crisp. Too much so, a sheen of artificiality. It was a feed from within the digitally-generated world of the Hub.

A bunch of The Blowback dickholes in their elaborate armor stood around a banquet table. Lying on the table was the cow-spider monstrosity that was the Hub version of Zoey Ashe. One of The Blowback kids was gleefully stabbing into her body with an elaborate dagger.

Zoey, the real one, said, "What the hell is this?"

Marti seemed confused by the question. "They've got you. There's nothing you can do. They've severed control."

"I'm several layers of confusion behind even that. Is *this* the feast?"

"Well . . . yeah."

On-screen, one of Spider Cow Zoey's hooves were being sawed off by another guy with a butcher knife, while the digital Zoey shrieked. He took a cartoonish bite out of it. A three-digit number appeared in midair and floated away, like a ghost.

"I don't know what I'm looking at. They're eating my Hub avatar? Why?"

"They won the *Battle of the Molten Sea*. They overran your estate. Over a thousand users, each commanding a division of a thousand NPC warriors, a million ground troops versus nearly half a million in the garrison. Took it with a flanking maneuver that locked up the AI on most of your bots until the wyverns could burn their supply caches. Fought all the way through them, breached the walls, took down the elite throne room guardians. Captured you, paraded you through the city. Did you not stay logged on for any of that?"

"I don't even know what any of that means. What are those numbers?"

Marti looked at her like she had just asked which end of the human the pizza goes into.

"Spoils. The currency, in the Hub?"

"Okay?"

"You were worth over ten million of them. You lose it all, forever, there's no way to get it back. You have to start all over with a new character. You'll start as a naked peasant."

"I don't care. Like I said, I don't ever go in there."

"Then who was controlling your side?"

"I don't know." Zoey watched as an entire leg was removed and cut into smaller pieces for other diners.

"Okay, then what did you think this was?" asked Marti. "The feast and all that?"

"I thought they were going to eat my cat."

"What? No. Ew. Who eats cats? *What is it with the cat?*"

"They sent people to my house. They had a drone, it flashed a big hologram meme at me."

"Well . . . yeah. To rub it in your face, that you were getting owned in the Hub. Wasn't that obvious?"

Zoey turned to Will. "So this *whole thing* was happening in the Hub. You know, the place I kept asking you to infiltrate, and you kept blowing me off because you thought it was dumb and pointless?"

Echo said, "Hey, the VOP just figured out the fake helicopter is fake. A, uh, stray dog came along and dragged the tarp off. With a little work they'll be able to reverse engineer the path the real helicopter took. They're coming."

"Recall ours," said Will. "Have it pick us up as close to this building as possible."

Marti asked, "Am I free to go?"

"You can go when I get my cat back," said Zoey, sharply.

Echo said, "Zoey, we can't keep him."

"No, she's right," said Will. "There's no reason to give him up without getting something in return, especially if Chobb has Budd and Andre. One way or the other, we need to force Chobb to the table. Work out a deal, get him to call this off."

"And by call this off," said Zoey, "you mean call off not giving my cat back."

That reminded Zoey—Knockoff Stench Machine needed water. There was a sink in the surgery room. She filled a shallow metal tray from the sink (it was probably used to weigh organs or something, but he wouldn't mind) and let him out to get a drink.

Watching her, Marti said, "I *really* don't think my dad has your cat."

"Then he'd better find him, if he wants his son back."

Marti paused for a beat and said, "I don't think that's as scary a threat as you think it is."

"What does that mean? That your daddy doesn't love you? Well guess what, Marti, he's mobilized an entire army to come wipe us out because we have you."

"My dad is coming for you because he can't be seen as weak. He hates weakness. He hates me. This whole thing he's had to do with the liver . . . he acts like it's my fault. Like I didn't try hard enough."

"That's very sad for you. My father abandoned me and my mom to a life of poverty, then when he died he bequeathed me a city full of powerful enemies. People like your father, in fact. And while your father may not care about you, I do care about my cat and I care very much about psychopaths taking my loved ones because they think it's some kind of game. Well, if your dad wants to play, I'll play."

Echo said, "I'm getting a call from the estate."

Zoey grunted. "Oh, *what fresh hell is this?*"

Zoey, Will, and Echo crowded around Echo's phone. On the screen appeared Carlton the butler.

He was holding Stench Machine.

35

Marti leaned over to see and said, "Isn't *that* your cat?"

"Is that really him?" gasped Zoey. "Oh my god, how did you do it? Oh my god . . ."

"I was preparing a late dinner for myself," said Carlton, "a nice piece of trout. He must have gotten hungry. Came out and hopped onto the counter."

"Where in the hell had he been?"

"I of course do not know."

"Why was he hiding this whole time? Why wouldn't he come out before, when we were looking for him?"

"Of course I cannot know that, either, but I would daresay that your cat may be something of an asshole."

Zoey felt a relief so profound that she was almost floating. It didn't last.

"Wait, so, this was all for nothing? Everything we did?"

Wu said, "We should be thinking in terms of extraction right now. How far out is the helicopter?"

Echo checked. "Two minutes."

Zoey motioned to Marti. "All right. Go home to your dick father. I don't care."

Will said, "That's the wrong move."

"We're not making moves anymore, Will. Our moves just make

things worse. If they really do have Budd and Andre, we'll work something out. Maybe he'll see this as a show of goodwill. No capital *W* there."

Echo said, "Just to confirm, it does appear that every available Vanguard of Peace vehicle and operative in the city has been rerouted to this location."

"Right. Let's get out of here." Zoey nudged the stray cat back into his crate and headed up the stairs.

"This isn't complicated," said Will from behind her. "Chobb has to strike back whether we give back his son or not. The transgression has already occurred and has become public."

"So?"

"So, an army is closing in on us and if they know Marti is on board the helicopter *they won't shoot it down.*"

"Well, then you'd better come up with some other way to keep them from doing that."

They all emerged onto a sidewalk and were greeted by a solid wall of human backs, most in some kind of costume. The crowd was now packed along the street, waiting for the Black Parade.

"How far out did you say the helicopter was?"

Echo was on her phone, with an expression Zoey immediately hated.

"Okay, what now?"

"Well, this isn't good."

"*What?*"

"It's not coming. It's, uh, returning to its owner. The rental period ran out and nobody paid for an extension."

Will clenched his jaw and muttered, "If Andre is still alive, I'm going to kill him."

Zoey, still staring at the sky, said, "What do we do?"

Will studied his surroundings, trying to think up options. He didn't look like he was succeeding.

"I think they're going to take us. Chobb's people. I don't see any way around it."

"That's not an option," said Zoey. "Maybe it is for you, but it isn't for me. Not for Echo, either. If you don't understand why, you haven't been paying attention."

Wu said, "If I need to extract Zoey apart from the rest of this group, then that's what I will do. So if you don't have a plan, then we will be on our way."

It was getting hard to hear him—a blast of thumping party music was approaching from Zoey's left. A small vehicle that looked like a glass capsule on wheels was rolling down the street. A scrolling message was flashing around the exterior, advertising the services of a booze misting pod. For a few hundred bucks you and half a dozen friends could sit in one and get a rolling tour of the city while slowly getting drunk breathing alcohol vapor.

This one veered off the road and the crowd parted as it bumped up onto the sidewalk, drunken people cursing it every step of the way. It rolled to a stop and the glass bubble opened, separating and rising like the sections of an orange. Sitting there, in white overalls that looked kind of like biohazard suits, were Budd and Andre.

Andre said, "Get on!"

They all started climbing aboard, leaving Marti behind, standing next to the crypt keeper by the front door.

Zoey turned to him. "Tell your dad I said hi. Hope the liver works out for you."

Andre pushed a lever and the segments of the glass bubble descended and sealed them off. The noise of the crowd outside was instantly muted as the cart rolled back onto the street. Andre and Budd both stank so badly of smoke that it stung Zoey's nostrils.

"We, uh, own this now," said Andre. "Only transportation we could come up with that could accommodate everybody under the circumstances. We tracked the chopper here, but I don't get a signal now . . ."

Will said, "Your buddy recalled it because the rental expired."

"Ah, right. Damn. Yeah, I got tied up due to events at the Screw." He gestured to the cat crate in Zoey's lap. "Is that Stench Machine?"

Zoey said, "No, it's a long story. What the hell happened back there?"

"So," began Budd, "it turned out the Rhodes Scholar residents of the Screw had stored some propane canisters behind that electrical box. After it overloaded, they ignited. It fried the drone, which happened to be right there, because that's our luck. Also set that side of the building aflame. So we felt compelled to go to the grounds ourselves to help evacuate the building. Think everybody got out okay, I know some got taken to the hospital on account of the smoke. Andre got some burns on his back from a piece of hot railing that fell on him. We've both been coughing up black mucus. Anyway, it gave us a close view of everyone who passed. See what they were carrying, in terms of critters."

Andre said, "But then another truck came along, heading toward the grasshopper factory, and I guess the VOP guys thought it was another attack. Fired a projectile intended to short out the motor. It should have just rolled to a stop, but instead the battery ruptured and the thing turned into a flaming wreck. It tumbled over and spilled its cargo, which was several hundred thousand bugs."

"This," continued Budd, "created something of a stampede in the crowd, and the rumor that this was all an act of sabotage, which it kind of was and kind of wasn't. We obviously were not tryin' to burn the building down."

Zoey said, "Well they surely knew we'd remotely hijacked the pee truck, it'd have been too much of a coincidence that the accident happened right when they were preparing to do their big Devil's Night feast."

Andre seemed mildly insulted. "We did no such thing. That *would* have been obvious. No, the truck was driven by a human, lots of trucks still are. Budd just paid the driver to get drunk off his ass and do the wreck. Guy had stumbled out slurring about how he steered to miss an armadillo in the road. Remember, the original plan was to come and go without them ever knowing we'd been there at all."

Zoey said, "Yeah, I guess that was a better plan."

"Not really," said Budd. "Melvin—that's the driver—spilled the beans to the VOP just minutes later. Told them everything, pointed us out while we were still tryin' to help people out of the building. We wound up getting chased through the fire and the crowd and the smoke and the plague of grasshoppers. Eventually got hit with stun sticks and put on board a transport to their headquarters. But lucky for us, and I'd say this was the only time luck smiled on us all night, Kowalski had been listening in on their radio chatter and made to intercept the vehicle. This resulted in something of a shootout between their security team and ours. I got grazed in the thigh and one of Kowalski's vehicles got blowed up. But long story short, we managed to get away in the end."

Andre said, "I don't know if you heard my last message but you've probably deduced that neither of us have got your cat in one of our pockets."

Zoey waved a hand. "Oh, it turned out Stench Machine was back at the house the whole time. Carlton found him."

Andre and Budd stared at Zoey in silence for what seemed like a very long time.

She asked, "Why are you wearing those outfits?"

Andre looked down at the white coveralls. "Oh, these come with the cart. Alcohol mist will mess up your clothes otherwise. Want me to turn on the vapor? It's gin, I think. Just don't light a match."

Ignoring the offer, Zoey pulled out her phone and found her mother's number on her contact list.

Echo said, "So, Titus Chobb's entire army is converging on this spot and we're rolling slowly down the street in a fragile glass booze cocoon."

"What favors do we got left to call in?" asked Andre. "Alonzo's got a convoy of treaded vehicles, look like tanks . . ."

Will said, "No, he wouldn't get here in time."

"If someone doesn't come up with a plan of action in the next thirty seconds," said Wu abruptly, "I am leaving with Zoey."

Zoey got no answer from her mother, as usual.

"Does anyone know where my mom is?"

Budd said, "Her plan was to spend the evening carousing along the parade route. People set up beer tents in various spots, she was at one of them. Or all of 'em. We've had one of Kowalski's people monitoring her."

"All right, tell them I need to get a message to her. Tell her to pack and meet me at the estate. We're leaving. Like she wanted."

Will said, "You are?"

"Yep. Of everyone in my circle, she's the only one whose advice actually makes sense. I never wanted this. Things aren't getting better. Wu, your job is now to get me safe passage to the estate and then out of the city."

Will made no effort to hide his annoyance. "So we're doing *this* again? This thing where you threaten to quit and then somebody has to talk you down? Is this just your process?"

"FUCK YOU!" screamed Zoey, and everyone flinched.

Well, everyone but Will. His expression didn't change. Zoey took a moment to gather herself.

"I . . . don't like what this life is doing to me. And my worst fear is that I'll start to like it. That I'll follow your advice and become the kind of person, the kind of *thing*, that thrives in this world. The kind of person who'll steal the organs of the poor to buy a boat. The kind of person my father was."

"Every time things get hard, you retreat right back to this place. Thinking of Arthur as this monster, ignoring all of the lessons you've learned. Everything you've learned about what power really means."

"And by lessons, you mean a pile of words to make victims sound like customers."

Wu said, "Perhaps you could have this argument at another time?

We need to establish a decoy transport that will appear to have Zoey in it, then we can—"

Will ignored him. "If you want to walk away, walk away. I'm done trying to talk you out of it."

"Oh, and if you think I'm putting you in charge, think again. I'm giving the money away."

"What does that even mean? You're still picturing your wealth like it's a pile of gold coins in your vault. It's not. It's a machine. You pay five thousand employees just to run your rental properties. Cleaners, maintenance, security. So you want to close it all down, fire all of them? Split up the cash and give it to the homeless in this big one-time payment that they'll spend within a month on drugs and booze? And then what?"

Budd, also trying to cut off the argument, said, "Kowalski's trying to get ahold of the guy who was watching your mother. Things are chaotic at the moment, the parade has started."

Will remained focused on Zoey. "And what becomes of the properties? They get snapped up by one of the million developers in this country looking to swoop in here and get a piece of the pie. Landlords who won't keep the tenants safe or the buildings warm. All of those people you fired, they'll wind up with a boss who'll treat them worse or they'll wind up on the street, get deported. How many of your workers are Mexican, Haitian, Filipino? How many of your women are Korean, Chinese . . . you want to see them get sent back? Every part of your machine will wind up under the control of men who don't know what a crisis of conscience even is. If you give up the money, you give up the power to make change."

"So you're saying I keep my power, but try to use it for good, to shape the world the way I see fit. In other words, the *exact* thing Arthur believed."

Echo said, "There are two helicopters right above us—"

Will cut her off. "Being against power is easy, Zoey, because you never, ever need to offer solutions or take risks. Exercising power in the right way is what's hard. This system favors psychopaths in the same way that basketball favors the tall. But Arthur's last act was to put his machine under the control of someone he thought could be better."

"Me."

"No. A fantasy version of you he'd created in his mind. He didn't know you. And you want to be better than him but you refuse to take a hard look at what being better actually means. If it means sick people die on the transplant waiting list because the government says it's illegal to let them buy organs, that's not being better, that's just not wanting to get your hands dirty."

"Meanwhile, I can't leave my house without getting torn apart by a city that hates me and, as I just found out, *has every reason to*. That whole time we were looking for Stench Machine, I had this nagging voice in the back of my head saying 'You deserve this.' I'm a part of the problem. So I guess that's two people who were right about this whole thing. My mom, and Titus Chobb."

Wu slapped the counter with his palm and said, "*I will put an end to this argument with force,* if I have to."

Echo said, "Our position is now being tracked from those helicopters. They know we're in here."

"All I ask," said Will, quietly, "is that before you run away, you watch the video from a month ago, from the night of the hostage standoff."

"None of that was on video."

"Not the stuff with you and Tilley, I'm talking about the videos from the scene outside the building."

"Why would I want to—"

"I heard from Kowalski," Budd interrupted, loudly. "And he, ah, says his people lost track of your mother. Hours ago. Blink search of her face turns up nothing, but of course it would if she'd put on a spontaneous costume at some point."

More to reassure herself than anything, Zoey said, "I've learned my lesson from the Stench Machine affair. We're obviously not going to assume an abduction this time."

Echo said, "We can track your mother's phone, if by some miracle she has it on."

Budd said, "Already doing that." He stared at his screen for a moment, perplexed. "Huh."

"Oh god," said Zoey. "What?"

"She appears to be, uh, *in* the parade."

"What does that mean?"

"Her phone is located inside one of the floats."

36

All told, about a hundred floats and balloons and several thousand performers would snake their way around the city over the course of the next three hours or so. More than a million people had crowded around the parade route the previous year, maybe twice that many had been expected this year. The city, and its reputation among tourists, was growing exponentially. If you took a trip to Tabula Ra$a, everyone knew, it was guaranteed you'd come back with a story to tell. There was no tourism board to advertise the fact. Blink did the advertising for them.

Over the summer, Zoey had been crushed to find out that her company would not in fact have a float in the Black Parade. Attending the event sounded like hell, but designing a truly mischievous float sounded like a blast. It turned out the parade organizers had banned Arthur Livingston from the event three years ago, after he'd rigged his float with an enormous catapult to fling whimsical projectiles at, and in some cases destroy, other floats along the route. The best Zoey's team had been able to do was convince the organizers to allow her back in next year, if all went well.

It wouldn't be a minor project. The average float in the Tabula Ra$a Devil's Night Black Parade was wide enough to occupy the entire street and as tall as many of the buildings it would pass. There was bitter competition between float makers—creative teams sponsored by local businesses and plutocrats—and they kept trying to top each other. Zoey was told that last year, one float was around two hundred feet tall, a massive mechanical Grim Reaper that seemed to float along the route. In its bony fist was a headless corpse dressed as a police officer, referencing a real event that had happened months earlier when a policeman was beheaded and hung from an overpass. That incident and its aftermath (including the revelation that higher-ups had been bribed to destroy evidence) had caused hundreds of officers to walk off the job, their positions never to be filled. That was how the Black Parade worked: the floats depicted in graphic, often cartoonishly exaggerated detail some horror from the dark underbelly of the city. A chance, organizers had always said, for Tabula Ra$a to confront and exorcise its demons.

And now, apparently, Zoey's mother was a participant. Somehow.

Echo was saying, "VOP ground units have now been dispersed along the parade route. Every outgoing surface street is being monitored."

Zoey only half-heard her. If she were still the type to become hysterical about her mother's safety, which she of course wasn't because she had resolved not to be, but if she was, she'd easily be able to put together a nightmare scenario in her mind. Chobb's thugs would have known Zoey's mother would be at the parade, would have been watching her, would be ready at a moment's notice to snatch her if they decided they needed leverage. Once they had done that, one of the creative, sadistic minds in Chobb's employ could have their way with her, and displayed her body in one of the horror-themed floats.

Will, once again seemingly reading her thoughts, said, "By far the most likely scenario is that Chobb's people picked up your mother and tossed her phone onto one of the passing floats, just so we'd have to chase it down while they moved her to another location."

Andre said, "Isn't it just as likely that some dude up on one of the floats spotted her in the crowd and invited her up there? They do that all the time, she's probably giggling and dancing with a guy in a Will costume."

"We just need to find a feed with the float in view," said Echo. "Here . . . oh. Uh . . . well . . ."

Zoey leaned over. "What?"

It was a drone's view of the parade, tracking a particular float that it turned out was actually very easy to spot. The float in question was a huge ball of flame, fifteen stories at least. The flames didn't look holographic—Zoey wasn't sure how they'd achieved the effect without the thing actually being on fire.

"It's supposed to represent the Goldstone fire. The float is about four blocks that way," she pointed. "Can already see the glow—look."

Zoey started to picture her mother tied to that float, burning to death. She squished the thought before it could fully form. No. She wasn't doing this. Fear was interest paid on money you didn't even owe. She tried to remember where she'd heard that. Oh, right. It was on a framed poster Arthur had kept in the conference room. She'd thrown it away when they redecorated.

Zoey heard a text chime on her phone. She held her breath, and looked.

Hovering above the screen was a message from her mother. Or rather, from her mother's phone. Two words:

COME ALONE

Zoey held up the phone, but didn't say a word.

Will barely skipped a beat. "All right. We've always known this was a possibility. Here's where we wish we had Marti to use as a trading chip, but—"

"Shut up, Will."

"Zoey. We've been through this situation before. This is a move we knew was out there for Chobb to make. He's made it. Now we make ours. This is exactly what you asked me to prepare for—"

"You think you're some kind of expert at reading people. But I'm telling you, buddy, you are *not* reading me right now."

Zoey looked out of the one-way glass bubble, at the crowd. All the giggling people, the dumb costumes. She tried to think of the last time she went somewhere and just enjoyed herself, drinking with real friends who made her laugh until she couldn't breathe. She couldn't even remember.

She met Will's impatient eyes and said, "I've got to say, it's a miraculous system you've built here. At one end you have an unthinkable act of evil, then the guilt for it gets chopped up and dispersed so that it comes out the other end as a cool breeze."

It was only now that Zoey remembered she had been holding this entire heated discussion while wearing the stupid Bonnie the Bonobo monkey mask. She pulled it off and blew hair out of her face.

She said, "Everyone, get yourselves to safety. Wu, you, too."

Zoey pulled up her phone and typed a response to the text:

I'LL BE THERE

Echo said, "You're not going alone. I don't care what you say. We stop, I'm getting off, too."

"Why? Because you care about me? If you do, then listen. You people remind me to listen to *you* ten times a day, are you capable of doing it? Any of you? I have to do this because this is what Arthur would never have done. I'm going down there alone and I'm ordering you to use that distraction to get yourselves to safety. Take this cat with you. Wu, you're relieved of duty. If I survive, I'll leave you a good review."

Zoey reached inside her costume, found a band in her pants pocket, and tied back her hair.

"Now, does somebody have a weapon I can borrow?"

Echo said, "I have something better."

37

Zoey couldn't help but notice that their operation was getting less sophisticated by the minute. A mission that began with an invisible helicopter, a giant robot, and Hollywood-quality wound makeup ended with Zoey alone, on foot, in a smelly rented costume of a bikini-wearing monkey. She was pushing through the crowd along the sidewalk heading back toward the oncoming parade, occasionally glancing up at the lights of at least two helicopters that were circling up there. She was using her phone to track the location of her mother's and it was, in fact, still creeping toward her at parade-speed.

Zoey reached the first float a few minutes later, out of breath and sweating in her stupid costume. She kept moving, largely ignoring the parade as it passed. She was vaguely aware of the crowd hooting and whistling when a particularly bawdy float or balloon went by, or groaning and jeering at one built around some intentionally terrible joke or bad pun. She heard everyone burst out laughing at one point and looked up to see a rolling fifty-foot-tall animatronic statue of the president sporting a grossly exaggerated stainless-steel penis. There'd been a rumor that he'd come to Tabula Ra$a to get an implant to combat erectile dysfunction. Behind and above him was one of the massive balloons, this one shaped like a crashing airliner, rigged to belch real black smoke behind it and to broadcast the screams of doomed passengers inside. The next float was a platform of actors on a set made up to look like a restaurant kitchen, one man in a bloody chef's costume feeding a pile of stuffed dogs into a sausage grinder, each crank of the wheel spurting "blood" out onto the crowd as it passed. Zoey had no idea what scandal that was referencing, you couldn't stay on top of them all.

The pulses of firelight were now just a couple of blocks down and it absolutely appeared to be an office building fully engulfed in roiling flames, somehow crawling down the street with the rest of the parade. Already Zoey could hear faint roars from the crowd where it passed. It was a stunning sight, and gave the impression that a strong breeze would cause the whole rolling inferno to tip over onto the crowd. A really good parade, Zoey thought, is one that can accidentally kill you at any moment.

She jogged a little faster. It was a cool night but the costume was stifling, her hot breath steaming her head inside the mask. No horror scenarios of what she would find ahead flashed through her mind. She was too exhausted for that. Plus, it would trigger all sorts of related thoughts she was not equipped to process right now, like the fact that she had spent hours tracking down a lost cat who wasn't even missing, while her actual mother may have been the one who was—

Nope. Enough of that. Until she knew what happened, nothing had happened. She had to be ready for whatever, or whoever, was waiting up there.

She could hear guitar music overhead now; a live band was playing on a stage thirty feet above the street, the platform held aloft by cables and balloons overhead. People in the crowd were throwing bottles at them as they passed, trying to knock them off.

And now, here was the burning float that contained her mother. Or her mother's phone. Or something.

The flames were definitely real, Zoey could feel the heat from where she was on the sidewalk. It was, as Echo had said, commemorating/mocking the infamous Goldstone building fire. That had been an office building in town holding several brokerage firms and other such businesses. When the blaze started, the alarm system and sprinklers both failed, or had never worked at all. Twenty-six people died, supposedly because the staff of one firm feared their boss so much that they stayed rooted at their desks even as smoke slowly filled the room. That boss had apparently told them they would all lose their jobs unless a certain report was finished by the end of the business day and without an alarm to give the order to evacuate, they just kept working. That was the story, anyway. The boss, who very much evacuated at the first sign of smoke, refused to speak of it in public.

The rolling re-creation of the building had no exterior walls, so that the burning victims inside were in full view. On each floor of the float were two rows of cubicles, each cubicle featuring a life-sized figure in a suit and tie working away at a computer. Everything was in flames— the desks, the chairs, the workers themselves. Fire rippled over their bodies, licking across faces that remained obliviously locked in concentration over some spreadsheet or other. Zoey figured they had to be extremely detailed animatronic dummies, ones designed so that the flesh would still cook and peel in an incredibly realistic manner . . .

Zoey studied the burning office inhabitants to see if there was anything that stood out. Not to see if any of them were her mother, of course, like if they had strapped her to a chair alongside the flammable dummies and set her on fire, her skin turning black while she screamed and the crowd cheered, because Zoey was past that, past imagining terrible things happening to her loved ones.

The tracking implied the phone was close, somewhere around that first level of the float. For all she knew, the phone was just lying up there, slowly getting melted. She needed a closer look, somehow. Well, the costume covered every inch of her body. It'd protect her enough to get up close, right? For just a few seconds? Long enough to see if any of the roasting human figures were . . .

Part of Zoey's brain was still trying to run the numbers on that plan while another part was already making her feet go. That damned hand cream.

She climbed over the barrier that had been set up along the sidewalk, then ran around to the front of the float and jumped onto its bumper. She'd had some idea that because these were decorative special-effects pyrotechnics that they somehow wouldn't be quite as hot as the flames you'd get in, say, an actual office fire. She now wasn't sure that was the case, absolutely feeling like she was being cooked alive in her ridiculous costume. She could faintly hear people yelling and gasping from the crowd. To them, this float had just gotten about 50 percent more entertaining. *Look, everyone! A drunk person could die!*

In front of her, the two rows of flaming cubicles on the first floor were separated by a walkway, just as they would be in an actual office. There was a gap in the flames wide enough for a person to dash through if they were wearing good protective gear or were very stupid.

She squinted against the flames and tried to study the burning figures, to see if any of them were . . . not animatronic. The ones nearest seemed to be performing the same looping mechanical movements, their flaming hands comically tapping keyboards and shuffling burning papers, everything made of some kind of material that was never fully consumed by the blaze. She couldn't see much beyond those first couple.

She heard someone shouting commands from the street behind her. A lone VOP security guard, jogging her way. Not because she was an organized crime queen with a bounty on her head, but because she was a presumably drunk idiot in a monkey costume climbing on a giant, rolling inferno. She heard a few hip people in the crowd yelling, "Bonnie! Where's Raja?"

The guard reached out for Zoey's leg and she pulled herself into the fire.

The air was instantly sucked from her lungs. Heat squeezed around her like a fist. What was she *doing*? She tried to shield her face with her arm. She ran forward, between the cubicles. The crowd was going insane, cheering like they were watching a daredevil jump a ravine in a motorcycle. Zoey tried to get a good look at each burning figure as she passed but the flames lashed out at her, flashing into her eyes, cooking her skin, *whooshing* and roaring around her like snarling de-mons. This was stupid, so stupid.

She rushed past the cubicles, sure these were just mannequins. This was all a stupid trap and she'd fallen for it. She reached the rear end of the float and jumped off, quickly trying to look around at herself to see if the costume was on fire.

It was. She felt it.

Zoey had to pull the zipper down the back. There were flames back there and she badly scorched her hand, even through the furry gloves. She was only able to yank the zipper down about halfway, but it was enough to get her shoulders out and shove the smoking suit of fur down to her feet.

She still had the mask on, so she was now just a woman in jeans, a sweat-matted HOW ABOUT I SLAP YOUR SHIT T-shirt, and a smol-dering monkey head. Would the cameras detect her identity judging from the neck down? They probably could map out her arm cellulite or something. Who cares, at this point?

The fiery float had pulled away from her and Zoey turned to see the back of it, to take one last look. There was a sign on the rear po-sitioned so it would flash to the crowd as a punchline, and in burning text it said, PROUDLY MAINTAINED BY ASHE CONSTRUCTION!

Zoey froze.

That . . . wasn't right, was it?

It's not like parade floats are held to some kind of journalistic stan-dards. Someone would have told her if that building had been her father's, that he was possibly to blame for its failing fire protection system and that, by extension, *she* was to blame for not fixing it.

While she stared, Zoey was swallowed up by a flock of dancers and a rapper who was freestyling insults to random people he found in the crowd. Zoey tried to step out of their way, then pulled out her phone and looked at the tracking info for her mother again . . .

It no longer showed she was in the fire float. She—or the phone—was ahead of Zoey now, moving down the parade. They were toying with her, she knew. She considered going back, finding the Suits, calling it all off. Then the VOP guy came around the fire float, yelling commands at her.

Zoey ran through the dancers, vaguely aware that the rapper was now also berating her. ("Get out the parade, Bonnie, you gonna get run over for real / these floats don't float, bitch, that shit's on wheels. Also can we get a round of applause for Bonnie's titties?")

Zoey looked back at her pursuer in time to see the yellow jacket get "accidentally" tripped by one of the dancers, who did an impressive job of managing to make it look like part of the choreography. Zoey ran, making her way back down the parade, having seen no sign whatsoever of her mother or her mother's phone or anything else. She ran around the next float. A quick glance to the side revealed it to be several actors in yellow VOP jackets comically brutalizing a young man who had stolen a loaf of bread, the victim on the ground yelling, "I told y'all, I paid for it! I got the receipt right here! Ow! Ow!"

Then she was moving through a group of marchers in Rasta costumes, or actual Rastas, one or the other. There were several huge Jamaican flags and they were towing the cables of a balloon shaped like an enormous joint, a mechanism spraying smoke down at the crowd from the lit end. If it wasn't weed smoke, it sure as hell smelled like it.

Her phone showed her target was still up ahead, somewhere.

Zoey passed some clowns who were tossing out little bags of pills like they were candy, then a group of strippers wearing little-girl dresses and holding oversized lollipops. Zoey tried not to think about that and jumped onto the front of the next float, her phone insisting her target was right there with her. Zoey saw the scene they had staged and sucked in a breath.

On one hand, this float seemed like it had been hastily put together, lacking the production value of the others. Many of the floats were the result of professional teams working sometimes years in advance, but this one featured only a clean white "room" (a floor and few pieces of furniture) and in the middle was a banquet table.

Lying on it was a man who was vaguely intended to look like Dexter Tilley. Same buzz cut, some crudely applied acne, drawn-on stitches in the appropriate spots. On his abdomen was piled loops of sausage and other meat parts they'd thrown on to suggest he'd been gutted, fake blood splattered over everything, running off the sides of the table and onto the floor. The man playing Tilley screamed for help, improvising lines about how he was being eaten, begging for death.

At the head of the table, sitting in front of a plate full of bloody guts, shirt and face smeared with red, was a person in a costume who was clearly supposed to be . . . Titus Chobb.

It wasn't like it was hard to get the costume together, all the guy had to do was shave the sides of his head, add some gray hair coloring, and put on a wrinkled work shirt and khakis. The fake Chobb stood up from his seat and turned to show the crowd a comically exaggerated erection in his pants. He shouted, "Look, I'm getting my youth back already!"

That's how quickly Budd's rumor had spread. This float would have already been in the staging area when the talk began to radiate outward from Budd's contacts. The ambitious designers of this one apparently tore down the original idea they'd worked on for who knows how long and threw together this scene with what they could get their hands on at the last minute, figuring that being on the cutting edge of a scandal would trump production value. From the reaction of the crowd—stunned into silence, with only the drunkest of them daring to laugh—they'd done it. They'd managed to actually cross a boundary.

The only other player on the set was a muscular guy they'd found to play Dirk Vikerness, who stood humorlessly behind "Chobb," staring Zoey down. They hadn't been able to find the armor, he was just in a tank top and black leather pants with a ridiculous glowing yellow codpiece. But they at least did get the stupid snake beard right. They'd even added an eye patch, as apparently word of him having died via scissors to the skull had hit the streets.

Zoey glanced down at her phone and saw her mother's signal crawl her way at the same moment the eye-patched muscle man was walking toward her, reaching out, grabbing her.

The guy on the table lifted his head and said, "Hey, that's Dirk Vikerness!"

By the time Zoey realized the same, she was flying through the air.

38

Zoey blinked. She had lost consciousness. She found herself lying in a pile of something somewhat soft but scratchy and for the moment, couldn't remember how she got there. She was staring up at the stars, the sounds of a parade all around her. She was in unbelievable pain.

Ah, now she remembered.

Dirk Vikerness, who it turned out was absolutely alive, had grabbed her by the neck, picked her up, and thrown her like it was an Olympic event. Zoey sat up on her elbows and found she was sitting in a huge pile of fake money. She had landed on the next float down from the Chobb cannibalism scene—if she'd missed and landed on the pavement, she'd likely have split her head open (she didn't know if this meant Vikerness had failed or succeeded with his throw). She sat up fully and realized that, in fact, she had landed just seconds ago—everyone nearby was staring, trying to comprehend what in the hell had just happened.

She made eye contact with a mostly naked Asian woman and said, "Hi."

Zoey tried to get to her feet in the waist-deep cash pool and immediately stumbled. She didn't seem to have use of her left arm or right leg and the back of her neck was wet with what she was pretty sure was blood. She'd banged it off of the edge, or something, when she landed. The Bonobo mask had fallen off at some point.

She heard a commotion from street level and knew that Vikerness was coming, would hop up here with her within seconds. She trudged through the drifts of fake money and looked back, for the first time registering the float she was on.

It was decorated to be an amazingly lavish bathroom, more ostentatious than anything in her estate, or anything she'd ever install there. Zoey had landed in a giant golden hot tub that could probably accommodate twenty people, full of bundled cash instead of water. Across from Zoey was a naked animatronic sex doll with a Zoey Ashe black-and-blue wig. It was mechanically grabbing handfuls of the cash and "washing" with it, rubbing it around its chest and neck. Standing around the tub were four female slaves, all in filthy rags that barely covered their privates, in ankle and neck shackles. They were actual women and had been fanning "Zoey" and acting like they were feeding her grapes.

She didn't need the backstory explained for this one. She suspected the parade spectators didn't, either.

Arthur Livingston, Zoey's father, had for years trafficked women from all over the world. He gave them safe passage to the USA in exchange for their services, sex work jobs they agreed to only in the sense that the alternative was starving in a refugee camp back home. Many of those women were still in Zoey's employ, because when Zoey had demanded they be freed, Will carefully explained that these women were not prisoners, that they had no other skills and would simply be snapped up by one of the city's other brothels or, worse, street pimps. Their new bosses would likely be men, likely be less generous with the pay, likely make less effort to keep them safe. They had nowhere else to go.

Zoey had told Will that she'd only agree on the condition that they were given time and money to get trained in something else, to do sales or coding or . . . something. He'd explained that they already had those programs, that Arthur had said the same toward the end of his life, but few took advantage due to language barriers, or the burden of childcare, or just not seeing the point in training for something that ultimately would pay less money. Words on top of words, the mortar keeping the bricks of the status quo locked into place. And, eventually, Zoey just dropped the issue. The same as her father had.

She yelled to the four slave girls, who were presumably just local actresses or models, "RUN! Get off the float!"

Zoey tried to do this herself, but there was Dirk Vikerness now, climbing onto the float with them. The girls just stared.

Zoey saw his bare shoulders . . . and there were the surgery scars. When he was rushed away to get help for his stabbed eyeball, he'd apparently decided to get an upgrade while he was in the shop.

Zoey grabbed her necklace and said, "Stop!"

He did not stop. Somehow, she knew he wouldn't. Still, she tried a string of similar words. No effect.

The giant man stepped forward and then, projecting his voice for the crowd, said to Zoey, "When you die, this city will throw a party. And I think you know it."

"Is my mother safe?"

He ignored this question, as Zoey had suspected he would. She was still standing in the tub of money, and actually wasn't totally sure she could lift her dead leg up over the lip. She was trying to stand in a way that would not reveal to him that at least two of her limbs now didn't work.

"As you can see," he said, in a tone that suggested a rehearsed line, "I have come back from the grave, stronger than before. When you see your father, thank him for bringing his invention into the world."

Dirk Vikerness lifted up his eye patch, and Zoey was sure that what she would find there was some kind of laser or plasma pulse thing embedded in the eye socket, something that would fire a beam and incinerate her.

"GO! GET OFF HERE!" she yelled to the four servant girls.

This time they listened, though they still didn't seem to grasp the severity of the situation. Everyone seemed to suspect this might still be part of the performance. They pulled free of their prop manacles and jumped ship.

Zoey tried to climb over the lip of the tub, struggling to lift her uncooperative leg. She found herself staring at the rows of spectators as they passed. To the tourists, this all must have looked like some kind of highly experimental theater.

Dirk Vikerness put his hands on his hips and Zoey tried to prepare herself to dive away from whatever flashed out of the man's replacement eye. Instead, his yellow codpiece opened. Out from it flew a length of thin chain, which ended in a wicked bloom of sharp spikes. The chain curled up into the air like a whip and then whooshed down in a blur, making impact right in the center of the tub.

There was a crash of blue energy and a shockwave that split the float in half, spraying a cloud of fake money and animatronic Zoey limbs in every direction. Zoey tumbled over the lip of the tub, then fell off of the float entirely. The float itself skidded to a stop, the axels shattered from the impact of Dirk Vikerness's electrified crotch whip. The crowd went wild, now certain this was part of the act. This kind of thing didn't *actually* happen to people, right?

Zoey landed hard on the pavement and struggled to suck in air. The wind had been knocked out of her. She tried to get up, and found she could not. Her limbs physically wouldn't respond to her commands, but also . . . she just couldn't. There was no energy inside her. Battery Discharge Error.

She lay there, looking up at the sky.

Someone in the crowd said, "Hey, I think that's her!"

Oh, well, it wasn't really a stealth mission anymore. Or any kind of mission.

"Yep, it's me," she muttered to herself. "Are you enjoying the parade?"

She knew Vikerness was coming. She knew he could splatter her like a beetle. And still she lay there, listening to the rumbling crowd, staring up at the stars, funny money wafting down like a ticker-tape parade.

And in that moment, she gave up.

39

The giant man with his absurd snake-beard came into view. Apparently the codpiece was not made to actually retract the crotch whip after use, as the chain was now dragging uselessly behind him, scraping along the pavement as he walked.

He loomed over Zoey and said, "They're not coming, by the way. Your people. If you were expecting them to show up at the last minute, you should know they're being pursued in the other direction."

"Sure. Hey, uh, I'm not gonna lie, I can't stand up."

He kneeled down over her. "Like a statue that has been toppled."

"Dude, I just want to know if my mother is okay."

He drew a knife.

"The challenge of our age," he said, "is pulling this lost generation of men out of the fake wars you've given them to fight and convincing them to fight the real ones. You know they're still celebrating killing your avatar? We will wake them up, one at a time. We are the children you sacrificed to your god, come back to have our vengeance."

"I want you to know that while you're making this speech, all I'm hearing is a series of fart noises coming out of your mouth."

He smirked and wrapped a rough hand around Zoey's chin. Holding her head still.

He brought the knife down and said, "First, an eye for an eye."

When Zoey realized what he meant to do, the fight-or-flight

mechanism in her brain finally kicked in and she found enough strength to get her hands up, to try to push him away, to grab at his face. Even without implants, he could have overpowered her without straining himself. Her thrashing around only added to his amusement.

A blade was moving steadily toward her right eye.

Then there was a sickening thud, and Dirk Vikerness's head bounced forward.

He just stared for a brief moment. Then blood dripped down onto Zoey's face. He reached back and felt his head, pulled away red fingers—

Another thud, then he slumped over on top of her. His body was twitching.

Someone was rolling the huge man off of her now. It was a very large, very drunk-looking woman probably in her fifties. Zoey didn't recognize her costume—she was dressed in a tank top and suspenders with filthy jeans, a bandanna around her neck. She had a sledgehammer in each hand. They were apparently not plastic props, as one was now matted with blood and hair.

She nudged Dirk Vikerness with her foot and said, "Did I kill 'im?" She then looked at Zoey. "What's goin' on here?"

Other people were crowding around now. They didn't seem to know what was happening, either. She heard one of them mutter her name.

Zoey said, "Get away from him!"

She scooted away from Vikerness, pushing backward on the pavement with her one working leg. He groaned and got up on hands and knees, blood streaking down his face. Grunting, growling. He raised a hand toward her. Zoey thought he was going to get up and grab a utility pole and smash her like he was swatting a fly, or unleash a bolt of lightning from his fist.

Instead, he hissed to the crowd around him, "You idiots, *that* is Zoey Ashe!"

He climbed to his feet and snatched his knife off the pavement, the blood running crimson zebra stripes across his face. He took a step toward Zoey—

He was tackled from behind. The woman with the hammers. He dropped the blade and another woman ran in and grabbed it.

"I've got his knife!"

Vikerness stood upright, the huge woman now clinging to him, the bloody man wearing her like a backpack.

"GET OFF ME!"

Someone from the crowd flew in and dove at his knees. Dirk went down. Someone else tried to get him in a headlock. People swarming in, strangers in costumes trying to gang-tackle the huge man like a fullback.

Vikerness snarled and flung everyone aside. One went flying, slamming into a storefront wall and going limp. This only inflamed the crowd. They closed in again, screaming curses at the enraged, bloody man. The big woman found one of her costume hammers on the sidewalk and smacked Dirk Vikerness in the back, and he fell to his hands and knees once more.

Then the woman who'd picked up the knife came running up, shouting, "He's got those implant things! I know how to disable it!"

She started wildly stabbing Dirk Vikerness in the ass.

This did not dislodge the Raiden capacitor, but it definitely got the man's attention. He spun on the woman and snatched her throat. The big woman with the hammer stepped up, screamed, and swung.

The impact of the hammer on Dirk Vikerness's skull was a sound Zoey was pretty sure she'd never forget. The huge man flopped to the ground like a sack of meat. Then the woman screamed and hit him again. And again. Finally she stood over him, huge chest heaving. The gang who'd felled the giant gathered around, stunned at the turn their night had taken.

The big woman said, "*Now* is he dead? If not I'll hit 'im with somethin' bigger."

She turned to Zoey, who'd never gotten up off the sidewalk.

"You all right, dear?"

"Yeah."

"You know this turd?"

"Sort of. This is Titus Chobb's right-hand man."

"I don't know who that is."

"Rich guy, employs a lot of people with guns. He was the guy in the float back there—it doesn't matter."

Others were tending to the person who'd gotten flung into the wall—a young guy, who was sitting up but with a blank expression. A girl yelled for an ambulance. Work crews were rapidly trying to figure out how to get the shattered float out of the way so that the parade could continue. Nothing stops the party in Tabula Ra$a.

The large woman, who Zoey decided was probably not a medical professional by day because she didn't seem to know the rule for not moving injured people, yanked Zoey to her feet like she was righting a knocked-over garden gnome. Zoey held on for support for a moment but found she could stand, sort of. Her left arm still didn't work. Several women, friends of the hammer lady, were trying to talk to her.

"Are you okay? Oh my god is that guy dead? Jenny, look at his scars. Are you okay? You've got blood on the back of your shirt, did you hit your head? I think there's an ambulance coming. Are you o—"

"Yeah, I'm okay, I think. Who, uh, are you people?"

"I'm Dani," said one of them, "that's Jenny, that's Shonda." The last one was the hammer lady.

"Hi. I'm, uh—"

"You're Zoey! Obviously."

A bystander said, "Who?"

Shonda said, "Oh, she's the one who got them to run the buses out to my trailer park. She's the only reason I can work in the city. And if you've ever used one of them free clinics, thank this girl right here."

"Oh. Thank you," said Zoey. "All that was . . . the very least we could do."

Zoey looked around, nervously. Her life had been saved because she had apparently gotten attacked in front of the only handful of people in this city who actually liked her.

"In fact," Zoey said, "I, uh, need to get out of here before the less-friendly people in the crowd find me."

ZOEY PUNCHES THE FUTURE IN THE DICK 305

On cue, Zoey heard someone pushing through the gathering behind her. She turned and braced herself, very aware that even a small child could knock her over in her current state.

Several teenage girls popped out. They were bouncing with excitement.

"Zoey! Zoey! Oh my god, we watched it all. Are you okay? Can we get a picture? Real quick?"

On one hand, this seemed like a less lethal threat than she was anticipating. On the other, she was having primal high school flashbacks. The girl who was asking was wearing tights with cat ears and a tail. Zoey got a homecoming queen vibe from her and wondered who exactly she wanted to show the picture to.

Zoey said, "Do what you want, but I'm not going to do anything to entertain you. The blood on my face isn't mine, if that's what you were hoping for."

The girl's face fell. "Oh. I'm . . . oh god, I'm sorry, I wasn't trying to be rude. I'm a fan, if this is a bad time . . . I'm sorry. I just wanted to say thank you."

"Oh. No, don't be sorry. I was—I just got attacked by a guy who launched a thing from his crotch. I assumed you were being sarcastic, I don't think I have fans."

"Seriously? You went in and talked down that guy who was holding that girl hostage? I named my cat Zoey."

Another of the teens, this one dressed as a nurse who's about to get fired for violating the dress code, said, "You want a drink? There's a vendor right over there."

"No, I've got a thing, I have to, uh, meet my mother somewhere. Hopefully. Oh, you guys are already taking the picture—should I wipe off my face?"

"Nah, the blood is badass. Smile!"

The cat girl and the inappropriate nurse squeezed on either side of her and a pink buzzing gadfly dropped in and snapped the pic of all three.

A third woman dressed as a futuristic schoolgirl in a glowing pink wig, who Zoey eventually noticed was dressed as Naoko from *My Hero Reo*, said, "Can I have a hug, or is that weird?"

And so Zoey hugged her and then she was hugging everyone and the whole time she could hear people nearby talking about what to do with the apparently dead guy whose brains were splattered all over the pavement. The destroyed Zoey Bath float was now being dragged slowly down the street by a pair of trucks, someone having decided to just make the shattered wreckage part of the parade. The crowd gasped as a gigantic Cthulhu balloon passed overhead, the tentacles on its face rigged to reach down and snatch at the crowd as it passed. People shrieked and laughed.

Zoey tried to pry herself away from her fans and largely failed, then two serious-looking men in suits showed up. Large men, not brandishing weapons, because they didn't have to. Behind them was a wall of yellow jackets, a whole swarm. Why hadn't they intervened a moment ago? Maybe they were all hoping Dirk Vikerness's demise would mean a spot had opened up for a promotion.

Shonda asked, "Who are these guys?"

"It's fine, I was expecting them. Thank you. Really."

One of the suited men said, "Ms. Ashe, we'd like to take you to your mother."

"Where is she?"

The other man silently pointed up and behind Zoey, to the top of Freya's Palace in the distance. Titus Chobb's stupid black blimp was parked up there, visible only as an oval void in the stars.

"I'll go, but you have to agree not to do anything to these people. They stopped that monster from killing me, that's all. If you want to blame somebody for Dirk's death, other than Dirk himself, then blame me."

"Mr. Vikerness was not an employee at the time of his demise and his death is not our jurisdiction. This way."

"You'll have to help me walk."

40

Zoey wound up in the back of an unmarked sedan. This made for an incredibly awkward silent car ride with her captors and, as she always did in such situations, she distracted herself with her phone.

She tuned in to Charlie Chopra, who was doing a broadcast from the scene of Dirk Vikerness's crotch assault on the Black Parade and his subsequent death by hammer. He was interviewing Shonda while, in the background, Kowalski was processing Vikerness's huge, muscular corpse, now covered with a sheet. Kowalski was carrying a tiny bloody object in a clear plastic evidence bag, presumably the capacitor someone had cut out of Vikerness's body.

Still, Zoey stared hard at the corpse, expecting the man to spring to life and start smashing everything into oblivion. She watched intently as they loaded him into the back of an ambulance parked on the sidewalk, his face covered, a limp hand flopping sadly out from under the sheet. In he went, the doors closing behind him. He would soon be put into the ground and the worms and bugs would not note that he tasted any better or worse than anyone else.

Zoey turned off the stream, then remembered the strange request Will had made earlier, that she go back and watch the video from the night of her hostage crisis. She'd had no clue at the time what exactly he'd wanted her to see, but now, she had a suspicion . . .

She browsed through archived feeds from the scene a month

ago, looking for shots of the crowds that had gathered to watch the Night Inn fiasco unfold. She started playback around the moment her leopard-print convertible arrived. There was the building with the Godzilla bite taken out; there was the thin yellow line of VOP guards holding back the gawkers.

She zoomed in on the crowd. She spotted some of the individual ringleaders they'd called out in their analysis earlier in the day, and in fact found the scruffy kid who'd led her into the room at the Screw to patch into her meeting (she wondered if that kid had survived the fire). When her leopard-print car pulled up, he and the rest were the first to start mooing and hurling insults. They were right by the spot where she'd parked the car, where they knew she'd hear them. Zoey saw herself get out of the car, hear the taunts, and say something about them to Will. Zoey remembered that she'd wanted to push the crowd back, but on the feed Will was saying something that she'd since forgotten, how he'd wished he could get the hecklers closer to the building.

Zoey turned up the audio, scrolled the video along the crowd by hopping across various feeds, watching every face. She counted. There were no more than twenty people actually yelling horrible things at her in that moment. About that many more stood around them, kind of looking spiteful but not really participating in the rage. Outside of that group she only found people who weren't necessarily *cheering* Zoey, but they were smiling, waving, trying to get her attention. A group five times the size of the trolls. Once she got to the periphery of the crowd, she saw faces that showed no sign of knowing who Zoey was, or why this girl in the table lamp skirt was even relevant to this situation. She accidentally hopped to a feed two blocks away and found only oblivious citizens strolling out of shops or ordering food from vending machines, only vaguely aware that there was a commotion over at the Night Inn and that they should probably steer clear.

In the end, it had just been that little group of yelling guys, so few that you could stuff them all into a single van. That's all it had taken to generate enough noise and ugliness to create the illusion that the entire species was against her. Will had wanted them even closer to Dexter Tilley to reinforce that belief that his people were an over-whelming majority, feeding his illusion of power and Zoey's illusion of powerlessness.

Out of curiosity, she switched the focal point of the feed, calling up all of the feeds that had been pointed at her.

Zoey's lifelong relationship with cameras was tumultuous and toxic. She could, if she was being honest, take a pretty damned good photo under the right circumstances. Looking upward a little, pushing the chest out, making her eyes big, just enough of a smile so as not to show her jacked-up teeth. But seeing her in a candid photo someone else took was like looking in a funhouse mirror, the camera turning her into a cruel mockery of herself. There was the little double chin, the fat rolls, the corpse complexion, the eyeliner that was never, ever drawn exactly the same on both eyes. An unlovable troll that would make guys turn off the bedroom lights so they could pretend she was someone else.

There, on these feeds, was that woman, only also looking scared to the point that she seemed sickly, fragile. It was horrible to see this version of herself and her impulse was to shut it off, look away. But she was also beginning to understand.

There she was, now recoiling from the wreckage of the spider robot, then steadfastly deciding to head into the building to face the mon-ster that had done that damage. Zoey tried to see herself as the crowd would see her, this lumpy, jiggly thing in a dumb outfit, clumsily clam-bering up the food truck, then slowly climbing the ladder, wind whip-ping around her lampshade skirt and showing her fat, polka-dotted butt to the crowd. Totally unequipped to face the threat that had smashed its way into the building but facing it all the same. There was a moment where her left foot slipped on a rung—Zoey didn't even remember that happening—and an almost comical gasp went up from the crowd. Scared that she would fall.

In his careful staging of the scene, Will had turned Zoey into an underdog, someone to root for. An everyday woman just trying to do her best in absurdly awful circumstances.

Once Tilley took her out of the room and away from the view of the cameras, the feeds had shifted to Will. He had immediately gone back down that ladder, actually sliding the last few steps, like he'd had tons of ladder practice in his life. He hit the ground already pointing and barking orders, coordinating with Andre and Kowalski. A team of firefighters dragged the food truck away and, a few minutes later, staff and customers started streaming out of the front entrance to cheers from the crowd. Cameras swarmed in as Will huddled with an armored team of Kowalski's men, chopping the air with one hand to emphasize commands as the men checked their elaborate guns.

Before they ran into the building, he swatted one guy on the shoulder pads and said, "Get her the hell out of there."

It was a clear narrative, and not *totally* inaccurate. Zoey sacrificing her own safety to occupy the superpowered psychopath so that her people could rescue the innocents. All of the important, complicating context that might muddle the story—that Zoey's side had inadvertently supplied that psychopath with his powers, that she profited from the plight of hostage and captor alike—was conveniently invisible to the cameras.

Before she could watch any more, the car rolled to a stop and her door was opened.

41

Freya's Palace hadn't really registered with Zoey the first time she'd passed through it; she'd had other things on her mind at the time. Now, in her state of shambling exhaustion, she decided the building was a modern wonder. The space was all creamy marble and gentle curves that had somehow been engineered to absorb all sound. Walking through the lobby was like stepping outside on a morning coated in fresh snow, a silence like a pair of soft hands over her ears. In the center of the cavernous lobby was the aquarium, a blue pillar that stretched up for five stories, the elevator running up through the center. As they approached it, Zoey could hear gentle trickling fountains. No signs flashed, no announcements played; the space was an oasis in the sensory assault that was downtown Tabula Ra$a. Zoey badly wanted to just lie flat on the floor and rest forever in Freya's peaceful embrace. She was pretty sure she had a concussion.

As Zoey and the two suit-goons rode up past the schools of startled fish, signs for the various spa services gently faded in and out on the screen as they passed their floors. Massage, beauty treatments, that sort of thing. Woman stuff. Then, at some point she happened to notice one of the floors was devoted to Cupid's Eros, the sex therapy company her mother worked for.

Wait.

Did she work out of this location? Why did Zoey not know that? Was that just a weird coincidence?

The elevator reached the glassed-in boarding area on the top floor where the looming black shape above them had swallowed the stars. Zoey stepped on board the Innerer Schweinehund to find Titus Chobb was sitting alone at a table, her mother nowhere to be found. Chobb, however, was hardly alone in the passenger hold—Zoey counted six VOP guards in full bumblebee armor. The two guys in suits were following her in, so that was eight men and those were just the ones she could see. All for little old Zoey.

All she had brought with her was a tiny object no bigger than a shirt button. It was in the front right pocket of her jeans and she actually had no idea if it had survived the altercation at the parade. But it was there, the lone object she'd been given before leaving the mobile vapor pod. She, in the end, had only one target. Nothing else really mattered.

"Please sit," said Chobb, sounding casual. "You don't want to be standing when we take off, the floor shifts rather abruptly. And you don't look like you are very steady on your feet even now."

"Where is my mother?"

"She's here. But we need to have a conversation, just the two of us. No competing voices in our ears to cloud our thoughts. Please, sit."

"What if I don't want to sit? Does anyone ever tell you no?"

"You can stand if you prefer. Just grab onto something."

Actually, she couldn't stand. She shambled over and managed to land her butt in the chair before she collapsed onto the floor. She ran her fingers over her front pocket, felt the tiny lump there. Titus had been eating some kind of dainty little salad prior to her arrival, which annoyed Zoey for several reasons.

He put down his fork and said, "I assume you know my son went public with the story. The details of his transplant, the truth behind Dexter Tilley's demise."

"Good for him. That's the story that could have been told all along. Then none of this would have happened."

"The bounty for your confession was of course lifted as well, by whatever anonymous donor had placed it."

Zoey tried to roll her eyes, but even those muscles were too sore to work properly.

"I want you to know," said Chobb, "that whole campaign against you, the unfortunate use of Mr. Tilley's corpse, that was all Mr. Vikerness, acting on his own. He was trying to solve a problem on the fly, in an extremely misguided way. Within hours of Tilley's disappearance, ugly rumors started to spread. Dirk was tasked with quelling that controversy. Still, I do not defend my former employee's methods, they were extreme and irresponsible."

"Convenient that he took all of that responsibility with him to the grave, leaving none for you."

"I do not absolve myself. However, I feel like you should in turn acknowledge that you took things too far by abducting Martius."

"Well, that of course was all Will Blackwater, acting on his own. Grossly irresponsible. And all of those other words you just used."

The airship jolted and Zoey once again watched the city fall away around her. The waitress emerged. She was now only partially nude, dressed as Eve, wearing a few leaves and a real damned snake that rested on her shoulders. She brought out a pair of delicately plated dishes of what looked like some kind of sliced pork with a side of glazed chunks of something or other. Zoey barely glanced at it.

"I know you haven't had dinner," said Chobb. "I'm told this should be to your liking. My chef, he can work miracles. Any raw material can become perfection in his kitchen."

"So, kidnapping my mother, was that Dirk Vikerness's idea, too? And trying to kill me down there just half an hour ago?"

"We'll discuss your mother in a moment. As for his actions tonight, I assure you that I had not been in contact with Dirk since his injury, out at the storage lockers. And even then, he was largely working on his own. His behavior had, unfortunately, become erratic. He was involved in that radical men's group that I never fully understood but regrettably had associated myself with. I will take responsibility for that as well. Sometimes you align yourself with parties with whom you believe you share a common goal, only to find that all along, you were the tail and they were the dog."

"I'll keep that in mind if I'm ever tempted to align myself with a murder cult in order to further my own selfish ends."

"Yes, surely you will never find yourself in such a situation."

Chobb sliced off a piece of the meat.

"Is that enough discussion for you to bring my mother out?"

"I assume you know that this radical group I speak of is also the reason you're here. Or perhaps you didn't know that? And I don't mean here at this table, but rather here in this city. My association with them goes back some years. I'm not proud of that."

"That's fascinating. See, the thing is, that hate group kind of isn't anything without your cash and backing. So I'd say it's *entirely* your fault."

Only then did it sink in for Zoey what exactly Titus had just said. About how this group, and by extension, Titus Chobb, was responsible for the current state of her life.

"Wait. Did you just confess to killing my father?"

"I will acknowledge that I set the wheels in motion. I provided financial backing and other resources to men I believed could help *contain* your father and his madness." Chobb studied her expression. "How do you feel about that?"

Zoey actually wasn't sure.

"My relationship with my father was . . . complicated."

"All relationships with fathers are."

"Does Will know you were behind that? If so, I'm not sure why you're still alive."

"We'll discuss that in a moment. But I want to say that I have barely known a moment's peace ever since I heard rumors of a grossly irresponsible technology that was only a modest investment away from becoming reality. Your father brought Raiden to life, putting the power to change human evolution in the hands of people who neither understood its implications nor were capable of understanding them. Your father built this city, and for that we are all in his debt. But in the end, he was overtaken by a deranged fantasy. If it had been up to me, none of it would have happened, including his tragic end. He just could not leave well enough alone. Both then and now, I went looking for allies as an act of desperation."

"See, you're trying to sell me on you being this remorseful by-stander in all this. But I know where you came from and I know what you are. You're a butcher. Wait, what am I talking about? A butcher actually gets his hands in the guts, does the work himself. You're the butcher's supervisor or something. I don't know. I'm tired."

"My guards have saved more lives than all of this city's doctors put together. Vanguard of Peace security staff have stopped twenty-three sexual assaults *tonight*. Meanwhile, due to your father's actions, the clock was ticking until the day one of his monstrosities would come and kick in my door. I still have nightmares about it."

"Okay, and twelve hours ago I talked to Megaboss Alonzo, who has nightmares about *your* armed thugs terrorizing his people."

"If my men do that, it's only because they are familiar with Alonzo's reputation. I heard he once ate a human heart."

"Look at you, operating with bad intentions because you assume everyone else is doing the same. It's like every awful person I've ever known works from the same playbook."

"It's just how the world works. In conflict, the side that takes the initiative wins. If you project that conflict is inevitable, the smart thing to do, the *responsible* thing to do, is to move immediately, end it before it begins. The longer you wait, the more both sides prepare and dig in, the worse the devastation will be."

"So you kill people in real life based on horrors that occur in your imagination. Got it."

Chobb shook his head, sighed, and took another bite.

Another man in a suit with a gun stepped out of the bar area—so that made *nine* guards—and said, "An aircraft is moving to intercept us."

"Thank you, Antonio." Chobb seemed unsurprised by the news. To Zoey, he said, "I assume that's Will Blackwater and his team in that aircraft. What is it you think he's going to try to do here?"

"What would you try to do, in his situation?"

"Win."

"And what do you think that looks like?"

"Attempt a violent extraction, even if it means everyone on board this craft is killed in the process, including you. If he negotiates terms, he establishes that taking you hostage is an effective way to extract concessions. He'd just be assuring that it happens again."

"Yeah, I think I remember him saying something about that. But you weren't going to do that to us when we had Marti on board. You weren't going to risk his safety just to look strong."

Chobb gave her a look as if to say, "I wasn't?"

Zoey reached into her pocket and brought out the object. It just looked like a little silver button, like it had fallen off someone's shirt. She kept it between her finger and thumb, under the table.

"So what was the point of luring me up here, then?" she asked.

"My goal is to try to talk some sense into you. Maybe we start by agreeing that we are both here because we failed to contain those we depended on to do certain labors on our behalf." He gestured to the plate. "Please, you must be hungry. If you're worried it's poison, we can trade plates."

Will had a rule about eating in these situations but Zoey was too exhausted to remember what it was. She was pretty sure you were supposed to eat, to show you weren't intimidated and to signal that you were there in peace and good faith. Also, she was starving.

She took a small bite of the braised pork or whatever it was, eating with her right hand while keeping the left under the table, with the button. The meat was, of course, excellent. Werner Wolff's reputation was of a man who could feed you your own shoe and leave you wanting to lick the plate.

Titus watched her. "I heard you're thinking about cashing out. Leaving town."

"What, did my mom tell you that?"

He gestured to the meat. "Do you like it?"

"It's pretty good." She took another bite. "What is it?"

"Surprised you don't recognize it. Based on what I've heard."

"I'm torn on the decision. On one hand, I hate this place because it's full of people like you. On the other hand, leaving means this place then falls into the hands of people like you and for some reason that also bothers me. I'm thinking I need to stay here and keep you in check."

"I see."

Zoey sliced off another bite of the meat. "I'm not going any further with this until you tell me where my mother is."

Titus put down his fork and laced his fingers, resting his elbows on the table.

"I'd seen your mother every day, for months. Did you know that? Though I didn't know that's who she was at the time. There is a cafe, in the lobby of Freya's. I stopped there every morning on the way up to my office. We always wound up in line together. She was outgoing, full of curiosity. Reminded me of Freya."

"She reminded you of . . . the building back there?"

"Freya's Palace was designed, built, and run by my wife, prior to her death. So then there she was, your mother, today at the parade. She came and found me at my spot along the route, came to plead on your behalf. And it all seemed very convenient. Very orchestrated. Like someone knew my weakness and went right for it."

"What did you do to her?"

Zoey put her fork down.

She looked closely at the meat on her plate.

"Zoey, there is a . . . cloud . . . that hangs over me. I can't explain it to you, because you haven't yet been down this road. All I can say is that something will happen in your life that will slice right through it, an inflamed wound separating everything that comes after from all that came before. The end of a career, the loss of a limb, the death of a spouse. And I'm not talking about some breakup in college, before you've even figured out who you are yet. I mean something that will hit you after you've come to believe the world is solid under your feet, thought you knew the shape of your life. It's like if one morning the sun just didn't rise. For me, it was Freya dying of cancer. Not just the death, but the original misdiagnosis, the year of fighting, the periods of false hope, the mistakes I made that may have cost both of us everything. After that day, after that red gash across the timeline, you look at your old photos and see a stranger looking back. Your mind gets pulled in so many directions that it loses its shape, becomes something unrecognizable. Monstrous."

Zoey couldn't speak. The tiny button was being squeezed between her thumb and index finger so tightly she feared she'd shatter it.

"Anyway," continued Chobb, picking up his fork to sever another bite. "Your mother made an impassioned appeal. And I listened. I offered to have her for dinner and she said yes. That's why we're having her for dinner tonight."

Chobb stuffed the hunk of meat into his mouth.

42

Zoey watched the man's jaw work.

In a low voice she said, "Where. Is. She."

Chobb set his fork down on the plate. Chewing. Staring directly at her with an expression that Zoey could not read.

He raised his voice. "Melinda?"

There was some stirring from the bar behind her. Zoey turned in time to see her mother emerge, some kind of colorful cocktail in her hand. Zoey would have stood if she could.

"Mom! Are you hurt?"

"No! You are looking a little rough, though."

Her mother sashayed over. From her walk, Zoey judged her drunkenness level at around a six. She took a seat, but not next to Zoey. She sat next to Chobb.

"I see you're eating," she said breezily. "Are we all friends now? Have you guys resolved your differences? I kept wanting to eat street food, these carts came by selling kati rolls—have you had one of those, they're like Indian burritos—and they smelled soooo good but Titus was like, no way, we're going up in the sky and having my man cook for us!"

Zoey looked at Chobb. "I don't get what's going on here at all, but are we free to leave?"

He said, "Well, it's a long way down if you walk out now."

Her mother laughed and gently slapped Chobb on the shoulder and Zoey felt like she was losing her goddamned mind.

"I don't want to leave yet," said her mother. "I haven't eaten! It's not even two in the morning, there are parties down there that don't even *start* until the parade ends." To Chobb, she said, "Excuse her, she's from a small town. Our stoplights used to start blinking at nine P.M."

"Mom, I love you, but this could all end in a big stupid helicopter battle that turns us into flaming chunks raining from the sky. And the drunk crowd down there will *still* think it's all part of somebody's float."

Her mother was touching Titus Chobb's arm.

Zoey said, "Okay, *what exactly is going on here?*"

"I will admit I was skeptical of her motives," said Chobb. "But I know people. And your mother is a . . . special woman. I've never felt a connection to someone so quickly. An intimacy. Melinda has . . . awakened some things in me. Things I didn't know were dead. I haven't had an evening like this since, well, maybe never."

Zoey stared daggers at her mother. "Mom? What did you do?"

"Now that's none of your business, little lady!"

"Okay," Zoey said, rubbing her temple like she was trying to massage away what she'd just learned. "My people are coming. Titus here thinks it's possible nobody survives that encounter."

"Only if we can't come to an agreement." Chobb raised his voice and said, "Antonio, what is the status of our visitors?"

Antonio poked his head out of the bar and said, "They have been forced to land by two of our air units. They'll be apprehended soon."

Chobb said, "Well, I would say that worked out for everyone."

The mostly naked server brought a third plate, for Zoey's mother. She sniffed the food, then glanced back at the woman and said, "Can you not afford uniforms for your waitresses?" She nudged Chobb playfully with an elbow. "I bet she's cold!"

Chobb looked embarrassed. "The girls work for Chef Wolff, a holdover from before I bought the place, he insisted they stay. He says it's all part of the food's presentation, the 'sensuality of anticipation' or some nonsense."

Zoey said, "Her name is Dasha, she was on his Blink stream. Be sure to leave her a tip, she has assholes for bosses."

Her mother said, "Eat your dinner."

In order to buy her a few seconds to think more than anything, Zoey took a bite of her side dish, which turned out to be some kind of fancy baked apples.

"So," said Zoey, "I will discuss this all with my mother later, *at length*, but the last time I was on the ground, I watched everyone who works for you come flying toward me like a swarm of locusts."

"To retrieve my son, yes."

"And now you have him back safe and sound. Unless that creepy funeral guy sold him for parts."

Chobb didn't reply.

Zoey said, "So here is the situation. Regardless of what your guy just said, you and I both know that at some point in the very near future, probably before we've all finished eating, my people are going to be here. In this room. Somehow, they'll be here. If they are able to get me and my mom out of here alive, what will you do in response?"

"If they are successful at extracting you, it will mean I am dead."

Zoey's mother said *"Titus . . ."* in a tone like she was scolding him for being melodramatic.

"Okay. Let's say your people stop them, then. They never show up. We land, you let me and my mother go. Then what?"

"Then I am also dead. Will Blackwater will come for me. And he will not stop."

"What if I give you my guarantee that I won't let him do that?"

"You just admitted a minute ago that you had no control over him."

"Actually, he did what he did because he thought he was acting in our interests. And he knows he can't come after you without starting a war. You have an army, you have people who'll take up your banner after you're gone, to retaliate."

"And yet, he will do it anyway. If I let you just walk out of here, it will be war. The city will burn. If he takes you by force, it will be war. The city will burn."

"So what in the hell are we supposed to do?"

"Get Blackwater out of the picture."

Zoey's mother said, "I could get behind that! Can you fire him, Z?"

That clearly wasn't what Chobb had in mind.

He said, "I did not bring you here to ask you to"—he shot a side-long glance at Zoey's mother—"terminate him. But if you agree to that course of action, I can, uh, deliver that news myself. Since he's coming to retrieve you, that puts you in a unique situation to assist me with that."

"So you want me to help you get him to lower his guard, so that you can conduct his . . . firing, here?"

Zoey's mother said, "Guys, I'm not stupid."

"That's why I brought you here in advance. To get you on board with this, the only path to peace. I was hoping your mother would help me convince you."

"No," Zoey said. "I won't help you kill Will Blackwater."

"Is his hold over you that strong? Do you really think if the roles were reversed, that he'd make the same choice, if he had a clear op-portunity to do away with you and take that seat at the head of the table? Don't project your own softhearted nature onto others, Zoey. It will get you killed. And don't for one second assume you know how a man like Will Blackwater thinks."

"And don't assume you know how a woman like me thinks. I said no, I meant it."

"Then it will be war."

"You don't want that. Think of Marti. Think of the danger that would put him in."

"That's not a factor," Chobb said, slicing off a piece of meat. He'd almost finished it. "One thing that recent events have taught me is that Marti will not be the one to inherit my empire. He should not have told you our family's private business. That made him a target and it's made me a target. He didn't have the stomach for this conflict any more than you do."

Zoey's mother said to him, "That's a good thing! For both of them!"

Titus scoffed.

Zoey said, "Well, I hope you didn't punish him for doing it. He was just trying to set things right."

"Punish him? Punishment would imply I still believed he could be corrected. He's not made of the right stuff and that's that. Do you know what it's like to invest seventeen years into offspring, nurturing them, passing on your wisdom, only to see all of your efforts die on the vine?"

"Well, I have a cat that won't do anything I say."

"Regardless, men in my position cannot be held back by sunk costs. You recover what you can and move on. I need to try again, to either make an heir or find one, and at my age my chances are dwindling."

"You're giving up on him? What happens to him now? Is . . . is he here?"

"In a way. He wasn't cut out for this world, that's all. Sometimes toughness is something you're born with. He was tender, as his mother used to say."

Chobb looked over at Zoey's mother. "What do you think of the meal? I was just telling Zoey here, the chef prides himself on being able to prepare anything. Is it . . . *tender* enough for you?"

She was chewing a bite of the meat. "It's amazing."

Zoey dropped her fork.

In a trembling voice, she said, "Where is Marti?"

43

Chobb met her eyes.

"Marti, get out here. We're having dinner."

Zoey heard grumbling and then out shuffled Marti from the bar, with his VR glasses on.

Zoey threw up her hands. "Oh, for the love of—"

Marti lifted the glasses just enough to see what was on the table, said, "I'm not eating meat," and left the room, seemingly not having noticed Zoey at all.

Titus said, "See? Always in that stupid game."

The bar guard, Antonio, stuck his head out once more and said, "It appears that Will Blackwater and the rest were not in fact on board the aircraft in question. It was unmanned. Maybe trying to draw our attention away."

"Thank you, Antonio."

Zoey said, "He's coming."

"You think he and his people are going to board this aircraft in midair?"

"*Yes.*"

Antonio cleared his throat. Apparently he hadn't finished speaking. "A separate team on the ground reported that they spotted Will Blackwater among a group entering the Lucky Cat hotel a short time ago, disguised as the cast and crew of an erotic magic show scheduled to perform tonight. It is believed they have since moved into one of the upper floors, but have blocked both the stairs and elevator to prevent being followed. Our team is attempting to find another way up."

That was the casino/hotel built to look like a giant golden *maneki-neko*. Zoey said, "Well, how about that."

Her mother asked, "They're in that big waving cat building? Why?"

"We're going to float right past it," said Zoey. "If we go the normal route. And I mean *right* past it. And pretty soon, if I remember."

Titus said, "That's correct."

Zoey said, "Unless we change course to avoid it."

Titus finished his food, wiped his mouth with a napkin, and said, "Why would I want to do that? Entire lives are wasted delaying the inevitable. I prefer to usher it along. If they're going to make some kind of ridiculous attempt to board this aircraft from a gigantic waving cat, well, I admit I'm actually eager to see it."

"Then I suppose I need to hurry."

Zoey put the little button on the table. It had a cobalt-blue pinprick of light in the center. Chobb jumped up and backed away, knocking his chair over.

This was in no way an overreaction. The magic of Raiden technology was that an astounding amount of energy could be packed into an object that size. Easily enough to blow a blimp out of the sky.

Zoey said, "Sit. My mother is right here, my goal is not to just kill all of us."

Chobb picked up his chair and sat, never taking his eyes off the device. When Zoey had said her good-byes to the team an hour earlier, she'd asked if anyone had a weapon. Instead, what Echo Ling had handed her was this button.

"How much time do I have, assuming that my people are going to launch a spectacular and lethal raid when we pass by?"

Chobb turned and looked out of one of the side windows. "Considering our golden cat friend is right there, I'd say about five or six minutes. See it?"

Zoey took a deep breath, her chest constricted by a band of bruises. In the most confident voice she could muster, she said, "I want to buy the Vanguard of Peace from you."

Chobb sat for a few moments to make sure he'd actually heard her. Then he burst out laughing.

"You think this is about money? You've got a lot to learn about men, sweetheart."

Her mother put a hand on his arm and said, "At least listen to her."

"Titus," said Zoey, trying quickly to put the words together. "I am going to give you everything you want. Everything you *really* want. The only problem is that it's going to be hard for you to admit that it's what you want, when you hear it. I know it's confusing, but just bear with me, okay? What I'm going to do now is make a series of statements and if I say something you *disagree* with, pick up your fork there and stab me with it. Just pin my hand right to the table. Ready?"

He glanced back over his shoulder, the gleaming gold skin of the cat building just ahead. "Time really is running short here . . ."

"First statement, this city *sucks ass*. You hate it here so much that you literally stay in the sky so you don't have to touch it. Second, you're *miserable* right now. Just in general, none of this is panning out the way you wanted. Third, you hate to lose. You'd rather *die* than lose. Fourth, you really do hate crime. It's not just talk, I get that now—you honestly hate it when innocent people are victimized and will do whatever it takes to stop it, regardless of what anybody else thinks. Fifth and final point, the future is murky because you have no one to take over your business, like you said. But it's not just the business that's in doubt, it's that mission, to keep people safe. And that bothers you a lot, because you don't want to let the victims down. Does all that sound right?"

In a thoroughly unimpressed tone, Chobb said, "Sure." Perhaps just as significantly, he did not stab Zoey with his fork.

"All right. So first, instead of all *this*"—Zoey swept her hand across the city outside the window with disdain—"I'm going to offer you control over an *entire economy the size of Germany.*"

This clearly caught Chobb off guard. "Am I about to hear that Will has seized a nation in Africa?"

"No, it's weirder than that. Here, I'm going to reach into my pocket—tell your men not to shoot me. I'm just getting my phone."

Zoey set her phone on the table in plain view, then brought up a live video feed that, upon initial viewing, appeared to be an anthill swarming with hundreds of thousands of ants who were in turn being overrun by an even larger swarm. Zooming in revealed a raging battle between men and creatures of all sizes, wielding elaborate weapons. An army trying to take a sprawling, walled city on a mountaintop.

"This is what Marti's doing on his headset back there. Echo showed me this. You see how this army here is all tagged with little red icons? Those are Dirk Vikerness loyalists, who just cast Marti out of their federation after he came forward with his confession. The ones tagged in green, those are your son's, he's leading an alliance of forces against them, including an army of Zoey loyalists, which until tonight I didn't know was a thing."

"Yes, this is the game he can't tear himself away from."

"It's not a game. It's real. No, listen. In every meaningful way, this"—she poked the phone with a finger—"is reality. The reason these guys care so much about these wars is that the stuff you see getting destroyed or captured here, they can't just click a button and start over. See that wall they're tearing down? There's a factory inside the Hub that makes bricks and there's a mine that produces the raw materials to supply that factory. There's a currency to purchase all of it that exists in the game and *only* in the game. The land they're building on is just like land in the real world; to build, you either have to kick somebody off their land, or buy it from them, or go out to the edge of the map and spend months clearing wilderness. It's finite, that's the word I'm looking for."

"Are you about to offer me a plot of imaginary land for my real-life business?"

"No. I'm going to offer you control of society's future. All of the stuff you see here requires work, *in the Hub*. It can't be bought with real money, there are no shortcuts or cheats. The reason is that when you make or grow something here, the final stage is to have it authenticated through a company called V-Terra—you pay a few pennies to certify it's real. A hundred million users in the Hub rely on it every single minute of every day."

"And you own V-Terra?"

"Well, it *was* owned by a Chinese billionaire. I had half-seriously asked Echo Ling if I could just buy the Hub out from under these guys. It turns out that's not a thing, but Echo dug into this and it then took Budd all of one hour to find out said billionaire is guilty of crimes that could quickly get him executed by his government. Budd has spoken to him and we are going to help him out of his jam, in exchange for ownership."

"And in the next two hundred seconds or so you're going to try to convince me that selling imaginary goods is a sound investment strategy for the future."

"You're not getting it. V-Terra doesn't sell imaginary goods. It *prevents other people from having them*. That, it turns out, is the stupid industry of the future. Look, the only reason there is value in having a big fake castle and golden armor is in the fact that other people *don't* have those things. That means these people in here finally have the one thing they can't get in the real world, and the thing they want above all else—status. The whole social order is reversed in here, if you or I logged in, we'd start at the bottom and we'd have no way to just buy our way to the top with real money—V-Terra bans anyone who tries. Work only counts if it's done in the Hub, which means to them, *we're* the societal dropouts, the maladjusted losers to be mocked and pitied. It's a whole new world for all of the poor souls who couldn't make it in this one.

"You, then, would pretty much be the king of that territory, taking a tiny cut of every single thing that's produced. It's potentially an *absurd* amount of money and it's a job you can do from anywhere. You can do it from the beach, in some country where the girls don't wear tops. The point is, *you wouldn't have to live in Tabula Rasa anymore.* You would be free of everything that's making you hate your life. You will have escaped the Badlands once and for all."

Zoey's mother clapped her hands together and said, "Ooh, we could go to Varadero! Like we talked about. The white sand . . ."

"And all I have to do," gruffed Chobb, "is abandon my home and my life's work. I'm sure Will Blackwater would like this 'deal' very much."

"That brings me to the next part. You don't like to lose and you absolutely do not want to lose to Will Blackwater, of all people. Trust me, I completely understand. That's why as part of the VOP buyout, you get *that* . . ."

Zoey pointed out of the window in the opposite direction of the golden cat, to a wobbly glowing shape in the distance. Her under-construction tower, shrouded in its childish hologram.

". . . the single most valuable piece of real estate in the city, which means it's one of the most valuable pieces of real estate in the world. Right in the heart of downtown, the spot claimed by Arthur Livingston himself all those years ago to lord over all he surveyed. You can do whatever you want with it, write your name across it in gold. No one in this city could ever look at the skyline and say Titus Chobb retreated or admitted defeat. And I promise you, Will Blackwater will absolutely *hate* that. It will torment him to the end of his days."

Chobb tried to suppress his reaction but did not do it in time. He clearly liked that part of the offer very much.

"And yet," said Chobb, exaggerating his gruffness a little, "the Vanguard of Peace will still fall into his hands, to add to the modified monsters he can turn out at any moment."

"No," said Zoey. "It falls into *my* hands. That's the deal. He never gets control."

"I don't mean to offend you, but whether or not he is given control on paper is meaningless. He will obtain it regardless."

"No," said Zoey. "He will not. Part of what you are betting on is me."

"You can't even see that Will set this up, that he sent you here to do this?"

"You can't even see that I know he *thinks* he did that?"

Chobb watched the digital battle play out on Zoey's phone. Zoey could see him teetering on the decision. Her mother touched his hand. He was almost making up his mind, on the cusp of a "yes" . . .

And then he withdrew. Chobb pulled his hand away, crossed his arms.

Zoey's heart sank into her shoes. The enormous golden cat was now right in front of them, its face filling the side window, the waving left paw giving it the appearance that it was beckoning them to pass on that side, like it was directing traffic. Its enormous eyes were windows and Zoey could see tables and people behind the glass—a fancy restaurant. If the Suits were over there somewhere, she couldn't see them.

Then, the paw stopped waving, grinding to a halt, held vertically as if it was telling them to stop moving.

Zoey pushed the little silver button closer to Chobb. She placed it so that it would be right under his face.

"Link that to your phone. It will come up with a prompt to activate it. If nothing else convinces you, that will."

Those had been Echo's only instructions. Zoey tried to make eye contact with her mother, to send a silent message. Chobb sighed and pulled his phone off of his belt. He fiddled with menus. From where Zoey was sitting, she saw his phone detect the device, a red "Initiate" button appearing.

He tapped it.

Zoey yelled to her mother, "GET DOWN!"

Zoey flung herself to the floor, landing hard on her injured shoulder. She almost blacked out from the pain.

After a moment, she realized no one had joined her down there. Whatever Echo's device was doing, it was doing it silently.

From above her, she heard her mother say, "Honey, are you okay?"

Zoey wasn't sure how long to wait on the floor. She slowly pulled herself back up to her chair to find her mother was now staring at her with great concern. Titus seemed mildly confused, then returned to scrolling through what seemed like a very long document on his phone.

"Sorry, I, uh, fell out of my chair."

"This data seems hard to believe," said Chobb. "They're saying crime dropped forty percent in Mumbai among regular users."

"Uh, sure. That's what was on that device. The . . . data. From the Chinese guy. I wasn't sure, my instructions were vague. And yeah, that's the point. People who get shut out of the real economy always go off and just make their own, that's human nature. Theft, contraband, all that. The Hub fills the same need, only nobody gets hurt."

Chobb kept scrolling.

"They've barely been profitable but they're expecting three hundred million users within the next few years. Network effects make it all but impossible for a competitor to come into the market . . ." He shook his head. "Even so, I've spent my entire adult life in private security. Why would I want to spend my golden years trying to make money in a field I know nothing about?"

"That," said Zoey, pointing a finger-gun at him, "is the best part. You're a novice in the Hub, you're right. But you know who isn't? *Your son, Marti.* Do you not see that he helped build a whole empire in there? And not with your money or connections, either. He did it with his own time, his own decisions, his own strategy. You say your son can't inherit your security empire and your conclusion is that it's time to throw away *your son*? How about you get a different empire instead?

You could run it together, the two of you, ruling over this magical kingdom in which anything is possible."

Chobb didn't answer. Zoey shot a nervous look out of the side windows.

There was a pop and a puff of smoke from the golden cat's shoulder, right at the joint where the waving arm met the rest of the structure. She saw people in the restaurant behind its eyes go wild, looking around, trying to figure out what had just exploded.

Then the cat's golden arm fell, rotating down like it was lowering a paw to stop the blimp. It had exactly that effect—the cat's arm jolted to a stop right in front of them and, a moment later, the blimp gently bumped into it. Everyone inside was jolted and the entire room tipped slightly to one side.

Zoey stopped her plate from sliding off the table and said, "It would appear they have initiated phase one of what looks like a very stupid plan to board this aircraft."

Chobb said, "Hmm." But that was it.

The engines revved, the pilot presumably trying to steer around the cat's paw. Then, incredibly, a tiny figure was running along the golden arm, hundreds of feet off the ground. They were holding some kind of a rifle. Zoey thought it was almost certainly Wu. He stopped and aimed his weapon, firing directly at them. It launched a projectile that unspooled a length of thin cable and thunked into the hull. Chobb rolled his eyes and sighed, sure that his floating office was going to wind up sustaining quite a bit of damage before this was done.

Zoey's mother gestured at the battle playing out on the phone and said to Chobb, "You can say all that isn't real, but your son, and your life with him, *that's* real. You know what isn't? This dumb wienie-wagging contest you've been tricked into having with Will Blackwater and all of the other reptiles just like him. *That's* the game, the one the world tricked you into playing, convincing you that winning it is worth losing your family, your life, your peace of mind. It's all so stupid, Titus. A game little boys make up on the playground and can't ever stop playing."

The airship was now attempting to fly in reverse, straining against the cable that was now attached to the cat's paw. Wu was running back across the arm, toward a gap in the shoulder joint.

Something was approaching from somewhere beyond the cat's arm, a small pair of bright lights growing in the distance.

Amplifying the tough-guy gruffness in his voice to almost comical levels now, Chobb said, "My own people will do their own analysis. Redo all of these projections. But if they agree with what I'm seeing here . . . I'll do it. To hell with it."

Zoey's mother said "Yay!" and hugged him.

"Don't celebrate too hard," said Zoey, studying the events outside the window. "There's a good chance we're still all about to die in a stupid blimp shootout."

Chobb said, "I still don't see how I won't wind up living the rest of my life looking over my shoulder, waiting for retribution from Black-water."

Zoey watched the oncoming lights outside her window and shook her head.

"You won't have to look over your shoulder. I said before that what you're banking on is my ability to get between you and Will. Well, Titus, we're going to test that ability right . . . now."

It turned out those moving lights outside belonged to a drone. It whizzed past the windows and then there was a crash and a noise like a robot getting his hand caught in his food processor. The drone had destroyed one of the engines. A moment later, an identical sound from the other side, a second drone hitting its mark.

The blimp stopped struggling against the cable. They were listing again; some silverware slid off the table and clinked onto the floor.

"They'll swing that paw back up," said Chobb, "with the cable attached. It will draw the passenger hold even with the top of the cat's head up there. At which point we will be boarded, presumably."

Zoey raised her voice to the nine guards, plus any others who may have remained hidden.

"Everyone stay calm! Will's plan is not to simply kill all of us, as far as I know."

Titus said, "Yes, stand down unless I give the order. Everyone got me? If I become incapacitated, well, you know what to do."

Soon, another cable was fired from the rooftop, from a flat spot in between the cat's enormous ears. It impacted the paw and a moment later, the cable was being pulled tight by some kind of apparatus up there, drawing the paw up vertically and dragging the blimp along with it, just as Chobb had said. As they drew even with the rooftop, there were the Suits, Zoey's people looking like fleas as they scurried around the Lucky Cat's rooftop cafe, frantically messing with their blimp-boarding equipment.

Wu was there with his rifle and he fired another cable. The hook on this one smashed through the side window and everyone jumped. The cable was then pulled tight and the hook grabbed the window frame, pulling them toward the rooftop, yanking them free of the paw, metal squealing and complaining every step of the way. They inched their way over, drawing close enough that Zoey could see everyone's nervous faces out there, her people jacked up on adrenaline and ready for action.

Zoey said, "If you don't want them to destroy your door, maybe go over there and open it?"

"I would not do that to a man," Chobb said. "To get all pumped up to breach a door, only to have someone just pull it open instead? I am not capable of such cruelty."

The blimp jolted as it forcefully contacted the rooftop. There was shouting from outside, commands for everyone to clear the door.

Chobb said, "Cover your ears."

An explosion blew the lock and the door was ripped open. A figure clad in sparkly red dove into the room and rolled.

It was Echo. She tossed a weapon to Zoey, who wasn't ready. It bounced off her right boob.

Zoey yelled, "Wait! I'm okay! I'm okay!"

Wu charged into the room next. He tossed a black sphere toward Zoey, like he was aiming for her face but missed high. When it reached her, it burst into a wadded-up cloth, which then spread and lowered over her, like an invisible hunter had thrown a sack over Zoey with the intention of hauling her away. It was actually a bulletproof fabric, intended to shield her from crossfire. She'd been briefed on it at some point.

Zoey frantically clawed the sack off of her, only to find that in the two seconds it'd taken her to do that, Wu was now behind Chobb, using him as a human shield, a katana at his neck. Chobb, Zoey thought, was doing an admirable job of staying calm. His guards were pointing their weapons, yelling commands. Wu was yelling back.

Zoey ran—well, limped quickly—around to get between the guards and Wu/Chobb.

"Stop! It's okay! Everybody!"

Andre entered immediately after, wearing a flashy red tuxedo, brandishing a gun with a barrel big enough that Zoey could have put her fist in it. He fired a projectile that bounced off the opposite wall and rolled onto the floor.

Zoey yelled "No!" just as the canister sparked and began spraying white smoke into the room. "Stop! Here . . ."

Zoey ran over to the smoking canister and kind of nudged it out the door with her shoe. She put her shirt over her mouth and nose, but the smoke just seemed to be for concealment, it wasn't tear gas or anything.

Through her shirt she said, "I'm fine! I'm fine! Everybody stop the rescue! Somebody kick that gas thing away from the door, some if it's still blowing in."

Everyone stopped yelling, at least for the moment.

Will was outside the door, it turned out, and he calmly kicked the gas grenade aside on his way in. He'd somehow had time to change suits and the bastard had a drink in his hand.

To Echo, he said, "I told you she was fine."

Wu slowly removed his blade from Chobb's throat and sheathed it.

Echo came over to Zoey. For the first time, it registered with Zoey that Echo was dressed as a magician's assistant, in tights and red sequins, apparently to coordinate with Andre as the magician. Unless this was some kind of progressive act where the roles were reversed.

Echo got a view of the blood on the back of Zoey's shirt. "*Are* you okay?"

"How do I look?"

"Like you died and were resurrected by someone who got distracted halfway through."

Zoey said, "Hey, when did you guys replace Echo with this talking trash bag full of fish heads?"

They were interrupted by a noisy wind outside. A helicopter was approaching. It didn't sound like Zoey's rental.

"Whose helicopter is that? Are a dozen more VOP dudes going to zipline down?"

"We reached out to Megaboss Alonzo for help," said Will, "but he flatly refused. We then sent Budd after him to try to change his mind, about thirty minutes ago. So without turning my head to look, I'm very confident in saying that is Alonzo's helicopter and that Alonzo did not send his men, but in fact came himself."

Will sipped his drink and the helicopter descended behind him. Its programmable skin was made to look like the scales on a snake and across the length of its undulating body were the words MEGA and BOSS alternately flashing in red.

Zoey, having to shout over the sound of the helicopter now, said, "So you launched this venture with no actual ability to get me off this rooftop? Just hoping that Budd and Alonzo would come through at this exact moment?"

"You hire the right people and trust them to get it done."

Andre ran out of the room and waved his arms at the helicopter. A moment later, the engine went silent, the helicopter having landed atop several pieces of cafe furniture in between the cat's giant ears. Out from the aircraft came Budd, Alonzo, and Alonzo's bodyguard, Deedee. Soon everyone was crowded inside the beached blimp.

"All right, everybody," began Zoey, "I'm not saying this under duress. We've come to a resolution. It will take a long time to explain and there are thousands of lawyer hours remaining to work out the details but . . ." She paused to take in and let out an exhausted breath. "I think we have it worked out."

Zoey's mother stood and said, "Everybody sit down! There are plenty of chairs. Titus's chef has enough back there for all of you."

Nobody sat. The blimp was tethered to an enormous cat's head with two destroyed engines and its door had been blown aside. The passenger hold now contained at least twenty people carrying a total of probably fifty weapons.

Zoey's mother said, "*SIT!*"

People started finding chairs. Andre propped the door closed as best he could to keep the cold out. Echo came and sat next to Zoey, across from Titus and Zoey's mother. Echo looked at them, then shot a curious glance at Zoey who waved her off with an "I'll explain later" gesture.

Zoey said, "Titus's chef has made a really good dish here, it's some kind of pork I think. And the side is . . ."

Chobb said, "Those are honey-roasted Sekai Ichi apples. As for the meat, as I said, I'm surprised you don't recognize it. Based on what I've heard, secondhand."

Zoey took a bite. "What is it?"

"It's wild game I caught myself. In fact, some would call it . . . *the most dangerous game.*"

"Dude, just tell me what it is."

"Wild boar."

Zoey was too tired to get whatever reference was being made there. "Yeah, it's good."

44

The boots of the armies never touched the soil, battling atop compacted layers of the dead. The broken corpses lay in heaps from horizon to horizon, discarded weapons jutting up like sprigs of a drought-stricken crop. And still, the battle raged.

"Your ex used to play this, right?" asked Echo, never taking her eyes off the monitor on the bedroom wall. "You think he's out there somewhere?"

"Oh, no," said Zoey, "he'd be hundreds of miles away from the battle, farming digital food and selling it to both sides at inflated prices. He'd have seen all of this as a big investment opportunity."

"That sounds hot."

"It was! Growing up where I did, having a guy who seemed to have it all figured out? Mmm. Yeah. And he'd spent his teenage years as a nerd, so he thought I was the hottest thing in the world. I thought he was going to have a heart attack the first time I took off my top. I should have known I was in trouble once he learned how to dress himself."

They were in Zoey's room. Echo was curled up in the chair with a glass of wine, Zoey was on her bed under the influence of the pain meds her nurse had left behind earlier (yeah, it turns out if you're rich enough, you can get somebody to come stitch you up right in your own bedroom in the middle of the night). Stench Machine would normally have been up there with her, but he was currently under the bed in a silent fit of rage over Zoey having brought another cat home. It was almost five in the morning and they'd been watching the battle since they'd gotten back to the estate an hour ago. The most recent development in the virtual war was that another army had swarmed in to support the remnants of Dirk Vikerness's garrison at the ruins of their citadel, nearly encircling Martius Chobb's invading force and cutting them off from their supply lines. Now a rear guard of Marti's was trying to hold them off so that the rest of his soldiers could retreat back to friendly territory, the withdrawing forces trickling across a single narrow bridge that was the only passage over a glowing river of lava.

Echo said, "This is the most stressful thing I've watched all month."

"Ooh, we should go find my castle on here."

"I, uh, think they razed it."

"So who built it? And the army, all of that? That wasn't you, was it? Something you were tinkering with behind the scenes?"

"I think your avatar was being run by an AI," said Echo, "mimicking your voice. Your army was made up of some real people and some bots."

"But who set it all up? Someone was organizing all of this with a fake me."

"My guess? Someone from The Blowback. As far as I can tell, 'you' showed up in the Hub right after the real you came home from the, uh, hospital last summer. They had failed to get you in real life, so they needed to pull you into their world. They got a whole bunch of followers to mine Spoils and built an army that would appear imposing, but that could be beaten. All so they could have a fight they could actually win."

"This is getting depressing. Will these guys spend the rest of their lives in here doing this?"

"Oh, I don't think so. Hopefully just their angriest years. A lot of them will probably wake up one day and see that thirty is around the corner and think, 'What the hell am I doing? I need to get a wife and a real place to live.' But in terms of giving them something to do in the meantime, it beats prison."

"It is a kind of prison, if you think about it."

Echo shrugged. "If you think about it, everything is."

"That chair isn't very comfortable. Do want to come over here on the bed with me?"

"No, I have to get going. The, uh, dogs need me."

45

Andre had retrieved the battered carcass of the Stench Reo robot from the park, which was now riddled with about ten thousand bullet holes. It no longer functioned aside from its ability to spout its catchphrases, but they propped it up in the courtyard and the kids were absolutely amazed by it. Zoey had put on most of her Naoko costume and since her own body was also beaten to hell, it looked like they'd added the damage on purpose. A girl and her mecha-cat, post-battle.

The Halloween party was an all-day affair, the first visitors showing up at about ten in the morning. They would come in scheduled waves, the first from a special-needs school Zoey had donated to, then after lunch would be the children of any employees from Ashe Enterprises who wanted to bring them. This included the sex workers, which had caused a huge controversy when announced (the lawyers, secretaries, and other white-collar types didn't want their kids around prostitutes and strippers, or to be seen with them in general—Zoey had told them they could stay home if they didn't like it). After that, the maze would be open to the public, though with several layers of security screenings that would be mostly invisible to those who passed through them. They were an hour into it, which meant it was the special-needs kids going through a low-key version of the maze with their parents, gently chased by a gang of Halloween staples like the whimsical, bumbling animatronic skeletons that at a designated point would trip and fall, bursting into a pile of disconnected bones.

Meanwhile, various junk-food vendors were doling out treats. From where Zoey was standing, she could smell the intoxicating scent of molten sugar from a booth where a Japanese guy was making teppanyaki popcorn on a flat iron griddle. He'd pile the kernels and oil inside a ring of sugar, then allow it to pop under a steel bowl. Kids were walking away with the warm, sticky clumps of popcorn in paper bags.

Zoey's arm was in a sling as she had in fact dislocated her shoulder, and she had stitches in the back of her head that were covered by her glowing pink wig. She'd gone light on the painkillers, though (they just made her sleepy), and as a result was standing there in a throbbing little pool of pain.

Megaboss Alonzo was talking at her and had been for some time, though little of what he said was registering. He was dressed as Batman, complete with the enormous white mustache that had been a staple of the character for a decade. She had been surprised when he had showed up at the opening of the maze with 2-Bladez in tow. The latter had apparently demanded to come, worried that the wiring in that skeleton was going to short out again. The man, now dressed as a pirate, had spent the morning hovering around that corner of the maze, making sure that the damned skeleton activated properly every time a group of kids passed.

Zoey sensed Alonzo was talking politics and said, "All that mayor stuff, that was Will's deal. I'm not into all that."

Alonzo groaned. "But by not taking a position, you're taking a position! That's the hell of politics."

"I just don't see how it will matter. You collect taxes and fund the cops, then eventually the voters and donors will say, 'Hey, I don't like these people over here, pass a law they can't help but break and then act like it's their own fault.' We'll be right back in the same boat."

"That's why you need a strong figure in that office! Somebody to stand against those tides! Did you know that in Japan, they've got this thing, it kind of just looks like a futon they've stood up on end, just a big cushion in a frame. When they've got someone who's drunk or crazy, they launch this thing at them and it just wraps them up like a burrito. Then they just tip it over and throw them in the back of a paddy wagon, take them somewhere to calm down. Next day, they're good to go. See? It'll be like that, give people room to make mistakes."

"For someone who is an actual professional criminal, you have a strangely utopian view of humanity."

"I can tell you from years of long experience that for every one truly evil man, there's a hundred wayward souls who just need to be put right. There are ways to set those people on the righteous path without handing them over to sadists to be treated like dogs."

"Okay, well, if you win and turn the city into a nightmarish dystopia, I'm going to show up at your office and say I told you so."

"So," he said, subtly shifting his posture, "what are you doing tonight, after the kids go home?"

"Nothing."

"Great, come to the club with me."

"No, I mean I'm planning to do nothing. An evening of doing nothing is incredibly important to me right now. I need it."

Wu appeared then, in a flannel shirt and jeans, an appearance so startling to Zoey that it might as well have been a Halloween costume even if she was sure it wasn't. Behind him was a boy and a girl, both in their late teens, who seemed very nervous to meet Zoey. Behind them was an annoyed-looking woman Zoey took to be Wu's wife, who seemed to silently disapprove of Zoey's very existence.

"Zoey," said Wu, smiling, "this is my son, Dennis, and my daughter, Rizza. Gary is away at Stanford. This is my wife, Mei."

"Hi!" said Zoey. They were all in matching flannel and jeans—wait, *was* it a costume? She was afraid to ask.

"Hello," said Mei, through pursed lips.

"I've heard a lot about you."

"Oh, I can't escape hearing about you."

To Wu, Zoey said, "See you at work tomorrow?"

Zoey vaguely remembered that she had maybe fired him the night before.

"If that is your wish, I will be here."

Zoey stuck out her hand to Mei and said, "Good to meet you!"

She shook Zoey's hand with the same enthusiasm she'd use to pull a wad of hair out of a drain. Wu then forced a joke and pulled his flannel family away to browse the snack stands around the courtyard.

Zoey sighed. She had about ten more hours of this ahead of her. She dug her tube of hand cream from her pocket, only to find it was empty.

46

That evening, the team did their Halloween gift exchange in the courtyard gazebo, close enough to hear the last of the kids passing through the maze, the skeleton in that corner giving chase and wiping out for probably the fiftieth time that day (at some point, Zoey had started to root for the skeleton to catch them). They had previously agreed to do this Secret Santa–style, everyone drawing a name to buy a single gift. Will never showed up, which was not a surprise as he'd said not to expect him. He was nothing if not dependable: when Will said he wasn't coming to your thing, you could bet he'd do whatever it took to not be there.

Echo had drawn Will's name and said she'd gotten him a Hawaiian shirt covered in animated parrots that shrieked a song called "Pretty Paris Park Parrot Party" loud enough to be heard from several blocks away. Budd drew Echo and had gotten her a five-year subscription to a cigar-of-the-month club. Andre drew Budd and got him a unicycle. Zoey drew Andre and gave him a pink Cow Zoey T-shirt, size extra-small, signed by Zoey. There was no gift for Zoey, meaning Will had drawn her name and he had apparently boycotted the entire affair.

Zoey listened to the skeleton rise and fall for maybe the last time. "It's annoying that Will didn't show up for this."

"Maybe that *was* his Halloween gift," said Budd. "He knew how aggravatin' you'd find it."

"Come Monday," said Zoey, "I want you guys to start assembling a list of everything. Everything we own, everything we do, out in the open and under the table. All of it. No more surprises. Then we're going through it and I'm deciding what parts I still want a hand in. If you've got a problem with that, too bad."

Budd said, "We'll have it in your hand by eight A.M. tomorrow."

"You don't have to pull an all-nighter, just make it a priority—"

"What he means," said Echo, "is that we already have that list. You asked for it a couple of months ago. After you got out of the hospital."

"Oh. Right. Well, I'll actually look at it this . . ."

Before Zoey could finish her sentence, she happened to glance over Echo's shoulder. Behind her was the exterior of the ballroom and she just happened to catch someone slipping inside the small door there. That, Zoey knew well, should not have been possible.

"Uh, hold on. I have to go check something."

Zoey limped over toward the door, mainly worried that some kid was going to activate Santa's Workshop and accidentally build a doomsday weapon. Not only should that door have been locked, but it should have taken an extraordinary effort to unlock it if you weren't a Suit.

Zoey reached the door, eventually, and poked her head inside the vast darkened room.

"Hello?"

Alonzo's bodyguard, Deedee, did not act startled to have been discovered. She was standing in front of Santa's Workshop, in the exact spot where Alonzo had stood a day earlier, which had been only hours before someone had gotten in and abducted Zoey's cat. She glanced back at Zoey, then turned away again.

Zoey approached slowly. "Is . . . Alonzo here?"

"He went home."

"Can I help you with something? You're Deedee, right? I don't think I ever got your last name."

"My last name is Dunn."

"Is Deedee like the letter D twice, like initials? Do they stand for something?"

"Dun-Dun."

"Is there something I can . . . wait, your name is Dun-Dun Dunn?"

Deedee sighed. "My father," she said, pausing to sneer at the word, "was a . . . *whimsical* man."

"Well, I see why you learned how to fight. Is there something I can do for you? That door was supposed to be locked."

"I'm sure it was." Deedee glanced around the room. "What is it like? To be this wealthy?"

"Ah, well, I don't think I know yet? If you'd asked me a year ago to guess what it's like to be rich, I'd have talked about fancy cars and big houses and vacations. But now I'm realizing that's like asking somebody in one of those Indian villages where they still don't have clean water how they'd handle living in my old trailer. They'd be like, 'I'd just sit around and enjoy my clean water all day.' It's kind of like that, you're beyond these basic needs but then there's this whole layer of new problems on top. Suddenly you're in charge of helping shape the world. I guess I could ask you what's it like to be strong, to know you can beat people up."

"You think that's what I do?"

"Aren't you Alonzo's bodyguard?"

"I protect my uncle from danger." She shot a brief glance back at Zoey. "Of all kinds."

"How did you get in here?"

"There are ways."

"Have you done it before?"

Deedee didn't answer.

Zoey asked, "You think I'm dangerous?"

"Yes. Because you don't really know what it's like to have a boot on your neck but you think you do. So you're going to slip right into the status quo. Same as all the rest."

"That thing with Alonzo going on camera and saying he was eating Tilley's heart, the thing that got us to come visit. Your idea?"

Deedee shrugged, as if none of that mattered now.

Zoey said, "What is it you want?"

"For me and the people I love to be able to walk the streets without fear."

"Isn't that what Alonzo is doing? With his mayoral run?"

"The change I want doesn't happen from the top down. It happens on the streets. If the people out there don't change, nothing Alonzo does will matter."

"Well, I don't want to be part of the problem, Deedee. I really don't."

"You are passing a stabbed man in the street and promising not to stab him a second time. That's not enough. The blade needs to be removed, the wound healed."

"You came in here for a reason. You want a weapon? Or are you looking to go all the way with implants?"

"I want, for the first time in my life, to enter an elevator with a man and not stand there with the knowledge that he can overpower me anytime he feels like it. I want to be able to go jogging alone, at night. And when I enter a room, I want the people there to take me seriously, because they know they have to."

"You think this machine can give you all that?"

"I'd like to at least find out. But where there's power, there's always somebody like you acting as the gatekeeper."

"Deedee . . . if you want it, if you *really* want it, come back in a week. We'd need to set you up with the surgeon, there are pre-op appointments, medical history stuff, training so that you don't accidentally rip your legs off. But I do want you to take some time to think about it. I'm telling you, getting a whole bunch of new power all at once, you can lose yourself. Forget why you even wanted it in the first place."

"And yet, you're keeping *your* money. And power."

"Yes."

"Then that, too, is my answer."

"If that's still your answer in a week, come back here."

"See you then." She turned to head for the door.

"Oh," said Zoey, to her back. "I have an extra cat, do you need one?"

"No."

47

Zoey had *just* eased herself into the tub when she got a call from Carlton saying Will was at the front door. Zoey grunted and decided she wasn't going to move. Let him come back in the morning. Then Carlton called again and Zoey cursed and dragged herself out of the water, did a cursory job of drying herself, and pulled on pajamas and a bathrobe.

Will wasn't in the foyer. Instead, she found him standing out on the cobblestones outside the big doors. She went out and let the doors close behind her.

She threw out her hands and said, "What the hell?"

"Can you be more specific with your question?"

"What the hell, *Will?*"

"Are you asking why I'm here? Or are you asking why I didn't share all of my information with you about the Tilley situation?"

Zoey answered with a silent glare. He knew damned well what she wanted.

"Look," he said, "you asked me to find out how to get to Titus Chobb. His weakness was his dead wife and his sick son. If I'd told you the strategy, you'd have vetoed it. So the answer to the question 'How do you get to Titus Chobb' was 'Find a way to exploit those weaknesses and don't tell Zoey.' The only way to carry out your order was to shield you from it."

"No." She stabbed a finger at him. "You're the one who got my mom that job at that Freya building. That's too much of a coincidence. You set that up and you did it *months* ago. You knew this was coming."

"I knew that the guy who instigated Arthur's death and was building a private army was going to eventually be a problem? You think that took some kind of next-level foresight?"

"And you got my mother involved, how?"

"She came to me and asked how she could help. I said she could keep an eye on this guy who was going to be a threat soon, talk to him, take his temperature. The rest, she did on her own."

"This city is full of absurdly hot twenty-five-year-olds you could have thrown at Chobb. There is no reason you had to pick my mother for that task."

"You think Titus Chobb wants a hot twenty-five-year-old? You don't think he can get that whenever he wants? He didn't need that; he needed what Freya had given him. He needed someone to give him permission to be the better version of himself. By making him feel like, deep down, he can still be a good man, that he could maybe even go off and have a whole new life with this woman, a fresh start. The same thing that captivated Arthur and probably several males your mother meets in the course of an average commute."

"That shouldn't be any woman's job."

"Fixing a clogged toilet shouldn't be any man's job but it's either that or let the house fill with shit."

"So you knew all the stuff with Dexter Tilley was going to happen, somehow?"

"What? No. That blew my plan apart. I wanted a rift between Chobb and Dirk Vikerness. The staff was loyal to Chobb, the people on the ground were loyal to Dirk. Nothing I've tried since Tilley has succeeded."

"But it all worked out exactly how you wanted anyway."

"Because *you* found a way. You convinced Marti to come clean. You and your mother somehow convinced Titus to abandon his life's work altogether. I'll never know how you sold him on that. I made a mess of the situation and you cleaned it up."

"God, you're so phony when you're trying to play humble. *I* think you're trying to butter me up to get me to ignore the obvious, which is that the Vanguard of Peace was your Halloween present, your prank gift to me. That this *whole* thing was orchestrated, by you, in some kind of misguided attempt to . . . what? Consolidate power?"

"It's strange how you simultaneously have an impossibly high and impossibly low opinion of me."

"You keep exceeding my expectations in both directions. You know I promised Titus that I'd keep you in line. Make sure you don't wind up running the city according to your evil desires."

"It seems like the first step in doing that would have been not telling me."

"Which raises a question in my mind that I still can't answer," said Zoey. *"What do you want?"*

"Right now?"

"Just, in general."

He shrugged. "I want what every man wants. I want to build something. Look around you. This house, all those buildings downtown, what do you think all of that is about? It's about leaving a mark. Not just the stuff you can see, but the connections, the systems. This guy needs a thing and has money, this woman on the other side of town has the thing and needs money. Find a way to connect those two and you've made the world a happier place. That's really all it is, all of civilization—just organizing those transactions. But the second you set yourself to building something great, a swarm of jackals wash in and start gnawing at it. Grifters, thieves, bureaucrats. Pretty soon, fighting them off is all you get done. What do *you* want?"

Zoey thought about it.

"I want to be comfortable in my skin. I want a little switch I can flip that decides whether or not people are paying attention to me. I want a daughter. A little nerdy daughter who wears dorky glasses and knows a million facts about dinosaurs. She has a little round face and hates dresses. Her name is Marcy."

"You think any of that's possible, in your situation?"

Zoey didn't answer. They stood in silence for a bit. It was cold, and the remnants of Zoey's bathwater had dampened her pajamas. She studied the cobblestones and tried to see if she could find dried bloodstains.

"How long ago," asked Zoey, "did your wife pass away?"

"The accident was four years ago this February, on the tenth. I don't know the exact time, she was gone before the ambulances even got to the scene. But would have been around three-fifteen in the afternoon."

Zoey studied her fuzzy slippers and said, "This summer, when I had my breakdown and woke up in the hospital . . . my mom said the paramedics showed up and found me passed out in bed. Pills and alcohol nearby. Then you called nine-one-one, she said, because Carlton was asleep and I'd sent Wu home. But you were there, for some reason. That's what she told me."

Will didn't answer, because she hadn't asked a question.

"But that story has never added up. Not based on what I remember."

Will just looked off into the distance, watching the giant jack-o'-lantern casting its orange glow around the front lawn, as if he was worried it would come to life and start rolling after them.

"My memory from that night isn't great," Zoey continued, "but it's not a total blackout, either. I did send Wu home, against his wishes, then took off in the convertible and found a trashy bar. I'd saved some of the pain pills from my surgery last year and took four of them, then drank a whole lot, really fast. I found this guy, big biker guy with a tattoo on his neck—or maybe he just liked the biker leathers—and dragged him back to the bathroom. So I remember that, that whole . . . sequence, and then he left me there and I stayed behind. I took off my dress and threw it in the trash, because it had . . . stains, and I remember that and then I remember that I was then lying on the damp concrete in my bra and panties and in that moment that floor just felt like a big puffy cloud I just wanted to sleep on forever. Then I blinked and I was in the hospital."

Will said, "If you say so. I wasn't there for that part."

"You weren't? Because that means *someone* had come and gotten me out of that situation and did it in a way so that no one ever found out about it. No staff at the bar ever talked, no customers talked, neither did anyone passing by outside. Not a single glimpse from a running Blink camera, not a single anonymous rumor leaked to Chopra. Not even the biker talked. I can't even fathom how that was accomplished. But it happened, and it happened because this mysterious, all-powerful person didn't want strangers to see me like that. Then that person proceeded to tell absolutely no one the embarrassing truth in the months since, not even my own mother. *Not even me.*"

"If you say so."

She sighed. It was like pulling teeth. "You should have been at the party today, Will."

"Just not my thing."

"Hey, I hate crowds, too. There's too many—"

"Variables to control. Yeah."

"Hating parties, that's the only thing we have in common."

He glanced at her for a microsecond before saying, "You think that's the only thing, huh?"

"Anyway," she said, turning to go back into the foyer, "for your performance this weekend, I'm giving you a six."

"I guess I'm getting better."

She went inside, closing the door behind her.

AFTERWORD

If you didn't already know, this is the second novel in this series. The first is called *Futuristic Violence and Fancy Suits* and it's not too late to go back and read it if you started with this one. It'll be like a prequel! And when beloved characters show up there who are conspicuously absent from this one, well, this way you'll know not to get too attached.

If you enjoyed this book and would like to see more adventures involving Zoey and the Suits, the best thing you can do is go out onto whatever social media thing you use and tell everyone you liked it. Now, the way social media works, these messages will travel further if there's some kind of outrageous statement attached, so maybe try something like, "You'll love this book if, like me, you agree that cannibalism should not only be legal, but *required*." If it doesn't get any traction, you can just keep adding stuff. ("Too bad we'll never get those laws changed as long as *women* are allowed to vote. Also, I never, ever tip.")

It also helps to leave an online review at whatever outlet is appropriate for your situation. If you're the type of reader who still likes to go outside the house now and then, you can even spread the word in real life. Maybe go to a pharmacy during their busiest time of day, walk up to the counter and throw a bottle of erectile dysfunction pills at the cashier, and say, "We no longer need those. We have *these*."

Then hold up all of my books, kind of fanned out in your hands. There are a lot of ways to go about it, these are all just suggestions. The point is that whether or not there are future books will be determined by the invisible hand of the marketplace, and word-of-mouth is everything.

Speaking of which, I should also note that one danger of writing about a hypothetical future in which an Internet-of-Cameras has reshaped society is that it is almost impossible to keep up with the speed at which the actual technology appears. *Futuristic Violence and Fancy Suits* was conceived in 2012 and finished in 2014. That means, for example, that doorbell cameras didn't exist when I first sat down to write it. Today, all of my neighbors have them and, sure enough, there's a social network/app called Neighbors where you can join up and watch other people's feeds. Did something terrible and/or hilarious happen in the neighborhood last night? Jump on and see it from every angle, follow the action down the street. So, yeah, it kind of looks like by the time I get around to writing a third book in this series, Blink will mostly exist in real life but will just be called something else. It's like when you read a futuristic sci-fi novel from the sixties and a character says something like, "I need to access the mainframe with my portable computer! Find me a DATA-NET port!" and you're like, "Man, this author was *way* off. What a dipshit." It's not my fault. I'm writing these as fast as I can.

Meanwhile, if these are the only books of mine you've ever read, you should know that I'm actually more well known for the gruesome and bizarre *John Dies at the End* series of horror novels. As of this writing there are three of those:

John Dies at the End
This Book Is Full of Spiders: Seriously, Dude, Don't Touch It
What the Hell Did I Just Read

Yes, those are real books, I'm not just making up titles here. The first book got turned into a movie that you can find on whatever device you watch movies on, the second became a *New York Times* bestseller. As of this writing, I'm under contract for a fourth book in that series, which may already be out on shelves by the time you read this. If you're reading this several years in the future and no such book exists, well, it's probably time to google my name to find out what happened to me.

Otherwise, please allow me to end this novel about corporations exploiting modern narcissism to trick citizens into building their own surveillance state by listing all of my many internet and social media platforms:

twitter.com/JohnDiesattheEn
facebook.com/JohnDiesattheEnd.TheNovel
instagram.com/jasonkpargin
johndiesattheend.com

Thanks, everybody.

—Jason Pargin
January 2020

A Preview of Jason Pargin's Next Novel,

If This Book Exists, You're in the Wrong Universe

The author of the Zoey Ashe novels also writes the deliriously grue-some John Dies at the End books, a *New York Times* bestselling series that has been adapted into a feature film. What follows is a preview of the upcoming fourth novel in that series, tentatively titled *If This Book Exists, You're in the Wrong Universe*.

"This is really about my wife," said the man with the parasite gnawing on his skull. "I'll let her explain."

He nodded to the chair next to him, where absolutely no one was sitting, then waited in silence like he was letting his "wife" speak. John, Amy, and I exchanged glances, none of us quite sure what to do.

The man was in his early fifties and had the kind of sad, droopy fea-tures that made him look like God hadn't finished inflating him. He had shown up at my apartment two minutes ago, saying he'd been dropped off by the police, who apparently hadn't stuck around to explain. He was now sitting at my kitchen table with me, Amy, and the empty chair, John leaning on the counter and fidgeting with the red-white-and-blue novelty cowboy hat in his hands.

The guy was now looking at us expectantly, like he was waiting for us to reply to whatever his invisible wife had just said. The parasite made soft grinding noises, a sound like an inmate surreptitiously sawing through prison bars. It was chewing away more of his skull, I guess—it had already made quite a hole up there. The parasite, or whatever word you'd use to describe the creature attached to the dude's head, had a body about the size of two fists, its sleek carapace a vivid purple. It had six long, black segmented legs, covered in bristles. It kind of looked like somebody had glued half a dozen fat centipedes to one of Prince's codpieces. The creature's legs were wrapped tightly around the man's face, one running under his nose like a mustache. Around its purple body was a ring of several eyes that twitched back and forth as if scanning the room, each moving and blinking at different intervals. Under the creature I could see a sliver of the man's exposed pink brain, surrounded by blood-matted hair. The victim seemed to not feel this at all and in general was clearly unaware of the creature's presence.

Amy finally broke the silence, bless her. "I'm sorry, can you explain why the police brought you here, again?"

The "here" she referred to was our apartment, which was small enough that the table we were sitting around overlapped the borders of the kitchenette, dining room, and living room. In general, I'm not sure either we or the apartment made for a reassuring first impression. Only two of the four kitchen chairs matched. Behind me, a window air conditioner was making a noise like it was being dragged down a gravel road. John was in the process of placing his garish American flag cowboy hat back atop his head; his outfit included a T-shirt featuring a photo of himself in which he was wearing the same hat and T-shirt he wore in real life. So the John in the photo was wearing a shirt featuring John wearing the photo of John wearing that shirt, creating a recursion that presumably continued for infinity. Below it was a pair of denim shorts that were too small. Much too small.

"Weren't you listening?" said the guy, suddenly exasperated. "Why does nobody listen? Eve and I went out to eat lunch at Loew's Steaks. The place was packed, because of the Fourth. We waited for an hour for a table. I sit down, we both order, the waitress brings my food but nothing for Eve. We ask—*politely*—what's going on with her order and the bitch talks to me and just ignores Eve completely. I demanded to talk to a manager, he comes over and does the same, won't even look at her. Right, honey?"

He glanced to the empty chair, then nodded in confirmation.

"Right. So at this point, I'll admit I got a little agitated. Some words were exchanged. Long story short, the cops come, smirking at us while we try to tell the story. Like they think it's funny. They take us to the hospital for some damned reason, that was a total waste of time. I talk to a doctor and the doctor turns around and calls the cops again. Nobody will give me a straight answer, like everybody's in on the joke but us. The cops finally bring me here and tell me to do whatever you say. They actually giggled as they drove off. I thought they were taking me to the loony bin . . ."

He trailed off as he glanced around at the apartment, scrutinizing it, now doing the exact same thing the purple creature on his head had seemingly done a moment ago: sizing us up. The man noted the centerpiece decoration on the kitchen table—a glass sphere in a brass frame with a floating severed finger inside it. The finger was pointed right back at him, wobbling slightly as it hovered in the center. He then looked toward the counter where there was a rusty iron box about the size of a human head, with a ragged hole where something had clawed its way out. Then his eyes flicked up to a cross-stitch sign hanging over the oven that said:

I'M 'BOUT TO DROP A NEW RECIPE ON YOUR FUCK-ING ASS

"Who are you people?"

I said, "Oh, that's John, this is Amy, my name is David. We, uh . . ."

"We work with the police sometimes," finished Amy. Well, that was definitely one way to put it.

The man seemed skeptical. It probably didn't help that I was wearing a T-shirt bearing a crudely drawn stars-and-stripes behind the words THIS FLAG NEVER FLAGS in a bombastic font (John had found it at a garage sale). Amy was holding a white straw hat and pink sunglasses in her lap, securing them with her right hand. She wasn't holding anything in her left because it didn't exist—that arm ended in a stump at the wrist. Old car accident. She was wearing so much sunscreen that the sweet chemical coconut stink was giving me a headache. When this guy had arrived, we had been on the way out to get a spot for the fireworks at the lake, and Amy knew she had to go in prepared, having descended from a tribe of freckled redheads in some sunless part of the world.

The parasite squeezed its legs around our visitor's head, digging furrows into his cheeks. I knew from experience that none of the parties involved in this incident—this guy, the cops, the doctors, the steak house waitstaff—had been able to see the little purple monster.

John lifted his patriotic Stetson and ran his hand through his hair, which at the moment was long enough to tickle his shoulders. "Let's back up," he said, replacing the hat. "Now, your name is . . ."

"Lou. This is Eve, like I said."

John glanced at the empty chair. "Sure. Uh, can I get you something to drink? Dave, what do we have?"

"Hmm, well, we have the beers out in the cooler in the van. In here we have . . . tap water that kind of tastes like it came out of a squirt gun, some cranberry juice, a bottle of 1985 vintage Austrian wine, and two cases of that Dan Aykroyd Crystal Head vodka—"

"Am I free to go?" asked Lou, somehow ignoring this amazing offer. "Why is everybody treating me like I got caught with a damned dirty bomb at the Vatican? It was a ruckus at a restaurant, who cares? No punches got thrown. Or, none that connected, anyhow. I don't know what's happening here."

"Is it okay if we ask a few questions?" asked Amy. "How long have you and Eve been together?"

"Why do you need to know *that*?"

"Please, this will only take a minute. We are actually here to help."

I was sure Amy believed that, but it seemed clear to me that regardless of what we did, this dude was already dead.

"Been with her about five months. Married for two. It's not official, got somebody local to do the ceremony back in May."

"And this problem, people acting like they don't want to acknowledge Eve, is this the first time it's happened? And if not, when did it start?"

Instead of answering, the man looked toward the empty chair, like his wife was answering instead.

When she'd apparently finished, he looked at us and said, "I'll take her word for it. My memory's not so good these days. Chemo messes with your brain cells. But like she said, she doesn't go out much. Got the agoraphobia, on top of her disability. Doesn't like crowds. But I told her weeks ago, we're going out for the Fourth, so get yourself right in the head, do whatever you've got to do, we're going out in public and we're gonna enjoy the holiday. That's no way for somebody to live, cooped up like that."

I asked, "What was her response?"

"Just what I'd expected. She pitched a fit. I waited for it to blow over and told her this was what we were doing, if I had to carry her out of the house." He smiled at the empty chair. "She eventually came around."

I found myself staring at the parasite and realized it was making eye contact with me with about three of its eyes. It's entirely possible that up to that moment, it thought it was as invisible to me as it was to everyone else, and now knew otherwise.

What is your game, here? I thought to myself, not entirely sure the parasite couldn't hear it.

I've been calling the creature a "parasite" because 1) half of all known living creatures are parasites, so that's always a fairly safe guess, and 2) it was allowing this guy to continue walking around and functioning as normal while it fed on him. That's what parasites do, climb on and leave the host healthy enough to do the hunting and gathering and fighting. It's a sound strategy if you can pull it off. As for why it would make him hallucinate a wife, I wasn't sure but also didn't particularly care.

I glanced down at my phone to check the time. We needed to get going; the good sitting spots around the lake would fill up fast (under the trees, where Amy wouldn't get roasted alive). I'm sorry if this seems cold, but it's not like this guy is the only one walking around with an interdimensional parasite leeching off his system. You've probably met somebody in that very situation in the last month. Hell, some of the people reading this are in that situation. Have you ever found yourself obsessively watching a TV show you don't actually enjoy? That probably means you're just watching your parasite's favorite show.

John said, "I want to try something, if that's okay." He dug into his front pocket and pulled out a quarter. He looked toward the empty chair where "Eve" was supposedly sitting and said, "I'm going to toss this quarter to you. I want you to catch it and toss it back to me."

Lou immediately looked outraged. "I'm sorry, is that some kind of sick joke?"

"It's just a test. It will only take a moment."

"How do you expect her to catch it?" shouted Lou. "Look at her. You can clearly see that her arms don't work. Got the nerve damage, on account of her disorder."

John dropped the coin to the table and sighed, defeated. He glanced at me with a look that said it all: *this is one of the few days of the year when this town's collective day drinking isn't considered a tragedy and we're missing it.*

To Lou, I said, "This may seem like another odd question, but do you get headaches?"

"No," he replied, over the gravelly rasp of the parasite munching on his cranium. "Why would I get headaches?"

John suddenly got that alarming look he gets when he thinks he has an idea, then positioned himself behind the empty chair and said, "All right, let me try this. Just stay where you are, Eve. Are you ready? Here we go."

John pulled the chair away from the table, then picked it up and lifted it above his head.

"Whoa!" said John. "Look at that. I'm the world's strongest man, apparently, because I just lifted your wife above my head like it was nothing."

Lou looked bewildered. "Are you out of your mind? She's standing right there. What's going on here? Am I being filmed? Is this a prank?"

I said, "I'm sorry, you've caught us at a bad time. We were just about to head to the lake to do that thing where we celebrate America's birthday by terrifying all of its dogs, so we've not been able to go through our normal meticulous process for evaluating a situation like ours. We're not trying to be rude, we're really not, but you have to understand that there's a narrow window in which you can get just drunk enough to not care that nobody has invented any new fireworks for the last thousand years."

"Then let us go," said Lou. "Hell, that's where we were headed, we were going to go after we'd eaten. So why are we here?"

I looked pleadingly toward Amy and then John, silently soliciting ideas. Normally the ideas were Amy's department, but she likely couldn't see the parasite and so probably didn't understand what exactly we were dealing with. John probably could see it, but I think he was out of ideas after the chair thing.

I sighed and said, "Look, I'm just going to rip off the Band-Aid. What if I told you that the reason people aren't interacting with your wife is because she doesn't exist?"

Amy recoiled. Usually we would try to use a little more finesse with this kind of thing, but, hey, you get what you pay for.

Lou smirked. "Now I know there are cameras filming all this. Where are they? Is this for YouTube or TV? What, you get everybody together to work out some elaborate prank and then I win a Hooter's gift card at the end?"

Amy said, "He's telling you the truth. There are exactly four people in this room. Well, let me clarify—David said that Eve doesn't exist, I should say that none of us can perceive her. She's real to you, that's clear, but it appears she's *only* real to you."

"How—"

"You have a, uh, condition," I said. "There's no easy way to explain it but it appears, from where I sit, that it's eventually going to kill you. Though none of us here are doctors, obviously. If you want to leave, we won't stop you. But something will have to be done about it at some point."

John said, "There's a chance you could become a danger to other people."

Lou scoffed and looked to the empty chair, then grabbed a patch of air and held it, like he'd put his hand on his invisible wife's forearm.

"You hear that, babe? You don't exist! I'll have to remember that at tax time."

John said, "I don't know how to explain your . . . condition because I don't know what you're ready to believe. So, let me just put it like this: there's an invisible parasitic creature, probably from another dimension, chewing on your skull. It's apparently making you hallucinate 'Eve' in order to manipulate you. Dave and I can see it but no one else can, for reasons that would take forever to explain. But any parasite's strategy is going to start with going undetected, the exact way it's hiding itself and preventing you from feeling the huge hole in your skull isn't really important in the long run, is it? Oh, right, it also has chewed a huge hole in your skull."

Lou stood, forcing a laugh. "You people are nuts. Come on, honey." He turned as if to go, then stopped and looked down at the empty chair. "What do you mean? That doesn't even—"

He became still, then sat down again.

"But," he began, but acted like he'd been sharply told to stop talking and listen for once in his damned life.

After a couple of minutes of this, he said, "Can you three step outside? We need to talk in private."

It was my home, so it didn't seem right that we had to go stand in the sun while he had his private conversation, but now didn't seem like the time to press the issue. We went out onto the landing of the rusty exterior stairway/bird toilet that led up to my second-floor apartment. When we closed the door behind us, Lou and "Eve" were already having a passionate heart-to-heart.

I raised my hand and said, "Who else votes that we just leave and go watch the fireworks?"

Ignoring this, Amy said, "Exactly what are you guys seeing?"

"He's got a creature on his head, sucking on his brain."

John added, "It kind of looks like a robot crab wearing a purple bicycle helmet."

Amy closed her eyes and let out a breath. We'd seen people in similar situations before, and if there's a cure, we never came close to finding it. You pull the parasite off and the guy's brain comes out with it. A team of a dozen of the world's best neurosurgeons could maybe do something if they actually possessed the ability to see the creature or the wound, which they almost certainly wouldn't. There was no need for the three of us to say any of that out loud.

"You don't see it at all?"

Amy shook her head. "I can sense something is there, but can't make it out."

If given enough time, she probably could. It was a skill one could acquire with practice, the way mechanics can tell what repairs your car needs just by looking at how expensive your shoes are. Seeing these entities had nothing to do with the anatomy of the human eye and everything to do with how the mind chooses to store memories—you might see it, but won't remember seeing it, even while you're actively looking at it. If you find that hard to grasp, keep in mind you've forgotten 99.99% of your life up to this point. Can you remember the face of a single cashier you've ever interacted with?

"So," I said, "which of the three options do we want to go with here?"

Again, I didn't need to state the three options, because they never changed: we could either A) let the guy go, B) painlessly kill him and then try to somehow kill the parasite (and these creatures could be *very* hard to kill), or C) make some token effort to remove the thing and see if, by some miracle, Lou survived. If that last one is your knee-jerk answer, that just means you're new to this. Knowing that there's a near-zero chance he survives, wouldn't it be better to sneak up from behind and quickly put him out of his misery, instead of making the poor bastard spend his final hours strapped to my bed while we try to wrestle an invisible monster off his face? And please note that when threatened, these creatures can do very nasty things to a human body and even nastier things to the mind, if not the soul.

Amy said, "He seems to be physically healthy at the moment, so we have some time to figure out what we can do for him. We could get an expert on the phone, maybe Dr. Marconi is around, maybe he knows somebody . . . I don't know. As long as there's life, there's a chance."

"She's right," I said. "We should tell this guy to go home and stay by the phone until we can figure out what's going on. In the meantime, we can go get drunk and watch fireworks, blow some shit up, eat some hot dogs. When we get up tomorrow afternoon, Amy can find some kind of freaky doctor or veterinarian who knows how to work on patients like this and if not, we can always kill him then."

John shook his head, oscillating his patriotic hat in the process. "Nah, we can't let the guy run around free with that thing controlling him. Did you see its eyes? It was listening the whole time, it knows we're onto it. Hell, it may be able to hear us out here, for all we know. What if we send him home and 'Eve' instructs him to go on a shooting spree? Or makes him build a little catapult to fling his own turds at a crowded playground?"

"Right," said Amy. "We have to keep him here, or somewhere, and keep an eye on him. You know what, you guys go watch the fireworks, I'll stay here and babysit Lou and try to contact somebody. It's fine, the Fourth always stops being fun once I'm the only non-drunk adult around anyway."

I said, "I'm obviously not leaving you here. If you're staying, I'm staying."

John said, "You're both assuming this guy's just going to hang out while you try to get on the phone with a . . . surgical exorcist, I guess? One who's working on the Fourth of July? So a surgical exorcist who hates America. The guy is going to demand you let him go and at that point, you'll either have to let him become a public health hazard or shoot him."

Amy said, "I don't want you shooting anybody today, even if solving a complicated problem by shooting it is just about the most American thing I can imagine. We have to get the guy to stay willingly."

"And since the parasite is controlling him," I said, "you mean we have to get the guy to stay willingly in a way that somehow won't alert the parasite that we're just stalling until we can get somebody to remove it."

John said, "I wish we had a tranquilizer dart, something like that. Just knock the guy out."

"There's actually no such a thing as a human tranquilizer dart," said Amy. "Same with knockout gas, it's only in movies, otherwise police would use it all the time. What we could do is—"

There was a noise from inside the apartment, something falling hard to the floor. Then an interior door slammed shut. All of our eyes snapped in that direction.

I muttered, "Get the shotgun."

We'd taken it out to the van earlier (we have a Fourth of July tradition where we soak bags of flour in gasoline, light them, and then blow them apart with buckshot). John ran down and returned with the shotgun a moment later, checking that there was a shell loaded into each of its five barrels. It was a custom item he'd just bought off the internet, and it had, to our knowledge, never been fired. But it had to have been of good quality, otherwise the maker wouldn't have charged a whole forty-seven dollars for it.

If I leaned out over the landing, I could peer into the nearest window a little and get a look inside. I saw one chair knocked over at the kitchen table, but no sign of Lou. I scanned the floor to see if "Eve" had detached and was maybe skittering around in there, looking for another brain to munch. I could detect no movement, but noticed the bedroom door was closed.

I made a hand signal to John to try to convey all of this, and he nodded as if he understood me. He readied the shotgun, checking that both bayonets were firmly attached. I threw the door open and then stepped aside. John went in, scanning the room with the five laser pointers that had been duct-taped to the barrels. Amy and I followed him in, and, finding the kitchen/dining room/living room empty, the three of us advanced to the closed bedroom door. There was a thump and the floor shook, like something heavy slammed against the wall. From behind the door came the sounds of rustling and a low, animalistic grunt, like someone or something struggling against their own body.

I held up three fingers to signal a countdown.

Three. Two. One.

I threw the bedroom door open. We all jumped inside, then froze.

Lou was completely nude, lying on our bed and frantically stabbing the air with his erection. His hands were groping the air above him, squeezing breasts that weren't there. Making passionate love to a woman only he could see.

The three of us stood in the doorway in silence—it was clear Lou either did not know we had entered or was too distracted to care— then slowly backed out and closed the door. We all sat down at the kitchen table without saying a word. We stayed there for the next thirty minutes, occasional howls of ecstasy filling the tiny apartment.

Finally, Lou emerged, looking sheepish, now clothed but still wearing the purple parasite like a jaunty hat. "I'm so sorry about that," he said, "we got to talking and realized that we may never get another chance. We, uh, cleaned up as best we could."

Well, I thought, *at least I won't feel bad about killing him now.*

He sat down at the table and started to pull out a chair for Eve, then silently slid it back into place. "She, well, she explained everything to me."

I made eye contact with the parasite. "She, as in, your wife?"

"Yeah. Eve, or the thing that created her in my head . . . whatever or whoever is speaking through her, we talked it out. I know Eve isn't real. Or, she isn't real in the way you would think of it. I know the chair is empty, I guess is what I mean. She said you guys spotted her and she doesn't want to keep up the charade."

"So . . ." I began, having been truly thrown for a loop by this, "you know you have a creature sucking on your brain? A purple thing with six legs?"

"Don't describe it to me, I'd rather not know. She—or it—offered to let me go look in a mirror, saying she would allow me to see her for real. I declined. I'm trying to keep my wits about me and I don't think that would happen if I saw the situation as it really was."

I thought, *that's probably how a lot of marriages are maintained*, but didn't say it.

Amy asked, "Did she explain why she's doing this? Or what her purpose is?"

"She's lost," said Lou. "She wound up in this world but doesn't know how. She needed a host so she picked me, because she detected that I wouldn't resist, not in my state. So she latched on and created this imaginary woman, my dream girl, to keep me pacified. To keep me mostly at home. It must have dug around in my thoughts, figured out what I needed." He shrugged.

"It was nice of her to come clean about it," said John. "You don't usually get that kind of honesty from parasites."

Lou scoffed. "She said that once she got to know me, she felt guilty about it. And it didn't work, anyway. She's dying. She can't survive here. And when she dies, I'll die. We won't make it through the night, no matter what anybody does. That's why she agreed to go out with me today, even though there was no chance it wasn't going to be a calamity. It's our last day. Our bodies will shut down and it's probably going to be very, very painful, she says. For both of us."

Amy said, "I'm sorry."

"Will you help me?" Lou asked Amy, having already identified which of us was likely to give him a yes.

"You just said nothing could be done," I said, kind of annoyed that this guy couldn't have had this epiphany on his own, before he screwed up our holiday.

Lou paused in a manner that I now recognized was him letting Eve talk, then said, "We want you to do it for us. If you don't mind."

"Do . . . what?" asked Amy. But she already knew.

"We would like this one last evening together. Then we want you to kill us. As painlessly as possible. Maybe a bullet through my head and her . . . it . . . at the same time. You guys have experience with this sort of thing, yes? That's why the cops brought me here? Afterward, put the gun in my dead hand and leave me wherever. Let everyone think I did it to myself. Everyone already thinks I went crazy, so . . ." He shrugged and wiped a tear from his left eye. The creature scooted one of its segmented legs aside so that he could do it.

I looked at Amy because this seemed like the kind of plan she would object to.

She said, "I don't think I can do that," which I noted wasn't the same as saying it shouldn't be done.

John said, "I can do it, if I get a couple of drinks in me."

"We could do it at the lake," suggested Lou. "In the woods, out away from the people, where we can still see the fireworks. Do it at the finale, when everything is going off at once, to hide the noise. Eve and I will sit there and hold hands and we'll go out together. Or it'll seem like we're holding hands, to us. You know what I mean."

I said, "You don't have any family or friends around here?"

He shook his head "no."

I realized it probably sounded like I was asking if he had loved ones who could help guide him through this difficult time, but what I was actually asking was if there was anyone who might raise a stink about the cops not looking too closely into his "suicide" (and they wouldn't). I didn't want to do it and then find out the guy's brother was our congressman or some shit.

Amy asked, "If Eve feels so bad about this, why can't she just detach herself? It's obvious that you're healthy enough to walk and talk, so why not go to the hospital, say goodbye to Eve and tell the doctors you need them to rebuild that side of your skull?"

"She can't. Her body is merged with my brain and nerves, all that stuff in there. It was the only way she could interact with our world, using my eyes and ears. There's no detaching, we're one thing now. If you gave me a gun I'd end it myself, but I don't think I can bring myself to pull the trigger. Too scared. And I know I sound more nutty with every word I say, but with what I've had with her over the last few months . . . I really don't mind. I haven't made much of my life, spent most of it high, getting fired from shit jobs. I said earlier that she detected I was too weak to resist the attachment and what she meant was that I didn't have much time left regardless. Got cancer, pancreas. But me and her have had such a good time together . . . it's been a gift, to spend my final months like this. I'm telling you guys, I'm okay with it."

Amy asked Lou to excuse us and led John and I back out to the landing.

I closed the door behind me and whispered, "This feels like a trap."

Amy glanced toward the kitchen and said, "How?"

"Maybe this parasite wants us to kill this dude, maybe that was the whole point. Maybe it spawned a hallucination purely to lead him to this."

"Why would she need us to do it?" asked John. "Eve can turn the dude's brain into sloppy joe any time she wants just by doing this." He twirled his finger around.

"Maybe it's toying with us. Wants to make us do it, just for the fun of it."

Amy asked, "So what do you suggest?"

I lowered my voice even more. "Well for one, it's irresponsible to take that creature out to the crowded lake. Maybe we get him out there and it jumps off this guy and latches onto somebody else's head. Maybe *that's* its plan."

"But he's been living among the public for months. She could have done that at the restaurant, the hospital, the cop car on the way over, anywhere."

John asked, "You think she's just telling the truth?"

"Why not? Not everything is an evil scheme."

I said, "Hold on. Are you now in favor of us taking him to the lake and shooting him in the head?"

"No. I don't know. How about we take him to the fireworks and let him eat a funnel cake and enjoy the night. While we're there, we try to talk him out of it. Maybe Eve is wrong, maybe there's a way to live on. Maybe we can find some kind of solution. I don't know."

John said, "I'm fine with that." He looked at me. "You want to make it unanimous?"

I shrugged. "I'm outvoted either way."

"The way I figure it, when you're given multiple choices with no way of knowing which one is right, you just do the easiest—that's called 'efficiency.' In this case, we pick the choice that lets us also go drink and watch fireworks."

Amy said, "Well, if at the end of the night we may have to, uh, cure this guy, then you probably shouldn't drink beforehand."

John adjusted his Stetson and said, "Oh, I'm gonna get drunk *as hell*."

If This Book Exists, You're in the Wrong Universe
**will hit bookstores in fall 2022 and will be
available for preorder in the spring.**

**For updates, follow Jason Pargin on one
or all of his social media channels:**

twitter.com/JohnDiesattheEn
facebook.com/JohnDiesattheEnd.TheNovel
instagram.com/jasonkpargin
johndiesattheend.com

JASON PARGIN is the *New York Times* bestselling author of the John Dies at the End series as well as the award-winning first book in the Zoey Ashe series, *Futuristic Violence and Fancy Suits*. His essays at Cracked.com have been read by tens of millions of people around the world.

Note: Jason Pargin's novels were previously published under the pseudonym David Wong, the author initially adopting the name of the main character in his first book. As of 2021, the novels have been published under his real name.

READ ALL OF
JASON PARGIN'S
BOOKS!